1

CHARLOTTE

The morning that everything fell apart, I woke up thinking it was going to be a perfect day.

To be fair—most of my days are good. Not that I don't have my moments like everyone else—a broken heel or a morning where I oversleep—but for the most part, my life has fallen into place exactly the way I wanted it to.

A comfy job working as an IT manager that lets me wear jeans to the office? *Check.*

A great group of friends who love getting brunch on the weekends? *Check.*

A condo apartment close enough to Lincoln Park that I have a good view from my balcony? *Check.*

A handsome boyfriend to share that apartment with, who also has a good job and shares a similar taste in what to watch on Netflix after a long day? *Check, check, and check.*

There have been times in my life, of course, when I've wondered if living a life according to a list like that is really making me happy. In college, I knew friends of my friends who did things like drive to the Grand Canyon on a whim, or book the next flight out of an airport without knowing where they'd end up. People who would take spontaneous weekend road trips and just pick a direction. People who didn't Google the menus of restaurants before they went there, so they'd already have some idea of what they wanted to order.

I've never been spontaneous, impulsive, or exciting. And I've always consoled myself that even if I do lead a pretty routine existence—it's worked out for me so far. Those other acquaintances, the ones who do all those impulsive things—they have maxed out credit cards and piles of student loan debt. They're complaining about being sick of dating apps and waxing nostalgic about the days when you could meet the love of your life over a loaf of sourdough at the farmer's market.

So maybe being *boring* isn't the worst thing in the world.

Jaz, one of my best friends, is waiting for me in the lobby when I step off the elevator five minutes after five p.m. She works for the same company that I do, in the HR department, and we usually catch a ride or walk home together, since she lives a block away from me.

"I have a stop to make," I tell her as I stow my badge in my purse, my designer mules clicking against the tile floor as I hurry towards the rotating glass door at the front of the building. "I need to pick up my dress for tonight from Velvet Luxe."

"Ooh, fancy." Jaz wiggles her eyebrows, catching up to me as we step out into the crisp Chicago fall air. "What's the occasion?"

"My anniversary with Nate." I can't keep the smile off of my face. "Five years. He got a reservation at Alinea for us. I've always wanted to go—I'm so excited."

Jaz whistles through her teeth as we stop, and I check my Uber app—these shoes weren't made for walking. They're cute, but I swear I was getting blisters today just sitting at my desk. She shrugs on a black leather jacket, tugging her hair over her shoulder. "Man, I need to find a boyfriend who will make reservations like that for me. I can't remember the last time Jay and I went out on a date. He's always so busy. Remote work doesn't mean more time off, that's for sure. And these game developers always have him in crunch for one thing or another."

"Make a reservation for yourself." I grin at her. "Or all of us. We

ENDLESS OBSESSION

A DARK MAFIA ROMANCE

ENDLESS DUET
BOOK 1

M. JAMES

PNK PUBLISHING

Copyright © 2024 by M. James

All rights reserved.

No part of this book may be reproduced in any form or by any electronic or mechanical means, including information storage and retrieval systems, without written permission from the author, except for the use of brief quotations in a book review.

could have a girls' night out. Celebrate our friend-a-versary—the whole group of us."

"Technically, that passed back in August," Jaz says, laughing as a black Toyota pulls up to the curb. "We all met at Northwestern, freshman year."

"Okay, so a belated celebration." The driver comes around to open the door for us, and I slide inside, Jaz following right behind me. The interior of the car smells like clean leather and pine, and I breathe in, letting myself relax back against the seat. This is the beginning of what I'm sure is going to be an amazing weekend.

Tonight is the special dinner Nate planned, and then tomorrow, I have a beer tasting booked at his favorite pub, followed by bar-hopping. Sunday, I even skipped my usual weekend brunch with Jaz and the rest of our friends, in favor of a lazy afternoon in. I'm hoping to order takeout, have lots of sleepy sex, and maybe take a long hot bath before I have to jump back into the week.

"Well, tell me what you think of it, and we'll discuss it next weekend. Since you ditched us for this one," Jaz teases lightly.

"You'd do the same thing if it were you." I can tell from her tone that she's not actually upset, though. An anniversary is a big deal. And especially this one, when I'm pretty sure there's a chance that Nate is going to propose. Jaz and I and the others have been speculating for weeks now, ever since I saw a jewelry store catalog in the mail. Nate isn't really the present-buying type, unless it's a very specific occasion, and he's never gotten me jewelry. So for a jewelry store to have his address, he must have been doing some shopping.

"Hopefully, he steps up his game this weekend, so you don't fall asleep mid-sex," Jaz retorts, and I shake my head.

"That was *one* time. *Once*. And I'd just worked an eighty-hour week. I think Ryan Gosling himself could have been down there, and I'd have fallen asleep."

"Not a chance." Jaz laughs. "I'm just saying, it doesn't sound like he's exactly rocking your world every night. Or even most nights. Any night?" She raises one perfectly threaded eyebrow, and I sigh, sinking back further into the seat.

"I mean—it's *not* that exciting," I admit. "I guess it's pretty standard, all things considered. But that's just how sex is. It's fun and feels pretty good, but it's not like—I don't know." I shrug. "All the stuff you see in movies and read in books. All those crazy fantasies. No one actually *does* that."

Jaz gives me a smug look. "No one?"

"Oh, come on." I narrow my eyes at her. "You? Seriously? You're telling me you've had that kind of sex?"

I see the Uber driver glance back at us in his rear-view mirror as I say it, and I wince, my cheeks flushing. "Not that we need to talk about this right now," I mumble. "Actually, we're almost there." I lean forward, gesturing to the sign a half a block ahead of us—white-painted and scalloped with the boutique's name written in wine-red script.

For as long as I've had any reason to buy special-occasion dresses—graduation, friends' weddings, nights out—I've been coming to Velvet Luxe. Not being a very adventurous person in any facet of my life, I was more inclined to go to a designer store like Dior or Chanel for those kinds of clothes—but one of our friends at Northwestern who was a fashion student used her trust fund to open it five years ago, right after we graduated. And, being good friends, we all made sure to get our dresses exclusively from her.

"Zoe!" Jaz calls out as soon as we step into the shop. She and Zoe have always been super close—they bonded on day one in our dorm over their three-letter names, and became inseparable shortly after, despite the vast difference in their career paths. She immediately goes behind the counter, giving Zoe a brisk hug, before turning back to look at me. "I hear you have a special order for Charlotte."

"I do." Zoe grins, tucking the pin between her teeth back into the cushion on the counter. "I'll go grab it."

A few minutes later, she emerges with my dress. It's absolutely stunning—a form-fitting, knee-length creation of cranberry-red velvet, with thin straps and a slit up each side that goes to mid-thigh. The neck is cut into a low scoop that reaches an inch below my breasts, reinforced with inner corsetry so that they'll be supported, with just the sides and a little bit of the lower curve showing.

Jaz whistles. "If he wasn't already going to propose, he will when he sees you in that. Ring or no ring. Damn, Charlotte, that might be the sexiest thing you've ever bought." She looks pointedly at my outfit for work today, which is pretty similar to what I wear most days. A pair of dark slim-cut jeans, a button-down shirt in varying colors and patterns, and sensible shoes. Today it was the leather mules with a heel *just* a little higher than usual. That turned out to be a mistake.

Getting out of my comfort zone usually does.

"I was surprised, too," Zoe says with a grin. "But if you're going to pick any night to go all out like this, this is the one. Five years together *and* Alinea? Girl." She zips the dress into a sleek black garment bag with *Velvet Luxe* printed on the top, and hands it to me. "He's going to have to pick his jaw up off the floor when he sees you." She twirls a dark ringlet that came loose from the messy bun atop her head. "Do some big curls tonight—old Hollywood style. Lipstick to match the dress—" She kisses the tips of her fingers dramatically. "Perfection."

That smile spreads across my face again, and I don't even bother trying to fight it. "I'll take a picture and send it to the group chat," I promise. "And now—" I wince, looking at my watch. "Shit, I have to go. I'm running five minutes behind."

Zoe rolls her eyes. "You and your schedules." She looks at Jaz. "You wanna hang for a minute? We could go get tapas. I don't have anywhere to be tonight."

"That sounds great." Jaz wiggles her fingers at me. "Have fun, Charlotte. Send pics. Of the dress *and* the ring," she adds with a wink.

I laugh, waving at them both as I call a second Uber, and hurry out to the curb.

I'm not actually sure that Nate is going to propose, for all that I've gossiped about the possibilities with my friends. We haven't talked about it much, outside of a few conversations where we discussed if it was 'time' based on how long we've been together. We've had all those talks about how we line up on various things, though—not directly saying the words *do we want to get married,* but discussing all the things that need to be talked through before promising to spend the rest of our lives with each other.

And we agree on those things. We both want to stay in Chicago, living downtown until our mid-thirties, when we'll look into buying a house in the suburbs. We agree on kids—we'd be okay if we didn't have them, but are open to the idea of one, no more than two. We both abhor debt and pay our credit cards in full every month. We agree on the places we want to travel to most—Spain, Japan, and England, in that order. Public schools over private, so our kids don't grow up to be snobs. We both value our alone time and our time with our friends. And if he has any issues with our sex life, vanilla as it is, he's never said anything. He seems satisfied, and I—

I have to admit, I'm curious about what Jaz was about to say in the car, on the ride over to Velvet Luxe. I can't believe that she's really ever experienced anything as crazy as the kinds of things that show up in fiction. I don't believe that's real—I've never known anyone who experienced it. If my friends' dating life is anything to go by, I'm lucky that Nate usually goes down on me just about every time—even if it's usually only for a few seconds and never does all that much for me. But I think that's on me, not him. I've never really been all that sensitive. Toys work well for me—but I've never found a man who really lights me on fire by touching me.

I just don't think that's reality.

Nate isn't home yet when I get up to our shared condo. I toss my keys in the porcelain bowl on the entry table, carrying the garment bag down the hall to our bedroom. It's neat as a pin, as always, decorated minimally, with the modern aesthetic we both like. A platform bed, two rosewood nightstands with black iron touches, and a matching rosewood dresser, a large television mounted on the wall above it. There's a dark grey ottoman at the foot of the bed that matches the dark grey bedding, and I lay the garment bag down on it, kicking my shoes off as I pad across the hardwood floor to the closet.

I have a pair of heels that will be perfect for this dress, but I never wear them. They're buried somewhere in the back of the closet, and I reach up to push a stack of Nate's weekend chinos aside to see if the box got shoved behind them, only to almost be hit in the head by something that comes tumbling off the shelf.

I catch it reflexively, feeling the velvet texture against my palm. My heart trips in my chest, and I look down at the small box in my hand.

He's actually going to propose. My pulse kicks up another notch. *This is good, right? This is what I want.*

I shouldn't open it, I know that. I should let it be a surprise. But I'm curious, and I nudge the seam of it with my thumb, opening the box a fraction before letting it close again.

What if it's not a ring? I reason, staring down at it. *What if it's— earrings, or something?* That would be a good reason to look—if I think it's one thing and it turns out to be something else, I might seem disappointed. I don't want Nate to think I'm unhappy with my gift, just because I thought it was a ring.

He's also going to be home any second, so I have to make up my mind. Actually, he should have been home already—but he works late fairly often. Today, of all days, though, I thought he would be on time.

Taking a deep breath, I flip open the top of the box, and my eyes go wide.

It *is* an engagement ring. An absolutely stunning one. The center diamond is pear-shaped and an exquisite quality, sparkling brilliantly even in just the light of our bedroom. There are three small round diamonds on either side of it, and it's set in yellow gold. Classic, with a unique twist. Exactly the style I showed him the one time that we did talk about rings, a little over a year ago.

It's perfect. My breath catches in my throat, and I feel my heart racing in my chest, nervousness prickling over my skin.

Nervous—excitement. Yes. Excitement. It's a big step forward, one of the biggest we'll make, so of course, I feel some apprehension too, but—

The sound of the front door closing almost makes me jump out of my skin. I close the box hurriedly, shoving it back behind the stack of chinos as I grab the shoebox out of the closet—at the very back, where I thought it might be—and close the closet door just in time to hear Nate's footsteps stop outside the bedroom.

He walks in a moment later. He looks as handsome as always—the picture of the clean-cut, all-American lawyer. Perfect charcoal grey suit, swept back dark brown hair, clean-shaven jaw. He sets down his messenger bag by the dresser, and smiles at me. "How long before you're ready to go?"

"Forty-five minutes? Plenty of time before our reservation."

"I'd expect nothing less." He chuckles, walking past me to drop a kiss on my cheek as he shrugs out of his jacket. "I'll change once you're done; it won't take me long. I might go fix myself a pre-dinner drink."

"I'll save myself for the wine pairings." I grin at him, carrying the garment bag into the bathroom. I can hear Nate just outside the door, getting out of his work clothes. "Don't forget, I have something special planned for you tomorrow, too."

"That's right, your anniversary surprise." He pauses. "I might have other plans on Sunday, though. I'll let you know. An old friend is in town for the weekend, and I don't want to miss the chance to grab a beer with him."

"Oh?" I try to keep my tone neutral, even as my heart drops a little. I tell myself I'm being unreasonable. Asking to have him to myself for a *whole* weekend is a lot. Especially if it means missing out on seeing a friend.

"No one you know," he says breezily. "Oh—shit. Work's calling. I'll be out in the living room, Char."

"Okay." I hate that nickname, but he started calling me that early on in our relationship, and it stuck. It's not *that* bad, and after all, one of the cornerstones of a healthy relationship is picking your battles. A silly nickname isn't a battle worth fighting.

I know for a fact what Jaz is going to say when she finds out Nate is ditching me on Sunday. But that means I'll be able to meet them for brunch, so it won't be *that* bad—

I reach for the seamless underwear I bought to go under the

dress, only to realize that in my hurry to hide the ring and act natural before Nate came into the bedroom, I didn't grab it. I check the time, reassured that I still have plenty to spare, and hurry back into the bedroom naked to find where I put it.

What if Nate walked back in? The thought flickers into my head as I dig through my top drawer for the Nordstrom bag, and I feel that small, disappointed swoop in my stomach that I sometimes do when I think about our love life. I'd like to think that we'd be late for dinner, if he walked into our bedroom to find me standing naked in the middle of the room, that he'd grab my hair and bend me over the dresser, unzip his suit trousers, and take me just like that. That he'd whisper in my ear that if I'm going to come, I should do it quickly, so we still have a chance of making our reservation.

I feel a throb of heat between my thighs at the thought, a tingle there, and I squeeze them together briefly, grabbing the bag out of the drawer as I try to shake the thought loose.

Because, the fact is, if Nate walked in right now, nothing would happen. He'd comment that I wasn't dressed yet, and then move on with whatever he came to the bedroom to do.

And that's fine, I tell myself as I head back to the bathroom. Men don't actually behave like that. *Maybe,* in some relationships, at the very beginning—but definitely not after five years. Having a stable, loyal, companionable relationship is much better than one that would just fizzle out anyway—

Something catches my eye, as I walk past the bed. Nate's phone—his personal phone, not his work cell—is on the nightstand. He doesn't usually leave it out—he tends to be picky about his things being put away—but I don't think anything of it, until it lights up a second time, and I glance over at the screen.

I don't mean to snoop. I've never felt that I have a reason to. I've never worried for a second about Nate's fidelity. But his phone is unlocked, the text bubbles popping up on the screen, and I see a woman's name.

Valerie.

Valerie.

Valerie.

It pops up a fourth time.

Someone from work, I tell myself. *A friend. A cousin he never told me about.*

But my gut tells me there's something off.

A fifth message.

Before I can stop myself, I dart forward, sweeping the phone off the nightstand as I duck back into the bathroom and close the door, leaning back against it. I tell myself that I'm not going to find anything. That this is all perfectly innocuous. That I'm going to feel foolish and guilty as soon as I read the messages.

But if I don't, I'm going to wonder all night. And I don't want to spoil our anniversary by my own silly anxieties.

I slide my thumb up the screen, opening the texts. And despite all my arguments with myself otherwise, I have a horrible feeling about what I'm going to see.

2

IVAN

"You need to come with me, *brat*."

"Good afternoon to you, too, brother." I don't look up from the padded leather seat where I'm sitting with my cheek against the headrest. Behind me, I can hear the soothing buzz of a tattoo gun, feel the sting of the needles as they pierce the skin of my shoulder repetitively.

I've been looking forward to this appointment for weeks. A little self-care, after a month that has, quite frankly, felt like a year. And now one of my brothers is here to interrupt it.

Lev, from the sound of it. My least favorite of my siblings. Not that I get along with any of them.

"We don't have time for this. You're needed down at the warehouse."

"Get Grigori to do it."

"Grigori is busy."

I grit my teeth, tilting my head up just enough to see the stocky, white-blond man standing a foot from the chair with his arms crossed over his hard-muscled chest. He's dressed to the nines as always, wearing a tailored dark suit and glossy dress shoes, tattoos climbing out of the sleeves and collar to wind over his hands and up his neck. His ice-blue eyes are flat and humorless.

I think I got my sense of humor from my mother. God knows neither my father, nor my three siblings' mother ever had one.

"There are plenty of men who can do what you need me to do." I'm staying vague because Alice, my tattoo artist, doesn't need to know exactly what I often get my hands dirty doing. I think she suspects, given what she knows of my background, but I don't need to make it crystal clear for her. She might stop tattooing me, and she's the best artist I've ever met.

She's also good at a lot of other things, although we quit fooling around a few years ago.

"And I'm telling you that I need you to come with me." Lev's face doesn't so much as twitch. "Or should I tell your father that spending time with your tattoo artist took precedence over family business?"

The way he emphasizes Alice in the sentence, the way his gaze flicks to her with just a hint of the icy threat that I know all too well, is what gets me to give in. I'll fight my brother on his bullshit all day, but I'm not going to let someone innocent get caught up in the violent mess that is my family.

"Fine." I twist my head around to look at Alice. "I need to call a raincheck on this. Can you cover me up and we finish tomorrow, maybe?"

"I'm booked until next week." The buzzing stops, and she sits back. "But I'll figure out where I can pencil you in."

"Thanks, *dorogoy*." I say it quietly, and she shoots me a look as she pumps green soap onto a paper towel and wipes it over my half-outlined tattoo. The sting makes me suck in a breath, but it's welcome.

"One day, I'm going to put that in a translator." She pats a bandage gently over the tattoo.

"You'd like it." I wink at her, and she rolls her eyes. There's a casual, friendly intimacy between us, the kind that only comes from knowing every inch of each other's bodies over the course of a few months spent rolling in the sheets together, until we mutually decided it was better if we call it quits. Now, we're good buddies.

Sometimes I do think she digs the needle in a little harder than she has to, though.

"You know the drill." She nods at the tattoo. "I'll text you with the next time you can come in."

"Sounds good." I glare at my brother. "Well? Let's fucking go, then."

He leads me out to the blacked-out Escalade waiting at the curb, sliding inside without a word. I follow, leaning my head back against the cool leather as I try to get my head in the right place for what I know is about to happen.

There's only one reason for us to be going to the warehouse, and it's going to end with me washing blood out of the crevices of my fingers later tonight.

It's not unusual for me to be called on for something like this. I'm one of my father's enforcers, but I'm not a grunt. Which means if Lev is demanding I go with him to take care of whoever it is that they have down there, there are only two possibilities.

It's someone who requires a particular special touch, someone they want good information from—or Lev wants to watch me, and see my reaction to whatever this man has to say.

There's not a lot of trust in my family, and no love. Loyalty, though, is expected. I'm not supposed to have the side jobs that pad my bank account. I should be entirely reliant on my family, even if my father only tolerates me and my brothers hate me.

Fuck that. I'm not going to allow my life to be ruled by people who want to see me fall. I've always relied on myself whenever I can, and I intend to keep it that way.

Regardless, this world that I live in is cutthroat—survival of the fittest at its finest. I can guess all fucking day at the reasons for Lev's demands, but when it comes down to it, the only thing that really matters is that I don't let him see me flinch.

No matter what.

The SUV pulls up near the warehouse. It's a shabby-looking

structure, one that no one would think twice about looking at. The kind of place that is just assumed to be barely standing, owned for the value of the land underneath it and nothing else. Which makes it a perfect spot for 'questioning' anyone who gets on the wrong side of my family.

Unlike a lot of the Bratva enforcers and soldiers, I don't get a lot of pleasure out of violence. There's a certain satisfaction to torture well done, to keeping someone alive long enough to get the information desired, making sure they spill their guts in exactly the way that I need them to. But I don't *like* hurting others in this way. I'm not a sadist.

At least—not *this* kind.

"You want to fill me in?" I ask as Lev and I get out of the car. He grunts, and for a moment, I think he's going to let me go in blind. But then he nods.

"Lower-level guy. I don't even know his fucking name, honestly. He was supposed to help run interference for the last shipment of women. Keep a lookout for any feds or anyone else coming in. He didn't do a very good fucking job, since that shipment got busted. Three of our best guys pinched, and a bunch of pissed-off clients that aren't going to get their girls. We think he tipped someone off."

"You think he's stupid enough to do that?"

Lev shrugs. "Maybe. Or maybe someone got to him and scared him. At any rate, he probably sang before, and he's gonna sing to you now. Let us know what happened, so we can dig out any other traitors and get this show back on the road."

I nod grimly, following Lev to the warehouse, keeping one step behind him so I can sort out my thoughts before I get in there.

The fact is, I know exactly what happened. That poor fucker who is about to end up in pieces didn't tip off the feds—or at least, if he did, he wasn't the only one.

That original tip came from me.

For months now, I've been working under an alias, feeding tips to the police and FBI about my father's criminal activity—at least, the activity pertaining directly to the human trafficking he's involved in.

I'm not trying to cripple his empire entirely—honestly, I don't give a shit if he sells weapons to the Irish or deals drugs. I couldn't care less about any of that. But I do draw the line at selling women.

Once he got into that business, I decided to make it mine to shut it down.

My chest tightens as I step into the warehouse. Despite the chill outside, it's hot and stuffy inside the metal structure, and it smells strongly of blood and piss. One look at the man hanging in front of me, and the dark stain down the leg of his trousers, and I know why.

I also feel like shit for what's about to happen to him. But I don't have any choice.

For the greater good, and all of that. For *my* good, because if anyone finds out what I've been doing, it's going to be me hanging up there instead of him.

That's not something I can allow.

I'm not a self-sacrificing man. I take no pleasure in the fact that this man is about to die, but I'm not the type to give my life for his— or for anyone. And that's what it would be, if my family found out the truth about what I've been doing.

Truthfully, I'll probably give him a better death than they would give me.

He's not squeaky-clean, anyway. No one who works for my family is. And likely, if I dug enough, I'd find something on him that would be worth stringing him up.

The man twists in the manacles holding him as I approach, his eyes widening with fear. "I—I don't know anything," he splutters, his bare toes scrambling for purchase on the concrete as he tries to push himself reflexively away from me. As if there's any getting away. As if there's anything at all he can do to escape his fate.

There are only three human reactions to a situation like this, though. Fight, flee, or fawn. He can't do either of the first two, and it's only a matter of time before he goes for the third.

They all do, eventually. And it never, ever works.

I ignore him for now, walking to the table at one side of the warehouse. "Get a tarp laid out," I call over to one of the grunts standing around, watching the scene unfold in front of them, and I hear the heavy *clunk* of boots on concrete as they jump to obey. I can feel Lev's eyes on my back. Now that I know the situation, I know he's watching me for hesitation. Watching for some sign that this is personal.

The tricky thing about being an informant is that sometimes, there's information that no one outside of the family would know. Sometimes, information gets disseminated among the family for exactly that reason—so my father knows if someone is leaking it. And it's a sensitive thing, to slip information to the feds that will help, without ever leaking anything that would mean my family knowing, beyond a shadow of a doubt, that there's a rat among us.

The thing is, I'm the kind of rat that's hard to trap.

I hear the low moan that the man behind me lets out, as I heft a metal toolbox onto the table and open the lid. I could do everything that I'm about to just fine with the knife on my belt and a pair of pliers that's already sitting on the table, but getting someone to talk is as much about showmanship as anything else. The sight of me opening up this toolbox, sorting through the implements inside, is making the man behind me think about what's possibly coming next. Warming him up to sing sooner rather than later.

The truth is, I won't use half of what's in here. Maybe not any of it. Not on this guy, anyway. But he doesn't know that.

I pick up the pair of pliers on the table, and stride towards him, grabbing a metal folding chair by the back on the way over. I set it down next to him, looking up at his pale face and bloodshot, wide eyes.

I set the pliers down on the chair with a heavy *thunk*, and he jerks, rattling the chains he's hanging from. His toes scramble against the concrete floor again.

"Now, now. Those toes are going to be plenty abused by the time I'm done with them. No need to rush things." I reach for the hunting knife in my belt, drawing it slowly out of the oiled leather sheath, and I see his eyes flick down, widening until it looks like they might pop out of his skull.

"*Please*—" he moans. "Please, please—"

I chuckle, running one fingertip over the serrated edge of the blade. "It's funny, you know," I murmur, raising the knife to rest the tip of it at the hollow of his throat. "There are really only two situations in life where I hear someone beg like that. One is a situation like this. Man trussed up in front of me, about to be asked all kinds of questions." I drag the knife down, catching the blade in the front of his sweat-soaked t-shirt, as I begin to cut it free. "The other is a pretty woman in my bed, all wet and waiting for me to give her all the things she's pleading for. Funny thing, too, is–"

I jerk the knife down sharply, ripping the front of his shirt open to reveal a skinny, pale white chest. He's hairless as a fish's belly, right down to the single stripe of dark hair that runs into his filthy pants. "Both times, more often than not, involve chains."

A grin spreads across my face as I dig the point of the knife into the man's belly, just above his navel. "Now, we're going to have a little talk. You're not gonna like a lot of what I do to you, but there will be less of it, the faster you answer my questions. But I want you to think about something else, too."

"What—what's that?" the man pants, looking down at the knife. That acrid scent of piss fills the air again, and I hear a *drip* on the concrete, between where he's hanging and I'm standing. I wrinkle my nose.

"Well, for one thing—and this wasn't what I was about to say—but you might wanna consider not pissing yourself for the rest of this interview. I don't like the smell, and I might just think about taking something off before it's time. If you know what I mean." I raise an eyebrow, and the man jerks backward, flailing in the chains. It makes him buck forward *into* my knife without meaning to, and the point digs into his fish-belly skin, sending a thick rivulet of blood dripping down his stomach.

He cries out, whimpering, and I laugh coldly.

I don't actually find any of this funny. I'm already thinking ten steps ahead of what happens next, because Lev is still watching me. My ass is on the line right now. Which is exactly why I'm putting on such a good show.

Award-winning. Oscar-worthy. If I were auditioning for *tough Russian guy who takes fingernails* right now, I'd have the part before another five minutes goes by.

"But what I was going to say—" I dig the tip of the knife into the small wound I've created, opening it further. "---is that you shouldn't just be thinking short-term. I know this all hurts right now. And it's gonna hurt for a while. I'm not going to lie to you about that. But think about your end, too."

"My—end?" The man lets out another shallow whimper, and I see tears starting to track down his face.

It makes me hate Lev a little more for this. My whole family, really. Because this guy is no operative. He's not tough or intelligent enough to actually have leaked anything, and I'd know that even if I wasn't the one who had actually done it. This man is a grunt. He's never going to be anything more than a low-level runner who is probably working for my family because he needs to pay off gambling debts or an overpriced car payment or some slumlord on the South side.

And he's going to die, painfully, because my father is too goddamn greedy to stick to just making money on guns and drugs. He had to involve human flesh in it—the unwilling kind. And some sacrifices have to be made, so that I can keep throwing wrenches in that operation.

"You're going to die today." I feel a shudder vibrate through the man at that flat declaration, and he lets out a sobbing moan.

"Please—"

"Don't waste your breath. You'll need it. And no amount of pleading changes that outcome. It wasn't even my decision, honestly. But *how* you die, is." I twist the knife again in the shallow wound, pushing it deeper, and the man cries out.

"It—hurts—"

"It does," I agree. "And what hurts even more, is me opening up your stomach the rest of the way, letting you stare at your own guts baking on the concrete while I leave you here to die at the end of this. It'll take a while for you to go, like that. In this hot warehouse, all alone, with no water. Nothing but looking at your own insides while the clock ticks away. Or—"

I step back, pulling the knife free. He's still hurting, but there's no new pain right now. After we go for long enough, that lack of fresh pain will start to feel good. Like a gift. A reward.

"Or, I can end you with a bullet. Fast, clean. All the pain will stop. Right now, I know you still want to live. You can't imagine bargaining for how you die instead of a chance to live. But we'll get there. Right now, I'm just telling you to think about it."

"Think about—" The man pants, looking down at me. Sweat drips off of the shaggy hair plastered to his face. He looks horrified. Frightened. I can't help but wonder who he's thinking about right now—who it is that he's never going to see again.

Or maybe there isn't anyone.

I know if it was me, hanging there right now, I wouldn't have anyone to miss. But honestly, it's better that way.

If there were someone for me to miss, then that would mean that there was someone that I'd be about to hurt by dying, who I wouldn't want to.

And I'm too good at hurting people to let that happen.

THIRTY MINUTES LATER, the muffled sound of a silenced gunshot mingles with the whimpering moans of a dying man. The moans go silent instantly, and the body slumps in the chains, hanging heavily over the gory tarp.

I let the hand holding the gun fall to my side, letting out a heavy sigh as I crack my neck in one direction and then the other. "Clean it up," I order the crew waiting on the other side of the warehouse, striding towards where Lev is waiting next to that damned toolbox.

I didn't actually use anything in it. But I wipe the pliers down, dropping them inside before I look at my still-glowering brother.

"Why did you kill him?" he demands sharply. "He didn't give you enough."

"He gave as much as he was going to." I close the lid of the toolbox. "That's why *otets* wants me to do these jobs, and not you. Because I know when they have nothing else to give."

Lev chuckles grimly. "So what? You should have kept going until he was dead. Maybe something else would have slipped."

Exactly what I wanted to avoid. I don't think this man—Bobby was his name, slipped out during one particularly fervent plea as I took off a toenail—knew jackshit about what I'm doing, or any of our operations, actually. He was just in the wrong place at the wrong time, working for the wrong fucking family. But there's always a chance that he did. That he heard something. That some fed was stupid enough to offer him a shot at getting out for information. Normally, they wouldn't work with someone as weak as Bobby, but sometimes the cops can be pretty fucking dumb, too. Especially the city police force, when they decide to start sticking their noses into things, hoping to find something that will let them show up the feds.

"Again, that's why I do this work." I stride towards the warehouse door, desperate for a breath of fresh air, even down here. The smell of blood and human waste is giving me a headache. "You do that—eventually, they start to realize that your promise of an easy death is bullshit. And then they get pissed. Rebellious. They'll endure all sorts of pain just to not give you anything else, since you lied to them." I step outside into the cool air, sucking in a deep lungful of it. "The promise of an end to pain is a great motivator. If you take that away, they have nothing to strive for. Nothing to bargain with."

Lev makes an irritated face. "Regardless, *otets* will be unhappy. All he gave were two names. Other low-level men. No real information."

"That's because he didn't actually have anything." I pull my phone out of my pocket, searching for a rideshare app. I'm not riding back with my fucking brother. "And now he's dead. We move on to the next one." *And I make sure my tracks are covered twice.*

"What the fuck are you doing? We're having dinner with family tonight." Lev tries to snatch my phone out of my hand, but I'm leaner and faster than he is. I move out of the way, hitting the next available ride.

"Maybe you are. I'm going to go get my fucking tattoo finished. And then—who knows?" I shrug, grinning. "Maybe a stiff drink and some pussy."

Lev is still glowering at me as I walk away. He hates everything about me; I know that. My attitude. My lack of giving a shit what he, and the rest of my family, think about me and where I came from. My popularity with women. The fact that I manage to not need our father, and to hell with whatever consequences that brings.

But I don't give a shit how he feels about it. I'm not going to change my life for anyone. And eventually, I'll find a new one.

One where I get to be only the man I want to be, and no one else.

3

CHARLOTTE

With every text that I read, I feel worse.

I press my back to the bathroom door, fighting a wave of nausea as I read them. I can't excuse any of it. I can't find a reason why these would be on Nate's phone, except the most obvious one.

The one that I never thought I had to worry about.

Valerie: *Are you going to call me tonight? I'm home all alone.*

Valerie: *Shit, I forgot you said you had a work thing. Maybe I'll send you pictures instead.*

Valerie: *I got a new toy. A big, thick cock bigger than yours. You like that, don't you? Seeing me take something so much bigger? Makes you feel like you gotta come over here and prove to me that you can still make me come with yours.*

Valerie: *I'll show you everything I do with it so you can punish me when you come over Sunday. Tie me up and make me beg for yours. I'm being a bad girl, aren't I? Begging for a bigger cock. You're going to stuff my mouth with yours so I can't beg anymore, aren't you?*

Valerie: *Look at me taking it.*

. . .

I CLAP a hand over my mouth as I reach the fifth message, the one that made me pick up the fucking phone in the first place. It's a picture of this 'Valerie' on a bed with a floral pink bedspread, on her hands and knees. Her legs are spread wide, and she's shoving an absolutely massive dildo between them, stretching her to the max.

It's much, *much* bigger than Nate's; I can say that for certain.

The fact that that's my first thought makes me want to break into hysterical laughter. The only reason that I don't is because I feel sure that if I do, I'll also start crying. Or maybe screaming.

I can't believe this is happening to me. I really, *really* can't believe it.

It's not even just the fact that he's cheating on me. It's the fact that it's *this*. That he apparently wants things he's never asked me for. That I would have been willing to try—hell, maybe *wanted* to try, if he'd ever given me a chance.

Instead, he just went straight for someone else.

I hear footsteps, and the sound of the bedroom door opening. Completely forgetting that I'm still naked, I yank the bathroom door open, pure, white-hot rage replacing every other emotion I might possibly have as I fling myself out of the bathroom and directly toward Nate.

He freezes, a look of utter shock on his face as he stares at me. I can't even imagine what I look like—buck naked with my hair piled up on my head, probably white-faced and wide-eyed, but he looks honestly terrified of me at this moment.

All I can think is, *good. I fucking hope he is.*

I've never felt violent towards anyone, not even the prior owner of the condo above us, who liked to play piano from ten to midnight every night, but right now?

I honestly think I could commit murder.

"Char, what the hell—" His gaze flicks sideways, seeing the phone in my hand, and it's his turn to pale. "I can explain—"

"No." I throw the phone at him, hard. It hits his chest, and he winces, staggering back a step as it drops to the floor. "I don't think you fucking can."

"Shit!" He presses a hand to his chest, looking down at the phone and back at me. "What the hell?" he repeats. "That hurt—"

"You're pathetic," I spit out. "'*That hurt?*' That's the first thing you're going to say to me?"

"Charlotte, sit down. Better yet, put some clothes on, and we'll talk. But we're going to be late for—"

"Oh, you want me to put clothes on?" I'm one second from clawing his eyes out. "Not *Valerie*, though. You like her better with her clothes off. Clothes off, and bent over, and shoving a monster cock up her pussy so you can punish her later for not wanting your pathetic one, apparently!"

Nate's eyes are almost bugging out of his head. I don't think I've ever said the words *cock,* or *pussy* before. Definitely not where he can hear me. Probably not even after one too many mimosas at brunch.

"Charlotte—"

"Don't you dare say you can explain," I warn. "I will rip your cock off myself if you do. There. I've said it *twice* now." I glare at him. "And it *is* pathetic! You don't even make me come, you piece of shit—"

"You've never complained!" He snaps back defensively. "And I thought I did—"

"You—" I press my fingers to my temples, feeling like I'm about to lose my mind. "That's not what we're talking about right now, Nate! We're talking about the fact that you're fucking *cheating* on me! With —with—" I look down at the dropped phone, the picture of Valerie on her hands and knees on the bed forever burned into my mind. "We have missionary sex." I sink down onto the edge of our bed, feeling angry tears threatening at the corners of my eyes. "Sometimes I get on top. Those are usually the only times I actually do come, by the way."

I press the heels of my hands into my eyes, trying not to cry. I do *not* want to cry in front of him. I want to be angry. *Furious,* even. I want to hate him. I want him to regret ruining this night forever.

But I don't want him to see me cry.

"You've never asked me to do anything like that." I point at the phone. "You've never asked me for anything at all in bed, actually. The few times I've brought up spicing things up, you've told me our sex life was perfect. Everything you want. That you're just not that adventurous. Well, that was clearly a fucking lie."

Nate runs a hand through his hair, looking at me warily. I can see his little lawyer brain going a hundred miles a minute, trying to work through how to get himself out of this. How to gaslight me into thinking I'm wrong about it somehow. That it's all just a big misunderstanding.

That's not going to fucking work. But before I throw him out, I want answers.

"I didn't ask you for those things because I respect you, Charlotte." He looks at me pleadingly, and I gape at him, unsure of what to even say to that at first.

So I guess he decided to go the route of excusing it, instead of trying to deny it. Those hot tears burn at the corners of my eyes again, and I have to fight them back. "You *respect* me?" I stare at him, the words sticking in my throat. "So cheating on me is somehow *respecting* me?"

"It means nothing! She means nothing, all of those things—they mean nothing." Nate is using his lawyer voice now, explaining, reasoning. "She has nothing to do with you, Charlotte. I love you. I don't feel anything for her—"

"Except arousal, apparently," I spit out. "She turns you on, clearly. She does all the filthy things you're imagining for you."

"It's just like porn, but—"

"But real?" I lurch up off the bed again, and Nate steps back. "I'm a *person*, Nate! Hell, *she's* a person. And now you're pissing me off even more, because you're making me feel bad for the woman you're cheating on me with, because you're talking about her like she's a fucking sex object—"

"I don't want to treat *you* like a sex object—"

"And I don't want to be fucking cheated on!" I'm shouting so loudly now that I'm pretty sure our neighbors can probably hear us, but I don't care. "I don't want to listen to my boyfriend explain to me how I should be grateful that he's treating other women the way he doesn't want to treat me. Which is just insult to injury, because I might *like* to be treated that way, Nate! Consensually, just in the bedroom! I might have fantasies of my own that don't involve thirty seconds of oral and missionary sex twice a week!"

"You want that?" Nate points down at the phone, disgust in his voice, and it's then that I understand.

He's ashamed of himself. Not for cheating, but for what he wants. He's disgusted by his own desires. He doesn't want to marry a woman who wants those same things, because then he'd be disgusted with her, too.

And I have no patience for any of this.

I stalk—still naked, but I'm past caring—to the closet. I throw open the door, going up on my tiptoes to yank the ring box out of the back where I re-hid it, and I spin around, throwing it at Nate's chest exactly like I threw the phone at him.

The box falls to the floor, next to the discarded phone.

"There," I spit out. "I hope you got a receipt. I found it earlier. I thought you might propose tonight. Honestly, I wasn't entirely sure I wanted to marry you," I add, every word laced with venom. I want it to hurt. And from the wounded look on his face, it does.

Good.

"But I thought you were good enough," I continue acidly. "I thought you were all the things I wanted. But I guess we were both wrong. Neither of us is really what the other one wants. And I guess the only thing we can be grateful for is that I figured it out before we made a big fucking mistake."

"Charlotte—" Nate holds open his hands. "Come on. We can talk about this. We'll go to therapy, if you want. Work through whatever is going on here—"

"What's *going on here* is that you're a cheating piece of shit who's too ashamed of himself to man up and ask for what he wants from the woman he wants to marry. Or maybe part of what gets you off is sneaking around. Either way, I don't want any part of it." I point at the door, doing my best to keep my finger from shaking. "Get out."

"Char—"

"*Get out!*" I scream it, so loudly that Nate flinches back, his eyes widening.

"Shit, fine." He grabs his phone off the floor in a rush, leaving the ring box there. "I'll call you, Charlotte, and once you've calmed down—"

"Don't," I tell him flatly. "Just get the fuck out."

"I'm going." He strides to the door, his features tightening. He hasn't won this argument, and I can tell it's pissing him off.

But I don't care. I stand there, ramrod straight, arms crossed over my chest, until he retreats from the bedroom, and I hear the slam of the front door closing.

Then, and only then, I sink to the floor and burst into tears.

—

Two hours later, I've calmed down enough to call Jaz. I could call any of our friends, honestly, and they'd be here as soon as they could. But I want Jaz. I know she won't bullshit me, but she'll also be nice about it. I don't want soothing platitudes right now. I want someone to tell me if I'm overreacting.

I don't think I am, but my mind has been going in circles, for as long as I've been sitting on the floor sobbing. Telling me that maybe this is just a bump in the road. That maybe Nate is right, and we could try therapy. That maybe we just need to work through our shit, and we could have a happy relationship. After all, love is about fighting for it, right? And maybe I've done something wrong, too, something to contribute to this—

That thought is what finally gets me up off the floor. I go to the dresser, wiping away tears as I dig through my drawers for underwear, a pair of leggings, and my favorite oversized t-shirt. I look at it in my hands, and press my lips together.

Is *it my fault?* Should I have been wearing silk and lace around the house instead of well-worn leggings and a band t-shirt that's three sizes too big? Would Nate have asked *me* to send him pictures of me fucking myself with a toy instead?

The minute I text Jaz, she answers within seconds.

CHARLOTTE: *Hey. Alinea is off. Some bad shit went down with me and Nate. Can you come over? I'm feeling pretty rough.*

Jaz: *Sure thing, babe. I'm out with Zoe, but I'll grab an Uber. You have drinks?*

Charlotte: *Plenty.*

Jaz: *Perfect.*

AFTER THAT, there's nothing to do but wait for her to get here. I drag myself into the living room, where I pour myself a full glass of pinot noir and grab the remote. I don't even know what to watch, but I need something other than silence, so I put on *Game of Thrones* and let it play in the background while I stare blankly at the dragons flying across the screen.

The episode is half over when I hear the buzzer go off. I open the door, and Jaz takes one look at me as she walks in before shaking her head. She shrugs her leather jacket off and hangs it on the brass hook on the wall, taking my almost-empty wine glass out of my hand and going to refill it as she pours herself a glass, too.

"What the fuck did he do?" she asks bluntly as she hands me back my wine, sinking down next to me on the dove-grey couch in the living room.

Now that I think about it, a lot of the stuff in this condo is grey. I don't even like grey that much. Or, at the very least, I'd add more accent colors.

Maybe I will, now that I'm never letting Nate back into this place again.

I take a sip of my wine, and another, and another as I fill Jaz in. By the time I finish, I've polished off the glass, and she has a murderous look on her face as she fills it up for me again.

"You've got to be fucking kidding me," she seethes. "I can't believe it. Like he's even hot enough to be—"

"Is it my fault?" I ask in a tiny voice, finally vocalizing the thing that I've been afraid of since I started reading those text messages. "Did I do something wrong? Is there something I could have done differently—should I have dressed sexier, or tried harder to figure out what he might want—"

"*Fuck*, no," Jaz spits out emphatically. "This is *not* on you, babe. In no way is this your fault. It's his fault for being a slimy, cheating piece of shit—"

I laugh, hiccupping a little, and press my hand over my mouth. "That's what I called him, too," I admit. "Well, not the slimy part, but—"

Jaz shakes her head. "You can do so much better than him. You *will* do so much better. But you're going to start by not blaming yourself for all of this."

"I never knew he wanted anything like that." I take another sip from the fresh glass of wine. I can feel the buzz starting to hit—I never drink very much, and rarely anything other than wine. Two big glasses of pinot noir is a lot for me. "I even asked a couple of times about his fantasies, and he never said—"

"What do *you* want?" Jaz interrupts, looking at me. "That stuff you found on his phone, is that something you want to do?"

"I mean—" I hesitate, taking a big swallow of wine for courage. "Not that specifically, I don't think. I don't want a man who wants to be humiliated. That just made me feel sad, I guess. Not for Nate specifically, because he's a piece of shit," I clarify, and Jaz smirks. "But just the idea of that. But that part about begging for it—" I bite my lip. "I don't know. There are definitely things I've thought about—"

"Like what?" Jaz latches on instantly. "Tell me. I won't judge you, I promise."

I narrow my eyes at her. "I'm not sure I believe you."

"I won't. Look—like I said in the car the other day. I've done some weird shit. And there's nothing wrong with that! Really. Everyone has fantasies. I wouldn't blame you if you had some crazy ones. Especially after being with Mr. Vanilla for so long."

"I mean—" I swallow more of the wine, and I can feel that I'm *definitely* buzzed now. A little more than buzzed, even. Probably on my way to being drunk. I might actually *be* drunk, I realize, as I try to gather my thoughts and feel like they're slipping and sliding all over the place. "A guy who focuses on me. I mean *really* focuses on just me and my pleasure. That's one."

Jaz snorts, and my eyes widen. "Hey! You said you wouldn't judge."

"I'm not judging, babe," Jaz promises. "It's just—that should be a basic requirement of every relationship. Sexual or otherwise. I don't mean he has to make it all about you *every* time, but at least some of the time—"

I frown. That definitely doesn't describe my sex life with Nate. He liked to keep things perfunctory—a little foreplay to warm me up, and then straight to whatever position he wanted to fuck me in. Usually missionary, occasionally me on top, once in a great while from behind.

Thinking about that brings back the image of Valerie on her hands and knees on the bed, and I wince.

"I think—maybe a guy who talks dirty, too," I admit, chewing on my lower lip. "Like one who would make me describe what I want. And ask for it." *Beg for it, even*, I think, squeezing my thighs together, but I'm not ready to say *that* out loud yet.

Jaz chuckles. "Promise, no judgment. But again, that's not anything crazy. You're still in the minor leagues of sex fantasies here, Charlotte."

I huff out a frustrated breath. "Okay, fine. What counts as a sexual fantasy to *you*, then?"

She laughs at that. "Lots of things. But what if I just showed you, instead?"

I frown. "I don't know if—"

"Not *me* personally." Jaz lifts an eyebrow. "Although you are very hot, Charlotte. Hotter than you give yourself credit for."

"So—what?" I finish my wine and set the glass down on the coffee table, a little unsteadily. The room is definitely starting to feel like it's tilting a little bit, and all the horrible feelings from earlier feel blurred and softened. I should go to bed soon. I'm glad that this happened on a Friday night, at least—I won't have to be hungover at work tomorrow or use a sick day to recover…both things that I've never had to deal with before. I don't ever get this drunk.

Yet another thing I can blame on Nate.

"There's a sex club downtown that I've gone to before," Jaz says, as casually as if she were telling me about a new restaurant we could try, and I gape at her.

"You've been to a sex club? I thought those just existed in movies."

She laughs. "No, babe, they're definitely real. This one is unique, too."

"How so?" I wrinkle my nose, flopping back on the couch as I try to see if I can get the room to stop tilting that way. I don't think I actually like being drunk.

"Everyone wears masks." Jaz grins. "It's completely anonymous, so all kinds of people go there—people who normally wouldn't want to be seen out at a place like that. Doctors, lawyers, you know. People who would have something to lose, but want to work their kinks out somewhere."

"And it's just a free-for-all?" My pulse kicks up a notch, and I feel uneasy at the thought—but also something else, too. A feeling of curious arousal. I'm—turned on by the idea. The thought of doing something with a complete, masked stranger sounds wild and impulsive, the kind of thing I've never done before. But I'm starting to wonder if I'm missing out on things by being so uptight. If I could have had all kinds of experiences over the last five years, that would have kept me from getting screwed over by someone like Nate.

"No, absolutely not," Jaz says firmly. "There are rules. They ask every new person about their fantasies, their limits, and they give you a bracelet that will fit what you're looking for. Everyone wears them and knows what they mean, so no one does anything or gets asked to do anything they're not comfortable with. And everyone has to submit a recent battery of test results from a doctor. Anyone with a regular membership has to update it periodically. And condoms are required for sex. So it's safe, too. They take it all very seriously."

"I—wow." I press a hand to my forehead, trying to think through the blur of the alcohol. "That's a lot to process. It sounds like you've been there a lot."

"A few times." Jaz grins at me. "No judgment, remember?"

"No judgment," I echo. "That's just—I didn't expect that."

"Do you want to go?" That grin is still plastered across her face. "We could go next weekend. Friday and Saturday nights are great."

I hesitate. I can't believe I'm even considering this. But I think of what I saw on Nate's phone, the picture of Valerie, all those dirty text messages. All of the things he asked her to do—and god knows how many other women—that he never even mentioned to me that he might want.

"Think of it as revenge," Jaz says with a gleeful look on her face. "Nate spent all that time cheating on you, and giving you mediocre dick in return. Now, you can go explore your fantasies with someone else. And while he's regretting losing you and the life you had together, you'll be learning all kinds of new things about yourself."

I do want revenge. Underneath the haze of the wine, I can still feel all the hurt and embarrassment and anger simmering. And even as outrageous as all of this sounds, I *am* curious.

"If I don't like it, we can leave?" I ask hesitantly, and Jaz nods.

"Of course," she assures me. "If you're uncomfortable, we'll go immediately. I won't even do anything with anyone, if that will make you feel better. I'll just stay by your side," she promises. "And wait for you while you find some hot guy to start making all your wildest fantasies come true."

"I doubt I'm going to do anything," I warn her. "But yes. Let's go. I want to see what this is like."

Jaz's squeal of excitement makes me smile for the first time since I saw those messages light up Nate's phone.

If nothing else, this will be an adventure. And I trust Jaz to shepherd me through it. I don't think I'm going to uncover anything new about myself, but...

There's always a chance. And I'm ready to start a new chapter.

4

IVAN

If any of my brothers ever saw where I live, they'd be horrified.

Not that there's anything wrong with it, as far as I'm concerned. The house I purchased a few years ago is nice enough, a Midwestern two-story that blends in with the rest of the neighborhood, with a basement large enough that I could fully kit it out with everything I need to operate. I bought it with cash—the less of a paper trail, the better—and registered everything that needed to be done publicly under a fake name. If my family dug hard enough, they could probably figure out who owns it, but I've covered my tracks as well as I'm able. Which is pretty fucking well.

Like I said, I'm a rat that's hard to trap.

The upper levels of my house look like any average home in the Chicago suburbs. Clean, neat, decently well-furnished. By my brothers' standards, I might as well live in a hovel, but it suits me just fine. I have a fancier apartment in the city where I take women, if I want to bring someone 'home' for the night. But this—this place is just for me. No one else comes here. No one else knows where it is. My own private lair.

The upstairs might look like a nice, normal home, but the basement looks like something out of *The Matrix*. Wall-to-wall computer screens and various tech, blinking neon in the dark. I sink down in my leather gaming chair, leaning my head back against it as I roll up to one of the screens and log on with an alias.

All of my various Internet personas are heavily encoded, layered under so much security that it would take someone as good as I am to hack into it and uncover my real identity. And very few hackers are as good as I am.

I'm good at three things. Violence, technology, and sex. The first two frequently interact with each other. The second two do sometimes. The first and last—never. That's the one area of my life where I consider myself a good man. A man with dark and deviant tastes, yes. But not one who would ever hurt a woman.

That's how I got in this position in the first place.

The screen lights up.

Wyatt8640: *Check-in, Viper.*

I let out a breath, running one hand through my hair as I start to type with the other.

Viper69: *A mouse was caught. He won't be squeaking to anyone else.*

My username is my own private joke. I know it irritates the feds that I work for that I have something so juvenile attached to it. But I like to remind them that I'm my own man. I'm feeding them information, but I'm not one of their serious, badge-wearing flunkies. I'll do things my own way.

Wyatt8640: *Make sure if they're squeaking, you're the one who hears it. I'll be in touch.*

The chat logs off, and I blow out a sharp breath.

I'm well aware of the position I've put myself in. I could end up in custody myself, if I step wrong. There's plenty the feds could pin on me, if they wanted to. I could probably negotiate a damn good deal, considering how much I've fed them, but that might not keep me from going behind bars. And if that happens, there are only two ways that ends.

One is with me in gen pop, where I'd die in a matter of days. As soon as my father discovered my betrayal, he'd have men on the inside after me, ready to spill my guts onto the floor.

The other is with me in permanent solitary, to keep exactly that from happening. And even then, my father would pay a guard to murder me. Prison means death, for me, if what I'm doing gets out. If I piss off the feds enough at any point to make it so that they don't protect me any longer.

But frankly, I'd rather die anyway than be behind bars.

I grit my teeth, running both hands through my hair. It infuriates me that I'm mixed up in this at all. That my father is so goddamn greedy that he couldn't be satisfied with the billions he already has, that arms dealing and drugs aren't enough. That he had to dip his toe into human trafficking, and make me feel the fucking moral compunction to stop him.

Now I'm here, playing a more dangerous game than I ever wanted to be a part of.

I shove myself up from the chair, heading for the stairs. I blink as I emerge onto the first floor, the light almost painfully bright after hours of sitting in the dark, with only the neon screens. I rub the heels of my hands over my eyes, hard, and head for the kitchen, where I know I have some good liquor stashed away.

I need a fucking drink.

There's a bottle of Belvedere in the nearest cabinet, and I pull it out, grabbing the first mug I see, and pour a healthy slug of it. Normally, I'd be a little more classy about it, even in my own home—get out a proper glass, pour a drink, and sit and sip it. But after the day I've had, I don't fucking care. I gulp it like water, pour a second slug, and gulp that too. And then I drop the mug into the sink hard enough to chip it, and stride upstairs to the bathroom for a second hot shower. I'm still finding blood in the crevices of my fingers, exactly as I knew I would. Some of it is probably from that man a week ago—some of it is from yet another man I was asked to take apart earlier today. Nothing to do with my own sins, this time. Just someone else who crossed my father, and had to pay.

There was a time when the violence felt like an outlet. Now, it feels exhausting. Pointless. And at barely thirty, I know I'm too young to feel such a bone-deep exhaustion with the cruelties of life.

I stand under the hot spray for a long time, hands braced against the tile, letting it run through my hair and down my back, over my muscles that are still wound tighter than a spring. Even the heat and steam can't help me unwind after the day I've had. I need something better. But it's too late in the evening to go out into the city to find a better distraction, and I want my bed. I'm fucking exhausted.

I turn off the shower, getting out and roughly drying myself off, walking naked into the dark bedroom and flopping down onto the bed. I close my eyes, feeling the pull of sleep already overtaking me, holding off just long enough for me to fumble for a blanket before I'm out like a light.

But sleep, for me, is rarely peaceful. And tonight is no different.

I'm back in the warehouse, the metal structure hot and stinking, but this time, it's me hanging from the chains, me with those hot iron manacles wrapped around my wrists, my bare toes barely brushing the concrete underneath me. My skin bared to the blade in Lev—my brother's hand, his smile wicked as he approaches me, a gleam of satisfaction in his eyes.

He's wanted this. Waited for me to fuck up. Thought about the day when he could do to me what he's always wanted to. What my other brothers want to do.

The tip of the knife digs in. "It's going to be slow," he murmurs. "I'm as good at this as you are, Ivan. I just never wanted you to know—"

The pain deepens in the dream, sharp and hot, and I wake with a jolt, sitting upright in bed. My palms are throbbing, and I realize where the bite of pain came from, that my hands were clenched so hard that even my short nails had dug deeply into my palms. I shake them out, dragging in a deep, shaky breath as I sit there in the dark, trying to regain my composure.

Cold sweat is prickling over my skin. *I need a diversion. I need to take the edge off. Something better than just picking up a girl in a bar.*

I reach for my phone on impulse, hitting the last text I sent, to one of my close friends. Leo is a good friend who has no direct ties to the mafia or Bratva or any other underworld group that I know of—he's just wealthy as shit, through a combination of being born lucky and making good investments after he came into his trust fund. I hang out with him fairly often, along with a couple other friends, and he's always good to get into trouble with.

Especially the kind of trouble I'm in the mood for right now.

Ivan: *Let's go out tomorrow night. Masquerade. I need to blow off some steam.*

I toss the phone onto the bed next to me, laying back against the pillows. My heart rate and breathing have returned to normal, but I'm a long way from getting back to sleep. That nightmare is far too close to being a real possibility, and fear churns in my gut, reminding me of what a precarious position I've put myself in.

The kind of things I've done, things like what I did to that man today, will pale in comparison to what my family will do to me if I get caught.

My phone buzzes, and I reach for it, squinting as I hold it up.

Leo: *Masquerade? Hell yeah. I'm in. I'll text Jonas and Brad, see if they want to go, too.*

. . .

I TEXT BACK a quick *sounds great*, and then toss my phone down again, closing my eyes. I only got a couple hours of sleep before the nightmare woke me up. At this rate, I'll be lucky if I manage a couple more. And I need to be better rested than that.

If I'm going to survive this, I need to be on top of my game.

—

I GET TO MASQUERADE, one of the best-kept secrets in Chicago, at ten p.m. the next night. I drove myself, glad for a chance to get my Mustang out of the garage, and I pull it up to the valet, giving the man standing there a pointed look as I hand him the keys. He's really more of a boy, probably nineteen at the most, and he's looking at the sleek black car with an expression close to worship.

"Don't fucking scratch it," I tell him, and go to join Leo and the other guys.

Leo is on his phone, talking rapidly to someone. Jonas is leaning up against the wall smoking a cigarette, and Brad looks impatient to get inside. I don't blame him. The kind of pleasures that Masquerade offers are enticing, and I'm looking forward to the night, too.

"Ready, boys?" I ask with a grin, and Jonas stubs out his cigarette as Leo holds up a finger, letting me know that he needs another minute on the call. We wait impatiently as he finishes up, turning his cell phone off. We'll have to surrender our electronics as soon as we get inside—one of the many rules of the club.

I turn to the smooth wall, a small steel box next to an almost invisible seam in it. I slip a key out of my pocket, turning it in the keyhole on the front of the box, and it pops open, revealing a number pad. Quickly, I tap out the passcode, and there's a slight rumbling sound as the wall parts, rolling back to allow us to walk in.

I pay an insane amount of money to be able to hold onto that key, to have the passcode, to be allowed the privilege of bringing guests here—each of which has to pay their own monthly dues to be allowed inside. Masquerade is an exclusive club, one that makes men pay dearly for their memberships. Women are allowed in much more freely, and less expensively, but Masquerade is owned by a woman—the wealthy widow of one of Chicago's former top mob bosses, if rumor is to be believed—and she ensures that only men who won't take undue advantages of the club's privileges are allowed to enter.

There are plenty of men who take issue with that, but I enjoy the exclusivity. I also appreciate the knowledge that every man inside the club is someone who knows how to behave like a gentleman.

Once inside, the door rolls closed behind us, leaving us in the dimly lit, smoky-scented entryway. The floor and walls are dark wood, with a thick wine-red runner leading to the stairs that go down to the door on the far wall. To my right are two wing chairs, a low velvet bench, and a small table for anyone waiting, and to my left is a long wooden desk, similar to the check-in desk at a hotel.

A beautiful woman in a crisp black skirt suit, her blonde hair pulled back in an elegant updo, is standing behind it. She smiles pleasantly at me, her makeup impeccable, her red lipstick perfectly applied.

"Your names, sirs?" She looks at the four of us, and I step forward first, handing her my I.D. She taps my name into the computer and nods as she pulls up my profile, giving me a slim black silicone bracelet to slip onto my wrist.

The bracelets here all mean something. Black means that I'm available for anything involving women, so long as it remains completely anonymous. Any inquiries into my identity, and the night ends.

While Leo, Jonas, and Brad check in and get their bracelets, I slip the leather gloves I brought out of my pocket. I like to be *completely* anonymous here, which means not even allowing my tattoos to show. I want nothing that would allow any woman I interact with here to recognize me outside of the club, if she saw me in passing. The absolute secrecy of this place is what allows me to relax, to feel free here.

To feel that I can do and be whatever and whoever I like, without worrying about what consequences it might have in the real world.

At the far end of the room, near the door, there's a basket with stacks of masks. There's every possible style that could be imagined, and I slip a black half-mask out of the basket—one that will cover the top half of my face entirely, down to the tip of my nose, leaving only my mouth and jaw exposed. Other than the top part of my neck, that's the only exposed flesh.

I've found, over the course of my visits to the club, that women find the level of anonymity I insist on extremely erotic. I've never had any difficulty finding a partner for the night—sometimes multiple. And no one has ever tried to cross my boundary.

I think they like the idea of being able to meet someone willing to fulfill their every deviant desire, who they'll never have to encounter anywhere else. Someone who will give them what they want without shame, without questions, without anything other than a matching eagerness to share in an exchange of pleasure.

And then they can go home, their secrets—and mine—safe behind these walls.

That's what Masquerade is all about, after all.

Leo and the others are less concerned about total anonymity. They wear the masks, of course—those are another requirement, much like the surrender of our cell phones—but they have their sleeves rolled up, top buttons of their shirts open, hands bare. They couldn't care less if a tattoo is seen, or if someone notices something about their features. For them, the possibility of getting recognized outside of the club is exciting, I think. The chance that someone might look at them across a restaurant or conference room or crowded bar and recognize another deviant, unable to say aloud what they've shared. The thing they have in common.

To each their own, I suppose.

We split off once we're in the club, each going his own way. Jonas and Brad like to share women, but I prefer to be on my own. I go straight for the bar, waiting my turn as the masked bartender comes up to me.

"Vodka, straight. Top shelf. Twist of lime," I order, and then I turn, surveying the room as I look for who might interest me for the night. My eye catches a slender blonde who is dancing next to another petite brunette on the dance floor to the left of the bar, swaying to the music. I see a yellow bracelet on her wrist—she wants whatever happens to her tonight to happen on the main floor, where everyone can watch. There's an orange one twisted around it—she's only open to oral sex. No penetration of any kind.

I glance away from her. She's beautiful, but I'm in the mood for something private tonight, not a performance. There's an auburn-haired woman further down the bar, alone, and I notice the black bracelet around her wrist. Only here for other women, then.

I've always liked the color-coded system here. No one's time is wasted, no one is asked for anything they don't want. It makes women, especially, more comfortable here, and that means a better time for everyone. This is a safe place, where no one is harassed or cajoled for what they don't want to give up.

This is a place for pleasure, and only that.

I hear the door open just as the bartender pushes my drink towards me, and I look over curiously, to see who's come in. The moment I do, I freeze with my hand on my glass, my attention instantly laser-focused on who is walking into the room.

The first woman who walks in is gorgeous, tall with inky black hair and bronzed skin, wearing a black bandage dress that's so short she couldn't bend over without flashing everyone in the room, her generous cleavage pushed up in the square neckline. She has heels that add four inches to her already statuesque height, and there's a confidence about her that immediately grabs the attention of everyone in the room who isn't already otherwise occupied.

But I don't even notice what color bracelets she's wearing, because it's not her that makes me stop and stare. It's the woman behind her.

She's just as gorgeous, with thick, dark brown hair spilling over her bare shoulders, and the hint of green eyes behind her black velvet domino mask. She's wearing a wine-red velvet dress that comes to her knees, surprisingly modest for this place, except for the slits on either side that run up to mid-thigh. The straps look fragile—so fragile that they look like I could break one with the twist of a finger, and that thought jolts straight to my cock, giving me the first swell of arousal that I've felt so far tonight.

I can tell that it's her first time here before I even look at the bracelets on her wrist. Everything about her demeanor, the way she steps into the room, the way she looks around, screams that she's not only a novice at this but that she's never done anything like this before.

Normally, that would be a turn-off for me. I like confident women, experienced women, women who know that this is a one-time thing. Women who will give as much pleasure as I give them, who will make the night a mutually beneficial experience for us both, and then walk away without a second thought.

But something about the woman in the red velvet dress grabs my attention, and won't let go. Her friend is saying something to her in a low voice, and I watch as she bites her lip, worrying it between her teeth. Her lips are painted the same wine-red as her dress, and all I can think about is what they would look like wrapped around my cock. What *all* of her would look like, wrapped around *me*. I can't take my eyes off of her. Even masked, she's the most beautiful woman I've ever seen.

She's mine tonight. And all that's left is for me to convince her of it.

5

CHARLOTTE

From the moment that Jaz taps in the passcode and we walk into the entryway of the club, I'm more nervous than I ever thought I would be in my life. A part of me just wants to go back home, change back into my pajamas, and curl up on the couch with a big glass of wine and some bad reality tv.

But I'm also excited and curious. I wait as Jaz checks in, breathing in the smoky scent that hangs in the entryway, glancing down towards the looming door at the end of the hall. There's a basket on a table just before it, and as I crane my neck, I catch a glimpse of what looks like masks.

My pulse races a little faster, and I smooth my hands over the velvet skirt of my dress.

Jaz convinced me to wear the dress that I'd planned to wear for my anniversary night out with Nate. She said it was the best possible cherry on top of the revenge that tonight will be, letting some other man touch me for the first time in five years in the dress that I was going to wear for my cheating boyfriend. And I couldn't argue with that. Besides, the dress was expensive, and it's the sexiest thing I own.

I'm just not sure that I'm actually going to let anyone touch me tonight.

When Jaz is finished, it's my turn to step up to the desk. I hand my I.D. to the gorgeous blonde with shaky fingers, and she looks at me appraisingly.

"First time?"

Is it that obvious? It must be. I nod, and she gives me a small smile, returning my I.D. after she types my name into the computer.

"Your friend has paid your entry fee. Since it's your first time here, I need you to fill this out, so I can give you the correct bracelets." She pushes a clipboard with a few sheets of paper on it and a fountain pen attached to it by a thin silver chain, and I stare at it blankly for a second before accepting it.

I hadn't been expecting paperwork. I suddenly feel like I'm at the doctor's office.

"You're welcome to sit over there." She gestures to where two wing chairs and a low bench are located, on the opposing wall. "Once you're done, bring that back, and we'll get you all squared away."

I nod, retreating to one of the chairs. Jaz sinks down next to me, tapping away on her phone. "We'll have to hand these over before we go in," she tells me, gesturing to her phone, but I barely hear her. I'm too focused on the questionnaire in front of me, which is filled with things that I've never even considered before.

The first question is easy—am I interested in only men, only women, or both? I check the box next to *men*, and move onto the next. I can feel my cheeks flushing as I read it—it's asking what types of sexual activity I'm interested in participating in. And from the start, it's making me feel woefully inexperienced.

I've never had anal sex. I would say my experience with oral is pretty limited. And sure, I've had plenty of regular intercourse, but only in the three most basic positions.

I'm in way over my head.

I'm so tempted to give the woman back the questionnaire and head home. But while I might be boring, I'm not a quitter. And the thought of retreating back to the safety of my apartment, while Nate is getting lewd texts and pictures from the women he's cheated on me with, feels worse than just being brave enough to try something new tonight.

But I truly don't know how to answer these questions. I've never been tied up. I've never been spanked. I've never had a reason to think about whether I want to watch others have sex in public or be watched myself. The thought sends a tingle of heat through me, but I don't know if I'm ready for that just yet. Maybe not ever.

Biting my lip, I stand up and walk back to where the blonde woman is tapping away on her keyboard. "Excuse me," I murmur politely, and she looks up at me.

"Oh! Are you finished?" She smiles, and I feel my cheeks heating even more.

"I—no. I just—I don't know how to answer most of these. I'm not very experienced with this sort of thing. Maybe this isn't the right place for me to go—" I hesitate, but her smile doesn't falter.

"Here." She looks at my paperwork, then slips two of the thin silicone bracelets out of the basket next to her—one dark blue and one a pale pink. "Dark blue means you're only interested in men. The pink means you're undecided as to your proclivities, and you want to explore." She pauses. "This club is very exclusive, Ms. Williams. Everyone should respect your space, and accept any no you give as exactly that. But, should anyone push you and make you feel uncomfortable, go to one of the bartenders. The safe word is *diamond*. If you say that to one of them, they will ask who is bothering you and make sure security escorts them out, while making certain you are safe. If you feel overwhelmed at any point and need a moment of privacy, there are two doors to the left of the main floor, both with mask symbols on the fronts. Those are quiet rooms. Type in the passcode —four zeroes—and you'll be able to go in and get some time to yourself." She pauses. "Do you have any other questions or concerns?"

I shake my head. I can't think of anything. I roll the bracelets onto my wrist, feeling nervous, but I don't want to turn back now. Everything she's said has given me a reason to feel better about the night, but it's still all so unknown. I have no idea how I'm going to feel about all of this.

"If you're ready, please hand over your electronics, and select and put on a mask before going through the door. And most of all, enjoy your night at Masquerade." The woman smiles. "This club is meant for pleasure, Ms. Williams. You should enjoy yourself. There's nothing to be ashamed of here."

I know she can see the blush staining my cheeks. It's not even that I'm ashamed—it's that I don't know what I want. I've never let myself think about it for all that long. It's always felt like a pointless exercise, like allowing myself to want things that are impossible. I'm not the kind of person to fantasize about what I can't have, much less what I thought didn't exist.

But now I'm being told that I *can* have it—at least some of it. Something *like* it. And I don't know what's behind that door.

Jaz grabs my hand as we walk to the basket of masks, squeezing it. "Relax," she whispers. "You don't have to do anything you don't want to do. But I think you're going to like it here."

"What have you done?" I whisper, taking a black velvet domino mask out of the basket.

"A lot of things." Jaz grins wickedly, selecting a matching mask.

"Private or in public?"

"Both." She laughs at my shocked expression. "It's amazing what a little anonymity will do for your inhibitions, Charlotte. No one here knows who you are. No one cares. And no one will ever know who you are outside of this place. In here, you're free to want whatever you desire. You're free to be yourself. No one will judge you." She fastens the mask, pinning it into her hair as she fluffs it over the string. "You can do nothing. You can do everything. It's all up to you."

I feel a rush of adrenaline as she steps forward, pushing the door open. I hear a steady beat, music flooding the room as we walk in. The volume is high enough that it gives the place a club-like atmosphere, but not so loud that I don't imagine that I'd be able to hear the sounds of pleasure if anyone started enjoying themselves out in the open. But it doesn't look like anyone has started *that* kind of show yet.

Yet being the operative word. On the right side of the main floor, I can see a variety of things that I don't quite know what they're going to be used for—but my imagination is already running wild. Padded benches with leather cuffs hanging at the front and back. A long padded table that looks to be about waist-high. Two lacquered X's, bigger than a person, against the back wall, with more leather cuffs hanging where wrists and ankles would line up. A long, lacquered cupboard next to them. I can only imagine what's inside.

The club itself is beautifully decorated. The lighting shifts from a soft pink to red to a hazy glow, and the floor is marble tile. The walls are hung in heavy velvet drapes with thick gold cords, giving the entire main floor the feeling of being a modern bordello—fitting, with the masquerade theme. The half-moon bar that's to the right, separating the areas for dancing and mingling from the section that looks to be for "play," is black lacquer with a marble top, matching the cupboards on the right. The seating to the left is leather and velvet, in black and red, with marble-topped tables. The dance floor is black lacquered tiles, standing out in the sea of marble flooring, with the DJ booth in the far corner, half-hidden behind more velvet drapes. And I see the doors that the blonde woman told me about, with the gemstone-shaped cutouts on the front—the quiet rooms.

A winding staircase leads up to the second floor, with a railing that circles all the way around. When I look up, I see doors along that level, and I realize those must be private rooms. My pulse kicks up a notch, thinking about what might happen behind those doors.

Or what might happen in the alcoves that I see on the right side of the room, hidden behind more velvet drapes. An in-between of public and private, close enough to where the play will be happening to still be a partial voyeur, but without the absolute exposure of whatever will happen on those benches eventually.

I swallow hard, suddenly imagining myself splayed over one of them. I don't know if the hitch in my breath, the sudden spike in my pulse, is out of fear or want.

"You okay?" Jaz asks, leaning in and I nod, my mouth dry.

"I need a drink." I start to walk towards the bar, Jaz staying right next to me, just as she promised. The bartender comes over immediately—it's not all that busy yet; it's still relatively early for a Friday night. He's a handsome man with dark hair—or at least, handsome so far as I can tell. A white theatre mask covers one half of his face, Phantom of the Opera style, leaving the other half bare. One blue eye twinkles at me cheerfully, and the half of his mouth that I can see curves upwards in a smile.

"What can I get you ladies?" he asks, his voice deep and rich, and a shiver runs down my spine.

"I—gin and tonic. Two limes." I fall back on my usual bar order when I want something other than wine, needing something familiar in this place. Something I can count on, that I'll be sure to like. And I definitely need something stronger than wine right now.

"A Gold Rush for me," Jaz says, sliding onto the barstool to my right.

"What's that?" I look at her curiously, as she leans forward, her elbows on the marble bar top.

"Whiskey, honey, and lemon syrup." She brushes a lock of hair out of her face. "A little smoky, a little sweet."

"I should try that," I say without much conviction—I've never tried whiskey before.

Jaz chuckles, taking her drink from the bartender as he brings them over, nudging mine towards me. "That man is looking at you," she says softly as she raises her glass to her lips. "In the half-mask, with the gloves. He hasn't stopped watching you since we walked in."

"How do you know that?" I hiss, taking a large sip of my drink. "He's wearing a mask."

"I can still see his eyes. And they've been on you since we stepped through that door."

Almost guiltily, I let my gaze slide over to the man Jaz is talking about. I spot him immediately—it's impossible not to. Even masked, he has the kind of presence that immediately demands attention. He's tall, with dark blond hair. I can't see his eye color from here, but I can see his build, fit and strong underneath the black button-down and suit trousers that he's wearing. He shifts slightly, and I can see the flex of his muscles in his arms and chest, tugging at the shirt.

And Jaz is right. He's staring right at me.

"Go talk to him," Jaz hisses.

"I—" I take another swallow of my drink. "I don't know if I can."

"Just try. If he puts you off, I'll be right here. But he's looking at you like he wants to eat you." Her voice drops. "And if you want him to, I bet he will."

A fearful thrill rushes through me at that. It sounds preposterous—the idea that he could do such a thing like that, here, when I don't even know his name yet. But he *could*. He could do it in front of everyone, or in one of those alcoves, or in a private room. He could do it without ever telling me his name, or me telling him mine. If we both wanted it, I could take that kind of pleasure from him, with no strings. No repercussions. Without ever seeing him again.

There *is* a strange kind of freedom in that. A kind of excitement.

Licking my lips nervously, I slide off my barstool, stepping towards him. There's an instant shift in his energy as I approach him. A moment ago, he was watching me patiently, observing, but he straightens a little as I approach, perking up like a hunter watching his prey. It sends a shiver down my spine, heat pooling in my stomach as I stop just in front of him, my hand clutching my drink for dear life.

"Hi," I manage. It sounds woefully inadequate for the situation, but I don't know what, exactly, *is* the opener for meeting a stranger in a sex club. *There should have been a briefing*, I think, swallowing back laughter. *A pamphlet, maybe.*

"Hello." His accent is British, crisp and formal, but there's a roughness to it, a sexiness that makes that shiver tingle down my spine again.

"I'm—" I start to say my name, forgetting the *anonymity* part of all of this for the habitual politeness that's intrinsically a part of me, when his finger suddenly touches my lips.

I forgot about the gloves that I noticed, when I first looked over and saw him. The leather is cool against my lips, and something about the strangeness of it sends that heat fluttering through me, warming me from the inside out. His finger drags down, the leather-covered tip pressing against my lower lip.

"No names. I take my privacy here seriously. This is all anonymous. You will never know my name, and I'll never know yours." His full lips curve in a sinful, promising smile. "That's part of the fun."

Another shiver washes over me. His hand drops, and I suddenly miss the contact. The feel of the leather against my skin. I bite my lip, my teeth catching where his finger was a moment ago, and I see his eyes drop to my mouth.

"Can I buy you a drink?" His gaze flicks to my wrist, looking for the bracelets. "Undecided. You're new here?"

"Do you come here often?" My cheeks flush as soon as the words leave my mouth. "Oh god, that was the stupidest line. I meant—"

"I know what you meant." His smile broadens, amusement written all over the part of his face that I can see, but it's not directed *at* me. He's not making fun of me. He seems to be genuinely enjoying my company—so far. "A drink?"

I nod. "I—yes. Thank you."

"Anything in particular, or should I choose for you?"

My teeth catch on my lip again. "What are you drinking?"

He chuckles. "I don't think you'd like it. Vodka, straight up, with a twist of lime."

I can't help making a face. I've never tried vodka, but I've smelled it before, and it smells like rubbing alcohol to me. Not anything I'd want to drink.

"You choose," I tell him bravely. "But not vodka."

That smile deepens. "Are you going to let me choose everything tonight?" There's that rasp in his voice again, promising something darker than his cultured British accent lets on. That heat blossoms through me again, but it's mixed with apprehension.

"I—"

"Don't worry." His voice is smooth again, soothing. "I'm only teasing you a little. Flirting. You don't have to do anything you don't want to do." He motions to the bartender. "Another vodka for me. And a gin and tonic for my new friend here. Two limes."

My mouth drops open as I look at him. "You knew what I was drinking?"

"I'm very perceptive." He smiles. "And gin has a very particular smell."

He shifts forward, moving towards me so that there's even less space between us now, less than a hand's breadth between him and me. He's close enough that I can feel the heat of his body, smell the woodsy smoke of his cologne. "A very particular taste, too," he murmurs, his gaze dropping to my mouth once more. "I'd like to find out what it tastes like on you."

"I—I don't know if I want to kiss." I'd thought about that earlier. Kissing feels sweet to me. Intimate. Something that you don't do with a stranger, only being used for sex. *Did Nate kiss any of his other women?* I wonder as I look up at the masked man in front of me. I'd imagine he did. I don't think men—especially a man like Nate—put that kind of weight on kissing.

I take a step back, putting a little more space between me and this stranger. My head is spinning, and I've only had one drink. This all feels so strange.

The things this man is saying to me sound good. *Too* good. They're the kind of thing I imagine someone saying after a date. Several dates. After wine and dinners and nights out. The sort of thing you warm up to. But he's saying them to me without ever even knowing my name—seconds after meeting me. He's introducing himself to me with seduction.

But that's what I'm here for. *Isn't it?*

I swallow hard as the bartender brings our second round of drinks. Those are also the kinds of things that *no one* has ever said to me. No one has ever said they wanted to taste me before.

The kind of men I date, men like Nate, men who wear polo shirts on the weekends and have investment accounts, don't say things like that.

"Is this too much for you?" The man tilts his head slightly, and I try to read what I can in his eyes through the barrier of the mask. His eyes are dark blue, I see, now that he's this close.

It doesn't look like he's judging me. It looks like he's being cautious. Making sure that this is what I want. That thought makes me feel more comfortable.

"I don't know what I want," I admit. "This is my first time in a place like this."

"I can tell." Once again, there's no judgment in his voice. It's just an observation. "We can just talk, if you like."

That startles me. This isn't the kind of club where people come to *talk*; I know that much. But he gestures towards one of the leather couches to the right of the room, far from the play area, where I can see a few couples starting to drift over. "We can sit down. Get to know one another. Anonymously, of course." His eyes glitter with mischief, as if he knows exactly how ridiculous that statement is. The entire purpose of this place is to *not* know each other. But I appreciate that he's trying to make me feel comfortable.

I glance back at Jaz, who makes an eager shooing motion with her hand. I bite my lip, stifling a laugh, and nod. "Okay," I tell him, and he stands up easily, with all the grace of a predatory cat, as his gloved hand wraps around mine.

"Come with me, then."

The feeling of the leather against my bare palm feels strangely erotic. I'm fully clothed, but he's somehow even more so, and that tingle runs down my spine again, trapping itself between my thighs. My breath catches in my throat as he leads me over to one of the couches, sinking down onto it as he drapes one arm over the back and looks at me expectantly.

I sink down next to him, crossing my legs at the ankle as I take a nervous sip of my drink. "You can't possibly have come here just to talk," I say softly. "I'm sure there's plenty of women here who would do anything you like right now. Without the need for all of this—foreplay." I bite my lip, and he smiles.

"You're already relaxing. Look at that—an innuendo." His smile reaches his eyes, and I look at his full mouth, that heat spreading through me again. *He's looking at you like he wants to eat you up.* Jaz's voice echoes through my head, and I clench my hands around my glass, the nervous butterflies fluttering through me again.

"I'm sitting here next to you because I want to be," he continues. "I'd rather be sitting here talking to you, than doing anything else, with anyone else, in this club right now."

A rush of emotion washes over me, tightening in my chest. He has no idea what that simple statement, said so blandly, means to me right now. The thought that anyone would rather be with *me* instead of another woman makes me feel breathless, and overly emotional for where we are—especially considering the fact that I'll never see this man again. I'm giving those words far more weight than I should. But I can't help it.

I came here because I wanted to feel desired. And he's doing that right now. He's giving me everything I need, already, with a simple statement.

Maybe Jaz was right. Maybe this place is exactly what I need right now.

I suck in a breath, gathering my courage as I take another sip of my drink. A part of me is still nervous and uncertain, wanting to run home to where things are familiar and safe. But my home is partially tainted now, full of memories of Nate, of all the times together that I thought meant more than they obviously did. If I go back right now, if I leave, it feels like admitting that he was right. That he needed to do those things with other women because I would never have done them with him.

I want to prove to myself that he was wrong. That he's entirely the asshole in this situation. And he *is*, because whether or not I ever would have done those things, he should have left me before he cheated on me.

It honestly would have hurt less.

That thought replaces my nerves with the anger I've been feeling off and on since I saw those texts. I'm hurt, sad, and unsure of the future—but I'm also furious. I'm furious that he did things like this with other women—that he probably went to clubs like this, that he played out filthy fantasies with them, that he never, ever even hinted to me that he might want me to try to satisfy him in some other way than what we already did. That he lied to me, and he never even gave me a chance.

I want to get back at him for hurting me like that. I want revenge.

This is a good start.

I take another sip of my drink, and turn to look at the man next to me. "What if I did want to do more than talk?" I whisper, the nerves fluttering through me with every word. "What then?"

He smiles, a lazy, lustful smile that's full of promise. His eyes drop to my mouth, then my breasts, my waist, sliding lower until his gaze has raked all the way down to my red-painted toes in my high-heeled sandals, and then back up again to my eyes.

"Then," he says slowly, his voice deep and rasping again, "Then I would do whatever you like, little dove."

Something jolts through me at the pet name. It sounds like an endearment on his tongue. And it sounds so much better than *babe*, or *baby*, the things Nate used to call me.

"What if I don't know what I like?" I take the last sip of my drink, my heart beating hard in my chest.

"Then we'll go slow, and find out what that is." His voice is full of promise, dark and rich, and I swallow hard.

"Can we go somewhere private?" I look up at the railing surrounding the second floor, and he nods, standing up with that same catlike grace as he holds out a gloved hand to me.

"Of course."

I catch Jaz's eye as the man leads me to the spiral staircase. Her eyes widen, and she gives me an enthusiastic thumbs up, mouthing *I'll be right here*, as she taps her now-full drink. I feel a flutter of guilt, knowing she's not hooking up with anyone because she wants to make sure she's there if I need her. *I'm going to have to make sure I do something nice for her,* I think as I follow the man up the stairs. Jaz is a good friend. The best kind of friend. And I'm lucky to have her in my life.

We stop in front of one of the doors. I notice that the one next to it has a golden tassel hanging from the knob, and I realize why when the man unlocks the door in front of us and takes a similar tassel off of a hook just inside the moment we step in. He hangs it off of the handle, and closes the door firmly, turning to face me.

"Well, you have me alone." He smiles that same slow, wicked smile. "I'm at your service."

Oh. A flutter of heat ripples through me at that thought. At the idea of having a man so blatantly sexual, so attractive, at *my* service.

I've always felt, in every sexual situation I've ever been in, that my own pleasure comes second. That anything I might ask for, any foreplay, any lead-up to the main event, is something that the men I've slept with have tolerated as a means to an end. What they *have* to do in order to get me aroused enough to have what they want.

This man seems to be treating *my* desires, *my* pleasure, as the main event. And I'm suddenly seized with a desire to push that as far as I can.

The problem is that I don't know how to vocalize what I want. I don't know what to ask for. I've never been in a situation before where I've felt that I *can*.

He seems to see my hesitation. He walks towards me, stopping a hand's length away once again as he looks down at me, his dark blue eyes unreadable behind the mask. "What's wrong, little dove?" he murmurs, and I swallow hard, wishing for another drink.

"I—" I think desperately of how to explain, of how much I *should* say, and I wish more than anything I were the kind of person who could fling herself headlong into this, without so much hesitation. I'm being offered everything that I thought couldn't possibly be real, and my own anxieties are on the verge of ruining it for me.

I don't want to let that happen.

He tilts his head slightly, studying me from behind the mask. I'm suddenly very grateful for my own—I feel less exposed, less vulnerable with it on. It keeps him from reading every emotion on my face, just as I can't entirely read him.

"You've come here for a reason," he says calmly. "I don't think it's just for pleasure, or you would have told me what you want from me already."

"What do *you* want?" It's the boldest question I've asked all night, but he just chuckles.

"I want your pleasure." He lifts his hand again, tracing my lower lip with just the tip of one gloved finger, that same motion that sends a tingling shiver down my spine again. "I want to find out what you taste like, little dove. Your mouth—or lower, if you don't want me to kiss you. I want to find out the sound of your moans when you come. I—"

"I don't come." I blurt it out, and he frowns. "Not usually, I mean," I amend. There have been a few times with Nate. But it's been rare. Rare enough that I could count on one hand. "Usually just—when I'm alone."

Something heats in his gaze at the mention of me touching myself. "I'd like to see that," he murmurs. "The way you make yourself come. But I'd rather teach you what it feels like for a man who knows what he's doing to give you an orgasm. Or more than one," he adds, that wicked smile on his lips again, and I stare at him.

"I don't think that's possible."

"Oh, it is." His voice is full of confidence as he takes another step towards me, and I back up, my pulse suddenly racing. "I could make you come more than once, little dove—I promise you that."

"I—" I lick my lips, and his eyes are instantly fixed on my mouth again.

"So you're here because you've been neglected." That smile turns into something more like a smirk. "Am I closer to the truth now?"

"I'm here because my ex cheated on me."

The moment it slips out, my face heats. I hadn't expected to say that. I hadn't meant to just blurt it out, but the man in front of me goes very still, his smile faltering.

"Someone cheated on *you*?" He says it with utter disbelief, as if it's such an impossible thing to imagine.

"I don't think it's that hard to believe," I murmur awkwardly. "I'm not that exciting."

He takes another step forward, his dark eyes fixed on mine so intently that I feel frozen to the spot. His gloved fingers capture my chin, his thumb touching my lower lip. He's not touching me anywhere else, but I feel that heat pooling in my stomach slide lower. I'm wet, just from him touching my lip. Aching, from the slide of leather against my skin.

"I don't know you well enough to know if that's true," he murmurs. "But I can see that you are beautiful. Sweet. Innocent. And no one should ever hurt you like that."

I look up at him, transfixed by the heat in his dark blue eyes, by the way he's looking at me from behind the mask. No one has ever looked at me like that before. No one has ever made me feel this desired with nothing but a look and a simple touch.

It's intoxicating.

"He never told me what he wanted," I whisper. "And then he did those things with other women. He said he *respected* me too much to ask for them."

That wicked smile tilts the corners of the man's mouth again. "That's bullshit," he murmurs softly. "But I can tell you one thing, little dove."

"What?" I whisper, fighting the urge to flick my tongue out, against the tip of his thumb that's still resting on my lower lip.

"In that case, I'd like nothing more than to disrespect you tonight."

That smile turns into a knowing smirk as he says it, and I have the vague feeling that the woman I am outside of this place—the one who never wears heels higher than two inches because they make her feet hurt and has a whole closet of basically-matching shirts—should be offended.

But whoever I am for tonight—I'm not offended. I'm curious. Intrigued. And I don't want him to stop.

"You deserve a man who will focus on your pleasure, and not on his own," he continues, his voice smooth and rich as that gloved fingertip brushes over my lip, his hand moving to cup my jaw. It's as if he doesn't want to give me even a chance to look away from him, as if he wants to keep my attention, so that I don't have the opportunity to get frightened and fly away like the bird that he keeps referring to me as.

"I—" I bite my lip. "I don't even know what I'm supposed to do."

The cool leather of his glove is warming against my skin. His thumb sweeps over my cheekbone, his gaze darkening with some secret knowledge of what comes next.

"If you want to find out," he murmurs, in that same husky, rich voice, "then go and lie down on the bed, little dove."

6

CHARLOTTE

As soon as he tells me to go and lie down, that urge to run flares up again. In a fight-or-flight situation, I'm definitely always going to choose flight. But this one is flight-or-fuck—and I'm dangerously close to picking the latter.

If I run now, it feels like admitting that Nate was always right about me. That I deserved to lose the relationship, instead of him being the asshole that never even gave me a real chance to be what he wanted. That's how it's felt all night, every time I've come up against one of these decisions.

Talk to the masked man. Have a drink with the masked man. Go upstairs with him. And then—

I hadn't even really noticed that there was a bed in the room. All I've been able to look at is him. But now, as I twist around to look for where it is that he wants me to go, I see the rest of it.

The room is warm and luxurious, continuing the sort of modern French baroque theme from downstairs. The walls are wallpapered a rich red, with a narrow window to the left, draped with gold. There's a plush, wide chair next to it, as well as a small table, and I feel my cheeks heat as I realize that the chair is the perfect width for a man to sit back in while a woman straddles his lap. My knees wouldn't even slide off the sides.

To the left of it is one of those padded benches, and I can't even begin to let myself think of what that's used for—all the reasons why this man might want to bend me over it or lay me back and use those leather cuffs to hold my wrists and ankles. I think of the feeling of his leather-gloved finger against my lips, and shiver.

To my other side, there's a cupboard on one wall, a set of drawers, and two more chairs. Directly ahead of me, in the center of the far wall, is a huge bed with a four-poster canopy. There are no drapes hanging from it, and I realize with another flush of heat that the canopy frame is meant for other uses. A myriad of different ways to potentially bind me to the bed, so that my partner in this room can have his way with me.

The masked man is eerily silent. He's waiting for me to decide, I realize—to either decide that this is all too much for me and leave, or to obey him, and go to the bed. I never thought I was aroused by the idea of obedience—by the thought of submission to a man—but this man wants me to submit to my own pleasure. It feels different, somehow. He wants me to obey, so that he can teach me all of the things I've been missing.

Taking a deep breath, I walk unsteadily towards the bed.

It's made up with a red silk velvet duvet edged in gold, similarly-colored pillows stacked three deep at the head of it. My heart is beating hard in my chest as I stop at the edge, afraid to look back at the man as I nervously kick off my shoes—wondering a second later if I was supposed to do that at all. He didn't tell me to. But I would never wear shoes in bed.

My teeth sink into my lip again. I'm overthinking this. I want to stop thinking so much. I want—

"I can help you with that."

I jump, covering my mouth with one hand to stifle my small yelp of shock. I didn't hear him move. I didn't realize that I'd said that last sentence out loud. But I can feel the heat of him now, standing behind me, *feel* his presence without even seeing him.

He gave me instructions, if I want this. I take a deep, shaky breath, and climb onto the bed.

No sooner do I lie back on the pillows, turning my head to look at him, than I see his mouth curve upwards in a wicked, almost satisfied smile. As if he's thrilled to see that I've obeyed him. As if *he's* getting what *he* wants out of this, instead of what he's promised, which is that this will be all about me.

A nervous shudder runs through me, a fear that I've been talked into something that isn't going to be what I thought, and I hold up a hand before he can move.

"Wait," I say nervously. "Do I—Ja—my friend said something about safe words. Something to say if I want you to stop. What do I—"

He chuckles, but there's no malice in it. "Normally, those words are for play where you're going to pretend not to want what I'm doing to you. There won't be any of that tonight. But if it will make you feel better, choose a word. Any word will do."

I search for something, looking around the room. "Paris," I blurt out, taking in the French-inspired decor, and he laughs again, softly.

"Paris, it is. Not something I can imagine screaming out at the height of pleasure whether I wanted to stop or not." He smirks. "And there's something else in these rooms, too. May I?" He reaches out towards my hand, and shakily, I nod.

It seems silly to be nervous about him touching my hand, when soon he plans on touching so much more. But I feel my breath catch as soon as that cool leather glides over my fingers.

He lifts my hand up, towards the headboard, and I almost pull it back. I think, for a second, that he plans to tie me up, and that both terrifies me and sends a bolt of heat through me at the same time— one that I don't have time to examine. Because a second later, I feel my fingers brush against the smooth wall—and something raised there, a round shape.

"A panic button." The man lets go of my hand. "There are others, but since I don't have plans to tie you up tonight, I don't think we need to spend time exploring all the safety measures in this room. The point is—you're safe, little dove," he says, his voice softening. "Nothing will happen here that you don't want. The owner of this club has gone to great lengths to make sure of that."

I feel a flicker of disappointment when he says he's not going to tie me up, followed by a sort of warm confusion. "You're worried about me feeling safe," I murmur softly, and his smile falters for a moment.

"You should always feel safe in a situation like this. Even in—*especially* in—the ones where you want to feel *unsafe* for a little while. Kink has rules, little dove. And the more dangerous and deviant the play, the more rules there are."

I bite my lip, unsure how I feel about that. My *life* is full of rules that I always play by. Full of me always trying to do the right thing, to be the perfect employee and friend and girlfriend. I want to forget about the rules for a little while. I want to be free of all of it.

But part of me is grateful to know that underneath it all, I'm safe here. And I can feel myself subconsciously relaxing, with every thing this man does to let me know that he's not here to take advantage of me.

At least—not in any way that I don't want him to.

"Now." His lips curl in that smirk again. "There are things I'd rather be doing with my mouth right now than talking."

A completely foreign sensation sweeps over me, from the top of my head to the tips of my toes, shivering over my skin at that. It's not like I've never had a man's mouth on me before—but just the way he says it implies that this will be unlike anything I've felt before. And I can't help thinking that maybe he's overselling it. That he has too high an opinion of himself, and that tonight is going to be just another disappointment.

Slowly, he moves onto the bed. When he's kneeling at the very foot of it, those dark blue eyes intent on mine for a moment, he lets his gaze drag down my body, so slowly that I can almost feel the weight of it. All the way down to my bare feet—and then he reaches out, his gloved thumbs sweeping up the inner curves of my feet as his hands wrap around my ankles.

Another shiver washes through me, my body twitching at the sudden contact. That smirk never leaves his lips, even for a moment. "Ticklish?" he asks, amused, and I shake my head.

"Not really." My voice sounds breathier than I think it ever has in my life, and he's only touched my *feet*. "I just—"

I feel my face flush, because I don't know how to explain what I'm feeling, and everything that comes to mind just makes me feel horribly naive and inexperienced. And before tonight, I didn't think I was. I've dated. I've had sex. I've had a handful of semi-serious relationships and one big, very serious relationship with Nate. But everything about this man makes me feel like a blushing virgin. Like I'm sixteen again, fumbling around in the back of a car with no real idea of what all these new sensations are or what I'm meant to do about them.

He's experienced, I tell myself, as his hands tighten around my ankles, spreading my legs apart enough for him to inch forward on the bed, kneeling in between my feet now. *He knows what he's doing. So he'll teach you what all this means.*

There's a relief that comes with that. With giving myself up to this man's knowledge, to his touch, to whatever it is that he has planned for me. I exhale a breath as his gloved hands slide up my calves, cool and soft, so supple and flexible that it would be easy to forget that they're gloves at all, and not his bare hands.

Except I don't think I *do* want to forget. It adds a layer of strangeness, of mystery to all of this, that makes it that much more erotic. Just like the masks, the anonymity, this entire theatrical display of hedonism.

His hands reach my knees, the hem of my velvet dress. My revenge dress, now, instead of one that was supposed to mark a special night in my life. A turning point. A new beginning.

But it occurs to me, as he begins to push the dress slowly up my thighs, that this night could still be all of those things. This could be the night that I discover something new about myself. Where I become the kind of person I've always envied from afar.

The kind who takes chances. Who prioritizes herself. Who lets herself *want*.

Someone who doesn't dismiss her own needs and desires as impossible.

Because this—what he's making me feel, felt impossible before this moment. It feels as if sparks are dancing over my skin, my lungs tightening, my skin growing hotter and more flushed with every inch that he pushes the dress up my thighs. The sensation of the cool silk lining against my heated skin makes me gasp, all of me sensitized with curiosity and anticipation—and he hasn't even touched anything that could really even be called an erogenous zone yet. He's touched my feet and my legs —that's it. And yet, I'm on the verge of panting, of whimpering, of *begging*.

I've never felt like this before.

He pauses as the dress reaches halfway up my thighs, his hands dropping to my knees. "How are you feeling, little dove?"

I look up at him helplessly, my lips parting, but nothing comes out. My mind feels foggy, like all I can think about is *more*.

"More," I whisper, and there's something knowing in his smile this time.

"Gladly, little dove," he murmurs, and his hands tighten around my knees, pushing them apart.

The movement shoves my dress higher up my thighs, rucked up around my hips now as he pushes my knees wide and flattens them against the bed, exposing the smooth black material between them. I'm suddenly thankful that I chose black, because I can *feel* how wet I already am, the fabric clinging to my folds, and I don't know if I could handle the embarrassment of him seeing how thoroughly soaked I am when he hasn't done—really anything, yet.

"Keep your knees against the bed," he murmurs, and another jolt of heat washes over me at the firm command, issued in that rich, smooth voice. "Or as close to it as you can." He pushes gently down on my knees again, a reminder to hold the pose that he's situated me in, and then those gloved hands start to skim up the inside of my thighs.

I can feel myself shuddering under his touch. I don't realize how hard I'm biting my lip, stifling any possible noise, until his hands suddenly pause at the very top of my inner thighs, and I open my eyes to see him looking at me.

"Don't be quiet, little dove," he murmurs. "I want to hear you through all of this. Every sound you make turns me on. Moan or beg or scream if you want to. I'll enjoy it all."

The idea of anything making me *scream* in bed sounds ridiculous. But I'm already on the verge of moaning. The only reason I haven't is because a part of me is embarrassed to let him hear how much I want it. How much he's already aroused me.

But if he *wants* to hear it—

His hands press down on my inner thighs, and I suddenly feel the firm press of one of his gloved fingers, between my legs. Over the wet material of my panties, just against the seam of my folds, rubbing there back and forth.

A gasping moan slips free. I can't help it. My hips arch up into his touch, a burst of pleasure rolling through me from the friction of his thumb, rubbing my folds against each other, against my clit.

He chuckles, but there's no amusement in it now. It's a dark, rough sound, a sound of masculine pleasure, and when he pulls his thumb away, I gasp.

"You need this more than you realized, little dove," he murmurs, and his hands slide up my hips, just beneath the crumpled velvet of my dress, hooking in the edge of my panties as he starts to draw them down. "I'm going to make you come so hard. And then I'll make you come again."

The promise in his voice sends another shudder through me, even if I still don't believe him. But it sounds like *he* believes it, and that's enough to make me wonder.

He slides the panties down my hips, over my legs, and as he pushes my knees apart again, back into that pose where he arranged me the first time, I feel the first temptation to resist. Because there's nothing between me and his hungry gaze any longer. Nothing except his own mask, which somehow makes me feel even more exposed, because he can see every wet, swollen inch of the most intimate part of me, but I can't read his face. My only hint at his emotions is in that ever-present smirk on his face, and heat blooms through me, my fingers curling into the silk-velvet duvet.

His eyes drop between my thighs, taking in all of my exposed, vulnerable flesh—and he *licks his lips.*

Like he's hungry. Like he can't wait to devour me.

My hips lift up off of the bed without my meaning for them to, a wordless plea, my body begging for something that I've never had and can't begin to imagine. But somehow, subconsciously, something in me seems to answer to that promise in his smile, in his eyes, hiding behind that mask.

He moves closer, stretching his long, muscular frame onto the bed between my legs. I realize with another flash of heat that he's still fully clothed, entirely covered except for the lower part of his face and the upper part of his neck, while I'm disheveled and half-undressed, naked from the waist down. His hands move up, his gloved thumbs resting on the seam of my folds, and I shudder at the touch, another moan slipping from my lips. I hear that dark, rumbling chuckle again, and then he leans forward, his thumbs parting me—and his tongue touches my most intimate flesh.

I feel it, flat and soft against me, wet and hot, dragging a searing line upwards from my entrance to my clit. My head falls back, my entire body reacting to the sensation after so much foreplay, and I cry out without meaning to, a shudder of pleasure rippling through me.

It feels better than any mouth on me has ever felt before. And it's only the first touch.

He pulls back slightly, his thumbs skimming over my soft flesh, and it takes everything in me not to beg him to keep going. But I'm not there yet. Not quite.

"I knew you needed this as soon as I saw you," he murmurs, his voice low and dark, his breath heated against my oversensitive skin. "But I had no idea how much." He leans in again, so close that I can feel the barest brush of his skin against mine. "Don't hold back, little dove. You can come as many times as you like. I want you to have as much pleasure tonight as you possibly can."

He says it like it's a given that I'll come. That I'll come again, and again. And I didn't believe him before, but now—as his tongue slides over me again and I feel another toe-curling wave of pleasure crash over me, I understand his cockiness. His *confidence*. Because I'm going to come, and I'm already so close.

His thumbs hold me open, his mouth pressed tightly now against me, his tongue sliding up to focus on my clit. He licks me in long, hot strokes, then circles my clit as my moans turn to gasping whines, the sounds coming from me like nothing I've ever heard before. They're certainly no sounds I've ever *made* before. But I can't stop. If *he* stopped right now, I *would* beg. Because I'm so close, so fucking close, and as those circles tighten, his tongue stiffening, I feel the muscles in my thighs seize, and I realize that what I've always thought was an orgasm has been nothing but a dim shadow of what I'm about to feel.

My entire body tightens, the sensations building to a singular, sharp point that suddenly explodes like a thousand fireworks, light bursting behind my eyes as my fingers claw at the blankets and my hips jerk upwards, grinding shamelessly against his face as I start to buck and writhe and gasp with a nearly incomprehensible pleasure. He's still licking, still keeping up those same intense circles, and I keep waiting for him to stop, but he doesn't. It draws out the pleasure, until I realize dazedly that the orgasm has ebbed, but the pleasure hasn't stopped. He's still going, and he's right—if he keeps this up, it feels like I *could* come again.

I'm still grinding against his mouth, gasping and making small sobbing, moaning sounds, and he slides one hand away from me, looping his arm around my thigh and over my stomach, effectively pinning me to the bed. I gasp at the pressure of him holding me down, another moan slipping from my lips, and his other hand moves down, two gloved fingers pushing inside of me as his mouth tightens around my clit and he starts to *suck*.

I cry out. It's very nearly a scream; the pleasure intensified even more at this new assault on my swollen, oversensitive flesh, and his fingers curl inside of me, the feeling of the smooth leather thrusting inside my body foreign and delicious at the same time. It feels like bare fingers and not, simultaneously, and I gasp, my hips rolling as much as they can under the weight of his arm as he thrusts his fingers back and forth, fucking me with them as he sucks harder at my clit.

I *feel* him groan as arousal floods me, soaking his fingers, his hand, his mouth, his chin. He must be dripping with me by now, but the embarrassment of it all has faded, replaced only with the desperate building need to come again. I've forgotten that I don't believe it's possible, forgotten everything except how much I *need* this, and I writhe under his grasp, riding his mouth to my second climax as his gloved fingers thrust and curl, his tongue lashing and fluttering against my clit.

He sucks harder, hard enough that I can feel how swollen my clit is, throbbing against his tongue, and the pressure builds to that sharp, sparkling point again—

He was right about making me scream.

It almost feels as if I black out for a second. I'm not aware of what my body is doing, of my hands scrabbling at the blanket or the bucking of my hips as I ride his tongue to my second climax. I'm only aware of sensation, of how impossibly good it feels, of how I never knew *anything* could feel like this, the cold strangeness of the gloves and mask and his fully clothed body nestled between my bare legs, only heightening everything. It's an experience like nothing I ever imagined, and I faintly hear my voice, shrieking out my pleasure as I take all of it from him, wave after wave, until it fades, and I lay limp and trembling on the bed.

I feel his tongue slide over me in one last long, lingering lick, before he pulls back, his fingers sliding out of me. I stare numbly up at him, speechless, as he looks down at me with that satisfied smirk on his face.

His lips are wet. So is his chin, glistening with my arousal. He sees me looking at him, and reaches up with one gloved hand, lewdly dragging it across his face. My mouth drops open, and I stare at him, at the unabashed, unashamed sexuality that drips from him.

He leans forward, two gloved fingertips pressing against my lower lip, and before I can react to what he's doing, he pushes them into my mouth. The leather is damp, salty and tangy from my arousal, and before I can think better of it, my lips close around his fingers as I suck the taste of myself off of him.

It's what he wanted me to do. I knew it, instinctively, even though I've never imagined doing anything like that in my life. But those dark blue eyes look startled, as if he didn't expect me to actually do it.

He groans, his head tipping back as he tugs his fingers free. It's only then that I think to look down, and I see the shape of his cock, straining in a thick, impossibly hard ridge against the front of his suit trousers.

My mouth goes dry. Unless it's some kind of optical illusion, he's *huge*. Bigger than any man I've ever slept with, for sure.

"That—turned you on?" My voice is a breathless gasp, still recovering from everything he just did to me. I don't think I can move.

His eyes widen again. "Is that a serious question, little dove?" His voice is still smooth and rich, that British accent clipping every word, but he sounds surprised by what I said.

I bite my lip, some of my self-consciousness returning. "I—I'm just used to guys needing to get fully hard again, after doing that," I half-mumble. "They always say it's distracting." I try to think rapidly of any man I've ever been with who didn't have to quickly stroke himself back to a full erection after going down on me for the cursory two or three minutes to get me wet enough to fuck—never enough to make me come—but I can't.

He snorts inelegantly, a little of the polished facade slipping, for a moment. Enough to let me see that he's playing a part, here. That the man here with me in this room, this club, isn't the man he normally is on the outside.

Whoever that is, I'll never know. I wait to feel disappointed, or robbed of something, but I surprisingly don't. I knew what this was. And it's been everything I could want.

"The taste of you makes me painfully hard, little dove," he murmurs. "I can't think of anything more arousing than making you come on my tongue. I'd do it all night, if we had more time."

"I don't think I could take it again," I admit, and he chuckles darkly.

"You could," he promises. "But maybe not tonight."

I swallow hard, looking down at that thick, threatening ridge again, straining against his fly. "What do you want?" I ask softly, starting to push myself up from the pillows. "Do you want oral, too, or—"

"I don't want anything," he says firmly, starting to slide off of the bed, and I reach out on instinct, grabbing one gloved hand. He freezes, and I look at him curiously.

"I don't understand." I frown. "You're turned on. You just said so yourself. You don't want to fuck me? Or use my mouth, or—" I feel my cheeks flush again, and I'm oddly hurt that he doesn't want me to return the pleasure that he just gave me.

His smile softens slightly as he stands up. "No," he says calmly. "I think you've had a lifetime of being expected to give something in return for any pleasure you receive. So I think for tonight, little dove, you should get to only take."

He sinks down into the chair next to the window, his long, muscled body relaxing into it. I can still see the evidence of how aroused he is, but he doesn't seem to be in any hurry to do anything about it.

I have the distinct feeling, though, that I'm being dismissed.

Slowly, I sit up the rest of the way, still feeling dizzy and a little shaky, as if I haven't entirely reinhabited my own body. I look for my panties, realizing that I have no idea where they ended up, and the man sitting across the room watching me seems to have no intention of helping me find them. The idea of looking around for them while he watches feels embarrassing, so I give up on the idea of them, tugging my skirt back down around my knees. Walking out of this place without my underwear is the least insane thing that I will have done tonight.

I slip my feet back into my shoes, glad for the low heels. Jaz tried to talk me into borrowing a pair of her stilettos, but I would tip right over if I tried to walk out of here in those shoes. I feel like a newborn deer trying to walk, as it is.

The man is still sitting there, motionless, as I walk past him. I look at him once more, silent and strangely handsome behind his mask, those dark blue eyes resting on me, and I try to think of what to say. I feel like I should say *something* before I leave, to the man who just made me come harder than I ever have in my life.

Twice.

"Thank you," is what comes out, and my face flames instantly. I'm painfully aware of how ridiculous it sounds. But he just smiles, one gloved hand resting on his thigh, close to that straining ridge in his suit trousers. I look at his hand, at those fingers that were inside of me, and another shiver runs down my spine.

"It was my pleasure, little dove," he murmurs. And then he leans back, his head resting against the back of the chair, and I realize with a flush of confused heat that he's waiting for me to leave.

He's waiting for me to go so he can finish himself off.

My eyes widen a fraction as that lust spreads through me again. I want to watch. I want to *participate*. I can envision myself going to kneel in between his legs, unzipping his trousers, and wrapping my hand around his cock as I slide it into my mouth, watching his expression change behind the mask.

My body goes tight at the thought, clenching, aching. But he's made it clear what *he* wants for tonight. And I have no more part in it, even if, for the first time, I *want* to give something in return for what I received.

I don't feel like a second thought. Like my pleasure is a necessary chore. And that makes me want to give him everything in return.

I bite my lip, wondering if I should push. But everything about him feels closed off, as if the night—with me, at least—has ended for him. And that feeling is enough to propel me towards the door, looking away from him reluctantly as I go to leave.

There's nothing else from him as I open the door. No parting words. He's utterly silent, as if he's ceased to exist, and my chest tightens as I step outside, closing the door behind me. I stand there, drawing in a long breath, and another jolt of lust ripples through me at the thought of what he might be doing right now.

I'll probably never see him again. I feel a flicker of regret at that thought—but it's overwhelmingly doused by a different one.

What else is out there that I've been missing this whole time?

7

IVAN

I'm so turned on that I can barely fucking think.

A part of me feels utterly insane for letting that woman leave without asking her to do anything to me. I *could* have asked for anything, and she would probably have done it; she was so drunk on pleasure after I went down on her. I'm pretty sure she was telling the truth about men having never made her come before. That orgasm—both of them—felt like a lifetime of pent-up desire flooding my tongue all at once.

It was one of the most erotic things I've ever felt. The way she gave herself over to it, not believing me when I told her what I could do to her, but willing to give it a chance anyway. The way she moved under me, the way she tasted, the sounds of her gasps and moans, and at the end—

The way she fucking screamed for me.

I would have committed terrible crimes to see her on her knees, flushed from two orgasms, her lips swollen and wet, wrapped around my aching cock. I would do worse to hear what other sounds she might make while I fuck her. To find out what she feels like, hot and wet and tight, fluttering around my cock. Truthfully, I don't know why I didn't keep her here to find out. She was more than willing. And I'm not a self-sacrificing kind of person. I'm not even a good man. Not the kind of man who gives up his own pleasure for the sake of others.

But I meant what I said to her tonight. Something about her cut me to the bone, touched things inside of me that I thought were long cold and dead. She deserves what I gave her—a night of pleasure that was only about her, that demanded nothing in return. She deserves to know what that feels like, to be selfish about her own needs. To take without having to give anything back. She's a woman who clearly has never gotten to be selfish in her life, especially in the bedroom.

Her comment about men always going soft after they went down on her made me see red—both because no man should ever be anything other than rock-fucking-hard after going down on a woman, particularly one like that—and also because the thought of any other man touching her sent a wave of possessiveness through me that I've never felt in my life before.

I've never felt that for a woman. My love life has been a string of casual girlfriends like Alice, one-night-stands, and the entirely anonymous encounters I've had here at Masquerade. I've never wanted to keep any of them. Never wanted to make anyone *mine*. But the thought of any other man teaching her all of the myriad ways that she can both receive and give pleasure that's clearly beyond her wildest dreams makes me feel murderous.

Which is yet another reason why I'm not a good man—because my telling her to leave without reciprocating wasn't entirely the altruistic gesture I made it out to be.

She won't be reciprocating tonight, but she will in the future. Because I have every intention of finding out who she is.

And I'm going to make sure no other man touches her until I decide if she really is going to be mine.

My cock throbs painfully at that thought, reminding me of my frustrated desire, of how long I've been hard without relief. I reach down, undoing my belt with one swift motion and tugging down my zipper, and my cock springs free instantly, jutting up stiffly.

For a moment, I consider taking off my gloves. But the leather is still soaked with her arousal, the sweet scent of her on my hand, and I want her all over me. I want to jerk off with her wetness still soaked into my fingers.

I feel myself throb again at that, pre-cum spilling down my shaft, and I let out a sharp hiss of breath as I wrap my hand around my shaft, my own arousal enough that I don't need to find where they keep the lube in this room. I've been dripping for what feels like hours now, soaking my boxer briefs the entire time that I was going down on my mystery woman.

Mine. The thought beats incessantly inside my head, again and again, a mantra as I slide my hand up and down my aching shaft. I close my eyes, leaning my head back as I surrender to the pleasure, to the feeling of slick leather against my hard cock, breathing in the scent of her mingled with my own arousal now.

I'm going to find her. I'm going to find out who she is outside of this place. She's been neglected in every way, treated as disposable, but I'm going to change that. And once she wants me outside of this place, I'm going to show her how she should have been treated all along.

I'm going to teach her what she deserves from a man.

My palm slides over my swollen cockhead, and I hiss again with pleasure, my back arching as I thrust up into my hand. I let my imagination take over, picturing her kneeling between my legs, her mouth, the wet tightness encircling my cock. I imagine her in my lap, that velvet dress pushed up to her hips again, taking my length over and over. Grinding against me, coming on my cock. Screaming out my name.

I no longer want anonymity, when it comes to this woman. All I want is her.

The orgasm hits me hard, fast, and messy, my cock going taut and solid in my fist as the heat explodes at the base of my spine and rockets upwards, cum bursting over my fingers as I stroke myself through it. My mouth falls open, a hoarse groan filling the air as I fuck my fist hard, cupping my other palm over my cockhead as I thrust up into it, filling my hands.

Her wetness mingled with my cum, soaking my fingers. The thought sends one more burst of pleasure through me, a last jet of my release arcing into my palm, and I shudder, moaning as the feeling recedes.

I can't wait to come inside her. Inside every part of her. I squeeze my cock, hips thrusting once more, and then I strip off my leather gloves, tossing them into the closed receptacle that's in the room for such things. I have a spare pair tucked into my pocket, and I tug them on, still conscious of not wanting anyone else downstairs to see my tattoos. I don't want to be identifiable here.

I realize that makes me a hypocrite, considering what I plan to do. But I don't even want her to know that the man she's going to meet is the one who made her come so hard tonight with his tongue.

I want no preconceived notions from her. No knowledge of me, until she's already fallen.

Standing up, I tuck myself back into my trousers, my mind clearer. And that's the most obvious sign that my plan is one that I need to follow through on. Because even now, in the wake of my own orgasm, my lust satisfied for the moment, I can't get her out of my head.

—

I WAIT, for the entirety of my trip home, for that feeling to fade. For me to realize that those feelings of obsession, of possessiveness, were born of intense arousal and nothing more. But she's still in my head when I park the car, when I unlock my front door, and when I slip into the secret house that I consider my real home. Not my family's mansion, or the apartment I keep in the city.

The space that is only my own.

It feels like I won't even be able to sleep until I know who she is. I leave the house dark, tossing my gloves onto the kitchen bar as I stalk to the door that leads down to the basement, able to find it easily, even in the darkness. I know every inch of this place intimately. I could walk through it in utter blackness, and never run into anything.

This is my lair. My place. The only thing I have that is entirely my own.

But soon, maybe, I'll have something else, too. Something to follow what I've already won tonight.

I can still taste her on my lips. The thought has me half-hard as I walk down the stairs into the neon glow of my basement, settling down into the leather chair, and I reach down to adjust my rapidly swelling cock. I shrug off my suit jacket, draping it over a stack of boxes as I shove my sleeves up to my elbows, ignoring the steady throb of desire in my groin as I log onto one of my computers.

I was the first man to ever make her come like that. The thought makes me groan as I start the process of hacking into the Masquerade's clientele list. At this rate, I'm going to need to get myself off again in order to be able to sleep tonight.

It's not easy, hacking into it. Whoever built their system did an excellent job of making sure that anyone like me who wanted to find out information about the people who go there would have a difficult time of it. It would take someone exceedingly skilled to get in.

Fortunately, I'm exactly that.

Once I'm in, I give a cursory glance at the photos as I scroll by. All I need is to find her. I have no intention of violating anyone else's privacy—my curiosity doesn't extend that far. I don't care who else avails themselves of the anonymous pleasures that Masquerade offers. All I care about is knowing who the woman with me tonight was.

Even though she was wearing a mask when I saw her, I recognize her bare face as soon as I see it in the picture. I recognize her mouth, her delicate chin, and the waves of dark hair falling around her face. Someone else, someone less trained in perception, might not pick her out. Might wonder if they had the right woman. But I know it's her.

Charlotte Williams.

Even her name sounds elegant. Restrained. The kind of woman

taught to keep her desires under wraps, to deny herself the things she wants, to expect perfection of herself but no one else.

But I want her unrestrained. Messy. Selfish. And tonight was the first twist of the combination that will eventually unlock her to me completely.

All I need is her name. From there, it's painfully easy to uncover everything about her that I could possibly want to know. It wouldn't be all that difficult to find a good deal of it just from a few quick Internet searches, but with my ability to hack into records and dig deeper, I can find out as much as I want.

She's twenty-seven. Graduated from Northwestern University with a degree in computer sciences. She has a handful of advanced coding classes under her belt—not enough for her to be anywhere near the level of skill that I have with computers, but enough that I'll need to be careful if I want to tamper with her devices in any way, or keep an eye on her electronically. She works at a major company in their IT department—a job that she's definitely overqualified for. She could do much better for herself, if she wanted to. If she had the confidence.

Or maybe it's that asshole ex of hers that was convincing her that she didn't *need* to do better, so that he could feel like the bigger man in the relationship. I do a little digging on him, too. Nathaniel Lake, thirty-two, an up-and-coming lawyer for a big Chicago firm. Corporate law, nothing noble or high-minded. I find an active membership at one of the other sex clubs in the city, and my jaw tightens, anger heating my blood.

So she was telling the truth. Her ex is a cheating son-of-a-bitch who never gave her an orgasm while going out and doing all the "disrespectful" things he wanted in bed with other women. That anger fuels me, and I do something that I rarely do for personal reasons.

I start to dig deeper into Nathaniel Lake.

A hack into his cell phone provider gets me a string of recent texts, a lot of them from a woman named Valerie, as well as a few others, all of them filthy. Full of fantasies that I can tell just from having spent a couple of hours with Charlotte that he never told her about.

I'm willing to bet that she would have tried a lot of them, if he'd ever asked. But once again, I'm not a good man—because despite the obvious emotional damage that this has done, I'm glad he never asked her.

That means that *I'm* going to get to be the one to introduce her to all the things she wants but has never known to ask for. The one who is going to teach her what it means to come from my tongue on her until she truly can't take any more. What it feels like to come on my cock while I fuck her in all the ways that she's been told she shouldn't be fucked. What it feels like to suck me off because she's desperate to taste me, not because she's been told she's supposed to.

Just the thought has me rock-hard, throbbing painfully as if I didn't already come once tonight. I reach for my zipper, drawing out my aching erection as I start to stroke myself in the neon glow of my screens.

And the whole time, I'm thinking of all the ways that I'm going to ruin Charlotte Williams for any other man.

—

Monday morning, I put my hastily assembled plan into action. The smarter thing to do would be to put off meeting her in person, giving myself time to meticulously plan out how I'm going to do this. But the truth is that I can't wait. I spent the remainder of the weekend unable to get her out of my head, constantly at least half-aroused and frustrated as hell with the memories of her spread out on that velvet bed for me. I woke up this morning from dreams of her, couldn't get out of bed until I'd made myself come again to thoughts of her, got hard in the shower just imagining her there with me. I need to see her again, with a near-desperation that's beyond anything I've ever felt before.

It would be alarming, if I could keep my thoughts straight long enough to really let that sink in.

I already know where she works. Figuring out a way to 'run into her' was as easy as hacking into her bank records. Unsurprisingly, she has a tendency to frequent the same cafe for lunch a few times a week. I have no idea if she'll be there today, but I'm prepared to stake it out every day until she is.

Hopefully, she'll be alone.

The way I dress for the day is just a different kind of mask. When I'm left to my own devices, I prefer comfortable t-shirts and black jeans or cargo pants. When I go to the Masquerade, with my faux-British accent and all my defining features covered, I wear a tailored suit. On occasion, for family events that I can't get out of, I do the same.

Today, I need to be the kind of man who could sit down to lunch with Charlotte Williams as she is day to day. Not the kind of man she met at the club last night, and definitely not who I really am.

I dig out a pair of dark brown chinos and a heathered, cream-colored henley shirt. Classy enough to look like a man of her social status out to lunch, not so overdressed that I might remind her of Nate—or of the man she met at the club last night. Despite all of my efforts to conceal my identity there, she has seen part of my face. I can't discount the possibility that she might suspect me, if she saw me dressed the way I was there.

That's not something I'm willing to risk.

Besides, I'm used to slipping into different identities. I do it online all of the time. Doing it in reality is only slightly uncomfortable. As I finish getting ready, making sure I'm clean-shaven, my hair styled neatly instead of the usual shaggy mess I leave it in, the man in the mirror has just become a different version of myself.

One that I think Charlotte will be attracted to. One that she could fall for. Someone different from her ex, but not so far outside of her comfort zone that she'll be afraid of me.

That's the goal, anyway.

The air outside is crisp and cool when I step out of the front door, fall coming in fast and hard now that it's close to October. I breathe in a deep lungful of it, feeling myself relax a little at the sensation of it in my lungs, soothing me. Fall and winter are my favorite part of the year. I like that the air is colder, that the world feels more empty, that it gets dark earlier. It feels like a state of being that I'm more suited to. It makes me feel like I belong.

It's the perfect day to drive my Mustang with the windows down, so much so that I don't even mind the early-morning Chicago traffic, or the fact that I'm up this early at all. But the possibility of seeing Charlotte again was enough to make the latter part worthwhile, all on its own. I turn up my music, leaning back in the leather seat, all thoughts of my family and what I'm forced to do for them, the dangers that I'm dealing with, and my dealings with the feds all fleeing my mind. All I'm thinking about is her, and it feels like that cuts through all the stress and worry and noise, leaving me lighter and freer than I have been in months.

I park at a garage a few blocks from where she works, locking the car, and starting a brisk walk to where I should be able to get a glimpse of Charlotte walking into work. A half a block away, as I cut through the crowd of commuters, I see her walking down the sidewalk.

Her hair is up, leaving her gorgeous face and long, slim neck bare. She's wearing dark jeans molded to her perfect body, a dark blue button-down shirt with the sleeves rolled up to her elbows, and a pair of black suede ankle boots. She pauses some yards away from the front of her building, and I watch her curiously from where I've stopped, leaning up against the corner of a nearby building within eyeshot as if I'm just waiting for a ride.

A car pulls up to the curb, and the other woman who was with her at the club gets out, giving Charlotte a quick hug before they both start walking towards the building. I'm not surprised—my research on Charlotte turned up the information that her friend also works with her, but in HR. I didn't dig much further than that on Jasmine Bakir—she's not the woman I'm interested in, and I had no desire to violate her privacy.

I'm not a monster or a stalker.

I just need to get to know Charlotte better. On a more even playing field. One where she'll be comfortable.

I watch her until she disappears into the building, through the glass doors, until she's gone from my sight. And then I push myself away from the wall, heading towards a coffee shop that I'm familiar with where I can wait until it's time to go to her lunch spot.

—

I GET to Cafe L'Rose an hour before most corporate lunchtimes start, not wanting to miss the window of time when Charlotte might come by. I settle down with a book—a recent mystery that I've been wanting to read—and my second cup of coffee for the day.

I'm not a superstitious man, or one who believes in coincidence, but even I find it ironic that the second time I meet Charlotte will be at a little French bistro, after meeting her for the first time in the Versailles-inspired luxury of Masquerade. And her safeword there —*Paris*. It's another sign of how obsessed I've already become that I can't help but think of it as a sign, when I know all of that is bullshit.

Just after noon, I look up to see Charlotte walking to one of the small, round iron tables out on the patio. My pulse instantly leaps into my throat, my senses all on alert—but I feel a sharp jab of disappointment when I see that Jaz is with her. The two women settle into seats on opposite sides of the table, saying something to their server that I can't quite catch, and I wonder if I should call it a loss for today. Finish my chapter and my coffee, and go home to deal with all of the things that I should *actually* be doing today. Come back tomorrow, and the next day, and however many days after that it takes to get Charlotte alone.

That would be the smart way to handle this. With her friend as a buffer, it's entirely possible that Charlotte might turn any advance I make down flat, completely shutting down the prospect of anything between us after my interruption of her lunch.

But I can't make myself leave. It feels like a physical impossibility, like I can't just get up and walk away. I watch as the server brings them water and takes their order, and I keep thinking again and again that I should just go, and try another day.

I *can't*. I can't walk away from her. That's just another reason that I should, but when I get up from my table, I already know that the direction I'm going to go in is toward what I've come to want more than anything else in the world.

Fuck the consequences.

"Excuse me, miss." My voice, when I stop a foot away from their table, is my own. Not the polished British accent that I use at Masquerade, that Charlotte heard last night, but my own second-generation Russian accent, the mixture of my family's thicker accent that I've grown up with all my life and the Americans that I interact with daily. "I'm sorry to interrupt, but I couldn't help myself."

It's the truth. I couldn't help myself. And when Charlotte looks at me, her head swiveling in surprise, the expression on her face is worth the chance I took.

This woman is going to be mine, no matter what I have to do.

8

CHARLOTTE

I'm glancing at my phone, checking for any urgent emails from work, and half-listening to Jaz tell me about her plans for this coming weekend, when a voice cuts through the air and makes me go very still.

"Excuse me, miss."

Just the sound of his accent is enough to make me curious, to make me look at him instead of waving him off, the way I'm instantly inclined to do. I don't want some strange man interrupting my lunch with Jaz, but when I look up, I'm glad that I did.

The man standing just next to our table is gorgeous. Tall, well-muscled, his arms rippling with tattoos that run all the way down to his hands and over his fingers, and climb to just above the open collar of his shirt. I can see a light dusting of blond hair on his chest, lighter than the dark blond hair on his head, and a glimpse of broad pectorals beneath the open buttons. There's more ink across his chest, and the first thing I think is that I want to know just how far down the tattoos go.

Did that night at the club really change me that much? I'm not the type to ogle men. Not the type to think about a stranger sexually—

even one this attractive. But I can feel my cheeks heating as I try to force myself to look up at his face.

He smiles at me, and for a second, I think I feel a flicker of recognition. There's something to his smile, a sort of self-satisfied, almost cocky smirk that reminds me of the man from the club. But he can't possibly be the same man. For one, I can't picture that man dressed so casually. There's an informal, relaxed air to this man that's completely different from the formal, precise way the masked man at Masquerade behaved.

That man had a British accent, too. Not the sort of Americanized Russian accent that this man speaks with.

"I'm sorry to interrupt, but I couldn't help myself," he continues. "I know it's awfully rude to disrupt your lunch, but I couldn't risk never getting the chance to meet you."

"I—" I blink rapidly, trying to get my thoughts under control, to think about this rationally. This man is a stranger, someone who just came up to me out of nowhere to flirt with me, and it should put me off. But either that night at Masquerade did crazy things to my libido, or my anger with Nate unlocked some deeply hidden part of myself, because all I can think is that I want to give him my number just so I can find out what he looks like with his shirt off.

And so that I can keep hearing him talk to me in that incredibly sexy accent. Every word out of his mouth sends a tingle through me, making my pulse race a little faster. I want to hear him say different things in it. Dirtier things.

"I'm sorry," he says, his smile turning regretful, and I realize that I've waited too long to respond. "This was far too rude of me. I'll go. I apologize again."

"No, wait." Jaz is the one who speaks up, pushing her chair back. "I'll grab my lunch to go and meet you back at the office. Sit down. Chat." She offers the man a brilliant smile, and then looks at me with an expression that very clearly says *get it together, Charlotte.*

"No, Jaz—we were having lunch. I don't want you to—" Even as I protest, I realize that I *do* want her to leave so I can talk to this man. His opening lines, his approach—none of this would have worked on the Charlotte that I was a few days ago, but in my current headspace...and especially after what happened at Masquerade, I want to try new things. I want to be open to new experiences.

I want to be impulsive enough to have lunch with a drop-dead-gorgeous stranger who approached me.

"It's fine. I promise." Jaz is already getting up, grabbing her phone and her purse. "I'll just tell the hostess to box up my order. I have some interview applications to go through anyway. The work just piles up, you know?" She smiles at the man. "Don't make me regret this," she warns him, and then she's gone, already tapping away at something on her phone.

I realize why when, a second later, her name lights up my screen.

JAZ: *You're looking at him like he's the second coming of Ryan Gosling. Just find out the man's name, for God's sake. And if he asks you out, say YES.*

Jaz: *Also, his accent is delicious. Don't you want to hear that moaning your name? Yes, you do.*

"I—" I look up at him, feeling like I'm floundering. "Well, you might as well go ahead and sit down."

He hesitates, then does exactly that. "I know this is all really presumptuous," he says, and the apology in his voice sounds sincere. "I think I lost my mind a little, when I saw you. I can't imagine that you're single, but if you are—I'd really like to buy you lunch."

"Why?" I blurt out. I can feel that I'm still staring at him, but I can't seem to relax. This is all strange, and I've never done anything like this before. I've never had lunch with a stranger. I've never had a stranger approach me like this in public—not in a way that I'd entertain, anyway. All of my dates have always been with friends of friends —people that I've been set up with—or men like Nate, who I met through some official channel. I met Nate in class, my senior year of college.

But I'm trying new things. And as I wait for his answer, I'm sure that this qualifies.

His mouth twists wryly, as if he's unsure if I'll like what he's about to say. "I know I'm not supposed to say that it's because you're beautiful. But you are. You're stunning. And I want to get to know you, so I can find out what all the deeper parts of you are that would make me fall in love with you regardless of how gorgeous you are."

"Did you get that from a book?" I bite my lip instantly, realizing how rude that must have sounded. "I'm sorry. Just—no one says things like that. I figured you would just tell me that it was because you thought I was hot, and leave it at that."

"You are." He grins, and it's captivating. It softens all the chiseled lines of his face, makes my heart beat wildly in my chest. "But I'm sure there's more to you. I just need the chance to find it all out."

I take a breath, but before I can say anything, the server comes back to our table. He has my chicken salad sandwich in one hand, and he looks at my new lunch date, raising an eyebrow.

"Can I get you anything, sir?"

"A water, please," the man says smoothly. "And I'll have—" he glances down at the menu. "The steak and gouda melt. Thanks." He hands the menu back to the server, and I take the plate with my sandwich; my appetite fled. I don't know how I'm expected to eat in front of this man. My stomach feels like it's in knots.

"What's your name?" It's the simplest, safest question that I can think of, until I can get my head straight again.

"Ivan Vasili." He smiles. "Very Russian, I know. But my family is very traditional."

"I'm Charlotte." I reach for my glass of water, my mouth suddenly very dry. "Charlotte Williams."

"It's nice to meet you, Charlotte."

I still can't decide if I should get up and leave. If I should be offended that this man has decided he can come and take over my lunch hour, just because he wanted to meet me. But being attracted to someone isn't a crime, and neither is talking to them. He's done his best to be polite about it, even apologetic about the parts of his approach that have been, admittedly, rude.

And he's gorgeous. I can't be upset about him leading with his opinion of my looks when at least three-quarters of the reason I haven't asked him to leave or gotten up to leave myself is because of how handsome he is.

The other quarter is because I'm curious about him, too.

"So tell me something about yourself." That smile is still on his mouth, and he takes a sip of his water, his expression openly curious. "What do you do?"

"I work just down the street. In their IT department." I'm not sure I want to give him the actual name of my workplace yet, even though that would be a relatively easy thing to find. He could just look me up on LinkedIn. But if this man is going to dig for information on me, I at least want to make him put in some effort. "What about you?"

"I'm an independent contractor." He grins. "Which is just a fancy way of saying I'm not good with routine, but I like money, so I've learned to be my own boss. I mostly deal with tech stuff, too. Some financials. A lot of it is locked behind NDAs, though, so I can't tell you too much."

The evasiveness makes me nervous. But it's not unheard of. There are parts of my job that I can't talk about. Sarah, another one of our friend group, works for the FDIC. She can't tell us about most of her job, and she has a laptop that she'd go to prison if anyone but her looked at it. There are plenty of legitimate jobs that can't just be talked about freely. I can understand the need for confidentiality when it comes to that.

"Tell me something more interesting than just what you do for work, though," he adds. "What about—hobbies? What do you like to do when you're not working?"

"I—well, I go to the gym. Yoga, cardio, that kind of thing. Nothing all that unique. I have a standing Sunday brunch date with my girlfriends. I like to read." I realize, with every word out of my mouth, just how dull my life sounds. No talk about travel or trying new restaurants or anything even remotely exciting. I wouldn't blame him if he just got up and walked away.

"A quiet life." He smiles. "That sounds relaxing."

I narrow my eyes at him for a moment, trying to figure out if he's making fun of me. It doesn't sound like he is.

"What do you like to read? I'm partial to mysteries, myself. I like a good paranormal thriller."

I can't help the slight shudder that runs through me at that. "I'm easily scared," I admit. "And I don't like books that are really tense. I read a lot of—I guess women's fiction is the genre. Stories about families, generational plots, that kind of thing. Low-stress."

"Is your job particularly stressful?" He looks at me curiously.

"No," I admit. "I guess I just—don't like to feel anxious. I don't like tension." I don't know this man well enough to explain the things I'm realizing about myself to him—that I'm anxious all the time in my daily life, that I always want to please others, to be the good friend and partner and employee that I feel I'm supposed to be. That the thought of pushing myself, of feeling tension or fear in my hobbies, makes me nauseous. That when I'm alone, I just want to feel peace.

Except—

I didn't feel peaceful at Masquerade. I felt out of my comfort zone. *Shoved* out of it, really, like a baby bird learning to fly. Terrified, quite frankly. But by the end of it—

By the end of it, I felt like a lifetime's worth of tension had been wrung out of me. Like all that buildup, all that tension and nervousness, was worth it for the exquisite pleasure that I'd felt at the end.

And now, I'm starting to think that I want to keep pushing myself. Beginning with this strange lunch date.

"You look like you're a million miles away," Ivan comments, and my attention snaps back to him as I feel myself flush.

"I'm sorry," I apologize quickly. "My life is in a bit of upheaval right now. I'm not as together as I usually am."

He chuckles. "You seem very together to me."

"It's a facade," I promise him. "One I'm very good at."

There. A moment of vulnerability. His face softens, and his gaze sweeps over my face, taking me in.

"I'd like to see what's under the mask, then."

A chill sweeps down my spine, and I feel myself go still. I look at him carefully, trying to determine if I was wrong earlier. If he could be the same man I met this weekend at Masquerade.

There's something about him—but no. Not enough. It can't be the same man. And anyway, the rules and protocol at Masquerade are all designed to avoid exactly that outcome—that anyone who plays there might find each other in reality.

It's just a coincidence. Or maybe I just attract men like that now. Cocky men with a mysterious edge to them. Maybe that's my type, outside of my comfort zone.

There's only one way to find out.

"I'd also like to take you out on a real date," he continues, as if he heard my thoughts. Something jolts in my chest, a feeling of fear—but also anticipation.

I'm afraid of what it would be like to go out on a date with him, of what that would mean. What happened at Masquerade had a tinge of unreality about it, something locked behind closed doors. But going out on a date means accepting that my relationship with Nate—five years of my life—is over. That what he did is unforgivable. That I'm finished with everything we had, because of what he did.

He tried to call me over the weekend. Then he texted me. He apologized. He said it was all a mistake. I ignored the texts, and by Sunday night, they got colder. He said I wasn't even trying. That I'm throwing away five whole years over something that can be fixed.

In the solitude of my apartment, I almost believed him. Over brunch on Sunday, Jaz and Zoe and Sarah and our other friends all told me in a chorus of *that's absolute bullshit* exactly what they thought of Nate's efforts. And my thoughts, all weekend and this morning, kept drifting back to that night at Masquerade. Wondering if I can ever go back to a relationship like the one I had with Nate, when I know what else is possible now.

I look at Ivan. *Could he make me feel that?* I don't know. I'm still not convinced that night is something that can be replicated in reality. But I want to explore. I want to find out what possibilities are on the other side of this relationship that has crashed and burned so spectacularly.

"I just got out of a relationship," I tell him hesitantly. "I'm not looking for anything serious right now. Truthfully, I'm not even sure what I *am* looking for."

That smirk returns, teasing the corners of his mouth. "It's just dinner," he says teasingly. "I'm not proposing."

I can't help but flinch a little at that, thinking of the ring I found in the closet. The ring that Nate has now—or that maybe he already returned. I can't be sure. Based on his calls and texts, I think he might still be hoping that I'll change my mind, that he'll get me back.

I want to close the door on that, as firmly as I can. So I take a breath, nodding.

"Okay, then. What about Friday night?" I don't have any plans yet. The best I had come up with had involved a bottle of wine and bad reality TV.

"Friday night it is." His smile widens. "Can I give you my number?"

It strikes me as odd that he asked to give me his, rather than asking for mine. But it also occurs to me that maybe he wants to give me the space to contact him, to be the one who reaches out. He's already come on strong by walking up to the table and introducing himself out of nowhere. I can only assume he's trying to make me more comfortable by putting the ball in my court.

"Sure." I pick up my phone, and he reaches out, sliding it smoothly out of my hand as soon as my Face ID unlocks it. It takes me aback, and I look at him, wondering if I should protest. He just took *my* phone out of my hand, after all. But there's something about it, a certain confidence, the way he smiles at me as he starts to type his contact information into my phone, that makes me think I'm overreacting.

He's charming and polite, and he hasn't done anything overtly offensive. I'm being too prickly, because of Nate. Too suspicious, because of who I am as a person. I need to give this man some breathing room to show me who he really is, or I'm going to ruin a good thing before it even gets started.

He hands me back my phone after a moment. "There." His smile softens again, and there's a sudden sincerity in it. "I know I came on very strong. Text me when you're sure about the date, and we'll decide where to go and what to do."

See? I let out a breath, relaxing as I realize that it was exactly what I'd told myself. He wanted to give me the chance to think things over. To text him and give him my number when I'm sure. "That's very thoughtful of you," I tell him, motioning for the server. Neither of us has touched our meals, and I'm going to end up getting mine to-go and eating it at my desk. My lunch break is almost over.

"I want you to be comfortable." He takes the to-go box from the server, that smile still on his face. "I'm hoping this is going to be the first date of many."

"Don't get your hopes up," I tell him, boxing up my sandwich and handing the server my card, before Ivan can hand over his. "I meant it when I said I wasn't looking for anything. But we'll see."

The truth is, I'm already far too attracted to him for my own good. I'm already thinking that I might want more than one date, too.

But what I *don't* want right now is to get attached. I want a chance to explore what that night at Masquerade awoke in me. I want a chance to try some of the fantasies that I've been thinking of ever since, before I get serious with anyone again.

More than anything, I want a chance to be free.

9

IVAN

By the time I leave Cafe L'Rose, I feel like I'm floating on cloud nine.

It all came together so much more easily than I expected. Her friend's willingness to bail on lunch to give Charlotte a chance to get to know me went a long way. It makes me want to send Jaz flowers just for the assist, but that's a bad idea. That might freak her out, and then I'd be back to square one.

I spent the weekend putting together the fake persona that I gave Charlotte. Vasili isn't my last name, but if she Googles me, she'll find a host of false records and planted information about me that will back up the story I gave her. A story about a purposefully vague career, so that I can keep track of what I'm telling her without slipping up.

Deep down, I know that this is all a very bad idea. That I'm mired in enough lies between my family and the feds. I don't need another story to keep up with, another host of falsehoods and secrets to keep straight.

I should forget about Charlotte Williams, and let her go on with her life, while I go on with mine.

But I can't. And I know she wouldn't want me as I am. Not until she's had a chance to get to know me better, anyway. If I tell her right off the bat that I'm Ivan Kariyev, that my family is one of the most dangerous criminal families in Chicago, that I have so much blood coating my hands that I could strip the skin away and still not be rid of it all, that I found her after that night at Masquerade because I hacked into every aspect of her life—she'd do more than just refuse to go out on a date with me.

She'd probably—and rightfully—call the cops. And then I'd have a whole other mess to deal with, even if nothing would ultimately come of it.

I don't need any more complications in my life. Charlotte is a lot more than a complication—my desire for her, my growing *obsession* with her, could rip a hole in the fabric of my entire life. But now that I've seen her, met her, *tasted* her—I can't get enough.

I can't shake her. The only thing that I can hope is that this is a passing obsession, and that once I've had her, I will have had *enough* of her. That this will burn itself out, and I can go back to my life as it was before.

That has to be how this turns out in the end. Because I can't lie to her for a lifetime. And if I'm being honest with myself, there is no other endgame beyond a temporary connection between the two of us. She's not the kind of girl to get involved with a criminal. And I can't keep her from knowing who I am forever.

I can for a while, though. Until I can get her out of my head.

—

The high I'm on only lasts until I get a call from Ani, the second of my brothers, telling me that there's a family dinner tonight. "Don't bother trying to get out of it tonight," he tells me curtly. "*Otets* will be furious if you're not there. He specifically said you were to be there, too. Don't make this worse for the rest of us."

There's a warning there, in his tone. A warning not to cause trouble, or he and my other brothers will find a way to make me regret it.

The last time I crossed them, I was left holding a gun to a woman's head while my brothers questioned her husband about a mistake he'd made with our father's bookkeeping. Pulling that trigger would have been a line they knew I'd refuse to step over. And it would have given them the excuse they need to tell my father that I need to be removed, myself.

That his bastard son is better off dead than a part of the Kariyev family. That I can't be trusted, even if I am my father's blood.

I'm expected to dress respectably for dinner. Suit trousers, a button-down, although I can roll up the sleeves and skip a tie and jacket. While I dress, I glance over at my phone repeatedly, sitting on the sink next to me.

When I put my number in Charlotte's phone, I also installed a tracker. It had to be done quickly, and it had to be embedded in her phone in a way that she wouldn't notice. A new app would be something she'd pick up on immediately. Something she'd look into, since she's also knowledgeable when it comes to tech. Instead, I got the information I needed from her phone, and used it to embed the tracker into an app already on it.

Right now, I've kept it simple. Her location, who's texting her, who's calling her. Not the actual texts themselves or the transcripts of calls. I don't want to pry that deeply, yet. But I do want to know where she is, and what she's doing—and with who.

For instance, if she goes back to Masquerade, I want to know. There's no way I wouldn't drop everything to go straight there, and make sure that she doesn't end up with a different man there. The thought of her in one of those private rooms, with some other man's face between her legs, makes my hands tighten around the edge of the sink counter hard enough for the granite edges to dig into my palms. The thought of her playing in *public* there, allowing others to see her as she's pleasured, as she comes, is enough to make me squeeze the counter so hard that I'd break it if that were possible.

No other man is going to get to touch her. Her pleasure, her lessons, all of the things that are about to be opened up to her on account of her ex's stupidity, are *mine*. No other man is going to make her come until I've had my fill of the sweet sounds she makes, until every other orgasm she has for the rest of her life is colored by the memory of all the times that it was *me* touching her.

The fact that I'd cross my family, risk angering my violent brothers and my father in order to intercept Charlotte if need be, should be enough to make me think twice about all of this. It should be enough to make me reconsider what I'm doing here.

But I'm not. I can't.

I've done drugs a handful of times in my life. I've never understood how people get addicted to them. How they'll do the things I've seen, make the deals I've witnessed, commit the atrocities that I know about, in order to get another high. But now that I've met Charlotte, now that I've had a hit of her—I get it.

I'm addicted. And all of my self-preservation has gone out the window in service of getting my next high. In service of making sure no one else gets a taste of what I want.

I drive myself over to my father's house. I don't want any delays between me and leaving, once I get the chance. And any chance I have to go out for a drive is one I want to take, anyway.

My father's mansion, on the outer edges of the city, is a sight. Dima Kariyev made a name for himself as a young man in Chicago, bringing over our family's name and influence from Moscow and establishing the family Bratva here. He's not the only Russian crime family in Chicago, but he's risen to be one of the most influential, and one of the most feared.

But fear and respect are two different things. My father and my brothers are known to be vicious. Men who have very little in the way of codes that they abide by. And those rules, those personal codes, are what gain respect from other men in this world. The knowledge that even in violence, there can be honor.

My father is a violent man, but one without much honor. My existence is proof enough of that. Men in this world are often unfaithful to their wives, but demanding that one of their bastard children be raised with the family, by their wife, is unheard of.

His wife hates me. I don't blame her for it.

I park my Mustang behind the row of other cars, all of them new and gleaming. Ani's Lamborghini, Lev's Rolls Royce, Niki's Maserati. They have an appreciation for money, but not for style or heritage. My Mustang is a classic.

More than that, it's a symbol of how little I want to do with my family. An all-American car, something with no ties to our lineage. Something that represents the world I'd rather be a part of, instead of the one I'm in.

Unsurprisingly, none of them have ever picked up on that. It's a silent rebellion, which, to my mind, makes it that much better.

I'm a few minutes late, the best I could get away with under the circumstances. I walk through the large foyer, my shoes clicking against the marble floor, and continue all the way to the formal dining room. My father insists on holding family dinners here, even though the six of us barely take up a third of the long table.

Dima, my father, looks up as I enter, his face already creased with displeasure. His wife, Katya, is to his right, my brother, Lev sitting to his left. Ani and Niki are both sitting next to Lev, which means I'll be forced to sit next to Katya, or further down the table, snubbing her. Treating her as less than my mother—which, of course, she isn't. Not really.

This is intentional. I'm fully aware of it. I'm also not about to allow any of them to see how they get under my skin.

I walk around the table, nodding respectfully to my father before taking the seat next to Katya. She turns to me, her face covered thickly with makeup, and I lean in, giving her an air kiss on each cheek, as she prefers. I can smell the powdery, thick rose scent of her perfume and makeup, and it turns my stomach.

It reminds me of my childhood in this house, and none of that is pleasant.

"You're late," Dima growls. "We were waiting on you. You've kept not only your father and brothers waiting, but also your mother. What do you have to say about that?"

That my mother isn't here. I wisely keep that thought to myself. "I apologize," I say flatly, forcing it out. "There was traffic."

"That can be planned for. Early is better than late. Better even than on time. Isn't that right, Lev?" Dima turns to look at his oldest son, who nods firmly. I'm sure he was more than early to dinner. Eager to please my father, so he can keep his place at his side.

That's the thing about having a family so vicious. Lev's birthright is his inheritance—the influence, connections, and most of the wealth of the Kariyev family when our father passes. But my family only observes the rules when they suit. If Lev angered our father enough, if he gave any hint that he didn't intend to continue on as Dima began, he could be removed easily enough. He could meet with an accident. And then it would be Ani's turn to prove that he's worthy of my father's name and empire.

I often wonder if Niki is relieved that it would take a lot for that particular inheritance to work its way down to him. I know I am. I also know Niki would try to have me killed the moment that happened, just to make sure that I didn't have the same idea.

Luckily for my brothers, I don't want any part of this. I'm not interested in my family's politics. And I have every intention of one day having enough money of my own that I won't need any of that from them, either.

Enough that I'll never need anything, from anyone.

The table is mostly quiet after that, until the first course is served—a mixed greens salad with a creamy dressing and a squash soup swirled with heavy cream. The food is the only tolerable part of these family dinners—my father employs an excellent cook. But it's still not worth what I have to sit through, not when I could get equally good food on my own without the stomachache that will inevitably follow.

We're halfway through the soup when Dima speaks again.

"I heard you questioned one of the men suspected of leaking the railyard location," he says, looking directly at me. "Lev also says you killed him before he could give much information."

Next to me, Katya flinches. "Dima, please," she says calmly, but her mouth tightens at the edges. "Can't we talk about something more pleasant?"

He ignores her. "Well?" he barks, setting down his spoon. One of the staff immediately springs into the room, clearing all of the plates, regardless of whether we're still eating or not. When Dima is finished with a course, we're all finished.

"I killed him when I was sure he had nothing left to tell us," I return flatly. "As I explained to Lev, the promise of a clean death is a bargaining tool. If the other half of that bargain thinks that is a lie, they'll no longer be forthcoming, and nothing they say can be trusted."

Dima laughs at that, a deep, hearty sound, as the next course is set out for us. Steak—tender-looking filet—with sides of roasted potatoes and spiced corn. He cuts into his steak first, and I can see that it's cooked black and blue, barely a step past raw. Very little turns my stomach, but in the present moment, something about watching my father slice through that still-soft meat makes the back of my throat burn with bile.

My appetite has fled, which is a shame. I like steak.

"You treat torture like an art," he says, chuckling. "My violence mixed with your mother's creative spirit, I think." He looks genuinely amused by the thought. "It's a means to an end, son. And I expect you to get that end. This is the second shipment of women we've lost. That's money that has to be repaid to buyers, unless we find a suitable substitute for them. Even then, they often want at least partial compensation for their wait. Those connections are fragile, Ivan. Those men can go elsewhere for their flesh. I want them to come to *me*. And with every shipment we lose, frays that trust. It damages my other business, too. Do you understand?"

He jabs the knife towards me, cutting the air as he says it. I don't flinch, but I can feel that squirming sensation in my stomach again. I'm not insensible to the pain that would be inflicted on me if he ever found out what I'm doing. The fact that I'm able to hide my fear of it doesn't mean I'm not afraid.

I glance towards Katya, wondering if I'll be able to read anything on her face. Surely, she, a woman, must feel something sitting here and listening to her husband discuss the sale of other women.

Unwilling women, being sent off to their buyers to be used and abused as those men see fit.

I also always wonder what she thinks when Dima brings up my birth mother. She can't have ever expected love or fidelity from him, but I know she resents being forced to raise me. But her face is smooth, impassive as she cuts into her well-cooked steak. If she feels anything at all about all of this, she's hiding it.

Which is likely the wisest choice she could make.

"I understand the difficulties that the leaks are causing. And I'll do all I can to uncover the source." It's a flat-out lie, of course. But every word I say is like tiptoeing around landmines. My father is greedy and cruel, but he's not stupid. He's smarter than I think my brothers give him credit for, especially Lev. It's difficult to keep the truth from him, and it will continue to be difficult.

"Do better." His voice is sharp, cutting, and it takes everything in me to nod, to give him deference, and keep my composure. To not tell my father what I really think of him.

It would be so much easier to turn a blind eye, as I have all my life to so much else in my family. I have no desire to be involved with *any* of their enterprises, not just what involves human flesh. But the rest, I can ignore.

Some things, though, are too evil for me to not do something about, if I can. And I'm uniquely placed to help these women, with talents that allow me to do more than most others could.

I just have to stay alive long enough to cripple this part of my father's empire entirely. Then, I'll stay long enough to let any suspicion pass me by—and then I'll take my money and my car and whatever else I want of my life, and go far away.

I'll start over. Maybe even as Ivan Vasili, instead of who I am now.

That makes me think of Charlotte. Of the impossibility of any real future with her. It goes beyond the fact that she's not the kind of woman who would want a criminal. I can't drag her into this world. I can't subject her to the kind of life I'll always live—one where my family will always be a threat, even if they're only in the background.

A life without her friends, without a family of her own, with only me for support.

I'm not the kind of man who can give a woman like her what she needs. The fact that I seem to need her like a drug doesn't change that.

All it means is that I need to get my fill of her, and then get clean. Teach her all the things that she's never been shown, make sure I've given her all those pleasures that she's never experienced for the first time, and then get her out of my system. We can give each other what we both want, and then I'll take off, leaving only good memories for us both.

After all, I tell myself as I finish dinner and say my goodnights impatiently, it's not as if she's going to get into a serious relationship with the next man she dates after a bad breakup. I'm already firmly in the rebound position.

It doesn't matter if there are other men after you. As long as you're the one she'll think of every time, long after you're gone.

That's what I tell myself to ease the sting of knowing that I won't be the last man to touch her, only the next. But there's no world in which I get to keep her. This temporary obsession is going to have to be enough.

When I get back home, I only pause to change into a pair of sweatpants and a loose t-shirt before heading down to the basement. I know my father has another shipment coming in, but I don't have all of the details, which means I need to be scanning the warehouses, docks, and railyards as often as possible to make sure that I don't miss any movements. The feds are expecting this information from me, and I'm in a precarious fucking position. Now that I've started feeding them some information, they expect a steady drip. If I start to slow down too much, or worse, stop, they'll turn on me as fast as my family would if they knew what I was doing.

I'm caught between two sides, and neither of them give a fuck about me.

I set my phone down next to the keyboard, keeping an eye out for Charlotte's movements. So far, all I've gotten is that she went grocery shopping at Whole Foods after work, and then went home. She's stayed there all night, texting her friends, and no one else. She hasn't downloaded any dating apps onto her phone.

That last is a relief. Both because it means she was interested in *me* today, and not just the prospect of going out with anyone—and also because it means I won't have to be distracted right now with figuring out how to place roadblocks in the way of any other dates.

This is already more of a distraction than I should be allowing myself. I know it from the way my thoughts keep drifting to her as I sift through the screens, viewing the various locations my father uses, as I scroll through saved footage of the day, looking for anything that I can pass on as information. I know it from the way I keep looking over at my phone, almost compulsively.

When I do get another ping for her, it's not from my phone. It's from one of my computers, one that I set up to monitor her online activity from home. I turn immediately towards the screen, logging on and looking to see what she's doing.

I feel an instant jolt of arousal. She's looking at porn sites. Only-Fans. And my lips curve up in a smile as I see her searches. *Masked men. Clothed man, naked woman. Masked sex.*

She's still thinking about me. She's in her apartment, alone, probably in whatever she wears to bed, looking up ways to get off based on thoughts of what we did together at Masquerade. My cock swells, thickening along my leg and tenting my sweatpants as I watch her pulling up videos, lingering on some of them long enough that I know she's watching. Maybe touching herself. Using her fingers, or a vibrator. She's wet by now, looking at all of this—just the thought brings back the memory of the sweet scent of her arousal, the way she tasted on my tongue. I feel the insistent throb of my own arousal, and I reach down, adjusting my now fully-hard cock. I squeeze it for a moment, pushing off the urge to slide it out and stroke myself until I come. I need to, badly—and I will. But I want to enjoy the feeling of need for a little while longer. I want to let myself be hard, aching, thinking of what Charlotte is doing by herself in her apartment. The feeling of being this aroused is almost as good as the orgasm that I'll have eventually—and that release will be made all the better by waiting for it.

The videos disappear, and I feel a swoop of disappointment. *Did she finish already?* I was hoping she'd draw it out, that I'd get to see more of what she wants. What sort of fantasies that she's exploring, now that she feels safe to do so.

I'm just about to give up and get myself off so that I can go back to focusing on work, when the monitor pings again. My attention instantly snaps to it, and when I look, I see that she's pulled up a website and started creating a profile.

It's a website I'm very familiar with. One that means she has at least a passing knowledge of the darker parts of the web, parts that she wouldn't be able to access without a VPN, and a bit of nerve.

I'm impressed—and more aroused than I ever thought I could be.

The site that she's logged onto is a chat site. One where users go to share all kinds of fantasies back and forth. There are forums to post pictures and share stories. And a messenger, for sharing those fantasies one on one. It's the online version of a place like Masquerade, a place with no real names and no faces allowed—except those are some of the only rules. Here, Charlotte could talk about almost anything she wanted, almost anything she'd be ashamed to admit, and she could find someone willing to listen. Someone to urge those fantasies on, to encourage her to lean into them. To seek pleasure from them. Someone who would get their own pleasure from listening to her describe all of the forbidden things she wants.

Jealousy, hot and thick, burns in my veins at the thought of anyone else reading those fantasies. Of another man stroking himself on the other side of a screen to the things that she wants, another man telling her the things he wants to do to her. Getting *her* off with those descriptions.

And in the wake of that jealousy, another thought springs to mind.

I have two identities with her. But there's a third one that's possible. Not just the masked man at Masquerade, which I might never be for her again, or the man who is taking her out on a date this weekend, the 'acceptable' version of myself.

This is an opportunity to give her a taste of who I really am. A way to be with her as myself, without her ever knowing that all three of these men are the same.

Quickly, I pull up the site on another of my monitors, logging on. I look for her username, and open up the messenger, typing out a quick message.

Venom69xxx: *I haven't seen you here before.*

For a moment, I wonder if she's even going to respond. A new user, especially a woman, is going to be flooded with messages. The thought that she might have answered someone else's request first makes my blood burn all over again, but I take a breath, forcing myself to stay calm. To ignore all my baser instincts before they ruin this for me.

And then I see the message that pops up on the screen.

CuriousDove24: *That's because this is my first time. ;)*

The breath leaves my lungs in a rush, a hot jolt of arousal scrambling all of my senses for a moment. It's not just the flirtatious comment about it being her first time, which is enough all on its own to make me feel like I can't think straight, but her *username*. I look at it again, thinking of that night at Masquerade, the taste of her on my lips, how badly I wanted her to touch me afterward.

That night must have meant a lot to her. It must have been more of a turning point than even I realized. My heart slams against my ribs as I try to focus, typing out a message before she thinks I've lost interest and answers someone else.

. . .

Venom69xxx: *What are you hoping to find here, dove?*

Calling her that feels like a risk. Like I'm tempting fate and taking a chance that she'll guess I'm the same man, but that's such a long shot, from her perspective. Most men that she would meet there wouldn't be able to track her down from the anonymity of the club to a dark web chat site. I've only been able to because of the lengths I've gone to, hacking into her personal information. And it's part of her username, after all.

The risk feels like a rush, too. The *good* kind of rush, not the anxiety that's so often felt like it's choking me since I started informing on my father for the FBI. That kind of risk feels like teetering on the edge of a dark hole, knowing there's death or worse at the bottom.

This kind is the kind that makes a man feel alive again.

CuriousDove24: *I don't really know. I just know that I want to figure out what it is that I like. I've never had the chance before. And I keep having these thoughts...*

There's that jolt of arousal again, but I ignore it. I'll get off at some point tonight, thinking about her, but right now, I'm more invested in this conversation. I want to know what she's thinking about. What kind of fantasies she's having. I want to know what my curious little dove is seeking.

I want to know, so that I can give it all to her.

Venom69xxx: *What thoughts are those?*
    CuriousDove24: *I don't know if I should say...*

Venom69xxx: *Isn't that why you're here?*

The chat goes quiet again for a moment, and I feel a jolt of apprehension, thinking that she might have changed her mind. That I might have lost my shot to find out what it is that my little dove is thinking about. But I can see on the other monitor that she hasn't logged off.

CuriousDove24: *I hooked up with a man whose name I didn't know.*

I lick my suddenly dry lips. She's talking about me—*to* me, of course, but she doesn't know that. Sharing our night together like it was some kind of forbidden fantasy. And it *was*, to her. Desire ripples through me, licking through my blood like tendrils of flame, and I want her so badly that it hurts. I want her here, now, with me. Not faceless, on the other side of a computer screen.

But she would never tell me these things in real life. Not as Ivan Vasili, the man she met today at the cafe, and definitely not as myself, Ivan Kariyev, the fourth son of a dangerous criminal.

Venom69xxx: *And that was out of the ordinary for you, I'm guessing?*
Curious Dove 24: *Very much so. I've always done the three-date thing before even a kiss. And I just got out of a relationship.*
Venom69xxx: *No better time to explore, I think.*
CuriousDove24: *That's what my best friend thought. And now—I think that's what I'm thinking, too. I want to explore more.*
Venom69xxx: *What kind of things would you like to explore, dove?*
CuriousDove24: *That man I hooked up with—he wore a mask. I think—I think that turned me on. Not being able to see all of his face. I think I want to do that again. It felt—dangerous. Wrong. Even though he was really very polite about all of it.*

Venom69xxx: *And you'd like a masked man who was less polite? ;)*

I wait for her response with my breath caught in my throat. I want to know what she's thinking right now. I want to know if she's picturing a man with rougher hands and less care for her well-being. I *do* care about her well-being, of course—but I could pretend not to. I could be the rough man that she wants. I could make her fantasies come to life, just for a little while.

I reach down, adjusting myself again. I can't remember the last time I was this hard for anyone other than her. My cock feels like an iron bar, and I'm desperate for relief. But not yet.

CuriousDove24: *I guess you could say I'm—curious. ;)*
Venom69xxx: *About what, exactly, dove?*
CuriousDove24: *I don't know if I'm ready to say all of it, yet. But I think—the man with the half-mask... I keep imagining his whole face covered. That the only way I can tell how much I'm pleasing him is by the sounds he makes. By his body language. I picture him waiting for me in my apartment. Sitting on the edge of my bed when I walk in. Telling me what to do from behind the mask—*

The chat stops. I close my eyes briefly, unable to ignore my own body's needs any longer. I slide the waist of my sweatpants down just enough to slip my cock free, my breath a tight hiss from between my teeth as I feel the relief of my hand wrapping around it. It's not going to be enough to do more than just take the edge off, but I'll take whatever I can get right now. I can't remember the last time I needed to come this badly.

I allow myself two long, slow strokes, sliding my hand down to the base and up again to the tip, using the pre-cum flooding from my tip as lubricant. And then I force myself to let go, reaching out to type out a response as my cock throbs in the neon glow from my monitor.

. . .

Venom69xxx: *What would you like him to tell you to do?*

Venom69xxx: *He's been thinking about you all day, after all. Distracted and so fucking hard. That's why he had to sneak in and wait for you. Do you want him to tell you to get on your knees for him? Are you going to give him that pretty mouth, since you made him wait all day?*

Her response takes a moment, and I start to worry again that I've scared her off. That even this relatively tame chatting is too much for her at this early point. But then I see the little dots at the bottom of the chat, and my pulse leaps as I see her username pop up again.

CuriousDove24: *Maybe he tells me to strip for him first. While he's sitting on the bed, fully clothed and masked. He makes me take everything off, so he can see what he's waiting for. And then—*

Fuck. My head is spinning. It feels like every drop of blood in my body has pooled in my cock—nothing else left to keep me functioning. My entire world feels hinged on knowing what she's about to type in response.

CuriousDove24: *He tells me to get on my knees. To—to undo his jeans and take him out. He's still fully clothed. I can't see any skin other than where he's tugged his shirt up out of the way, and his—*

CuriousDove24: *That's as far as I got.*

I'm not entirely sure I can type a response. I don't know if I can manage words in any format right now. This wouldn't be nearly as erotic as it is if I didn't know exactly who was on the other side of that screen, but I *do*. I've seen her in the flesh, sweet and innocent and shy, and I can picture her biting her lip right now, picture her hand moving between her legs, her fingers slipped inside of her panties as she nervously gets herself off.

And I would bet money that she just came, and that's why she's suddenly backed off.

Venom69xxx: *Were you touching yourself while you told me all of that, dove? Did you just come thinking about the man sitting on your bed, telling you to strip and suck his cock?*

I suck in a breath as I wait for her response. If she really did finish, and she's regretting any of this, right now is when she'll run. She'll log off without another word, and I might never hear from her again—at least not like this.

But if she's still curious, she'll respond.

CuriousDove24: *How would I type if I were doing that? ;)*

I thought all the blood in my body was already in my cock, but I feel another surge of arousal all the same, making me feel briefly dizzy. Charlotte is hot as hell when she's talking dirty, but it's somehow even better when she's flirting. When she's teasing me like she is now, playing coy. The need to see her in person right now, to touch her, feels like what the worst craving for a drug must be. I want to see her biting her pretty, full lip. I want to grab her chin in my fingers and tell her what the punishment is for being a little tease. I want to see her cheeks flush when I say it.

I'm not in love with this woman. That's not an emotion I'm capable of—not an emotion I can allow myself to feel, not when I live my life the way I do. But I'm sure as hell in something else, neck deep and drowning. Need. Lust. *Obsession.*

V ENOM69XXX: *You tell me, dove.*
    CuriousDove24: *Are you going to punish me if I lie?*

O H, *my fucking god.* I tilt my head back, breathing deeply as I wrap my hand around myself again, unable to deny myself a moment of relief after that.

V ENOM69XXX: *Would you like it if I did?*
    CuriousDove24: *I don't know. I think I might.*
    Venom69xxx: *So tell me the truth, dove, or I'll have to think of a way to punish you, the next time we talk.*
    CuriousDove24: *You think about that, Venom.*

J UST LIKE THAT, she's gone. I look over at the monitor tracking her activity, and I can see that she's logged off, leaving me with only that last teasing, parting shot.

If I wasn't a hundred percent sure that it was her, that it's Charlotte, I wouldn't have believed it. The woman I met at Masquerade wasn't brave enough to tease like that. But she seems to be getting more daring. Behind the anonymity of a computer screen, she's spreading her wings, just like the nickname I gave her.

I can't wait to find out what happens next.

10

CHARLOTTE

I'm glad, when I leave Cafe L'Rose after my strangely interrupted lunch, that Jaz and I don't work in the same department. She's going to want all the details, and I need some time to get my head on straight.

A little over a week ago, I would never have given the time of day to a stranger who walked up and interrupted my lunch. But a little over a week ago, I was also just about the furthest thing a person could be from single. The lack of a ring on my finger was the only thing keeping me from that next step.

Now, I'm the opposite. About as single as it's possible to be. Short of the calls and texts from Nate begging me to reconsider, I'm completely free of any ties. And the fact that I haven't gotten any of those calls or texts today makes me hope that maybe he's given up.

I'm honestly surprised that thought doesn't make me feel worse. I would have thought that I would want him to try harder to get me back than that, even though I have no intention of actually going back to him. But now—all I feel is relief at the idea that he might be out of my life completely.

That night at Masquerade whetted my appetite. Showed me a glimpse of what I've been missing all of these years by being so careful, so perfect, so focused on what I'm *supposed* to do and want and not what I actually want. And now—

Now I'm curious. So curious that I actually let Ivan Vasili give me his number.

Am I going to text him? Am I really going to go on that date? The questions rattle around in my head as I walk the two blocks back to my workplace, tugging my camel-colored peacoat closer around me. It's a chilly day, the wind picking up and ushering in fall, and I'm ready for it. Fall is my favorite time of the year.

It's not even like it's going to be all that different being single this fall, I think grimly as I walk back to the elevator and up to my desk. Nate was often too busy to go on leaf-watching and apple-picking dates with me. He always blamed work for why he didn't have nights free to curl up in front of the fireplace and play board games with me, or why we couldn't take a long weekend to a cabin in Michigan and stay on the lake. I always told myself that I was lucky he encouraged me to do those things with my girlfriends instead—that he didn't want me to be home and waiting on him; he just was working too hard to join in.

Now I know that while some of it might have been work, part of it was that he was cheating on me. For how long, exactly, I don't know. But at least for a while.

I turn over the idea in my head of asking Ivan to go on one of those cozy dates with me. At first thought, it seems funny to think of asking the handsome, heavily tattooed guy who came up to me today to go walk through a pumpkin patch—but maybe I'm just judging him too much on his outward appearance. Maybe he *would* do something like that with me.

Maybe I should ask.

Pushing the thought of him out of my head, I try to focus on work for the rest of the afternoon. I have plans with Jaz and the rest of our friends to get drinks after work, and I don't want to be running late.

Jaz is already waiting for me in the lobby when I come down. She must have changed in the bathroom while she was waiting—she's swapped out her black pencil skirt and silk blouse-and-jacket combo from work today, into a pair of form-fitting jeans and an off-the-shoulder striped top in cream and blue that shows off her bronzed shoulders and sharp collarbones, her black hair piled on top of her head now to show it off even more. She's swapped out her shoes, too, into a pair of stiletto ankle boots that make her a couple inches taller than me.

Next to her, I feel frumpy in my jeans and button-down shirt. Maybe, as I'm turning over this new leaf, a wardrobe update is going to be in the cards as well.

"I feel like I need to go home and change," I mutter, as we walk outside to catch the Uber Jaz called. "You always look so stylish."

"You're fine," Jaz reassures me, as we slide into the back of the SUV that pulls up. "You look like *you*."

"Maybe I don't like how *me* looks anymore." I tilt my head back against the cool leather seat, breathing in the scent of pine air freshener that's hanging thickly in the air. "Maybe I should change things up."

Jaz chuckles, opening her purse to find a mirror and lip stain. "The night at Masquerade really did a number on you, huh?"

I look nervously towards the Uber driver, to see if the mention of the club sparked any recognition. The whole point of the anonymity is that no one will know that I went to a place like that. But he doesn't so much as glance back in our direction, still entirely focused on the traffic ahead.

"It made me curious," I admit.

"Curious enough to give that gorgeous guy at lunch your number?" Jaz swipes a dark cherry stain over her lips and then turns to look at me. "Please tell me that my eating lunch at my desk wasn't wasted."

I can feel my cheeks heating. "It wasn't," I mumble, looking away and pretending to search for something in my own bag. "But he gave me his number. I guess he felt like he was being overbearing and wanted to put the ball in my court."

Jaz's eyes widen. "Seriously? Okay, he sounds like a catch. Hot, tattooed, with that accent, *and* thought about your feelings?" She fans herself. "Girl, if you don't take him up on that date, I will. Give me those digits if you don't want them."

The instinctive reflex that I feel to hide my phone startles me. Do I really feel possessive over a man's *number*? A man I don't even really know? That feels odd to me.

"I think I do want them," I say instead, dropping my purse back into my lap. "He *was* polite, at least after that initial thing of interrupting lunch. And he said he just wanted to get to know me better. He wants to take me out on a 'real date.' His words."

"Well, you should text him," Jaz says decisively. "See what his idea of a real date is."

"I'm going to. I think." I chew on my lower lip as the Uber pulls up to the curb outside of the restaurant where we're meeting Zoe and Sarah. "But I want to make him wait a little bit. I'll text him tomorrow."

"Good for you. After that bullshit Nate pulled, you deserve to have a man waiting on you." Jaz hops out, waiting for me as I follow her. "You deserve to have some time to do whatever the fuck you want, honestly."

"I told him I wasn't looking for anything serious," I admit. "That I just got out of a relationship and I want to explore my options for a little while."

"What did he say to that?"

"That it was just dinner. In like—a teasing way." I can't help the small smile at the corner of my lips, remembering that. It made me like him more, the easy way that he brushed past that, as if he wasn't put off at all by my reticence. As if he's willing to give me the space I need—or work for what he wants.

I want to be worked for. I want someone to prove that he's going to do what it takes to make me happy—that my happiness matters to him. I want someone who is going to put in the effort. Because the more I look back at my relationship with Nate, the more holes I see in it. The more things I see now where he just didn't try, where he assumed I'd always be there waiting when he had time for me. And if

I'm going to get serious with anyone in the future, I don't want that in my next relationship.

I want someone who would burn down heaven *and* hell for me, if that's what it took for us to be together.

And I want someone who can make me feel like the man at Masquerade did. Who makes me feel those flames between us, every night that we're together. I'm still not sure that I believe it exists in reality, but that night was enough to make me wonder.

To make me want to look for it, before I resign myself to the idea that it doesn't exist in a real-life relationship.

The tapas restaurant we're grabbing happy-hour drinks at is one of my favorites. It's a rustic, open-floor concept, all dark woods and iron, with huge floor-to-ceiling windows that let all the light in, flooding the space. The seating is an eclectic arrangement of low-to-the-ground couches in bright, jewel-colored velvets, with dark wooden tables set between them. With the weather being as nice as it is, some of the windows are opened, letting in the brisk, fall-scented air.

Zoe and Sarah are already seated on a mustard-yellow velvet couch, drinks in hand. Sarah is still in her work clothes—a sleek, fitted pantsuit in dark blue, with a cream-colored silk shell blouse underneath it and her blonde hair neatly wrapped up in a bun atop her head. Zoe looks every bit the fashionista, her wild, black ringlet hair in a cloud around her head, wearing a streetwear-styled khaki cargo skirt with an asymmetrical hem and assorted pockets, along with a dark green, one-shouldered tight top that shows off her toned stomach and shoulders. She has a cocktail in one hand, and Sarah is sipping at a glass of wine.

"We ordered a charcuterie board while we were waiting," Sarah says, taking another sip of her red wine. "It should be here in a minute. Charlotte! I'm so glad you made it." She gives me a sympathetic smile, and I know what she's thinking—that she's surprised I feel up to socializing. But the truth is that the last thing I want is to be stuck at home alone, thinking about all the reasons why my relationship with Nate failed. I don't even want to be at home thinking about the possibility of this new date with Ivan. I want to be out with my friends, feeling normal. Feeling like my life hasn't changed all that much just because I'm now single.

"I hope you found a way to put that dress to good use," Zoe says, tilting her cocktail glass at me. "That was too hot of an outfit to let it go to waste."

"Oh, she did," Jaz says with a smirk before I can stop her, reaching over to take the gin fizz that the server brings her. I ordered a glass of pinot noir, and I raise it to my mouth to try to hide the flush on my cheeks.

"Oh?" Sarah looks intrigued, grinning at me. "Do tell."

Out of our close foursome, Sarah is the one most like me. She's been single for a few months, but her last relationship lasted three years. She's more adventurous than I am—she's traveled out of the country, for instance—but she also tends to play things on the safe side. And we have a similar style. Sleek, buttoned up, conservative.

Zoe is more like Jaz. Wilder, more impulsive, impetuous, fashionable. Extroverted, whereas Sarah and I tend to be more introverted. Even our tastes in food and drink tend to run similarly. Zoe wouldn't think twice about hearing where I went wearing that dress, but I can only imagine the look on Sarah's face.

I don't know if I can get out of admitting it now, though.

I take another sip of my wine, mentally trying to run through all of the ways I could turn this conversation to some other topic, but I've already hesitated too long. Sarah grins. "Okay, now I know it must be really good."

"Come on," Zoe pleads. "Tell us. I want to know it didn't just hang sadly in your closet." She bats her long eyelashes at me, and I sigh, glaring sideways at Jaz, who is grinning unrepentantly.

"I went to Masquerade," I mumble around the lip of my glass. "Or, more accurately, Jaz took me there."

"I did." Jaz doesn't look the slightest bit embarrassed by the fact that she went there, or the fact that her taking me there implies she's been there often enough to introduce someone new to it. But then again, I wouldn't be surprised if at least Zoe already knew about that side of her. Zoe is equally adventurous and wild, and she'd be the type to readily not only listen to those stories, but join in.

Jaz is my best friend, but clearly, my reticence to do and try new things led her to never tell me about those adventures. Not until recently. Clearly, she thought it would make me so uncomfortable that she didn't share that part of herself with me.

It makes me wonder what else my friends don't tell me, because they think I might be shocked or judgmental. If there are other things I don't know about the people I care most about, because I've always been too reserved to share them with.

I don't want to make Sarah feel like that. I don't want my friends to continue to not be open with me—and that means not holding back with them, either.

"What is that?" Sarah asks, and there's a knowing look on Zoe's face, a curl to the side of her mouth that tells me she does know *exactly* what Masquerade is.

"It's a club," I manage, feeling my cheeks heat a little. I want to be brave enough to tell my friends about my adventure, but I suddenly feel horrifically embarrassed, thinking about what that means. That they'll know I hooked up with a stranger. I didn't have *sex* with him, not *completely*, but I did things with him that I wouldn't have thought I would have done with anyone I didn't know, not all that long ago. I did, arguably, *more* than I have with men I've been in relationships with. More than I did with Nate.

No one I've ever dated made me feel the way the stranger at Masquerade did. And I've never come like that with anyone before.

"It must be an interesting club, to make you blush like that," Sarah says, smirking, and I see Jaz look at me out of the corner of my eye.

"What's more interesting is that Charlotte has a date," she interjects quickly, and I feel a deep wave of relief—and gratitude, that Jaz picked up on how uncomfortable I am and changed the subject for me.

"What?" Zoe and Sarah both immediately look at me, eyes wide. "With who?"

"A *very* hot guy who interrupted our lunch today. Tell them, Charlotte," Jaz urges, and I'm more than happy to turn the subject to Ivan, and away from my experience at Masquerade. And either they're so interested in him that they forget about it, or they picked up on how uncomfortable the topic made me, because they don't ask about the club again.

I explain all about the lunch, and how he gave me his number after asking me out on an 'actual date' to 'just dinner.' I *don't* tell them about how he took my phone out of my hand to put his number into it, because I already know how they'll all react to it. Pretty much how I reacted at first.

And I don't want anything to taint this. I know that part of this whole process of trying new things is not letting others' opinions matter so much to me, but I don't want any negativity around this. I want to go out on my first actual date since Nate broke my heart with all of my friends excited and happy for me.

I know they'd tell me that taking my phone out of my hand is a red flag. But they didn't meet him and see the other things he did. The way he apologized for interrupting lunch. The way he flirted and teased and made sure to give me space to confirm the date on my own.

"Okay, this is perfect," Sarah says enthusiastically, refilling her wine from the small half-carafe in front of her. "This is your first *real* date since that asshole broke your heart."

My friends have tried very hard to avoid using Nate's actual name when talking about him. It's honestly endearing.

"And, it sounds like it's with a real smoke show," Sarah continues. "So this is fantastic. Is he the type you settle down with?" she adds, looking at me and then at Jaz.

I bite my lip, at the same moment, Jaz shakes her head.

"Nah. I mean, not Charlotte, anyway." She grins at me, patting my hand. "I'm just saying, a super-tattooed bad boy is Charlotte's rebound, not her future husband. And you shouldn't be thinking of him like that right now, anyway. You shouldn't think of *anyone* like that until you've had a chance to really get out there, you know?"

I nod, taking another sip of my wine. I know Jaz meant well, so I don't want to let on how much that stung. I could tell her, maybe, if it was just the two of us, how something about what Nate did snapped something loose in me. How I don't know if I *want* to be the 'perfect' one anymore, the one who is absolutely going to settle down with a golden retriever of a boyfriend instead of someone more interesting and edgy and mysterious. No one would think twice about Jaz or Zoe getting into a relationship with someone like Ivan.

Although, I do have to admit, none of us would believe that it would *last* with them, either.

"I definitely told him I'm not looking to be exclusive," I tell them firmly. "And I'm not."

"Good for you, girl." Zoe tilts her glass in my direction. "Don't let any man tie you down for a *while*. Find out what it's like to be hot and single now that you're totally independent and on your own."

I roll that last statement around in my head, in the Uber on the way back to my apartment later, my thoughts a little fuzzy from the wine. Zoe was right about that—I haven't been single since Nate, and that was my senior year of college. There's a whole part of my adult life, my *real* adult life, where I've been committed to one person. There's an entire world of dating that I haven't gotten to experience, and my chance to do that is now.

My mind drifts back to the man at Masquerade. I can't get him out of my head—his confidence, his utter assurance that *I* was what he wanted and no one else, his smooth British accent, and the way he touched me. The way he made me forget all my insecurities, all my anxieties.

The way he made me just *feel*.

My head falls back against the seat of the Uber, that warmth pooling through me again, an unfamiliar ache spreading over my skin, down into my veins. I always thought I didn't really have much of a sex drive, but now I'm starting to wonder how much of that was me, and how much of it was the fault of the men I slept with. If I was so convinced that sex was boring and unfulfilling for me that I just turned it off, even though it had the potential to be so much better.

If I had my own membership to Masquerade, I'd be tempted to tell the Uber driver to take me there instead, just so I could see if the man from the other night was back again. Or maybe—

I don't have to be committed to him. The thought feels bold, startling. He was a one-night stand, not a new relationship. I'm free. If I went back to the club, I could sleep with anyone I wanted there. *Do anything I wanted.* Participate, or just watch—

The thought of watching sends another flutter of heat through me. I swallow hard as the Uber driver pulls up to my building, and I slide out of the car, heels clicking against the lobby tile as I take the elevator up to my apartment.

My *empty* apartment. Where I can do and fantasize about whatever I want, now.

11

CHARLOTTE

As soon as I'm inside, tossing my keys in the porcelain dish, I go to pour myself another glass of wine as an idea takes shape in my head. I walk down the hall, unbuttoning my work shirt, slipping out of my clothes. I dig around in my upper drawer for a pair of loose cotton sleep shorts and an oversized t-shirt, my gaze straying again and again to the laptop sitting on my desk by the window.

Nothing about my outfit is sexy, but that doesn't matter. I'm here alone. No one will bother me. And I can do something that I haven't done in a very long time—

I don't usually watch porn. I've been absurdly reliant on one of a few trusty toys I have to get off over the years, when I have been in the mood and frustrated with the incompetence of men to get the job done. And when I do use them, I either look up erotic stories online or just fantasize in my head.

But I want something different tonight. I want to *feel* different.

Taking a deep breath, I sit down at my desk and open my laptop, taking a big gulp of my wine as I do. I don't know why this feels so much riskier than any of the times I've read erotica or fantasized alone before, but it does. There's nothing safe or vanilla about the things I want to look up tonight.

At first, I open a fairly well-known porn site, typing in *masked man,* and then a moment later, *sex with a masked man.* But after pulling up a few of the videos, it doesn't give me the feeling I'm looking for.

It all feels so overproduced. Impersonal. It *feels* like watching actors, and that's not what I want.

Even with the anonymity, my encounter at Masquerade felt personal. It felt real.

I pull up sites with actual profiles, scrolling through, but nothing feels quite right. And then something pings in the back of my mind, something I remember hearing a few of the guys in one of my computer classes in college talk about. I remember it specifically because, at the time, I was so shocked by it.

It was a chat site, one on the dark web, accessible with a VPN and a decent bit of willingness to explore parts of the Internet that most people either don't know about or consider better left alone. I remember them talking about finding women to chat with who had dark, kinky fantasies that they were embarrassed to talk about with anyone else. I also remember them laughing and talking about how much better it was than porn.

Isn't that what I am? A woman discovering dark, kinky fantasies that I'm ashamed to tell anyone about?

I bite my lip, taking another long drink of my wine. I have a VPN on my laptop. Most people I know who are knowledgeable about computers and IT are, even if they never use it for anything remotely out of the ordinary. It's like a doctor taking vitamins, because they know all the ways that the human body is vulnerable. I've just never gone onto any site that might be deemed questionable.

But I'm curious. I'm more than curious—that night awakened a craving in me that I want to explore. And despite my racing heart and apprehensions, I find myself looking for that site that I remember hearing about all those years ago.

It's less difficult to find than I would have thought. I hesitate as I make a profile, chewing on my lip as I try to decide on a username. I remember the man at Masquerade calling me his *little dove*, and I find myself smiling a little as I type out **CuriousDove24** into the field.

It feels like a little inside joke for myself.

I'm too nervous at first to try to chat with anyone. But there are forums, too, full of posts of users describing fantasies that they'd like to play out. One of them is a description of wanting to be chased by the woods by a man wearing a Jason-style mask, and as I read it, I can feel myself starting to get turned on. I can feel my thighs squeezing together, my breath coming a little faster as I picture exactly that —*maybe* not the hockey mask, but a different type. A skull, maybe. Chasing me through a dark field, or the woods, knowing that he's going to catch up to me eventually. That he's going to make me do whatever he tells me to.

My breath hitches as I navigate over to the link for videos. With every link that I click on, every gulp of wine, I start to feel less and less self-conscious, all my inhibitions floating away on a mist of arousal that makes me feel as if my body is winding tighter and tighter with every moment that passes. I feel warm, achy, *needy*, like I did that night at the club. A longing for pleasure that I've never experienced with anyone that I've been with.

And then the chat box pops up, in the lower right-hand corner of my screen.

I hurriedly pause the video that I was watching, snatching my hand away from where it was resting at the very edge of my shorts, on the verge of sliding under them, and peer at the box.

Venom69xxx: *I haven't seen you here before.*

My breath hitches again, for an entirely different reason this time, mingled fear and anticipation pooling in my stomach. But that's exactly the feeling I'm looking for. That feeling of toeing the line, of doing something risky, mixed with the possibility of the pleasure that I didn't believe existed before this.

I fight back the urge to just close out the windows and run away from the whole thing, knowing that I'll just end up back here if I do. I *want* this. I just have to find the courage to reach out and try it.

So, fingers trembling, I reach out and type back the first thing that popped into my head.

CuriousDove24: *That's because this is my first time. ;)*

The admission feels vulnerable. And I don't know if it's better or worse that there's a screen between us this time, instead of that vulnerability being in front of a real person, the way it was at Masquerade. At least this time, whatever I say, I don't have to see this man at all. Whatever his reactions are, I won't know. And I never have to talk to him again, if I don't want to.

That feels freeing. It's enough to keep me going, chasing that high, that feeling of reckless adrenaline mixed with pleasure. I can feel the slick ache between my legs, begging me to do something about it, but I wait, wanting to see what he'll say next.

Venom69xxx: *What are you hoping to find here, dove?*

It's such an honest question that it catches me off guard for a moment. *What am I hoping to find here?* An audience that won't judge me, maybe. An outlet for the things I'm thinking and feeling. A way to explore. An easy escape, if it gets to be too much.

But I'm not sure if I'm ready to tell him any of that, yet.

. . .

CuriousDove24: *I don't really know. I just know that I want to figure out what it is that I like. I've never had the chance before. And I keep having these thoughts...*

Those thoughts are rushing through my mind, now. Fantasies of being told what to do, of being chased, of being *taken*, all by a man with his face hidden, giving me orders from behind that shield.

Venom69xxx: *What thoughts are those?*

That urge to run hits me again. But instead, I hedge it just a little longer. *What will he do to pry it out of me?* I wonder, and that feels daring. Like what I want to be.

CuriousDove24: *I don't know if I should say...*
    Venom69xxx: *Isn't that why you're here?*
    CuriousDove24: *I hooked up with a man whose name I didn't know.*
    Venom69xxx: *And that was out of the ordinary for you, I'm guessing?*

I stare at the last message for a moment. It felt like such a huge admission for me, but his reaction is a reminder of where I am—the kind of person I'm undoubtedly talking to. This man has probably had plenty of sex with women whose names he didn't know. An anonymous hookup, to him, probably isn't worthy of a VPN and an anonymous chat site.

    I could discount it as him mocking me. But there's something about the overall tone of the conversation that makes me think he's not. That he's genuinely curious about what has led me here, to this point. And I can't see the harm in telling him.

    After all, it's not like he has any idea who I am.

. . .

CURIOUS DOVE 24: *Very much so. I've always done the three-date thing before even a kiss. And I just got out of a relationship.*

Venom69xxx: *No better time to explore, I think.*

CuriousDove24: *That's what my best friend thought. And now—I think that's what I'm thinking, too. I want to explore more.*

Venom69xxx: *What kind of things would you like to explore, dove?*

I BITE MY LIP. Now is the time to be honest about what I'm thinking. The time to explore further, if I really want to.

I reach for my wine glass, swallowing the rest of it in one large gulp, and start typing.

CURIOUSDOVE24: *The man I hooked up with—he wore a mask. I think—I think that turned me on. Not being able to see all of his face. I think I want to do that again. It felt—dangerous. Wrong. Even though he was really very polite about all of it.*

Venom69xxx: *And you'd like a masked man who was less polite? ;)*

A JOLT of arousal shoots through me, that hot, tight feeling sweeping over my skin. My hand drifts towards the edge of my shorts again as I swallow hard, reaching out to type with my other hand.

CURIOUSDOVE24: *I guess you could say I'm—curious. ;)*

Venom69xxx: *About what, exactly, dove?*

CuriousDove24: *I don't know if I'm ready to say all of it, yet. But I think—the man that I hooked up with had a half-mask on. I keep imagining his whole face covered. That the only way I can tell how much I'm pleasing him is by the sounds he makes. By his body language. I picture* *him waiting for me in my apartment. Sitting on the edge of my bed when I walk in. Telling me what to do from behind the mask—*

I CAN FEEL myself getting wetter, the thin cotton of my sleep shorts clinging to my skin. My teeth dig into my lower lip as I wait for Venom's response, my hand skating under the edge of my shorts to brush my fingers over the outside of my pussy.

I'm so wet that I can feel it just from that. I suck in a breath, unable to keep myself from going further after that first touch. I dip my fingers in between my folds, tracing my fingertips over my clit, and it's so swollen and sensitive that it startles me. I've never been this turned on when I touched myself before.

VENOM69XXX: *What would you like him to tell you to do?*

Venom69xxx: *He's been thinking about you all day, after all. Distracted and so fucking hard. That's why he had to sneak in and wait for you. Do you want him to tell you to get on your knees for him? Are you going to give him that pretty mouth, since you made him wait all day?*

THE MOAN that slips from my lips startles me. I gasp, my two fingertips moving more insistently, back and forth, rubbing over my swollen clit as that image springs into my head. The man from Masquerade, but with a full mask this time, sitting on the edge of my bed. Waiting for me, waiting to give me orders to make up for how long I've kept him waiting.

I'm already close. Usually, it takes exactly the right fantasy and *just* the right amount of stimulation—always with a toy—to get me there, but I'm on the verge of coming just from my fingers. But I don't want it to be over yet—and I have a feeling that as soon as I come, I'm going to be too embarrassed to keep talking. My arousal is what's driving this interaction right now, entirely. I pull my hand away, biting my lip as I type a response.

. . .

CuriousDove24: *Maybe he tells me to strip for him first. While he's sitting on the bed, fully clothed and masked. He makes me take everything off, so he can see what he's waiting for. And then—*

CuriousDove24: *He tells me to get on my knees. To—to undo his jeans and take him out. He's still fully clothed. I can't see any skin other than where he's tugged his shirt up out of the way, and his—*

CuriousDove24: *That's as far as I got.*

I DON'T GET FURTHER than *maybe he tells me to strip for him first*, before I can't take not touching myself. I'm too turned on, too close to the edge, and I hit the button for my voice-to-text on my laptop, the added eroticism of describing my fantasy out loud only driving my arousal higher as I push my hand back under my shorts and frantically rub my clit. I'm so close, so very close to what I need—and I can't stop. I need to come, and other than the night at Masquerade, I can't remember ever needing to come this badly.

I picture myself being ordered to my knees, staring up at this faceless, masked man while I reach out to undo his jeans, my hand wrapping around his cock as he pulls his shirt up and out of the way, revealing taut, toned skin—

In my head, it's tattooed, just like Ivan, ink stretching across his muscled abdomen, the man from Masquerade, and Ivan, and this man on the other side of the computer screen all mingling together into a fantasy that pushes me over the edge, my clit throbbing under my fingertips as my hips buck upwards into my hand and I moan helplessly, gasping as an orgasm stronger than anything I've ever given myself before crashes over me.

I don't want it to stop. I keep stroking my fingers over my clit even as it ebbs, staring at the screen as I wait for Venom to respond, trying to catch my breath.

. . .

Venom69xxx: *Were you touching yourself while you told me all of that, dove? Did you just come thinking about the man sitting on your bed, telling you to strip and suck his cock?*

My breath catches, my brain momentarily shorting out. *How did you know?* I want to ask, but I realize immediately how foolish that makes me sound. Of course, he knew. I'm on a website designed for exactly that. No one is sitting here and just *talking* all night, and the fact that I even doubted for a moment that he would know what I was doing tells me just how naive I really am.

Too naive, probably, to be going down this path. But I can't stop now. Not when I feel like I'm on the verge of uncovering so much more that I never knew I could have.

And, as my brain clears, that other part of me takes over. The more daring part. The part that agreed to the date with Ivan today, the part that flirted a little with this man at the beginning of the conversation. A part of me that I never knew existed before, that can be coy, flirtatious, and teasing.

One that I want to keep exploring.

CuriousDove24: *How would I type if I were doing that? ;)*

A smile spreads across my lips as I sit back, waiting for his response. This is a site meant for sex, but I want a little flirtation, too. And now I want to see what he'll say back. If he's just gotten what he wanted, too, and will disappear.

Venom69xxx: *You tell me, dove.*
    CuriousDove24: *Are you going to punish me if I lie?*

. . .

I FEEL another flutter of arousal through my stomach as I type it. *Is that something I would want, too?* I don't know—but this feels like a way to explore it. A way to test if I would want a man who I lied to about something like that to find out, and punish me. To spank me, maybe, or tie me up and tease me—

Venom69xxx: *Would you like it if I did?*
    CuriousDove24: *I don't know. I think I might.*
    Venom69xxx: *So tell me the truth, dove, or I'll have to think of a way to punish you, the next time we talk.*
    CuriousDove24: *You think about that, Venom.*

I LOG OFF ABRUPTLY, my heart racing. *The next time we talk.* I had expected anyone that I talked to would be a one-off thing, that I wouldn't run into the same person twice. But he makes it sound like he's going to be waiting to see that I've logged on again.

Like I've caught his attention enough that he's going to be waiting for *me*.

After feeling like a second thought for so long, that feels heady. The rush of it feels like it could be addictive. I bite my lip as I look at my now-dark laptop screen, feeling more than a little shocked by what I just did. Like that night out with Jaz, it's beyond anything I've ever even thought of doing before.

I get up, leaving my wine glass on the desk as I go to take a shower before bed. Another small rebellion, since Nate was always so particular about having the apartment perfectly clean at all times. But he doesn't live here any longer. *I* do. And if I want to leave my wine glass out until the morning, I will.

There's no one here to tell me what to do any longer.

Not unless I want there to be.

12

IVAN

If I thought I was on the way to being obsessed with Charlotte before, it's nothing compared to how I feel after that chat. There's no going back now.

Everything that happens after she logs off is quick and messy, my arousal driven to the point that all it takes is a few harsh strokes and the memory of her hinting that she might want me to punish her, and I'm covering my hand with my cum. Minutes later, as I'm in the bathroom upstairs washing up, I look up into the mirror and let out a sharp breath, gripping the edge of the sink.

What the fuck am I doing?

I know this only ends badly. I want more of her. And I've created the perfect way to have her—both possibly in real life, as myself, where I can play the gentleman she's told herself she wants...and online, where I can be the depraved masked man that she's allowing herself to fantasize about more and more.

The man created from a night that she doesn't even realize was me.

It's twisted and fucked-up, and I know it is. I know it's wrong. But I want all of her. I want her pretty and sophisticated on her lunch break, and I want her tipsy and daring and wicked. I want her buttoned-up, and I want her messy. I want to know every facet of her, and this is the perfect way to do exactly that.

In real life, I'll get to find out who the Charlotte is that everyone else sees. I'll get to find out who she is as a woman—a *real* woman.

And online, I'll slowly pull the threads of who she wants to be, and unravel all those fantasies until I uncover her darker side. A side that just might want me, no matter who I really am.

Shit. I look up at my reflection, shaking my head at myself, but my thoughts are already running off to a place that I know is impossible. Charlotte would never fit into my world, and I should never want her to. I should never want to bring someone so beautiful, so naive, so *normal* into the fucked-up criminal underground of the Bratva. Into a world that thrives on breaking and using women, even if I've never done that myself. Someone will want to. And if I ever failed to protect her, I could never live with myself.

But my mind is already spinning the fantasy. Deep down, I know if she ever finds out that these three men—the masked man at the club, Ivan, and Venom—are the same man, she won't want me. I know she wouldn't want a man who is a part of the Bratva. But if I make her fall for me before she ever knows, if I make her admit all her deepest desires to me, and if I show her how those pieces of myself connect...

Maybe she won't be able to walk away from me, either.

FRIDAY, all I can think about is the fact that I have a date with Charlotte this evening, one that I've planned meticulously all week. I have a meeting with a distributor for my father first, but once that's done, all I have to do is go back home and get ready, and then pick her up.

It's difficult to focus on anything else. She hasn't logged back onto the site all week, and I feel like I'm starving for her. I went as far as to follow her twice in the morning, to see her walking to work, but that's all I managed, with the other responsibilities that I have. I didn't dare interrupt her lunch again. I didn't think I could make up a good enough excuse for that twice.

She texted me on Wednesday, to confirm the date. Ironically, I got the text as I stood across the street watching her go into her building, my phone pinging with her name as I leaned against a brick wall at the corner of one of the alleys and watched her dark hair fluttering in the breeze around her face, wishing I could wrap a piece of it around my finger.

CHARLOTTE: *Sorry it took so long for me to text back. I just needed some time to make sure this is what I wanted to do. Just out of a relationship and all of that.*

Ivan: *No, of course. Take all the time you need. I wouldn't want to pressure you. I know it might have seemed like that, the way I introduced myself, but I just couldn't bear the thought of letting you go and possibly never seeing you again.*

OF COURSE, I know that I would have seen her again, if that day didn't work. I don't like the way the text budges up to a lie, but I tell myself that it's the truth. What if she had never come back there? I couldn't have stood losing my shot with her. And I couldn't stop myself from trying.

It's only a lie in the most technical sense.

CHARLOTTE: *So, how does Friday night look for you? I'm free. For 'just dinner' on an 'actual date.' ;)*

Ivan: *You remembered. I have an idea for 'just dinner.' You'll love it. Friday it is. I'll pick you up if you send me your address? How does eight-thirty sound?*

Charlotte: *Perfect. I'll send it over on Friday morning.*

. . .

CAUTIOUS. *Good girl.* It's the first thing I think when she says she won't send me her address until Friday morning, because it's the smart thing to do. Of course, I already know her address, and a lot of other things about her. That guilt pings in the back of my mind again, telling me that all of this is not the way to begin, if I want to keep her. That every one of these lies and secrets and omissions will build on one another until I'm caught under the weight of them, with no chance of having Charlotte in my life.

But there's no possibility that she would have me any other way.

I keep playing that conversation over and over in my head, along with the night at Masquerade and the online chat, as I'm driven to the bar to meet my father's distributor. She hasn't texted me since then, other than to send me a pin of her address this morning, and that's contributed to the feeling that I'm starved for contact with her. That I *need* her, in a way that defies logic.

The bar is a dive near the South side, one that my father owns. There's a black Buick with darkened windows parked in the back, visible when the car I'm riding in pulls into the back as well. I would have preferred to drive myself, but my father insisted on sending his driver for me this morning. I know it had nothing to do with my comfort, and everything to do with him wanting control over my movements. Possibly also someone to report on where I go after I leave and if I stopped anywhere beforehand—the driver isn't someone I recognize. A new hire, maybe, and potentially also a spy.

Either way, I don't make a fuss. That's more suspicious than just going along with it.

It's five o'clock, but the bar is still dark and quiet. This place is more of a front for business than anything else; shabby enough on the outside—it fits right in with everything else, drab enough that it gets only a handful of customers. The ones that are here are sitting at the cracked wooden bar top, on worn green leather stools, talking to the worn-looking woman pouring them shots. I spare her a glance as I walk in through the back door—she looks like she was pretty once, but her blonde hair is greying now, put up in a pile atop her head, and what was once probably a pretty damn good figure has softened in a way that doesn't flatter the frayed low-rise jeans and black tank top she's wearing.

I see the shadow of the man I'm supposed to meet in the back. He's folded into the furthest booth, a sweating glass of water and another of beer in front of him, both mostly untouched. In the shadows, I can't make out any of his features, but I see the ring on his forefinger that I was told to look out for—a heavy gold ring with a star in the center.

The bartender gives me one glance and then straightens up, pushing the shots over to the waiting customers before starting to look busy polishing glasses. I'm dressed casually in black jeans and a thin black hoodie, military boots finishing off the look, but I suppose there's no mistaking one of the boss's sons. There are probably pictures of us all in the back for reference—or to use as a dartboard.

God knows I've used my father's picture that way often enough.

I slide into the booth, over the cracked green leather. The man lifts his head, and I see a smooth, almost boyish face, two days' stubble, dark eyes that are nearly black. "Karyiev," he says flatly, and I nod.

The ironic thing about meeting my father's distributor in this place is what it is that he'll be moving. Party drugs, high octane coke, molly, and LSD, all of which will be sold at top dollar in my father's establishments by other dealers who will take their own cut. This man is probably worth as much as I am, but we're sitting here in this dingy bar. The musty, sour smell barely covered by the sharp scent of lemon cleaner and new alcohol, while the jukebox plays whatever the bartender or one of the patrons chose at a muted volume. Right now it's something by Linkin Park, which I'm not fond of. The sound is grating.

"My father wants the shipment done by this weekend," I tell him quietly, my voice pitched low. "Delivered and parceled out to the other dealers to move. We're running low on product, so he wants a higher volume this time. The Black Cat and Fantasy clubs especially moved twice as much as we expected."

The man picks up his water glass, taking a sip. "I have as much allocated as last time. He wants it this weekend, but wants a higher volume? Then he'll have to pay more."

I know he's right to ask it. My father sprang this on me, too, and I'm well aware that it's a big ask. I also know he put me in this position to see what I'd do about it. "He'll pay the usual rate for the product. No additional fees."

The man snickers. "You ask for anything in a hurry, you pay a premium. The Kariyev *pakhan* should know this."

He does know it. I let out a slow breath between thinned lips, frustrated that I'm here at all, frustrated that I'm dealing with a situation that I know my father has made purposefully difficult. "I'm the messenger," I say flatly. "I'm telling you what Dima wants, and what he will give. All I need is for you to nod and say yes."

"You're not the messenger." The man leans back, giving me another look at those near-black, unsettling eyes. He crosses his arms over his chest, and the sudden pull of the material of his shirt gives me a glimpse at where his gun is hidden—at least one, anyway. I never go into a situation assuming that I know all of the weapons someone has on them, and so far, I've always walked away alive. That's probably one of the reasons.

"You're Kariyev's son," he continues. "So don't bother telling me that you're not in a place to bargain or make concessions, because you are."

Less so than you think. I'm not Lev, to have my father's ear and his trust. Even Lev would only need to put a foot wrong once or twice to lose those things. If I make a choice my father dislikes, I'll pay for it. There's little I can do in this situation, especially when I'm fairly sure that Dima has no intention of paying a rush fee for anything.

But I also don't want this man thinking that I'm disposable, or powerless. That's always the wrong card to play in these situations.

"There are no concessions to be made," I tell him evenly. "And the price is the price. I'm here to discuss logistics, not negotiations."

"They became negotiations when you said you wanted more product. It's a thirty percent upcharge to rush product, Kariyev. If you want to try to negotiate that, you're welcome to." He smiles at me, and I feel my jaw tighten.

"How do you feel about negotiating with the wrong side of my blade?" I growl, leaning in and keeping my voice low.

The man chuckles. "You're not going to kill me. I know how much of your product I provide. Your businesses couldn't handle it. And you think word wouldn't get out? That I don't have ears and eyes that know where I am today? Not easy to get another distributor, if you murder one like me."

I move fast, like a striking snake, out of my side of the booth and into his in a flash. I crowd in close to him, preventing him from drawing a weapon, and grab his arm, wrenching it around as I press him into the corner of the booth.

With my other hand, I slide my knife free, resting it against my leg. "Threats and money work wonders," I murmur, my voice pitched very low. Low enough that no one else will hear. "And maybe I can't kill you, but I can take a piece. A little blood. A pound of flesh to make up for your extortion."

I already knew I couldn't kill him. He's right about that. There's no world in which we can take out one of the main criminal distributors in Chicago, and not suffer a blow worse than paying his upcharges. But I also know that I can get away with threatening him. And everything that's happened so far has only served to piss me off enough to follow through on that. My father's manipulations, this man's arrogance, the fact that time is ticking closer and closer to when I'm supposed to meet Charlotte, and this meeting is threatening to encroach on that.

"I'll drop it to twenty-five percent upcharge," he sneers, and my patience snaps.

With one swift movement, I angle the knife under the table, pressing the point into the crease of his thigh. "There will be no fees. The shipment will be finished by Sunday, ready to distribute and start selling in our clubs by next weekend. Or I'll see to it that not only will you be walking funny for the foreseeable future, but you also won't be availing yourself of any of the perks that come with visiting some of those clubs? Understood?" I tilt the knife, pressing it close to the edge of his dick, and the man squirms.

I can *feel* his resentment. "You're going to pay for this," he hisses between his teeth, and I smile coldly.

"No. I won't. Because if anything changes over this little disagreement, I'll start calculating just how many fingers you actually need to do your job." I press the knife in a little more firmly, enough that I feel the denim of his jeans start to give way beneath the tip of it.

"Fuck you, *shchenok*," he growls. "There will be a reckoning, Kariyev. I promise you that. One way or another."

He's not Russian, and his Russian is bad, but I still understand what he said. And it fucking pisses me off. "Right now, all I care about is that you do what I came here to make sure you handle." I stay right where I am, his arm twisted back, the knife pressed into his groin. "Are we done *negotiating*?"

"Fine. Get that fucking knife away from my fucking cock, and I'll make sure it's done." He glares at me like he wants to spit in my face, but he does nothing more.

"Finally. A little fucking respect." I smirk, taking the knife back and moving away from him. "Your money will be paid on delivery. I'll have a guy there with the cash for you."

I'm sure as hell not going to be that guy. I have a date tonight, and this meeting is already running long.

By the time I get back to my place in the city—where I had the driver pick me up this morning, because I sure as fuck didn't want my father hearing anything about my other house—I have barely enough time to get ready for my date with Charlotte. I left clothes at the penthouse, figuring if I somehow get lucky enough to bring her back home tonight, I'd want to make sure this place was exactly how I'd like it to be.

I have a regular housekeeper who comes by to make sure it's clean —I'm rarely here enough to make a mess of it, but I still check to make sure that my instructions are followed. There's good wine in the rack by the refrigerator, everything is neat and orderly, and the bed is freshly made. I light a candle in the living room and bedroom before

I go to take a shower, wanting it to feel like it's lived in. She'll notice something like that, I think, if the space feels stale and cold, like it's often unlived in.

When I finish getting ready, I feel like a different person than I was this afternoon. I chose a light grey suit for tonight, with a very pale blue shirt and no tie. With my hair styled neatly and freshly shaved, I look nothing like the guy who threatened a drug dealer in a dive bar just a few hours ago.

Glancing at my phone, I can see I have just enough time to grab the car I plan to take tonight from the garage, and head to her place. One more look in the mirror, and I grab my keys, heading out to the elevator.

This is the moment I've been waiting for. And I don't want to screw up a single second of it.

13

CHARLOTTE

I can't shake the nerves as I start to get ready for my date.
    Jaz helped me pick out the dress yesterday from Velvet Luxe, a silky dark blue dress with a diagonal hemline and an off-the-shoulder neckline. She comes back to my apartment with me after work, relaxing and sipping a glass of wine together until it's time to get ready. Then she perches on the edge of my tub, waiting for me to come in to do my hair and makeup.
    "Oh my god, you look stunning." Her eyes widen as I walk in, still barefoot. I don't want to be in the heels we picked out any longer than I have to—Jaz finally convinced me to buy a pair higher than two inches, telling me that wearing my usual kitten heels with this dress would constitute an *actual* crime.
    "Thanks." I bite my lip, glancing in the mirror. Much like the dress I picked out for my failed anniversary dinner—that I then wore to Masquerade—this one is sexier than what I would normally wear. I feel like half my chest is exposed, even though it's not that low-cut. But my collarbones and shoulders are shown off in a way that seems sexier to me than even a very deep v would be, and the balconette bra I'm wearing under the dress has my cleavage pushed up to look firm

and supple in the gently curving neckline of the dress. The silky blue material clings to my every curve, necessitating more of that seamless underwear, and I feel my cheeks heat a little at the memory of the masked man at the club slowly sliding them down my thighs.

"Ooh, you look like you're thinking about something fun. Picturing Ivan later tonight without his shirt?" Jaz grins at me, taking another sip of her wine, and I shoot her a glare.

"I'm not going home with him tonight," I tell her firmly, getting my curling iron out to start heating it up. "He'll be lucky to get a kiss."

Jaz pouts. "I thought new Charlotte was going on the date tonight."

"She is." I clip a large part of my hair atop my head, leaving the bottom layers free to curl. "But what if I actually like him, Jaz? I told him I'm not looking for anything exclusive, but that doesn't mean that I don't want to see where it goes. If I'm interested in more than one night, then I can't sleep with him on the first date."

Jaz rolls her eyes so hard that I think they're going to disappear for a second. "Anyone who says that is either a dick or living by some *really* outdated rules," she says, shaking her head. "Plenty of men date women who fuck them the first night. Case in point—" she gestures to herself. "Remember that one guy I dated like two years ago? Jax?"

"How could I forget? He was really into the matching names thing." I let a curl slide free and let down more of my hair. "You slept with him on the first date?"

"Girl, do you remember how hot he was?" Jaz looks at me wide-eyed. "I let him put it in my ass on the first night. And he still dated me for eight months. Trust me, men don't play by those stupid rules."

"You—" I can't quite get past the first part. "Never mind. I don't want details."

"Oh, don't tell me you've never done that." Jaz takes another gulp of her wine. "Okay, actually, I believe it. And Nate would have never *disrespected* you enough to ask." She rolls her eyes. "But I thought maybe some other guy, before him—"

"It's not like my love life has been all that prolific," I tell her dryly. "So no. I haven't done—that."

"Try it," Jaz suggests cheerfully. "It can be pretty hot, in the right circumstances."

I'm not really sure what those circumstances would be. But I also don't have time to ask, because I need to finish getting ready in less than thirty minutes, and my hair is only half-styled. Jaz has distracted me more than I should have let her.

By the time I'm done, my dark hair is loose and bouncy, with thick, fluffy waves, my makeup done in muted shades of champagne, with a dark nude lip. I slip on the sharp-toed, high-heeled shoes that Jaz talked me into buying—although I made sure to get them in nude and not red, so they'd go with more—and suck in a deep breath as I grab my clutch.

"It's going to be great," Jaz reassures me. "You're going to have a blast. And I'll clean up here and then go home, just in case—" She wiggles her eyebrows at me, and I shake my head.

"I'm not sleeping with him tonight. But thanks for cleaning up." I give her a quick hug, and then head to the door.

When I get downstairs, I see Ivan waiting in the lobby. I see him before he sees me, and my breath catches, heat sweeping over me.

He's undeniably gorgeous. He was when he interrupted my lunch, and he's even more so now, in a perfectly tailored light grey suit, his dark blond hair styled away from his face, and his strong jaw perfectly clean-shaven. I can see his tattoos peeking out of the suit, down his hands and in the open space where the top two buttons of his shirt are undone, and the contrast between the dark ink and the expensive suit sends a shivery feeling down my spine.

I've never dated a man with tattoos. Never slept with one. Logically, I know tattoos aren't really all that wild, and half the people in my department either have a few I've seen or probably have some hidden away. But it's more than just the fact that this man is tattooed. There's something about how he wears them, the presence that he has and the way they're a part of that, that makes me feel like I'm approaching something dangerous. That he's a wild predator, and I'm tonight's prey.

It should terrify me, but like a mouse hypnotized by a snake, I only want to draw closer to him.

He turns, and the way his gaze sweeps over me, taking me in from forehead to toes with a sudden heat flaring in his eyes, makes me feel electrified. I can see the way his lips part, the breath he draws in as he looks at me, and no one that I've ever gone on a date with has ever made me feel this beautiful with a single look—made me feel this wanted. He hasn't even said a word, and I feel like his entire world has just narrowed down to only me.

"I'm glad you didn't stand me up," he says with a grin, and that smile softens the perfectly polished, dangerous edge of his look tonight. "I was starting to get worried."

"I'm five minutes early."

"I thought you'd be so excited, you'd be down ten minutes before." He flashes me that grin again, and it takes everything in me not to playfully sock him in the arm. But we're not that close yet. I can't be that casual with him on a first date. *Can I?*

"I thought I should keep you waiting." I smile back, to let him know I'm just teasing, and he chuckles as he leads me out of the front door of the building.

"For you? I'd have waited all night. But they might have towed my car." He gestures to the vehicle waiting for us, parked at the curb, and I briefly freeze, staring at it as if I'm not sure I'm seeing correctly.

I don't know a lot about cars, but I know enough to know that there's an Aston Martin parked at my curb—silver with a black leather interior, bringing to mind James Bond. I've ridden in some nice cars, but nothing as fancy as this.

Nate would be so fucking jealous, I think as I look at it, and immediately feel bad. This man deserves better than to just be an outlet for my rage and pettiness toward my ex. But the thought is there, all the same.

"This is gorgeous," I breathe as I step towards the car, and Ivan opens my door for me. "I've never seen anything like it."

"I was hoping you'd say that." His gaze flicks over my dress again, and down to my legs as I slide into the car. "I also didn't mean to match you tonight." That grin returns, and I realize what he means as I take in the powder blue color of his shirt.

"It's not dark enough to be matching," I tell him with a laugh as he gets in. "But I see why you would think that. It's nearly white, though. In the right lighting, no one will even notice."

"Oh, good." He puts the car into gear, his mouth quirking up as he glances over at me once more. "I wouldn't want you to think I was stalking you."

The statement feels so ridiculous that I laugh again. And I realize, as he pulls into traffic, that I've laughed more in ten minutes in this man than I did in probably the last six months with Nate—-at least that I can remember.

I don't want to keep comparing. But it's hard not to. And that, too, makes me think of if I'll have another date with this man. At some point, if we keep seeing each other, the past will start to fade away. It really will become about just he and I. And I wonder what that would look like.

I can already tell he's different from anyone I've ever dated before. But surely not *so* different that this couldn't possibly be real?

Sinking back into the soft leather of the seat, I run my fingertips over the buttery surface, taking it all in. Ivan is obviously much wealthier than I realized when he approached me at lunch. It's not something that matters to me in a man—I never cared that Nate made top-dollar lawyer money at his firm. I make enough on my own to keep myself in the style that I like, and I don't need or want to rely on a man to buy me things. That's not my love language. But there's something about the way Ivan wears his wealth that's attractive to me.

Nate liked to be flashy. He liked to order the most expensive bottle of wine at a restaurant, get the items on a menu that were so rare the price wasn't even listed. He kept a brand-new Corvette garaged, even though he almost never drove it and knew nothing about cars. He wore name-brand suits to the office, even buying a couple of Tom Ford suits to wear to meetings. It was always about others *seeing* that he had money. And I'm just now realizing how off-putting that was to me.

But Ivan seems to treat it like it's a second skin, one that he's comfortable in, with no need to show off. And that makes me like him more.

"Where are we going?" I ask curiously, and he flashes me a grin.

"Are you alright with it being a surprise?" he asks, and I nod, my eyes widening a little.

"Of course," I tell him quickly, a warm feeling washing over me at the idea that he's putting in effort for this date. That it matters to him that he makes a good impression with me, instead of just assuming I'll fall at his feet.

"I want to impress you," he says, as if he can hear what I'm thinking. "I figure I might only get one shot at it, so why not go all out?"

"You've already impressed me," I admit, rubbing one hand over the soft leather of the seat again. "On time—early, even, the car, and now a well-thought-out date that you want to surprise me with? You haven't missed a step yet."

"That sounds like the bare minimum I should be doing." He turns the car smoothly down a side street, and I see that we're nearing the nicest part of downtown Chicago. The view is beautiful, as it always is—there are cities with bigger skylines, but I never get tired of ours. "It sounds to me like men haven't been treating you the way they should, Charlotte."

"Maybe not," I admit. I let out a slow breath as Ivan slows the car, pulling up in front of Ascent, a new Michelin-starred restaurant that I heard a couple of my coworkers talking about just the other day. I press my lips together, a thrill of excitement fluttering through me, and I can feel Ivan's eyes on me as he opens his door, taking in my reaction.

I watch as he hands his keys to the valet, coming around to open my door. I look up at him as he holds a hand out, putting my hand in his as he helps me out of the car, and I feel a slight jolt as my skin touches his.

I told Jaz I wasn't going to sleep with him tonight, but that might prove harder to do than I expected.

Just that thought startles me. I've never slept with *anyone* on the first date. Never even come close. And the idea that I might have to exercise self-control to keep myself from doing it tonight momentarily blurs my thoughts as I step out of the car and up onto the curb next to Ivan.

"Are you alright?" he asks, his eyes crinkling a little at the corners. He looks amused, but not in a malicious way.

"I'm just caught off guard," I tell him honestly. "I didn't expect all of this." I glance back at the Aston Martin. "Honestly, I'm still not past the fact that you picked me up in James Bond's car."

"He made me promise to have it back to him by midnight," Ivan says, not missing a beat as he takes my hand and tucks it into the corner of his arm. "So we should probably be getting to dinner, shouldn't we?"

I can't help but laugh at that, nodding as a smile spreads across my face. Ivan feels warm next to me, solid, someone that I can lean into. Someone who will plan an entire night for us, without me having to do a thing.

A pretty, polished-looking hostess is standing at the front of the restaurant, dressed in a dark red bandage dress with her brown hair slicked back into a smooth bun, her makeup absolutely perfect. She flashes us a toothpaste-commercial smile as we walk up to the dark wood hostess' stand, looking directly at Ivan. I don't miss the way her gaze flicks enviously over him, and that gives me a bit of a warm glow, too. Whether or not this goes anywhere, he's with *me* tonight.

"Reservation for Ivan Vasili," he tells her, and she motions for us to follow her through the dimly lit restaurant.

It's beautiful, clearly new, furnished in dark wood with gold accents, greenery lining the tops of the walls that we walk past on our way to the dining room. Faint string music is playing in the background, and Ivan and I are led to a dark wooden round table with matching chairs upholstered in red velvet, the place settings resting on gold chargers. We have a view of the kitchen from the small, walled-off area where the hostess brought us, with only four other tables around us, two of them occupied. This is clearly an exclusive area of the restaurant.

The red and gold remind me of Masquerade, and I sneak a look at Ivan as he pulls my chair out, looking for some hint of recognition. *Could it be him?* I wonder for a brief second as I sink into the chair. *Is all of this some hint that he's the man from the club, and he tracked me down?*

But it's not possible. Jaz extolled at length how carefully encrypted the records at Masquerade are, and how difficult it would be for anyone to uncover the identities of the people who visit there. I'm honestly not sure I would have gone, otherwise.

It's a coincidence, that's all. If I were a more superstitious woman, I might say it seems like a sign.

"What do you think?" Ivan asks, as the hostess leaves us there to wait for our server, and I look around at the surroundings.

"It's gorgeous." I bite my lip, reaching for the soft white cloth napkin to arrange it on my lap. "I don't usually go out to places this fancy."

I start to tell him about the plans for my failed anniversary dinner, but I bite my tongue. I'll tell him eventually, if this goes anywhere, but it strikes me that maybe talking about my ex isn't the best way to start off a date that Ivan clearly planned to be special. I wish Nate wasn't so much on *my* mind, but it all still feels so fresh. And I can't help thinking that this kind of attention is what I was missing all along. Not the flashiness of the date, but the thoughtfulness behind it.

"Good evening." The server's voice interrupts my rambling train of thought, and I look up to see an older man with a trimmed, greying beard and neat black uniform setting a carafe of still water on our table. "Would you like sparkling as well?"

"No, thank you," I say at the same moment that Ivan does, and I bite my lip to stifle a giggle. I'm not sure he would appreciate that.

"We're going to do the chef's choice menu," Ivan says smoothly. "With wine pairings." He glances at me as the server walks away. "I hope it's alright that I arranged that already. It's the best way to experience the restaurant, I'm told. And I wanted this to be as special as I could possibly make it."

"It sounds wonderful," I tell him honestly. "I've always wanted to go to a restaurant and do that. I just haven't gotten to yet."

He grins. "I'm glad I could make all your dreams come true."

I swallow hard as he says that, reaching for the carafe of water to pour myself a glass. I can't let my mind run wild with all the dreams that he possibly *could* make come true, in just one night. I'll end up making choices I might regret later, if I do.

The server brings our first course—two small white China dishes with what he says is slivered chicken liver topped with a thin dusting of caramelized sugar and jalapenos. I raise an eyebrow, looking at Ivan, and he shrugs, his mouth quirking up on one side.

He waits for the server to pour the wine pairing—a dark red, we're told, with pepper and berry notes—and then chuckles. "Well, I don't know how I feel about this one. What a way to start, right? But let's see what it tastes like."

He looks up at me as he says it, and the sly expression on his face makes me feel like we suddenly have an inside joke, a secret, like we're embarking on an adventure together. I smile back, reaching for my fork as I cut off a delicate slice.

"It's actually really good." My eyes widen a little as I chew, the salty sweetness bursting over my tongue in the instant before the spice of the jalapeno hits. "I would never have ordered that on my own, but it's delicious." I reach for the glass of wine, which, of course, pairs perfectly with it.

"I would never have tried it either," Ivan admits, taking another bite. "But that's the point of a menu like this, right? To make you try new things? Broaden your horizons, when you might not have tried them otherwise?"

I feel a slight flush hit my cheeks as he says it. It no longer entirely feels like he's talking about dinner. It feels a little like he's talking about dessert—and not the one they're going to serve us here.

"Do you go out to places like this often?" I try to switch the topic, reaching for my wine glass again.

"I've honestly never been to one of these Michelin-starred restaurants before," he confesses with a grin. "I don't go out as often as you might think."

"So, what made you decide to do it tonight?" I know I sound a little incredulous, but I can't help it. I'm sure this man goes out on plenty of dates, and it makes me wonder where else he takes them. Much like bringing up my ex, though, I feel like that's something I shouldn't ask on a first date.

"Well—" he pauses as the server comes back to take our plates, replacing them with the next course. It's a baked scallop in a thick coconut sauce, set in the middle of a shell, with small wisps of seaweed and caviar on top. "I thought if I was going to try this new experience, I wanted it to be with you."

The statement, said as casually as he does, takes me aback for a second. "Why?" I blurt out before I can stop myself. "I think—I think I'm actually the most boring one of my friend group, really. If you wanted an exciting evening, you should have asked Jaz out."

He cocks his head slightly as he picks up a fork and deftly slices off a piece of his scallop. "I don't think you're boring at all." He reaches for the wine, a sweeter pairing this time. "I think you just need to find what excites you."

"You don't even know me." There's a hint of defiance in my voice, and I wonder why I'm arguing *for* this man to find me boring. It's the last thing I want, but there's some part of me that doesn't want anything about this interaction to be fake. I was grateful for the mask at Masquerade, but *this* man—something about him makes me want to be sure he's seeing the real me, from the start. To be certain that if this goes anywhere, it's because he wants *me*, and only me.

I've barely even gotten to know him, but I have a strange, and slightly uncomfortable feeling that if I were to find out that he wanted me because he thought I was something different than I am, I would be devastated. Maybe it's just because my last relationship ended because of lies, but it feels imperative to me.

"That's the point of this date, isn't it? To get to know each other?" He smiles, taking another bite of scallop. It's perfect, buttery sweet, with just a hint of spice in the coconut sauce, but I'm thoroughly distracted by the conversation we're having now. "Maybe I'm just a good judge of people."

"So what do you think of me, then?" I reach for my wine glass, feeling nervous for the answer. I'm not sure I want to know what he's going to say in response to that. I'm not sure that I'm ready to hear it.

"I think you just need the opportunity to come out of your shell. Someone like your friend—" he pauses, as if thinking of exactly how he wants to say whatever it is that he's going to say next. "She's confident in who she is. I bet she knows everything she likes, and takes charge in every situation. And that's a good quality. But what I think is even more interesting is someone who doesn't yet know all of that, but is trying to find out. Someone who is learning about themselves. And I'd like to see who you become as you do that."

I blink, startled by the raw honesty of the statement—and by how true it is. "I told you I'm not looking for anything exclusive," I remind him, and he smiles.

"It's just dinner, remember?"

"That sounds like a lot more than just dinner." I bite my lip. "It sounds like you're looking for something serious. Like you want a relationship, and not just a—a—"

"A fling?" he supplies, that grin quirking the edges of his mouth again. "I don't have any preconceived notions of what I'm looking for."

We're interrupted again by the server returning, this time bringing us another set of small plates with a quail leg set on a small pressed spoonful of mashed potatoes, a pool of egg yolk beneath it. He pours the next wine pairing, and I start to say something else about not wanting anything serious, but Ivan speaks first.

"Why is it that you think you're boring?" he asks, and I hesitate. I'm a little afraid that whatever I say is going to convince him of it.

"I—" I let out a slow breath. "I'm not spontaneous. I'm not the kind of person who books a vacation on a whim, or who tries a new hobby without researching it to death first and doing a cost/benefit analysis on the amount of time I'd have to put into it to know if I'd like it or not. I'm not a person who likes adrenaline or who takes risks. I've never traveled outside of the country. If you'd told me where you were taking me tonight, I would have tried to look up a menu to see what I'd want to order beforehand. This dress is by far the sexiest thing in my closet. And—"

"Well, I'm not sure *that's* true," he says, a smirk on his mouth, and I flush a little, thinking of the dress I wore to Masquerade. But there's no possible way he knows about that.

"None of those things make you boring," he continues. "I'm inclined to think that it just means that there hasn't been anyone who made you feel comfortable enough to try acting differently, without fear of how they'll react if it doesn't go entirely right. If you don't like your food and want something else, if you end up disliking the place you chose to go on a whim. That they'll accuse you of ruining the fun instead of finding ways to make it enjoyable anyway—or just cutting the plans short."

"What would you have done if I didn't like the food here?" I look at him curiously. "You planned this whole date so carefully. Wouldn't you have been offended?"

Ivan chuckles. "No. Not at all. We would've left and found somewhere else to go."

I'm startled by his response. I take a bite of the tender quail, wanting a moment to think about what to say in return. Nate would have berated me for not being adventurous enough, for not appreciating his effort. "I think I might just be a little bit of a homebody," I admit. "Or at least someone who really likes their routine. I tend to do the same things every week. Lunch at the same cafe, happy hour with my friends once or twice a week, brunch on Sunday."

Ivan shrugs. "There's nothing wrong with enjoying staying at home. I happen to really like my house, myself. And I like my time alone."

I think about that as I finish the dish, wondering if maybe I've been too hard on myself all of this time. If maybe Ivan is right, and I just need a partner who won't make me feel small and lesser if I don't enjoy the leaps I might try to take.

After all, isn't that what happened at Masquerade? I took a leap with Jaz, knowing that if I didn't like it or if it was too much, she'd take me home and never make me feel bad about it. It makes me wonder what it would be like to have a partner who didn't make me feel bad, either.

The last course is brought out to us—a delicate piece of honeycomb with vanilla ice cream and a puff of spun sugar, served with a sweet port. I'm surprised to see how quickly Ivan digs in, and it makes me laugh a little.

"You have a sweet tooth."

He looks up at the observation, that same smirk at the corners of his mouth. "That surprises you?"

"Well—yeah."

One eyebrow slowly rises. "Why is that?"

"I—-" I feel guilty for saying it, suddenly, like I'm judging him. "The tattoos," I say finally. "I don't know—I just thought you wouldn't like sugar as much as you clearly do."

He laughs, and I'm relieved to see that he doesn't seem to be offended. "I'm different to you, aren't I? Different from the men you usually date."

Now *I* feel a little judged, but I can hardly say anything after what I just said to him. "Yeah," I admit. "You are."

"Well, now you know the two aren't mutually exclusive." He sips at the port, clearly still amused. "Here's to a night of new things."

I blush a little. I don't think I'm missing the innuendo in that sentence. "I loved all of this," I tell him honestly. "But you really didn't have to do all of this to impress me. I'm much easier to please than this. I mean—" My blush deepens, as I realize all of the ways that sentence could be taken.

"Well, I know I said it was just dinner, but—" Ivan pauses. "I also have tickets to a show for us, if you're up for that. I don't know how you feel about the theatre, but *Les Misérables* is playing at Chicago's Broadway right now, and I've heard it's good."

I laugh, shaking my head at him. "You're right, that isn't 'just dinner.' But I'm more than happy to continue the night for a little while."

"Good." He looks pleased. "I like spending time with you, Charlotte."

"I feel the same way about you." I bite my lip, feeling nervous at the admission. "And I like—all of this." I look around at the restaurant. "But I really am just as happy with simple dates. I want you to know that. What I want is—" I hesitate, wondering if this is too much. If I should be telling him what it is I want when, just a little while ago, I made sure to emphasize how much I wasn't looking for anything serious.

"What do you want?" He looks at me keenly, as if I'm on the cusp of telling him something vastly interesting, and I'm not sure how that makes me feel. I don't think I'm really all that interesting, and I can't help wondering if he's faking the interest to get me to go home with him. It's clear that he finds me attractive, but what I can't figure out is why it would be more than that.

"I want someone who wants to spend time with me," I tell him simply. "No matter what the date is. I want someone who's just happy that we're together."

His gaze doesn't leave mine, even for a second. "What is *your* preferred date then, Charlotte?"

He hasn't tried to shorten my name once, I realize. It's yet another thing that makes me like him more than I probably should.

I feel pretty certain that as soon as I tell him the truth, this carefully-crafted interest of his is going to start to fade. But I reason that that's what I would want. I don't want lies and pretense. I don't need promises of forever, not right now, but I do need someone who will tell me the truth. So if he thinks my idea of a fun afternoon is silly, wouldn't it be better to know now?

It's a test, but I think it's one worth giving him. I don't think he's the type to want to go on a casual, ordinary, get-your-hands-dirty kind of date, not when he drives an Aston Martin and takes me out to one of the most expensive dinners in the city, but now I want to know.

"It's fall—my favorite season—so if I were choosing the date, we'd go apple picking," I tell him. "And then we'd take them home and try to bake something together with them, and we'd get changed afterward and go to a movie. Just a normal movie, at a normal theater."

To my surprise, he doesn't flinch. He doesn't look put off. He grins —a real, wide grin, and nods. "Alright, then. That's our next date. Apple picking, baking—which I'm very bad at, by the way, so plan to either put me on dish duty or for the pie to be inedible—and a movie. I'm all yours."

That last sentence sends an entirely inappropriate flood of heat through me. "I'm not—" I start to say, and Ivan chuckles, interrupting me.

"---looking for a serious relationship. I know, Charlotte. You've told me. Enough times that I'm almost offended." The smile that's still on his mouth tells me that he isn't, really. "I understand that you're just out of a relationship—with a guy who is obviously a complete moron, by the way—and you want to explore. That's fine. I get it."

I look at him suspiciously. I can't help it. I don't know Ivan well, yet, but everything about him looks like he would be possessive. Like he would hate the idea of sharing me with anyone. And a small part of me wishes that he would say that he doesn't want to. That he won't be satisfied with anything less than making me entirely, completely his.

"Most men wouldn't like that," I say slowly.

Ivan smiles. "I'm not most men, Charlotte. I think you'll realize that sooner rather than later. And something else that you're going to figure out, once we've spent more time together, is that I want *you*. All you need to realize is that I'm capable of being and giving you everything you need."

It's the most arrogant, high-handed thing he's said all night. The possible crack in his veneer of casual carelessness.

But it also takes my breath away.

His dark blue eyes hold mine, as he reaches out to touch my hand, sending another shiver down my spine. "I'm fine with you exploring, Charlotte, because I want you to be all in when you realize it."

It feels hard to speak, for a moment. I feel my fingers involuntarily curl around the tips of his, not wanting to let go of his hand. "Why?" I ask softly, and something gleams in his blue eyes, an emotion that I've never seen before and can't entirely read.

"Because, Charlotte," he says softly, "when that happens, it'll be it for us both. Forever."

14

IVAN

I was a little afraid that my declaration might have scared her off. And I saw the shock in her face before she quickly hid it, saw the moment that she heard me say that, and wondered if I was crazy.

I'm pretty sure I *am* crazy. I'd have to be, to say that to a woman I've only talked to three times, a woman who would never, ever want me if she knew who I really was. But it's the truth.

I didn't mean to say *forever*. But when it slipped out, I didn't want to take it back.

And that's how I know I've really lost my mind to this woman.

Of course, I have every intention of making sure that no one else goes on a date with her. I'm not going to allow anyone to manage even coffee with her. But she doesn't need to know that. And if she needs the illusion of having the freedom to explore until she's fallen for me, then giving her that can't be any worse than what I'm already doing.

I've committed sin after sin already against the way a relationship should happen. I've already crossed lines that she doesn't even know she needed to draw. But I keep telling myself that it's fine. That she doesn't need to know. That I'll figure out the consequences when the time comes.

I'm willing to play whatever game I need to in order to buy myself the time I need to win her over.

The rest of the evening goes off without a hitch. We get our seats at the theatre, and the hardest part of all of it is keeping my hands off of her in the darkened room. I can barely pay attention to the play, because so much of my attention is wrapped up in her. Every breeze wafts her scent towards me, the smell of coconut from her shampoo, and the sweet honey scent of whatever fragrance it is that she's wearing. It brings back a memory of Masquerade that is entirely inappropriate for where we are, and I feel my cock stiffen abruptly, thickening along my leg and straining the fabric of my suit trousers. I shift in my seat, trying to push away the memories of how she felt on my mouth, hot and wet and sweet. The memory of her taste on my tongue, like the honey that she smells like.

God, I want to pull my cock out right here, yank her onto my lap and fuck her in front of all of these people. That fantasy only serves to make me harder, thinking about Charlotte impaled on my cock in the middle of this theatre, the man behind me a front-row witness to the pleasure on her face as she comes all over me.

I'd have to kill him after that.

The thought is so sharp, so unexpected, that it quells my arousal a little. This possessiveness is unlike me. I've fucked women on the public play floor at Masquerade before without a thought. Their screams of pleasure as everyone else witnessed how well I fucked them only adding to my own enjoyment. Charlotte shouldn't be any different—-but the thought of anyone else seeing her eyes flutter and her mouth drop open with pleasure, the thought of anyone else witnessing her climax...it makes me feel murderous.

Like it should belong to me, and only me, ever again.

My hand tightens on my leg, curling into a fist as I fight not to reach over and touch her leg. I haven't touched her at all tonight, which has required an immense amount of restraint on my part, but now I wonder if it's been too much. If she's going to think I'm uninterested, because I haven't tried to touch her at all.

If she only knew how hard it is for me not to fuck her right here.

Slowly, I reach out, resting my hand on her knee. A jolt runs up my arm, like touching an electric wire, the feeling of her silky dress against my bare fingers making me ache. A touch that simple shouldn't make me hard, but my receding erection comes back to life in an instant. I'm painfully stiff just from the curve of her knee against my palm.

I hear her soft, indrawn breath, and I wonder if she'll pull away. But instead, she reaches out, her fingers grazing along the side of my hand—and then her hand curves over mine, resting there.

For the remainder of the play, we sit there like that, holding hands. And not even when I was a fucking teenager have I ever been so painfully turned on by that alone.

—

When I drop her back off at her apartment, I walk her to the front door. I wait to see if she'll try to lean in for a kiss, and when she doesn't, I don't push it. I just smile at her, taking in the shy, almost hopeful expression on her face, and let the moment pass.

"I'm going to hold you to that apple-picking date," I tell her, and the smile that spreads over her face, one that tells me she's impressed that I didn't push her for a kiss, makes it all worth it.

When I get home, I head straight downstairs to the basement, before even changing out of my suit. I have a strange conflict about whether I hope she'll be online or not—on the one hand, my arousal is raging out of control, and I desperately want her to tell me what she's fantasizing about right this moment, so we can get off together. But at the same time, that would mean that right after our date, she would have gotten online hoping to talk to who she believes is another man.

I don't know whether to be relieved or disappointed that, after an hour of waiting and checking my camera logs, she never comes online.

I'm supposed to go with Leo, Jonas, and Brad to Masquerade again tomorrow night. But my usual anticipation for it isn't there. Charlotte has invaded my mind so completely that the thought of doing anything to another woman—or having anything done to me—doesn't hold the appeal that it usually does. When I think of sex, all I can think of now is her.

That will change, after I've had her. It has to. Maybe it will take a little while to fuck her out of my system, but sooner rather than later, I'll get tired of her. The obsession will wane, and I'll come to my senses and remember that a woman like Charlotte has no place in my life long-term.

But for now, it's painfully clear that she's all I want. It's clear after my shower, when I go to bed and can't fall asleep until I get off to the thought of her coming on my tongue, and it's clear the next night at Masquerade, when I turn down every advance, choosing instead to watch the show on the main floor while sipping vodka, and then get a private room to stroke myself alone to that same memory.

I haven't been inside a woman for weeks now. And it's all because of her.

It's even more clear Sunday morning, when I follow her to her brunch. She'd mentioned on our date that she has a standing weekly brunch with her girlfriends, and the text thread that pings on my phone from hers tells me all the details. They're going to a place called Amuse-Bouche, a trendy brunch spot that I've passed a number of times but never had any interest in going to, and I take an Uber from my house to downtown, waiting until I get a ping from their group chat mentioning where their table is before going in. I'm wearing black cargos and a black t-shirt, with a black baseball cap and aviator sunglasses, and thankfully, the chill in the air means that I can add a jacket to that, which only adds to my ability to shroud myself in a corner on the outside patio.

With my laptop in front of me, I'm able to keep myself hidden enough that Charlotte and her friends shouldn't notice me, and if they do, neither she nor Jaz will figure out who I am. There's a small risk, of course, but that's a part of the rush, I'm realizing. Just like the two other identities I've shrouded myself behind to keep tabs on Charlotte, both of which aren't completely foolproof. But they're close enough to it that the odds of her figuring it out are low.

There's no real reason for me to be here. It's another symptom of what I know is becoming an increasingly concerning obsession with every passing day. But I feel a *need* to see her. To know if she likes sweet or savory. If she orders a mimosa or a Bloody Mary or doesn't drink alcohol at brunch at all. To *watch* her.

I wish I understood it, because it would make me feel slightly less insane. I'm not a voyeur, normally. I'm not someone who has ever become obsessed with a woman. And I'm not someone who is prone to addiction. I've smoked cigarettes, and I drink, and I've done drugs now and again, and it's always been easy for me to pick them up and put them back down without issue. But for the first time in my life, I understand that craving for a hit.

I can't hear what they're talking about, but it doesn't really matter. What I want is to watch *her*. And that's exactly what I do, for the next hour and a half. I watch her order a mimosa, watch the server bring her a plate of eggs Benedict with smoked salmon, and study her face as she talks. As she laughs. I shift under the table, angling myself so that no one else out here on the patio can see that I'm rock hard just from watching this woman's lips move.

Lips that I want so desperately around my cock.

I'm disappointed that I have to leave before her brunch is over. But I have a meeting with the FBI agent that I'm feeding information to, and I can't push that off. The last thing I can afford to do is get on their wrong side. All it would take is one misstep, and they could bring my entire world crashing down in an instant.

I pay for the waffles I barely picked at, stow my laptop away, and leave out of the side gate so that I don't have to walk past the table that Charlotte is at. And then I call an Uber to the South side diner where I'm supposed to meet Agent Bradley.

Adam Bradley is a massive thorn in my side. He knows the barrel they have me over, and he doesn't seem to think that my informing on my father over the trafficking of women pays for a lifetime of other sins. If he had permission from his higher-ups, I have a feeling that he'd find some reason to throw me in prison anyway faster than I can say *laundry list of felonies*.

But he doesn't have that permission, and I have no intention of giving him a reason to ask for it. It just makes me curse my father even more, because it's *his* crimes that have sent me to the other side, anyway. If not for this, I would never have come this close to an FBI agent. Not in a million years.

He's sitting in the back of the diner when I arrive, in plainclothes, wearing a baseball cap not entirely unlike the one I wore to watch Charlotte at the restaurant. I've taken mine off, which feels better—I'm not really a hat guy. I stroll into the diner as if I don't have a care in the world and slide into the booth opposite him, even though my insides feel wound tighter than a violin string.

"That's bad for your gut." I point at the mug of black coffee in front of him. "Especially on an empty stomach," I add, noticing that there's nothing else there. Just the coffee, and the unpleasant expression on Bradley's face.

"This whole job is bad for my gut." Bradley's frown deepens. "What do you have for me, Kariyev? Make it good."

"Was the entire shipment of women that you managed to get out of there before my father's buyers showed up not good enough for you? Or are you not really in this for the women, and the only joy you get out of this job is not actually helping people, but taking others down?" I raise an eyebrow. "And here I thought better of you."

"No, you didn't." Bradley gives me a look that tells me that he's not interested in my sense of humor, which isn't a surprise. He never is. "I want information, Kariyev. *Real* information. Or I might have to start putting the screws to you instead, if I think you're holding back on me."

"You get what I know. I don't know exactly who in my father's employ is setting these deals up. I also don't have client names. Not yet. And I've been a little preoccupied with making sure that no one who *isn't* involved in this starts squealing about me, because I keep getting dragged out to the warehouses to cut pieces off of guys who don't actually know anything. Makes it hard to spend time figuring out who does."

"So get involved." Bradley's glare doesn't diminish. "Tell your father you want a cut of the flesh trade. Tell him you want to buy a girl for yourself. I don't fucking care how you do it, but get in there and get me names."

"I handle the drugs." I let out a sharp breath, pausing as the pretty waitress walks over to ask me if I want anything. On another day, I would have enjoyed the view more than I am—she's way too pretty to be working here, with gorgeous chocolate-brown eyes and mounds of thick dark hair that are meant to have a man's hands buried in them. It's piled up on her head, a few pieces falling free, and her uniform is just a bit too tight on her.

Not all that long ago, I'd have left my number on the receipt. But I look at her, and all I can think is that while she's drop-dead gorgeous, she's not Charlotte. And Charlotte is all that I want.

Nothing is stopping Bradley, though. He's looking at her like he wants her to melt all over his mouth, and I find it amusing. For all that he works as one of the government's righteous avengers, he's at heart just a dog like the rest of the male species.

Not that I've ever been much better. I do at least manage to keep my tongue in my mouth until I'm asked not to, though.

"I'll have coffee," I tell her. "Cream and sugar. And some scrambled eggs with a side of salsa, if you don't mind." This diner has surprisingly good salsa, and I could use some actual food. The lemon-berry waffles at Amuse-Bouche were good, but not all that filling.

"Coming right up, handsome." She winks at me, and I search for the desire to flirt back. It should be there. It's almost always there. But once again, all I see is the image of Charlotte's laughing mouth, her head tossed back as she sat across the patio from me earlier without even knowing it.

A tingle of heat runs down my spine, and I push it away. My

libido has been out of control lately, and I don't really want to be sitting across from Agent Adam Bradley with a hard-on.

"I handle the drugs," I repeat. "And my father knows I don't like the trafficking. He's not going to believe me if I suddenly say I want in on it. He knows I'm not particularly motivated by money, and he already considers me a pain in his ass, for the most part, because I don't kiss it like my brothers do. He's not letting me in on that."

Bradley listens to me with the bored air of a man who really doesn't care what I'm saying, but is going to let me finish. "I don't give a shit," he says, when I'm done and the waitress has left again, this time after depositing a cup of coffee in front of me, liberally dosed with cream and sugar. "Figure it out, Karyiev. That's your problem, not mine. Mine is to make arrests. Yours is to get me the information I need. I don't care how you do it. Just do it."

He throws down a ten-dollar bill on the table, gets up, and strides out of the diner.

Shit. I rub my temples, looking down at the plate that's slid in front of me, my appetite entirely gone. It's clear the feds are getting impatient. And why wouldn't they? They're not going to be skinned alive if my father gets wind of what I'm doing. They're not going to prison to get a shiv in the kidney if I don't deliver the information I've promised. Nothing is going to happen to Adam Bradley except a good talking-to from his boss, and maybe a reduction in his Christmas bonus.

Meanwhile, I'm staring down the very real possibility of looking at a grave from the wrong side.

I gulp the coffee, poking at the eggs for a minute before giving up on eating anything additional, and toss some cash down on the table with a generous tip for the pretty waitress, before getting up and heading for the door.

I very nearly run face-first into Lev on the way out.

For a second, I think my heart is going to stop. It takes every bit of self-control I have to keep my face schooled into an expression of neutral surprise, and not the bone-chilling fear that sweeps through me at the sight of him, at the thought that he might have been watching. Waiting for me.

At the thought that I might be the one in manacles before the day is out, bleeding onto a filthy concrete floor.

"Lev." I raise my eyebrows, looking for any hint of anger. Any satisfaction from him that he's about to be the end of me.

"Brother." He crosses his arms. "Why am I not surprised to find you here?"

"Why am I not surprised you're looking for me?" I shrug, leaning back against the stained wall as I reach into my pocket for a pack of cigarettes. I don't smoke often, but right now, I feel sorely in need of one.

"*Otets* has a message for you. He sent me to track you down and let you know."

That cold feeling in my gut spreads outwards. Once again, it takes everything in me to school my expression into something neutral, that doesn't give away the feeling churning in my stomach, threatening to send that coffee and two bites of eggs right back up.

I don't care what anyone says; it's not cowardice to have a healthy fear of pain and suffering, even of death. And I have far too intimate a knowledge of Bratva torture methods not to feel fear at the thought of them being applied to me.

"What's that?" I raise the cigarette to my lips and light it, at this point more for the sake of having something to do with my hands and mouth than anything else.

"He has a job for you."

The fear eases a little. What remains is not because I've been caught today—clearly, I haven't, but because it's apparent that someone is tracking me. There would have been no reason to know that I was at the diner otherwise.

Lev might have seen Bradley leaving, or he might not. He might have noticed him and later figure out that a federal agent was at the same diner I was, or not. All I can count on is that Lev isn't smart enough to add two and two together, which I'm grateful for right now. His stupidity often frustrates me, but just now, it's a boon.

"Okay." I suck in a deep lungful of smoke, letting the nicotine buzz through my veins. "Spit it out, Lev. I'm on pins and needles here."

As usual, the expression on my brother's face tells me that he wants to hit me. The fact that I'm quicker than he is probably the only reason he doesn't—he lost many a fistfight to me throughout our childhood.

"There's a charity gala coming up next Friday night. Some nonprofit." Lev waves his hand, clearly not giving a shit about that part of it. "Petrov's daughter is going."

"Yuri Petrov?" I frown at the mention of his name. Yuri Petrov is another Bratva patriarch, the *pakhan* of a family that my father considers to be his direct rival. The fact that his daughter is already being brought into the conversation sends an uneasy prickling sensation over my skin. "I don't kill women, Lev. *Otets* knows that."

"Ah, lighten up." Lev cracks a sarcastic smile. "You're not going to be asked to kill anyone, Ivan. What you *are* going to do is take Sabrina to the gala, as her date."

I narrow my eyes. "Why?" If it were anyone other than my father requesting this, I'd assume this was some kind of start to an arranged marriage, one I would strenuously object to. Not because there's anything wrong with Sabrina—I've met her before, and she's a pleasant enough woman, beautiful and tolerable to talk to. But I'm not about to be roped into any union against my will.

I already know it's not that, though. It's going to be something worse than that.

"Our father has settled on his revenge for the injuries Petrov has done him over the years." Lev smiles coldly, leaning against the wall opposite me, as if this were a normal conversation to have outside of a local diner. "She's going to be taken and sold. And you're going to ensure that happens."

Shit. I manage to keep my face blank, but my mind is already spinning ahead. If Sabrina Petrov is going to be kidnapped and trafficked, then I'm gong to have to do something to interfere in that. I have no particular affection for her, but I'm not about to allow her to be sold because of our fathers' rivalry. But more than that, this is a possible opportunity.

Before my little chat with Bradley, I would have done everything in my power to get out of this. But it's clear that I need to provide some kind of information that he considers valuable, and soon. This might be a way to do exactly that.

I groan, stubbing out my cigarette on the wall, because Lev will be suspicious if I agree too quickly. "I'm not going to be able to get out of this, am I?"

Lev's smile widens. "No," he says with satisfaction, and I can tell he's enjoying this. "And she's a virgin, Ivan. So no playing with her before she's handed over."

I grimace. "Not even a hand job in the bathroom?"

"Absolutely fucking not. She's to be handed over exactly as she is now, pure as the driven snow."

"Fine." I push myself off of the wall. "It's not like I had any other Friday night plans," I add sarcastically, and Lev's expression grows even more pleased.

"You do now. Don't fuck it up," he adds, calling out after me as I start to walk away. "*Otets* patience is waning."

"So is mine," I mutter under my breath.

"What's that?" Lev asks, and I grit my teeth, not bothering to turn back around.

"I said, send me the details. I'll adjust my calendar accordingly."

And with that, I start to walk down the street, back in the direction I came. I'll call an Uber before too much longer, but for right now, I need the fresh air.

If I can pull this off, I might both be able to save Sabrina Petrov, and get Bradley enough information to get him off of my ass for a while.

If not—

That doesn't bear thinking about.

15

CHARLOTTE

I have high hopes for my Sunday morning, until I wake up to texts from Nate.

Nate: *Char, just call me.*
   Nate: *Char, babe. You're being really unreasonable.*
   Nate: *Don't tell me you've got some other guy over there already, and that's why you're ignoring me.*
   Nate: *Were you just waiting this whole time to be a slut?*
   Nate: *I'm sorry babe, I'm just going crazy not hearing from you. My brother is getting sick of me crashing on his couch.*
   Nate: *We can talk this out. Just call me. You're not going to throw away five years just like that, are you?*

JUST READING the string of texts before I've even gotten in the shower makes me feel tired, and douses some of the glow I've been riding on since my date with Ivan. *That* couldn't have gone better, so much so that I've been looking forward to filling Zoe and Sarah in on it at brunch. Jaz already knows, obviously—-I texted her nonstop the minute Ivan dropped me off at my apartment after the play. She's of the mind that the fact he didn't even try to kiss me is concerning. I think it's gentlemanly.

It made me feel like he really cares more about spending time with me than anything else. Like he really does see more about me that he likes than just my appearance.

I ignore the messages from Nate, tossing my phone back on the nightstand before going to shower and get ready for brunch. If anything, the date with Ivan made me that much less interested in rekindling anything with him. In fact, I'm starting to wonder if Nate's cheating was a blessing in disguise. Sure, it hurt to find out about, and it made me feel like shit at the time—but I feel like my eyes have been opened since then to everything that I was missing.

Brunch is at Amuse-Bouche, one of our favorite spots. Zoe and Jaz are there first, and I get a text from the group chat just as I'm getting out of the Uber, letting me know that they have a table. When I get there, there's already a pitcher of pineapple mimosas that they're sharing, while picking at a plate of cinnamon knots.

"Heyyy!" Jaz exclaims as I sit down. "Oh my god, I can't wait for you to tell Zoe about your date."

"I'll wait for Sarah to get here." I settle into my chair across from Zoe, noticing an odd-looking man out of the corner of my eye, sitting at the far end of the patio. He's dressed all in black and wearing a leather jacket and cap, focused intently on something on his laptop screen. Something about him sends a shiver down my spine, but I shrug it off. There are all kinds of eccentric people in the city; there's no reason to think there's something particularly off about him.

Sarah comes flying in a few minutes later, breathless. "Sorry I'm late," she says, dropping into the empty seat next to me right as the server brings me a mimosa. "I had to go to a board meeting last night that they decided to hold at Grapevine, that new wine bar, and we ended up staying out a little too late. I overslept."

"No worries," Jaz says cheerfully. "Brunch isn't supposed to be stressful! You get here when you get here."

"Was it a meeting for that nonprofit you're on the board for?" Zoe asks, and Sarah nods.

"I'll tell you all about it in a minute. But first, I want to hear about Charlotte's date."

The whole table—even Jaz—is rapt as I fill them in on the details: the restaurant, the play, the second date he agreed to, the lack of a kiss at the end. Zoe frowns when I say that last, unsurprisingly a similar reaction to Jaz.

"Okay, but if a guy didn't want to kiss me at the end of a date, I'd be worried," she says with a frown. "Like maybe he was just into me as a friend."

"I definitely don't think it was that." I bite my lip as the server brings our breakfast orders: smoked salmon eggs Benedict for me, a vegan omelet for Zoe, a ham and Swiss croissant for Sarah, and avocado toast for Jaz. "I could definitely feel that there was—something there. I think he was just being polite. Maybe he picked up on the fact that I didn't want to take things too far on the first date."

"You were pretty clear about that with me." Jaz shrugs. "So maybe he did pick up on those vibes."

"He agreed to go on an apple-picking date with me next weekend." I can't help but smile at the memory of that conversation. "I really didn't think he would, but he seemed—I don't know, kind of excited about it. Which was surprising."

"I would not have pegged him for the kind of guy who would go apple-picking," Jaz agrees. "So yeah, he must really like you. Even without the kiss."

"There doesn't *have* to be a kiss on the first date," Sarah argues. "I've had plenty of good dates that didn't end in a kiss. Colin didn't kiss me until date three."

Jaz smirks. "And how did that go?"

"Aw, that was a little low." I give Sarah a sympathetic smile. She's only a couple of months off from that breakup, and I know she hasn't been out much since. Much like my relationship with Nate, she expected that one to go for the long haul.

"Well, that brings me to what I was going to ask," Sarah says with a small laugh. "Like I was saying, I'm on a board for this nonprofit. My work has been encouraging us all to get involved with some charity work, and I picked this one—it helps fund inner-city schools. Anyway, there's a gala for it Friday evening."

"A gala?" Jaz looks at her curiously, and Sarah nods.

"They hold them now and then, dinners for fundraising. Seven hundred dollars a plate," she adds, and Zoe whistles.

"I'm a trust-fund baby, and that's too rich for even my blood," she says with a laugh. "But some of them buy dresses for the evening from my boutique, so I can't argue that it's not stimulating the small-business economy," she adds, still laughing.

"Who goes to something like that?" I ask curiously, and Sarah shrugs.

"Politicians, wealthy investors, those kind of people. Anyone important who wants to be seen doing good. Some people who do... less than savory business, too, but who need to seem aboveboard. I don't doubt that there's some money that gets laundered through their contributions. But I guess overall, the nonprofit sees that as a lesser evil."

I can't help the shocked expression on my face. I know, of course, that there are criminal operations in the city—there are in every big city. I know that there are a few that have been caught because they've slipped up somehow with the federal organization that Sarah works for. But I always thought of them as secret, shadowy, like creatures living underground. It never occurred to me that they might be out and about in the real world, among all of us, doing something as outwardly charitable as contributing to the betterment of city public schools.

"It happens all the time," Sarah adds, clearly seeing the look on my face. "Anyway, I was going to ask if one of you wants to come with me as my date. I don't have one, and I'd rather not go alone. It feels a little depressing, especially since Colin was going to go with me before the breakup."

"I can't," Zoe says apologetically. "Like I said, people get dresses from Velvet Luxe for these things. I'm going to be exhausted by then.

I'll want to go home Friday night and soak in a hot bath with some trash TV, not be out chatting up the creme-de-la-creme of Chicago."

"I have a date," Jaz says with a grin. "With a *super* hot guy I matched with on Tinder last night. I love you, Sarah, but there's no way I'm putting this off."

"Charlotte?" Sarah gives me an entreating look, and it's on the tip of my tongue to tell her no. The gala sounds exhausting, to be honest, and I'm not really good at parties. But I can see from the look on her face that she really, really wants one of us to go.

"Sure," I tell her, and I can see the look of relief on her face instantly. "It'll be a fun excuse to dress up and eat whatever constitutes a seven-hundred-dollar a plate meal," I add with a laugh, and Sarah grins.

"It's probably not going to be as good as what you had out with Ivan," she cautions. "It's definitely over-inflated. But still pretty freaking good. And you'll have fun, I promise."

"Are you going to come get a new dress?" Zoe asks with a smirk, and I sigh.

"I guess I'm going to have to. I probably need a long dress, right? The velvet one or the one I bought for my date with Ivan won't work?"

"You do need an evening dress," Sarah confirms. "A lot of people rent one if they don't want to commit to buying."

"Come on, come give your credit card a workout at my place," Zoe says. "I'll make sure you look fabulous. You'll leave with so many numbers."

"I'm not sure I want that," I say with a laugh. "But okay. My credit card really is getting a workout lately, though."

I notice, as we start to talk about dress options, that the man at the far side of the patio is packing up. I really have no reason to look at him—he's just an eccentric patron—but something about him keeps drawing my attention. I watch him in my periphery, trying to figure out if I've seen him somewhere, but I can't place anything. It's just a feeling, and then he's slipped out of the side gate and is gone.

"Let's go when we're done eating, actually," Zoe says enthusiastically. "I'm closed on Sundays, so it'll be like you're getting your own private shopping experience." She grins. "I have some new dresses that just came in that you'll look *incredible* in."

I'm not entirely sure how I feel about going shopping for an evening gown on a full stomach of eggs Benedict and mimosas, but Zoe is so enthusiastic that I can't tell her no. "Okay," I agree, finishing the last of my eggs and slipping my wallet out. I can tell that Sarah and Jaz are eager to go and play dress-up, too, and Sarah looks so relieved to have a "date" to the gala that I don't want to do a single thing that might burst her bubble.

And truthfully, this morning is exactly what I needed. The uncomfortable feeling left by Nate's texts has dissipated, and I'm back to feeling excited about the next time I see Ivan. Excited about my future.

It also occurs to me that if I *were* still with Nate, there still wouldn't have been anything stopping me from going to the gala with Sarah. No date that I would have had to cancel or disappointment from him that we wouldn't get to spend time together on a Friday night. I can hear what his response would have been in my head: *Oh good, now you won't be lonely while I'm working late. I'm glad you have something to do. Enjoy yourself.*

On the surface, it seems like a good thing. For a long time, I really believed that it was, that I had a good, well-adjusted partner who didn't care if I was out having fun without him because it meant his hard work wasn't impeding my life. But now, I'm realizing that I was just always a second priority. I was never as important as his job. He wasn't passionate about it, but he still put it before me.

He put a lot of things before me, apparently. Including other women.

We all pile into an Uber to go to Velvet Luxe, tipsy on mimosas and giggling the whole way. Zoe unlocks the door with a raised eyebrow and an air of secretive mystery that makes it feel like we're doing something we're not supposed to—even though it's her boutique. Sarah and Jaz flop onto the jewel-toned velvet couches in front of the three-way mirror, and Sarah lets out a sigh.

"I was going to wear something I already had in my closet, but now I'm starting to think I should get something new. You have so many gorgeous things here, Zoe."

Zoe beams. "I just got the new fall line in. I'm so excited. And Charlotte, I have the *perfect* thing for you. Hold on, and I'll go grab it for the back. Maybe I'll pull a couple things for you too, Sarah," she adds with a wink, just before disappearing into the back of the store.

"I love how perfect all of this is for her," I murmur as we watch her go. "She's been so passionate about it since college. And it's all worked out."

I want to feel that passionate about something. I've always enjoyed tech and working with computers; there's something about it and the changes that it's continuously making in our world that I find compelling, but I don't spend my days voraciously reading about the latest innovations or talking to my friends about it in my off time. Zoe lives and breathes fashion, and Jaz lives and breathes adventure. Sarah isn't particularly passionate about her work, but she loves the influence that it gives her to work on projects for nonprofits like the one throwing the gala Friday night. And I—I just kind of float, from day to day, in a life that has never felt particularly unique or interesting.

*What if it's not something that I want to be passionate about, but some*one? That seems like it goes against everything I'm supposed to want as an independent woman, that I shouldn't crave a person that I can lose myself in, and who will lose himself in me. But I think of what Ivan said at dinner the other night—that once I realize that he's the one who can give me everything I want, what we have will be forever—and it sends a shiver down my spine that feels *good*. It feels anticipatory, like what should frighten me is instead unlocking a craving that I didn't even know I had.

"Here we go!" Zoe emerges from the back of the store, holding an armful of gowns. "Charlotte, this is perfect for you." She hangs one dress in front of one of the velvet-curtained dressing rooms, and the other three in front of another. "Sarah, try these on." She directs us with all the authority and confidence of a military general, and Sarah and I jump to obey just as quickly. This is Zoe's domain, and all of us listen to her when it comes to our fashion choices.

For something like this, anyway. Zoe has long bemoaned the fact that I haven't changed up my day-to-day wardrobe in half a decade.

The dress that she chose for me is gorgeous hanging up, and when I slip into it, I have to admit that her choice was flawless. It's a deep burnt orange silk, with fluttery straps and a boned bodice with stiff cups that push up my breasts to their best advantage. The gathered skirt flares out, with a slit that goes up to my upper thigh, and there's a lighter-colored, feathery leaf print all over the entire dress.

It's stunning with my dark hair and light green eyes, and I feel like an autumn princess. I feel beautiful. And I suddenly wish that Ivan was going to see me in it on Friday night.

When I step out, there's a gasp from Jaz, and Zoe has a satisfied look on her face. "I *knew* it would be perfect," she says, spinning her finger to indicate that I should do a twirl. "You're stunning."

"Oh, my god. It's perfect," Sarah echoes, stepping out of her own dressing room a second later in a dusty blue satin dress with a scooped neckline, thin straps, and two high slits that make her look like a much sexier Cinderella with her blonde hair and icy blue eyes. "We're going to be the prettiest belles at the ball." She grabs my hand, spinning us both around, and the smile on her face makes spending my Friday night at a stuffy charity dinner entirely worth it. "We'll take them. And Charlotte, I'll buy yours, since you're agreeing to be my date."

"You don't have to do that," I start to argue, but she shakes her head firmly.

"It's the least I can do."

After a little more chatter, and Zoe putting the dresses in garment bags for us after Sarah pays, I head home. I opt to walk, because the day is crisp and chilly, with the sun filtering through the trees in that specific way that it only seems to do at the beginning of fall, and it feels good.

My life is better without Nate. I believe that more and more with every day that passes. I just need to figure out what comes next.

Or maybe I don't. I shove my hands down into the pockets of my coat, wondering if maybe I *don't* need to figure everything out just yet, or for a while...or maybe not at all. Maybe what my life would benefit from is me just letting things happen, for a little while.

After all, I've been doing that for the last week or so, and it's been good. Better than things have been in a while, really.

A feeling prickles up my spine, and I twist around, suddenly getting the sensation that someone is watching me, or following me, maybe. But there's no one there, and I do my best to shrug it off as I pick up my pace a little, reasoning that I'm probably just jumpy because of the texts Nate sent me this morning. Now that I don't have my friends with me to distract me, I can't help thinking about them again, and his hot-and-cold attitude sends a shiver of discomfort through me. Not to mention the way he called me a slut—which doesn't exactly fit with his excuses that he never asked me to do the things he wanted in bed because he *respected* me too much.

I push the thoughts aside, imagining instead that it's the man I was talking to online, Venom. That he tracked down my information, and he's the one following me. I picture a fit man in dark clothes—maybe like the clothes that the man on the patio at Amuse-Bouche this morning was wearing—with a mask over his face, slinking through the shadows as he trails me home.

I picture him slipping into the service entrance to my building, following me into the elevator just before the doors close. I picture gloved hands like the man at Masquerade's sliding around my throat, his thumb pressing into the hollow of my jaw, holding me back against the wall of the elevator as I watch what's happening to me in the other mirrors on either side.

Another shudder runs down my spine, but this time, it's excitement. I feel it pool in my stomach, hot and thick, clenching between my thighs. It's all impossible, of course—there's no way that Venom could have tracked me down. Websites like that are in that shadowy corner of the Internet for a reason, where everything is encrypted, and identities can be hidden. But that's precisely why it's so erotic, because it *is* so impossible. An impossible fantasy that makes my mouth go dry while my panties are suddenly wet, clinging to my skin as I speed up my pace *this* time because I want to get home.

I want to be alone with my fantasy.

Fifteen minutes later, I'm upstairs in my room, fumbling to open the drawer next to the bed as I lay back against the pillows. I barely get the zipper of my jeans down before I push the small bullet vibrator into my panties, holding it against my clit as I let my head fall back, hips arching up to meet the sweet pleasure of the vibration against my most sensitive spot.

It takes me seconds to come to the fantasy of my masked man hovering over me, holding me down on the bed by my throat as *he* pushes the vibrator against my clit, edging me with it until I'm pleading for him to let me come, begging for release, and then—

The orgasm crashes over me, wracking my body with several seconds of white-hot pleasure as my back arches, a ragged moan escaping me as I come hard. I'm panting by the time it ebbs, sinking down into the mattress as the afterglow wraps itself around me like a thick fog, and I close my eyes as I toss the toy aside. It felt so good, but I want more.

It's dark outside when I wake up from my orgasm-induced nap. I clean my toy and put it away, changing into a pair of leggings and an oversized t-shirt as I go to make myself something for dinner. I settle for heating up leftover Thai noodles, eating them cross-legged in front of the TV as I watch a rerun of a house renovation show on HGTV. But as I watch a moderately handsome man and his pretty blonde wife slam hammers through drywall, my mind keeps drifting back to that website, and Venom.

I can't resist the urge to log back on again. Not just to talk to anyone, but to talk to *him*. I feel a little guilty about it, knowing that I just had a wonderful date with Ivan, with another one planned this weekend—but isn't that why I'm doing this? Why I told him that I don't want anything exclusive, so that I can experience for once in my life what it's like to do what men do? To *not* dive in head-first and close myself off to all the other options?

The urge doesn't leave as I finish my dinner and clean up. I pour myself a glass of wine, tapping my nails against the glass as I try to talk myself out of it, but I find myself walking down the hall to my room anyway, my mind already ten steps ahead.

Getting myself off to thoughts of him this afternoon didn't make me want it less. It only made the need to experience more of this feel even more intense. More demanding.

I log on, scrolling through some of the videos, checking every few minutes to see if Venom is online. Watching the clips of women getting fucked in bondage by men with their faces covered, running through mazes until they reach a room where a man is waiting for them, getting fucked in a roomful of mirrors with a different man on each end—all of it turns me on, making me feel warm and shivery at the same time, but none of it quite gets me there, to the point where I feel like I can't do anything *other* than touch myself, like I felt when I chatted with Venom last. I don't feel that aching, desperate *need* to come.

I'm about to give up and log off when I see his name pop up suddenly, and for a brief second, it feels like my heart stops in my chest.

VENOM69XXX: *The pretty dove came out to play tonight. You know what a snake does to a pretty little bird?*

MY HEART COMES BACK to life, stuttering in my chest as I suck in a breath, quickly typing out a response.

CURIOUSDOVE24: *Why don't you tell me?*

I KNOW it's not the most daring response, but I don't think that matters. What matters is that it feels daring to *me*. I feel breathless, excited, flirting with this man who is so much more than a stranger, separated from me by walls of data and an anonymity that I won't ever be able to breach.

A moment passes, and another, until I wonder if he's going to respond at all. And then a message pops up, and for a second, I forget how to breathe.

Venom69xxx: *He eats her.*

16

IVAN

Even before Charlotte became an obsession for me, I've never gone to Masquerade twice in one weekend. But the guys had such a good time that they want to go again Sunday night, and rather than deal with their questions as to why I *don't* want to leverage my membership and get to fuck one of the myriads of hot women there who could fulfill my every kinky fantasy, I go along.

This time, I don't get a room to myself, even after I've watched the festivities on the open floor. I sip my vodka and watch, getting gradually more and more turned on by what amounts to live, public pornography, the sounds and smells of sex drenching my senses as the night wears on. I sit there, my cock aching, and my thoughts keep drifting back to Charlotte.

I don't want to get myself off here tonight while I think about her. I want to do it while she tells me all the things she wants me to do to her, while she doesn't even know that it's me.

As I finish my third drink, I motion to the bartender so that I can pay my tab, too eager to stay at the club any longer. I want her, not the noise and fog of sex all around me. And I can't wait even a moment longer to have at least some part of her.

In the neon glow of the screens in my basement, I strip out of my suit, tossing it over a stack of boxes as I pull on a pair of sweatpants, shoving my still half-hard cock down. I'm fully erect just from the anticipation of chatting with her by the time I've logged on, and when I see her username in bold, telling me that she's logged on, I don't have the patience to play coy.

Venom69xxx: *The pretty dove came out to play tonight. You know what a snake does to a pretty little bird?*

Her response comes almost immediately, faster than I thought it would. Almost as if she were waiting for me.

CuriousDove24: *Why don't you tell me?*

In an instant, I'm so hard that I can't stand it any longer. I push my sweatpants down around my hips, freeing my cock and giving myself a couple of quick, hard strokes before I respond to her. I'm already slick with pre-cum, and I can feel the veins throbbing against my palm. If I don't control myself, this will be over faster than I want it to be.

Venom69xxx: *He eats her.*

Just like that, the memory of her in Masquerade comes flooding back, the sweet taste of her on my tongue, the way she moaned and mewled as I licked her, the way she came all over my face as if she'd never been properly eaten out before. I'd be willing to bet that she never had.

I want to taste her again. I want to fuck her. I want her to scream my name. *My* name.

I'm getting off both on the fact that she has no idea that all of the men filling her fantasies right now are the same one, and I desperately want her to *know* that it's me, all at once. It's a dichotomy that's fueling my lust to an almost unbearable degree.

My hand wraps around my cock again as I wait for her to respond, stroking in long, slow passes of my palm over my throbbing length. I sink my teeth into my lip as I groan, letting my head fall back against the chair as my hips lift up, fucking my fist for a moment until I can't take it any longer, and I have to pull my hand away before I come. My balls tighten, that heat licking at the base of my spine, but I refocus on the screen, tearing myself away from that pleasure that's so close to overcoming me.

CautiousDove24: *Maybe she wants to be eaten.*

Fuck. I stroke myself again, that one pass of my hand from the base of my cock over the too-sensitive tip, almost sends me over the edge. I want her so badly it hurts.

Venom69xxx: *Hard to eat you with a mask on, dove. But there are so many other ways I could make you come.*
    CuriousDove24: Tell me.
    Venom69xxx: *Only if you tell me what you're doing right now.*

There's a pause, and I run my hand up and down my length again, my vision blurring slightly as that knot of pleasure tightens at the base of my spine. I *need* to come, but putting it off is only enhancing the pleasure, building that delicious ache that's an exquisite torment.

I don't edge like this often, but I'm well aware of how good it can feel. And I can't wait to imagine that I'm coming all over her face by the end of this.

CuriousDove24: *I—I'm touching myself. Thinking about you.*

That almost does me in. I pretty much knew that was what was going on, of course, but seeing her tell me like that makes me throb without even touching myself, so much pre-cum spilling down my length that, for a moment, I almost think I've lost control of my orgasm. I reach down, roughly squeezing the base of my cock with my left hand as I type with my right, staving off the explosion for as long as I can.

Venom69xxx: *Tell me how, exactly.*

I'm not sure what prompts me to do it, but I'm so aroused that I'm definitely not thinking straight.

On the far end of my desk, near the last of my monitors, there's an off-white mask in the shape of a skull. I bought it while I was out the other day, imagining a scenario exactly like this, and wondering if I'd go through with it. I'm still not entirely sure that I won't scare Charlotte off if she's actually confronted with her fantasies.

But right now, all the blood in my body is in my cock, and it's the only thing I'm thinking with.

Slipping the mask on, I reach for my phone, leaning back and taking a selfie. In the neon glow and scattered shadows, my abs look impeccably chiseled, my blond hair swept back so that she can't see much of it. The shadows blur my tattoos to the point where they're unrecognizable—it's the only reason I'll allow her to see me shirtless. Otherwise, I'd be too worried that I'd get far enough with her as Ivan for her to see me in the light without a shirt, and start piecing this all together.

Ivan is taking this slow with Charlotte. But I don't know how long I'm going to be able to resist her, especially once *she* starts pushing that side of things.

Quickly, I upload the photo to my computer, making sure it's scrubbed of all metadata before I send it. It pops up in the chat under my last message, a bad, blurry selfie of an unidentifiable man in a mask.

Venom69xxx: *I'm watching you just like this dove. My hand is wrapped around my cock right now. Tell me what you're doing. Tell me what you'd want, if I were there.*

CuriousDove24: *I—I'm just wearing a T-shirt and panties. It's not very sexy—but I just slipped my fingers under them. I'm so wet, I couldn't wait any longer. I thought about using a toy, but I wanted skin on skin. I wanted to imagine it was your fingers on me. You ordering me to spread my legs for you while you held me down by my throat. I can't see your face, just hear your voice, and you tell me you're going to punish me if I try to run. That if I lay there and let you have me, you'll make me come before you fuck me.*

God. I grit my teeth, not daring to touch my cock after that. I can feel myself throbbing with every word, my cock straining upwards, desperate for something to sink into, something hot and wet wrapped around it.

No. Not *something*. Charlotte. Charlotte's mouth, her pussy, her ass—

CuriousDove24: *Oh god, you're so fucking hot. I don't think I've ever actually said that to a guy before. Not like that. But I also haven't...*

Venom69xxx: *Haven't what?*

CuriousDove24: *This. Masturbating for someone. Telling them what I want. Are you doing it too? I wish I could see your cock. I'm so wet...*

Venom69xxx: *Do you have a dildo in those toys of yours that you mentioned, dove?*

I ALLOW MYSELF ONE LONG, slow stroke as I wait for her answer, my head spinning with thoughts of what I want to do to her. I imagine taking her from her apartment to my penthouse in the city, keeping her locked up there for days, as I teach her every depraved thing that I want to do to her. As I make her body mine, and mine alone. As I make her come so hard that she forgets anyone else ever did, even herself.

I want to ruin her for other men, for toys, for her own fingers. I want her to crave my touch until she can't come, unless it's with my fingers, tongue, or cock. I want to *own* her.

"Fuck!" I growl, squeezing my straining cock until it almost hurts, staving off my climax once again. I don't know if I'll be able to do it a third time.

CuriousDove24: *Yes.*

Venom69xxx: *Good. Go get it. If you're as wet as you say, you won't need lube, so don't you dare use a drop. I want just your wet pussy all over my cock. Tell me before you slide it in, dove.*

MY HEART IS BEATING SO hard that I'd almost be concerned, if I had enough presence of mind to think about something like that right now. I watch the screen with my breath caught in my throat, my fingers still pressing around the base of my cock as I wait for her.

CuriousDove24: *I'm about to put it in. Please tell me I can. I need to come so badly. I need this. Please.*

Venom69xxx: *Good girl. You're so pretty when you beg like that. Tied down on your stomach with your hands and feet all wrapped up in that soft rope. You sucked my cock so well earlier, dove. Now you get to be fucked with it. And if you come all over my cock just like I want you to, you can have my cum, too, pretty dove.*

CuriousDove24: *Oh god—fuck, it almost feels too big. I needed this so badly. I need you to fuck me.*

Venom69xxx: *I'm going to slide it in nice and slow, dove. You'll take every inch of my thick cock. Fuck, dove—I'm stroking myself right now, thinking about this. Let me know right before you come. We'll come together.*

I GIVE up all pretense of waiting. My only goal right now is to hold off my own climax long enough that I don't come before she tells me that she's about to. I start to stroke my slick, aching length, gripping the base tightly at the end of each stroke, moaning every time my fingers and palm slide over the swollen tip. I rub pre-cum around the head, hissing through my breath as I imagine that I'm just barely dipping into her tight pussy, making her beg for it before I thrust into her again, hard. I want to do exactly what I just told her—tie her down on her stomach with her head at the end of the bed, feed her my cock until I'm dripping with her saliva and she's begging to be fucked, and then make her come hard while I pound into her.

I'm so close. So fucking close. I'm panting, my muscles wound tight, desperately trying not to come, until I see the message that I'm dying for pop up on the screen.

CuriousDove24: *I'm about to come, Venom. Your cock feels so good, I can't hold off. Please let me come. Please, please...*

Venom69xxx: *Come for me, pretty dove. I'm going to come so fucking hard for you.*

. . .

I IMAGINE that it's her pussy clenching around my cock, instead of my fist, as I pump it hard, staring at the screen. Miles from here, Charlotte is fucking herself while she pretends she's coming around her mystery man's cock. The thought sends me over the edge, imagining her pretty mouth open on a moan, her body tightening around that silicone length. I've never been so fucking jealous of a toy in my life as my legs splay open and my hips thrust up, the orgasm shattering me as my cock explodes.

Nothing that I've done with my own hand has ever felt this good before. My eyes are shut so tightly that I see colors as my cock throbs and cum sprays over my hand, over my thighs, probably ending up in places that I'll have to clean up later as I come so fucking hard that I feel dizzy, like I'm going to pass out. I moan her name as I come, the sound spilling from my lips as all of that built-up pleasure explodes from me, and I shudder as more of that sticky heat spills over my hand. I can't remember ever coming this much before, or this long.

"Charlotte—*fuck*, Charlotte—" I fuck my fist hard, my oversensitive cock still spurting, dragging out my climax until my balls feel sore and drained. I've never come this hard from *sex* before. I feel foggy afterward, disoriented, and it makes me wonder what it would feel like to fuck her.

It occurs to me, for the first time, that it might not just be me who ruins her for anyone else.

She's ruining *me*.

I swallow hard, blinking at the screen as I reach for tissues to clean up, but Charlotte has already logged off. Whether it took me too long to come to my senses, or if she came to hers and fled out of embarrassment, I don't know.

But what I do know is that I can't wait to see her again.

MONDAY MORNING, I find myself watching her walk into her building for work again, as I lean against the wall opposite the street. When she and Jaz disappear from view, I head down the street to a cafe, getting a coffee and puttering around on my laptop until I can head to Cafe L'Rose and pretend to run into her again for lunch. I don't get much in the way of work done—all I can think about is her, and last night, and our date this weekend. About the fact that I don't know how long I can hold off actually getting her into bed. The desire to have her in reality is fast outstripping the satisfaction that her internet fantasies are giving me, and I need more.

That doesn't change the fact that *more* is a distraction.

Right now, I should be thinking about the gala on Friday, and how I'm going to stop my father from selling Sabrina Petrov into sex slavery. I should be thinking about how I'm going to foil his plan and get information to Agent Bradley without getting caught. I should be forming an intricate, foolproof plan that won't result in Sabrina getting hurt or me ending up on the wrong end of Lev's hunting knife.

Instead, I'm thinking about how Charlotte tasted on my tongue, and if the rest of her will feel as soft as her pussy did against my lips.

At eleven, I make my way over to Cafe L'Rose. Charlotte isn't there yet, as expected, and I make myself comfortable, scrolling through articles on my phone as the server brings me a beer and an appetizer of spinach dip with pita chips. I don't eat them, leaving them there instead to make it look like I've just arrived to get lunch.

Just shortly after noon, as usual, Charlotte walks in. This time, she's alone, and my pulse spikes. I'd been prepared to interrupt her and Jaz, again, but this is even better. This gives me an excuse to walk over and talk to her.

Once she's seated with a glass of lemon water, I get up and walk over to her table. She looks up at my footsteps, and I catch the barest hint of alarm in her expression in the instant before excitement takes over.

I know exactly what that is. It's her subconscious telling her that I'm dangerous, that in this moment, she's prey. That she should run, instead of what she does, which is smile invitingly as she tries to smother some of her obvious excitement.

"You're here again." She bites her lip. "Jaz is working through lunch today. Do you want to join me?"

"I can't say no to that." I slide into the chair opposite her easily, as if there's nothing engineered or strange about this at all. Just a happy coincidence.

"This is twice now you've been here on my lunch break. If I didn't know better, I'd think you were stalking me." She says it with a teasing grin, light-hearted enough that I know she's joking. It calms the momentary spike of alarm that I felt, thinking that she might be on to me.

But she's not. She's not even trying to find something wrong here. She trusts me, more than she should, and that sends a spark of guilt through me. It's not that I don't know that what I'm doing is wrong.

I just want her too much to care.

"It's not stalking if you tend to eat at the same place," I tell her with that same light, teasing inflection in my voice. "Besides, who says it's you that I'm here for? This place has the best steak sandwich I've ever eaten."

"You should try their chicken salad." She relaxes back in her seat, her green eyes sparkling. She's incredibly beautiful, even like this, dressed in a button-down shirt and dark jeans with her hair up in a ponytail. My thoughts immediately shift to images of that ponytail wrapped around my hand, of her bent over a table like this one while I—

I blink them away, clearing my throat. I need to get laid. Because the truth is, I like Charlotte for more than just how much she turns me on. It's just that right now, it's hard to think past the need to satisfy that with her.

"I'll order that today, then." I grin. "I'll try something new."

I emphasize the last part a little, reminding her of our conversation at dinner the other night. And I think she picks up on it, from the way her mouth twitches.

"Okay, then," she says. "I'll order the steak sandwich."

"About that apple-picking date," I start to say a few minutes later, once our orders are in, and I see her face instantly fall.

"You changed your mind, didn't you?" She tries to cover her disappointment with a tiny laugh. "I had a feeling you'd think about it and decide that wasn't your thing."

I feel a jolt of anger at that. Not towards her—but because clearly, she's had that done to her before. Promises broken, because some guy decided that his fun was more important than hers, always. Disappointment over her desires never being prioritized. It's clear she's been let down more than once.

That stops now.

"Not at all," I assure her, and I see her eyes brighten instantly. "I just wanted to tell you that I do have plans Friday night. Something I can't really get out of. So I was going to ask if you were free on Saturday for our date. Apple-picking, pie-baking, a movie at a sticky theater, the works."

Charlotte laughs, picking up a napkin and throwing it at me. "Just because it's a *normal* movie theater doesn't mean you have to make it sound so gross. Have you ever even been to a movie theater before?"

"Of course I have." I grin at her. "I'm rich, but I'm not some kind of shut-in. Or a celebrity that can't be seen out in public."

It's actually been a long time since I've been to the movies. What I can't tell Charlotte is that I haven't been since I was a kid, when I'd use my allowance to sneak out and go hide at the theater for an entire day, watching movie after movie so I could avoid my stepmother's cold disapproval and my brothers' abuse. I can't tell her that the smell of old upholstery and buttered popcorn feels a little like a haven to me.

But what startles me is that I'd like to. For the first time in my life, I find myself wanting to open up to her completely. To show her all the dark corners of myself that I've kept hidden all these years. I want to do more than unravel her entirely, so that I know her better than anyone else ever has—I want her to unravel me, too. And that terrifies me, enough that I almost stand up and call it all off.

Obsessing over Charlotte is dangerous enough. Falling for her like that would be catastrophic to us both.

The server brings our sandwiches, and Charlotte smiles, reaching for half of hers. My stomach growls a little—steak, aioli, blue cheese, and avocado with a generous helping of au jus is exactly what I wanted today. But the spontaneous fun of switching our orders is better than that.

It's helping to break Charlotte out of her shell.

"Oh god, that's really good," she admits as she takes a bite. "You're right. It is the best steak sandwich I've ever had."

"Told you." I grin, taking a bite of my own sandwich. To my surprise, it's equally good, rich and creamy, a perfect mix of savory and sweet. "That's really good, too."

Charlotte nods, reaching for her napkin. There's a drop of juice on her lip, and I swallow hard, forcing back the urge to lean across the table and thumb it away. "As for the Saturday date," she adds, "that's perfect. I have Friday night plans that I can't get out of, too, so that works out great, honestly."

Instantly, jealousy floods me. I haven't seen anything from her phone to suggest that she's on dating apps or that she's been texting any other men—other than her asshole ex, who speaks to her in ways that make me seriously consider murder—but that's not the only way to meet someone. She could have met someone in person, maybe at work, and made plans that way. My thoughts instantly spiral, heading down a path of a dozen different ways that I can figure out how to stop this in its tracks. No one is taking her out on a date except for me.

"Oh?" I try to say it as casually as possible. She was clear that she didn't want exclusivity yet, and on the surface, at least, I agreed to it. So I can't let her see that I'm jealous. If I do, she'll break things off immediately, and I'll lose her. "A hot date?" I smirk at her, forcing my tone into something resembling playfulness.

"If you count my friend Sarah as a hot date—which most men would, I think, then yes," she says with a laugh. "She's on the board of this charity—" Charlotte bites into her sandwich, letting me squirm for a moment before she finishes her sentence. I'm half-wondering if she has a date with this friend Sarah, and trying to decide how that makes me feel, before she puts me out of my misery.

"They're throwing this gala, Friday night. She just went through a breakup a few months ago, and she asked me if I'd be her date for it. It's not exactly my idea of a wonderful Friday night out, but I told her yes, because I could tell it meant a lot to her." Charlotte shrugs, taking another bite of her sandwich. "And it could be fun, right? In between all the stuffy speeches from politicians or whatever, I'll get to eat an expensive dinner, and Sarah and I will dance and play it up just to get all the millionaires hot and bothered, and then I'll go home and crash."

She grins, clearly enjoying the idea of the plans she and her friend have made, but inwardly, I'm panicking. I'm well aware of what gala she's going to—because it's the same one I'm supposed to accompany Sabrina Petrov to.

The same one where my father's men are planning to abduct Sabrina, to sell her off later to the highest bidder.

There are any number of reasons why I don't want Charlotte at that gala—I don't want her within a hundred miles of men who are part of my father's human trafficking ring. I also don't want her anywhere near anything to do with my family. I don't want them to know about her, and I don't want her to get even the slightest whiff of my association with the Bratva.

All of those things should be the primary concerns that I'm thinking about right now, but instead, the one that comes to the forefront of my mind is that if Charlotte is at the gala, she'll see me with another woman.

After what she's just been through, the last thing I want is for her to think that I'm seeing someone else. Even if she's insisted she doesn't want to be exclusive, and there's nothing technically wrong with that, the idea that she might believe that my interest is anything but entirely wrapped up in her makes me feel like I'm going slightly crazy. Because the truth is, I can't think of anyone *but* her.

I start to open my mouth to tell her *something* about it, just so she's forewarned that I'll both be there and that I'll have a 'date,' but Charlotte suddenly holds up a finger, giving me an apologetic look as she answers her phone.

"Yeah? I'm at lunch. Oh—okay. Yeah, I can come back. I'm leaving early, then. Okay. Be right there."

She tucks her phone back into her purse, that same apologetic look still on her face. "I'm sorry," she says, pulling out her wallet. "I have to run back to work. There's a tech problem, and my boss is about to go into a big meeting. I'm really sorry."

"Don't worry about it. I'll get lunch," I add, as I see her about to put some cash on the table for her meal.

She frowns. "Are you sure? I—"

"It's fine," I assure her, and she flashes me a smile before jumping up from her chair, hurrying abruptly away from the table and towards the door of the cafe.

I watch her go, a strange, tight feeling in my chest. I want to go after her, but I can't. I feel helpless to fix a situation that I can see spiraling out of control, and that, more than anything, makes me feel more than a little unhinged.

I have a feeling that whatever happens at the gala Friday night, it's not going to be good.

17

CHARLOTTE

I'm more excited, getting ready for the gala Friday night, than I thought I'd be.

I brought my dress over to Sarah's apartment, and now we're in her gorgeous pink and gold and quartz bathroom, getting ready side by side like we're in high school again.

"This is why I can't move in with a man," Sarah says dramatically. "Can you imagine any guy being fine with a bathroom like this? He'd try to change my whole aesthetic, or make me move in with him to his bachelor pad. Colin complained *so* much every time he spent the night."

"It's stupid," I assure her, and in my opinion, it is. Sarah's apartment is a luxe feminine dream, all soft cream-colored carpets and blush textiles, with pink and white striped wallpaper accenting some of the rooms. Her bed is one of those four-poster canopy beds with gauzy fabric draped around it, like a grown-up princess, and every time I come over, I feel like I've entered some kind of fantasy land. It feels like her own private haven, and one of the things that made me detest Colin was how hard he tried to convince her that they should move into a more "polished" apartment of their own.

Now that I think about it, though, a lot of the dreary greys of my own apartment that I'm thinking about updating were because of Nate. He liked it, and so I never thought about what *I* might like instead.

"A man can pry my pink bathroom away from my cold, dead hands." Sarah leans forward, rolling another piece of her blonde hair up in a hot roller before pinning it. She grins at me as she puts the final one in place. "I'm going to go get dressed."

I slip into my own dress as she goes into the bathroom, leaving the back so she can zip it for me—I can't quite reach it. My own hair is still wet, tucked up into a towel on my head, and I plug in my curling iron as I unzip my makeup bag and start on my face for the night.

An hour later, we're both ready. Sarah looks like Cinderella in her blue gown, her blonde hair loose in thick Hollywood curls around her face, her makeup soft and flawless in delicate rose and champagne shades. I went for darker and more glamorous, curling my dark hair and pinning the front back, adding bronze eyeshadow, a cat eye, and dark brown lipstick to match the autumn tones of the dress.

"Look at us." Sarah smiles as she looks at our reflections in the mirror, wrapping an arm around my waist and pulling me close for a hug. "Thank you for coming," she adds. "This will be so much fun because you're here."

I squeeze her back, just as her phone buzzes, telling us Uber is almost here.

The gala is being held at the Natural History Museum, a dark blue carpet rolled out along the steps, making it and I point it out to Sarah as we step out of the Uber. the Oscars," I whisper to her theatrically, and she walk up the stairs towards the lights at the suited doormen are waiting to check our Sarah's invitation, since I'm her plus one.

Inside, string music fills the cavern are spaced out among the exhibits, a the far end, with tiles put down for room. As Sarah leads me toward

I recognize—one of the older partners from Nate's law firm, and my chest seizes with a sudden cramp of alarm.

"Shit," I whisper. "I didn't even think about the fact that Nate might be here."

Sarah looks in the direction I'm staring, biting her lip. "I didn't see his name on the guest list," she murmurs. "I would have said something if I had. I knew the main partners would be here, but he's not anywhere on—"

"Maybe he won't be here." I bite my lip, sinking into the chair where a small name card with my name written in black script is tilted against a China plate.

"And if he is," Sarah says firmly, "then he'll just see what he's missing out on. You, looking like *this*." She waves a hand up and down in the air, gesturing at me, and I manage a small, nervous smile.

"You're right," I tell her, and she is. If Nate is here, he's going to be alone, and he's just going to see me dressed to the nines and enjoying a night out with one of my best friends. I don't want him to see that he's crossed my mind for even a second. I just want him to see me happy and having a good time—without him.

That's the best revenge, right?

Still, I can't help keeping an eye out for him as the night progresses. There's speeches from Sarah's boss and other members of the charity about the purpose of the dinner tonight, interspersed with the courses of the meal—which, while delicious, are probably not worth seven hundred dollars. There's a crab bisque, and Caesar salad to start that is phenomenal, and after that, a starter of delicate crab lollipops with red wine glaze and scallops with a lemon butter broth, followed by filet mignon with gorgonzola cheese crust and red potatoes. I'm more than happy to dig into the meal, enjoying each bite, and Sarah and I are deep in conversation about what I want to do to renovate my apartment when I suddenly see Nate out of the corner of my eye.

For all that, I told myself I didn't care, and that I just want him to see me enjoying my evening, the tender filet feels like it turns to cardboard in my mouth. Even more so when I see the woman on his arm, and I drop my fork next to my plate, swallowing hard.

I see Sarah follow the direction I'm looking in. Nate is in one of his Tom Ford suits, a light grey one, and an absolutely *stunning* woman is on his arm. She has dark auburn hair pulled back in an elegant updo, and she's wearing a dark green silk dress that almost looks black. It's simple to the point that it would be boring, if it didn't cling to her so perfectly, outlining every inch of her perfect body in a way that's alluring without being *too* sexy. She's wearing diamond waterfall earrings as her only jewelry, drawing attention to her sculpted shoulders, swanlike neck, and sharp collarbones, and I stare at her until Sarah elbows me, bringing me out of my jealous haze.

"She's not that hot," Sarah says, seeing my expression.

"She looks like a movie star." I watch them walk to their table. Nate doesn't see me, which feels like a small blessing, but I still feel like I'm crumbling inside. Not because I want him back, or because I still love him, but because—I can't even really explain why. I don't want to be on his arm instead of that woman, and yet, I wanted him to be suffering for what he did. I wanted him miserable, sleeping on his brother's couch, wishing he hadn't fucked up so badly. Not swanning into this ridiculously expensive gala with the hottest woman I've ever seen on his arm, without a care in the world.

"Stop it." Sarah pokes me again. "Okay, she's hot. That doesn't mean anything. So are you. All it means is that either he paid her to come with him, someone bribed her into it, or she hasn't figured out how shitty his personality is yet. Either way, he's still the guy who cheated on you and broke your heart. If he doesn't realize how badly he fucked up yet, he will eventually."

I know all that is true, and I clearly remember all the texts I ignored, where he begged me to answer him because he clearly *has* realized he's fucked up. I don't know what's going on here or who she is, but I do know that Sarah is right, and it shouldn't matter.

It still doesn't change the fact that I desperately feel like I need to escape.

"I just need some air," I tell Sarah, taking a gulp of my wine before pushing my chair back and hurrying towards the opposite end of the room, where I see a curving set of stairs. I follow it up, hoping to find a private place where I can be alone for a minute, and see a door at the top, what looks like it might lead to a fire escape or maybe just a storage closet. At this point, I don't really care.

I shove the door open, chilly air hitting me in the face, and realize that it leads out to a small balcony.

A balcony that Ivan is standing on, leaning on the railing as he takes a drag off of a cigarette.

For a moment, I don't believe what I'm seeing. The door slams shut behind me, and I jump, letting out a small squeak as Ivan straightens abruptly, turning to look at me as his eyes widen with startled recognition.

"Charlotte." He blinks, the cigarette held limply in his fingers, and I can feel that my mouth is hanging open.

I can't believe I've unexpectedly seen Nate *and* Ivan, within ten minutes of each other. I don't know what Ivan is doing here, or if seeing him is going to make the night better or worse, but I'm seriously considering getting an Uber and going home.

If it weren't for Sarah, I definitely would. All I can think is that *if he knew he was going to be here, why didn't he tell me?*

Unless he's keeping secrets, too.

"I—" I swallow hard, trying to think of what to say. I take a few steps forward, suddenly shivering in the chill air, and Ivan's gaze sweeps over me, his usually dark blue eyes darkening even more as he takes in my appearance.

"You look gorgeous," he murmurs, flicking the cigarette away as he walks towards me. There's something prowling in his walk, an intent in his eyes that sends a shiver down my spine—but a good one. I'm reminded of the feeling I had walking home the other day, when I imagined my masked man stalking me.

My breath catches in my throat as Ivan stops a few inches away, his gaze sweeping over me once again. We're alone out here, and I can't help but think of all the things he could do to me, all the ways he could touch me. We haven't even kissed, but he looks darkly handsome in his suit, his blond hair styled back away from his face in a way that makes the sharp lines of it look even more chiseled than usual, and my mind is running wild with fantasies that I hadn't dared to think of before when it came to him.

As if out here, for just a moment, we're in our own private world. One that no one can inhabit but us.

"I meant to tell you I'd be here," he murmurs, reaching out to brush his thumb along the edge of my jaw. The touch makes me tremble, for reasons that have nothing to do with the cold. If anything, I feel hot suddenly, warmth blooming through me just from the simple brush of his finger against my skin. "You had to leave lunch in a hurry, or I would have said something."

I swallow hard, trying to find my voice. "That was Monday," I whisper, a sharp breeze blowing my hair around my face as I speak. His finger catches one of the pieces, sliding down the length of it before he releases it, and that sends another jolt of heat down my spine for reasons I can't even begin to explain.

This man does things to me that I didn't think were possible. That I didn't think were *real*. And I want more of it, even if some deep, instinctual part of me is shouting that there's something dangerous about him, too. Something primal, feral, that I'm not seeing.

That I'm responding to, when instead I should be running away.

"You could have texted since then," I manage. "You could have told me. You had four other days—"

"I wanted to explain in person that—"

"Ivan?" A sweet, lyrical voice floats across the balcony as the door opens before Ivan can finish his sentence, and my heart drops to my feet.

I have no right to be jealous. None at all. I know that, not when I told him that I didn't want to be exclusive, and yet my stomach twists at the feminine voice, at the sight of the woman walking out onto the balcony.

She's gorgeous, with blonde hair cut into a soft collarbone-length bob that's curled around her face, accentuating the delicate lines of it. She's waifishly thin, dressed in a shimmering rose-gold dress with a square neckline and a peplum waist, designed to give the illusion of hips. She looks at Ivan curiously, but without jealousy, and it makes me wonder what's going on here.

"We should get back to the party." Her blue eyes flick over to me, sliding over me with a cool assessment, and my stomach turns.

"So should I." I break away from Ivan, fleeing towards the door, even as I hear him call my name after me. I can't stop, though. Even though I have no right to be upset, I am, and I can't stand hearing an explanation, no matter what it is. On the heels of seeing Nate with his date for tonight, I can't deal with hearing about why Ivan is here with another woman.

One that he could have warned me about, and didn't. He could have warned me about all of this.

The door slams behind me, and I try to pick up my pace, but strong, masculine fingers suddenly wrap around my wrist, yanking me back. I can smell Ivan's cologne, and fear and desire both collide in my chest, making me gasp as he pulls me back.

Out of sheer instinct, I try to pull away, and in the momentary struggle, I feel his shoe step on the hem of my dress, a ripping sound cutting through the thick air between us. I freeze, spinning to face him just as he backs me against the wall of the stairwell.

"You tore my dress," I whisper. "That was expensive. Sarah bought it for me, and now—"

"I'll pay for it. Whatever it costs." He moves closer, crowding me in, and my pulse kicks up a notch, fluttering in my throat. This close, I can smell not just his cologne but his skin, warm and musky, the masculine scent of him filling my senses. His body is pinning me to the wall, hot and hard, his hands landing on my hips and skimming up my ribs.

"I don't want you to get the wrong idea," he whispers, those dark blue eyes searching mine. His hips press closer, and I bite my lip, stifling the sound I want to make at the feeling of him pressing against my thigh. He's hard, a thick, solid line against me through the fabric of his suit and my dress, and I realize with a flush of heat that he's *big*. Bigger than any man I've been with before.

"The wrong idea about what?" I can hear the bitterness in my voice. "You being here with another woman?"

"You could have been here with another man." His hands slide up to just below my breasts, fingers gripping as he holds me firmly in place. My pulse is beating wildly, my heart on the verge of pounding out of my chest. No one has ever touched me like this before. I've never felt so helpless, so trapped—or so completely, thoroughly aroused.

If Ivan tried to fuck me in this stairwell right now, I'm not entirely sure I would tell him no.

"You said no exclusivity." His dark eyes glitter. "Isn't that right?"

"Yes, but—" I try to swallow, my mouth dry. My head feels foggy. I can't think past the feeling of his hard cock against me, his hands rubbing up and down my ribs, as if he wants to feel me through the silk and boning of my dress. As if he's imagining the sensation of my skin against his palms instead. "I—"

"You were jealous. Because even though you can't admit it, you want me all to yourself." He leans in, his mouth skimming along my ear, and it takes everything in me not to moan. My knees feel like they're turning to water, the weight of his body against me the only thing keeping me upright. "But I have good news for you, Charlotte. I don't actually care about the woman with me tonight."

"You—" I blink, trying to make sense of that in my lust-fogged mind. "So why are you here with her?"

Ivan lifts one shoulder in a careless shrug. "Family obligations. Easier to say yes to my father than to say no. I really did want to tell you at lunch, before you had to run, to avoid exactly this. Although —" His hips rock against me again, and my head falls back against the wall, a breathless gasp escaping my lips. I've never wanted a man inside me as badly as I want him right now. I want to know what he feels like, hot and hard, sliding against my stomach as he kisses me, nudging inside of me as I wrap my legs around him.

"Now, I'm starting to be glad I *didn't* tell you," he murmurs, his lips ghosting over the shell of my ear again. "Because if I had, I don't think we'd be here like this—" His hips press into me again, and this time, I can't help the small, whispery moan that escapes my lips. "*Doing* this, right now."

His mouth drops to my lips as he surges against me, and the kiss is like nothing I've ever felt before. It's hard, urgent, *hungry*, his mouth devouring mine as his hands grip my wrists and pin them against the wall, holding me entirely captive.

My lips part underneath his, and his tongue sweeps into my mouth. He tastes like wine, dry and earthy, and my body arches into him involuntarily, wanting more. I never knew a kiss could feel like this, that it could make me hot all over and shivering at the same time, my body tight and aching for sensations that I've only ever imagined, so soaking wet that I can feel it.

His teeth catch my lower lip, and he sucks on it briefly, his hard chest pressed to mine as he holds me there, our mouths connected as the kiss slows. My pulse is beating wildly in my throat, and I tip my chin up, wanting more of the desperate, devouring kiss. Wanting more of *him*.

But then I hear the door click above us, and I know this moment is about to come to an end.

"Ivan." That musical voice floats down the stairs. "It's cold outside. And we need to go back to the party."

If nothing else, the utter carelessness in her voice makes me believe him. There's nothing about this woman that suggests that she's angry to not only have found Ivan out on the balcony with me, but then having to wait outside while he kisses me recklessly in a stairwell. Truthfully, she doesn't seem to care at all. If anything, she seems mildly annoyed that her evening is being interrupted.

Ivan pulls back, breathing hard, his carefully styled hair messy around his face. He runs his fingers through it, pushing it back, and looks down at me with a heat in his gaze that nearly makes my legs buckle. "We'll finish this later," he murmurs, his voice husky and full of promise, and then he turns, nodding to the woman as he starts back down the stairs. She follows without even bothering to look at me, trailing behind him as they both disappear from view.

I stand there, breathless for several moments, my head spinning as I try to piece together what just happened. It all feels like it happened in a rush, faster than I could process it.

When I feel like I can breathe again, I look down at the hem of my skirt. It's torn at the edge, but nothing so bad that anyone will likely even notice. Nothing that will stop me from going back to the table and resuming the evening.

I suck in a slow, shaky breath, trying to regain my composure. I want to believe that Ivan is telling me the truth, that there's nothing between him and the oddly detached woman. I want to believe that he's as fully mine as he claims to be, even though I know that isn't entirely fair to want.

Slowly, I walk back down the stairs, going to rejoin Sarah at the table. I scan the room as I sit down, noticing that Ivan is sitting at the very far end, next to the woman in the rose-gold dress. She's barely even looking at him, her gaze off somewhere in the distance, her expression utterly bored. By contrast, when I look for Nate, I see that the woman he came here with is animatedly chatting with him, her long diamond earrings swaying back and forth as she speaks, fluttering pale hands tipped with sharp nails.

Not a fellow lawyer, then—no one could do casework all day with nails like those. I tear my gaze away, telling myself that it doesn't do any good to fixate on what the woman with Nate does. At the end of the day, it doesn't really matter.

"Are you alright?" Sarah asks concernedly, putting a hand on my arm. "You look a little flushed, and you were gone for a while. Do you need something? Another drink, maybe?"

"More wine would be nice," I admit, licking my lips nervously. Dessert was brought while I was gone; there's a cold dish of crème brûlée at my place setting. I pick up a teaspoon and chip at the sugary crust with it, just to have something to do with my hands.

Sarah nods, waving one of the servers over, and replacing my empty glass of wine with a full one. I reach for it with trembling fingers, and when I glance over at her, her expression is still concerned.

"Do you want to just call an Uber and go home?" she asks, a small line appearing on her smooth forehead. "It seems like Nate being here really upset you. I would have warned you if I'd known, I promise."

"It's fine," I reassure her quickly. "I know you would have. But maybe—" I look up just then, seeing Ivan escorting the woman onto the dance floor, his hand on the small of her back, and my stomach clenches. "Okay, yeah. Maybe I should head out. I'm sorry—"

"Don't be," Sarah says firmly. "I totally get it. I'd feel the same way if Colin showed up with a new woman on his arm. Just be safe getting home, okay? Here, I'll call you a ride."

I start to protest, but she's already tapping away on her phone. I try not to look in the direction of the dance floor, but my gaze keeps drifting that way anyway, to where Ivan and the woman in the rose-gold dress are swaying back and forth. She's looking at him intently, now, and while she doesn't look entirely happy, it does look like she's finally paying attention to him.

A wave of exhaustion sweeps over me. I know it's not fair for me to be jealous, but I can't help it, and trying to fight the irrational feeling is making me tired. I get up and give Sarah a hug, grabbing my clutch and walking briskly towards the entrance, forcing myself not to look in their direction again.

I'll talk to Ivan about it later, when my head is clearer. Right now, I just want to be home, out of this dress, and in a hot bath.

That's exactly what I do as soon as I walk into my apartment. I strip out of the dress, hanging it up carefully in front of my closet with every intention to take it somewhere to have the rip mended—and possibly send Ivan the invoice—and draw myself a hot bath with rose-scented bath oil. I sink into the silky hot water, closing my eyes as I reach for the glass of wine I poured myself, and try not to think about how completely upside-down this entire evening went.

My thoughts drift back to the kinky website, and Venom. I could log on tonight, and see if he's there. But a sharp pang of guilt stops me from taking that line of thinking any further.

I already felt a little guilty for talking to two men at the same time.

It's not the kind of thing I've ever done before all of this. But after my encounter with Ivan tonight, I feel even more guilty.

If I was upset that he was at the gala with another woman, it feels wrong to get online and chat with another man tonight, to say and do the things that I did last time. Just the thought of him kissing that other woman the way he kissed me tonight sends a burn of jealousy through me—and I can't help but think that means that, at least for tonight, I shouldn't try to see if I can talk to Venom.

This is exactly why I told Ivan that I didn't want anything serious. But it seems like my heart—and my conscience—is determined to get in the way. This is my time to be free, to explore things. To find out what I've been missing for so long. I can't do that *and* demand that Ivan wait around for me until I'm ready to make things serious.

Except—that seemed like it was exactly what he was going to do. Like he was promising me, at dinner, that he was going to wait for me. And as unfair as it is, and even though I didn't ask him to do that, seeing him with that woman tonight felt like a betrayal.

We'll talk about it later, I tell myself. I'll stay off of that site, and I'll wait until tomorrow, when Ivan and I can talk about it outside of the heated environment that we found ourselves in tonight.

I feel sure that we'll figure it out then, and it will all be fine.

I just need to talk to him.

18

IVAN

The last thing I wanted was to leave Charlotte there on the stairs after that kiss.

What I actually wanted was to scoop her up in my arms, carry her into the nearest empty room, and slide under that dress so I could reacquaint myself with what she tastes like. Or better yet, just fuck her up against the wall.

From the way she was squirming against me, I wonder if she would have told me no.

I'm still half-hard by the time Sabrina and I get back to our table, my mind still in that stairwell. The sound of her breathy moan in my ear, the scent of her, the way she arched against me, the sweetness of her mouth—all of it is driving me crazy. I don't want to think about anything other than her right now.

Unfortunately, I have to. Because what I also need to do is get Sabrina Petrov to safety.

I have a plan, one that I put together to the best of my ability over the last few days. It's what I've been entirely focused on, outside of my other responsibilities to the Bratva—and it's why I didn't find the time to text Charlotte and warn her not only that I'd be at the gala, but that I'd be there with a 'date.'

That, and the fact that I didn't want to try to explain it over text. But I didn't have a chance to try to have lunch with her again. I was too busy trying to figure out how I'm going to pull this off tonight and still have all my body parts attached at the end of it.

"She seems nice." Sabrina's voice is so bored that I can't tell if she's being sarcastic or not. She seems more than a little displeased to be here tonight, and I don't know why. I don't think my company is *that* hard to tolerate, but maybe I was wrong. "Is she your girlfriend?"

"No," I say shortly, my gaze flicking over the tables around the room. I didn't see Charlotte earlier, and I look for her now, trying to see where she's sitting. I finally spy her near the front of the room, sitting next to a beautiful blonde in a blue silk dress who is leaning close, murmuring something to her with a concerned look on her face. I can only assume that must be Sarah, the friend that Charlotte mentioned.

"Do you have a girlfriend?" Sabrina asks, tapping her spoon against the crème brûlée in front of her, and I suck in a breath, reminding myself to be patient. I need to get her to the men who are going to guarantee her safety, and to do that, I'm going to have to let her in on the plan.

This is the hardest part. There's no easy way to tell someone that they're about to be a victim of human trafficking, and that if they don't listen to you, the one springing the words *human trafficking* on them, that that's exactly what is going to happen.

"I don't," I tell her, trying to soften my tone a bit. The music picks up, and I turn towards her. "Come dance with me," I suggest, holding out a hand, and Sabrina gives me a suspicious look, but rises gracefully from the table and puts her hand in mine.

A good deal of her coldness is a shield, I know that. She's a Bratva princess, raised to close off her emotions since she was a child, bred to fulfill her father's whims and nothing more. Now, she's about to be used as a pawn for *my* father's revenge, and I refuse to allow that to happen. Not on my watch.

I just need her to believe me, and since we don't know each other very well and our families are enemies, that's a lot to ask.

I lead her onto the dance floor, hating the fact that if Charlotte looks in this direction, she'll see me dancing with Sabrina. I don't care that I have just as much right as she does to be out with someone else, I don't want to be. And I don't want her to *think* that I want to be.

I want her to know that I'm hers. That there's no other woman in the world who makes me feel what she does from just a touch. Just a kiss. That I'm dangerously obsessed with her.

That as soon as she lets me, I plan to make her entirely mine.

I suck in a breath through my teeth, reminding myself to focus, that I can't be this distracted right now. That I need to be paying attention to Sabrina, and how I'm going to get out of here.

As the music swells, I splay my hand over her lower back, pulling her closer. "Listen," I murmur, leaning in so that my mouth is close to her ear. I force every thought of Charlotte out of my head, every impulse to think about how ten minutes ago, it was her ear this close to my lips, her scent filling my senses. The last thing I want right now is to get a hard-on with Sabrina close to me, especially considering what we're about to talk about. "Why do you think we're here together tonight?"

Sabrina pulls back slightly, her expression a little displeased. "Well," she says slowly. "Frankly, I'm assuming that our fathers have come up with a time-honored way to put their rivalry to bed...by putting us in bed together." Her smile is humorless. "I assume this is the prelude to some sort of marriage arrangement. I've put off all my father's suggestions for too long, so I suppose this is the price."

"Am I that bad?" I can't help myself. I don't have any interest in her, either, and this has nothing to do with what we need to talk about, but her comment has needled me anyway. And now I want to know.

She smirks. "No offense, Ivan, but bad boys aren't really my thing. And you have *edgy and dangerous* written all over you. Honestly, I'd like a boring man. My life has been exciting enough. I'd like one who brings me flowers like clockwork every Tuesday after work, and who looks at me like I hung the moon. But I'll never get that, not with my father pulling the strings."

I raise an eyebrow, keeping my voice low as I speak. Between the music and the hum of conversation, as more couples come onto the dance floor, I should be able to ensure that only Sabrina hears what I have to say.

"Well, that's not why we're here tonight. But don't be too relieved," I murmur, pulling back just enough that I can look directly into her eyes. I mindlessly run my fingers up her spine as I speak and we sway together, putting on a show of dancing romantically rather than having a serious, potentially deadly conversation. "I'm here because something bad is supposed to happen to you tonight, and I'm supposed to help facilitate it. But instead, I have every intention of getting you out of here."

Sabrina tenses in my arms. "What is it?" she asks tightly, and in that moment, I'm grateful both that she's smart, and that she's the daughter of a *pakhan*. The dangers of this world aren't strange to her, and she's prepared to face them. Her lack of shock and disbelief will make this all so much easier.

"You weren't too far off the mark about our fathers and their rivalry. But mine doesn't want peace. He wants revenge. And he plans to use you as the means of it." I tighten my grip on her, schooling my face into an expression of desire, the way I should be looking at the gorgeous woman in my arms, even as I speak faster before the song is over. "He's expanded his business to trade in flesh, Sabrina. And he plans to have you taken tonight, to be sold. I'm supposed to help bring you to the men who will take you to the next stop. But instead, I'm going to take you to the men who will get you to safety."

She manages to keep her expression smooth, too—which is fucking impressive, in my opinion—but her eyes clearly show how frightened she is.

"What kind of men?" she asks, and I spin her in a circle, bringing her back into my arms as I lean my mouth very close to her ear again.

"FBI. They'll get you away from here. Things will be—things will be different for you afterwards, Sabrina. I'm sorry about that. Your life is going to change. But it's the only way to keep something much worse from happening to you."

I look up, and I see three men in crisp, tailored suits making their way onto the dance floor, from three different angles. To anyone else, they just look like guests seeking out their plus-ones, but I know who they are. They're my father's men, and they're closing in on Sabrina. I know what I'm supposed to do now. I'm supposed to come up with a reason for her to follow me into the rooms to the right of the main floor, where I'll take her down a hallway where four other men are waiting. I'm supposed to drug her and hand her over to them.

But I don't intend to do any of that.

"I need you to trust me," I whisper to Sabrina, just as a heavy hand closes on my shoulder.

"What the *fuck* are you doing with my girl?" A tall, muscled man spins me around, his eyes narrowed, his cheeks a bit pink as if he's been drinking too much. "You told me you weren't going, you bitch—"

Sabrina's mouth is hanging open, the shock on her face entirely real, which is all I need from her. "I don't know what you're talking about," I snap, playing dumb for the Bratva men closing in around us. "But you need to get the fuck out of here, friend. She's here with me."

"I don't fucking think so. That's *my* girl. Sabrina, just come with me." The man's voice turns pleading, his eyes fixed on her. "We can work this out, baby. It doesn't have to be like this."

"Don't come near her," I growl, my hands clenching into fists. "She's my date, asshole. Whatever you want, you can talk about later. *After* she and I have enjoyed our night."

Out of the corner of my eye, I can see my father's men backing down. They can't afford to create a scene by involving themselves in this, not when it could escalate into violence and the police could be called. To them, this looks like Sabrina has been seeing someone without her father's permission, and he's decided to crash the party. Anywhere else, my father's men would kill him without a thought and take her. But this is too public, which is exactly why my plan might work.

The man lunges forward, shoving me aside, hard enough that I almost actually fall on my ass. "Come with me, Sabrina," he snaps, grabbing her arm and yanking her towards him, the picture of a jealous, angry boyfriend. "I want to know why you've been lying to me."

And then, low enough that only Sabrina and I hear it, he murmurs into her ear: "Agent Brooks. FBI. I'm going to get you out of here."

Sabrina's face softens instantly, and my respect for her kicks up a notch as I realize she's a better actress than I would have ever given her credit for. "I'm sorry," she says, loudly enough that the other men can hear it. "I should have told you. It's just, that fight—" She keeps talking as Brooks leads her off the dance floor, one arm going around her and pulling her close, his pace quick as if he can't wait to get 'his girl' alone to talk things out.

I know, of course, that he's trying to get her to his car as quickly as possible. It will be a matter of minutes before my father's men call in outside reinforcements to go after them. Whether Brooks gets her out of here or not is in his hands, now. I've done all I can.

I think it will be enough. I also know which men my father sent to handle this now, at least the first few of them. That will be good information to feed to Bradley.

"Congratulations on fucking things up."

The growl behind me is Lev's. I know it before I even turn around. My chest tightens, because even though the plan went off without a hitch, and there's no real way to trace the fact that the FBI got ahold of Sabrina before she could be kidnapped back to me—I still need to tread carefully. And this is still not going to be good.

Lev is angry. My father is going to be fucking furious. And nothing is going to stop either of them from taking it out on me.

"Looks like virginal little Sabrina had an angry boyfriend," I say dryly as I turn around. Lev glowers at me like he wants to punch me. And he might—-once we're not in public.

I wish I had an excuse to not leave with him.

Quickly, my gaze flicks back to the table where Charlotte was sitting. She must have seen all of this, too, and I'm not entirely sure how I'm going to explain it away tomorrow when I see her. I also really, *really* don't want her to see me standing here with Lev. I doubt she would know who he is, or be able to easily find it out, but it's a chance I don't want to take.

But when I look over quickly at the table, she's gone. Not just her, but the small clutch purse that had been sitting on the table, too. Her friend is nibbling at her dessert and looking at her phone, and her demeanor doesn't suggest that she's waiting for Charlotte to come back.

I think Charlotte went home. And while I should be relieved that not only is she not seeing this, she might have missed *all* of it, all I feel is a sharp stab of disappointment that she's gone.

Lev snaps his fingers in my face. "Pay attention, brother," he growls. "We're going to go talk to *otets* right now. And you're going to explain to him why, instead of coming home with the good news that Sabrina Petrov is headed to the auction block, she got dragged off by some nobody boyfriend that she shouldn't even have. *You're* going to explain why you didn't stop that. Why *you* failed."

I don't say anything, which I know pisses him off even more. He wants me to argue, so he can hold his authority over my head, the fact that he *can* order me home to face our father. But instead, I save everything I want to say for the moment when I do.

"Aren't you going to say anything?" he snaps, and I shrug.

"No point in repeating myself twice, is there?" I smirk at him, enjoying the cold fury that washes over his face, and then I pivot, striding towards the entrance to the museum. I'll end up in Lev's car on the way back. He'll want to keep an eye on me. But there's no reason I can't get to it first.

—-

LESS THAN AN HOUR LATER, I'm marched into my father's mansion and to his large, opulent office, led by Lev. The men who were supposed to help kidnap Sabrina have slunk off, unsurprisingly having no desire to face my father. I'm sure their punishment will come later, when he's done with me.

My father's office is dominated by a massive mahogany desk, surrounded by bookshelves filled with books written in Russian. He takes pride in the fact that most of what he reads is in the mother tongue, and derides his sons—except for Lev—for not knowing the language very well. I speak it passably, as do my other brothers, but only Lev is fluent enough that it's hard to tell that he's second-generation, born and raised in the States. It is, like everything else in his miserable life, his way of sucking up to our father.

Dima is standing in front of the fireplace, still wearing a crisp suit despite the hour and being at home, sipping on what looks like a glass of straight vodka. He doesn't turn as we walk in, and I feel a cold tendril of fear lick down my spine as Lev locks the door behind him. I don't know what comes next, but I can't imagine it's going to be pleasant.

"Tell me what happened, Ivan." Dima's voice is cold and hard, and it's clear from his tone that he already knows. He just wants to hear it relayed from me, in my own voice.

I step forward, taking a deep breath. I can feel Lev's heavy presence at my back, a foreboding reminder that I have no friends in this room. That my family is that only by blood, and not affection. That even in this room, I only have a part of the former. Lev is my father's true son, his heir, and I'm a bastard. Half his, half a woman who he didn't care about enough to ever even say her name to me growing up.

"Everything was going according to plan," I say calmly. "I was dancing with Sabrina when I saw your men come in. She was very —receptive to me, as we were dancing." She wasn't, but there's no way for him or Lev to know that. "I thought I wouldn't have any trouble convincing her to slip away with me. Your men would have followed, as planned, and joined the ones waiting in the back room. But before I could suggest that she and I go somewhere more private, a man showed up and accosted me. A boyfriend, apparently."

Lev makes a scoffing sound behind me, and I turn slightly, arching an eyebrow.

"I'm sorry," I say coldly. "Do you think he was someone else?"

"We haven't gotten any intelligence that Sabrina had a boyfriend, or any male contacts outside of her father. There shouldn't have been anyone to worry about." Lev's voice is flat, rote.

"Because I'm sure that if the virginal daughter of Yuri Petrov had a boyfriend, she would have let that get out in a way that someone else could find out about it," I snap back sarcastically.

"There." Dima turns around, his hand tight around his vodka glass. "That's the first problem. If the Petrov girl had a boyfriend, we *should* have known about it." His eyes are fixed on Lev as he says it, and for the first time since everything went down, I feel the tiniest bit of tension ease from my shoulders. At least I'm not the only one bearing the weight of Dima's wrath tonight. It seems that he's angry with Lev as well. "If she's not a virgin, that severely decreases her value."

"But not enough not to kidnap her." Lev's tone is cool, entirely unaffected. "Ivan, you were aware of your part in this. Did you look into her at all? Did you find any signs of a boyfriend?"

"That wasn't my job. I have nothing to do with the trafficking." I shrug. "You told me to show up as her date, made it clear that I had no other choice. So I did it. I wasn't told I was supposed to do homework beforehand."

Lev moves so quickly that I don't see the blow coming. One instant, I'm smarting off to him, and the next, I'm doubled over, coughing as his fist to my side drives the air out of me for a second.

"Answer with respect," he snarls, grabbing my shoulder and jerking me upright as I cough again.

"The answer is the same," I mutter. "I wasn't aware that I was supposed to do more than show up and play Sabrina's date."

"That job was Lev's," Dima says flatly. "If there was a boyfriend, we should have known about it. But my question now is, why the fuck did you allow her to leave with him?"

His voice is icy. I'm not surprised that he knows the details. I already assumed that someone had filled him in before we got here. "What would you have liked me to do?" I ask archly. "Cause a scene in the middle of the gala? Isn't that why your men backed down, because that's exactly what we needed to *not* do?"

Another blow from Lev, his fist driving into my ribs. This one I anticipate, but it doesn't change the pain, or the way it drives the air from my lungs.

"Speak to your *pakhan* with respect!" Lev snarls, and I straighten with effort, ignoring the throbbing pain in my ribs.

"He's also my father." I put all my attention on Dima, because, at the end of the day, how he feels about this is what really matters. What he believes. Lev can posture and hurt me all he wants, but Dima is the one who holds the keys to my life and death. He's the one who I really need to convince, when it comes to my involvement in all of this. "I did my job, *otets*," I tell him flatly. "I did exactly what was asked of me. I believed that we would let her go before causing a scene that could shed unwanted light on what you're doing here, so that was how I proceeded. I'm sorry if that was the wrong call."

I'm not sorry, of course. Not at all. But I *sound* like I am, enough that I think that surely my acting will pay off. That my father will believe me.

He tosses back the last of his vodka, setting the cut-crystal glass aside as he pushes up his shirtsleeves. "Be that as it may," he says stiffly, "You were the one who took point on this, Ivan. I gave you an important responsibility. I trusted you with my revenge. With a prize that I valued a great deal. And I see now that I was wrong to do that."

Dima walks up to me, a few inches from my face, and his smile is utterly cold, without a trace of warmth in it. "You are my son, Ivan, so I will treat your failure more kindly than I would if you were only one of my men. But it is a failure nonetheless." He nods to Lev. "Hold him, son."

I barely have time to register the relief that my father at least doesn't suspect me of something worse than mere failure, before I feel the solid crunch of his fist connecting with the bones of my face.

It hurts. *God*, it fucking hurts. It hurts every time he hits me, again and again, as Lev's iron grip holds my elbows, threatening to twist them in ways that will leave me far worse off if I try to fight.

I could fight. I might even win. I'm formidable with my own fists, and I'm quick. My father is old, and I've taken Lev in a fight plenty of times before.

But I know there's no point. If I don't take this punishment now, like the man that my father wants me to be, then there will be a worse one waiting for me later. So in the interest of my own skin, I let him hit me, again and again, until I can feel my face swelling and taste the blood dripping onto my lips.

Dima steps back, shaking his hand as he looks at me narrowly. "There," he says, with a satisfaction that no father should get from hitting his son. "Let him go, Lev."

Lev releases me with a grunt, and I stagger in place, willing myself not to stumble, not to fall. I refuse to end up on my knees in front of my father, no matter how badly he's hurt me. I'm determined to walk out of this room under my own power, no matter how difficult that is.

"Are we done here?" I ask thickly, through my swollen mouth, and I feel Lev tense behind me. Not out of concern for me, I know, but out of hope that he might get to punish me further. That he might get to enjoy watching me be humiliated even more.

My father's eyes darken, and for a moment, I think Lev is going to get his wish. But instead, Dima steps back, picking up the decanter of vodka and pouring two glasses. He picks them both up, holding one out to me.

"Drink," he says, in a commanding voice that brooks no argument. And because I refuse to let my father see me flinch, I take the glass and lift it to my lips as he takes a drink of his.

The pain of the vodka touching my cut and abraded mouth is excruciating. I can feel my eyes watering as I gulp it down, forcing the pain to the back of my head. Reminding myself that this could only be the tip of the iceberg, if I falter. If I let my father see that there's more to this story than I'm telling.

"This could have been so much worse for you, son," my father says coldly. "Think of this, the next time you're given a job to do. And consider the price of failing again." He takes a deep drink of his vodka, tossing the rest of it back before setting his glass down, and looks at me evenly, an expression on his face that tells me he expects me to drink the rest of mine.

So I do. I ignore the pain, and I drink, refusing to allow so much as a single sound of pain to slip out. And when I swallow the last of it, I hold out the glass, and Dima takes it from me.

"Get out," he says harshly, jerking his head towards the door.

I can't obey fast enough, but I leave with a measured pace, striding to the door and opening it. When I step out into the hall, I let out a sharp breath, pressing one hand flat against the wall as I struggle against the wave of nausea and pain that washes over me. One step at a time, I head for the front door of my father's mansion, my head swimming now that I'm out of his sight.

A black SUV is waiting outside, a uniformed driver standing next to it. It's then that I understand, with a heavy feeling in my chest, that I won't be going back to my house tonight. My father wants his driver to take me home—both so he can claim that he looked after me after hurting me and so that he can keep tabs on my whereabouts, undoubtedly—and that means I can't go where I want to without clueing my father in to my secret house.

I'm not willing to do that, so instead, I end up at my penthouse, walking into the unwelcoming darkness of it as I shut the door behind me and struggle to stay on my feet.

I barely have the strength to make it to the bathroom, let alone turn on the lights as I go. I stumble with my hand on the walls towards my bedroom suite, the apartment unfamiliar enough to me that I might as well be in a hotel room. This place is a front, a cover. I barely spend any time here. And it's not where I want to be right now.

Where I want to be is with Charlotte.

The thought is so abrupt, so startling that for a moment, it yanks me out of the fog of pain. *This*, what's happening right now, is why I *shouldn't* be with her. Why all my stalking and all my inappropriate desires can only lead to a brief period of time with her, not forever. Because this life, the kind of life where my night can end with my eyes swelling shut and my nose and mouth bleeding, isn't the kind of life a woman like Charlotte belongs in.

It's not one she would ever want, and it's not one that I want for her.

I find the strength to flick on the light when I reach the bathroom, and I wince as I see my reflection in the mirror. My face is already purpling with bruises, a cut from my father's signet ring down one cheek, my lips split in a few different places. My nose isn't broken, thankfully, but it's damaged. My face is covered in blood, and although I haven't looked at my ribs yet, they're either bruised or cracked. I can feel it with every painful breath.

I don't have the energy to clean it all up. Instead, I stumble to the shower, turning on the hot water as I strip my clothes off. The room swims as I pull my shirt over my head, and I stumble, falling onto my knees on the soft bathmat as I grip the edge of the tub and try not to throw up.

I've been hurt before, but never like this. Never this badly. And what I want, more than anything right now, is to not be alone. Not just that, but for it to be Charlotte who is sitting here next to me. I want her soft hands on me, her voice in my ear. I want *her*. And that realization, when there's not a chance in hell I could do anything sexual with her right now, makes my head swim for a different reason.

I don't know her well enough to feel like this. To want her for reasons that have nothing to do with sex. And I can't think straight enough to try to unravel what it is about her that makes me feel this way, when no other woman ever has.

When my clothes are a pile on the floor, I half-crawl into the shower, sitting on the cold tile floor as I push myself under the spray of water and let it rain down over me. The heat stings, burning as it washes the blood away from my wounds, but I lay my head back against the wall and let it drench me.

I'm tired of this game. Not the game I'm playing with Charlotte, but the one I'm playing with my father. And sooner or later, I'm going to have to come up with a plan to get out.

The blood swirls in the water, pooling around me, turning pink as it slides down the drain. I watch it listlessly, and as the exhaustion swims over me, I realize that I have another problem. One that I didn't think of until right this second, as I watch my own blood swirl down my shower drain.

There's no way I can go on a date with Charlotte tomorrow, looking like this.

19

CHARLOTTE

When I wake up in the morning, my head aches as if I have a hangover, even though I really didn't drink all that much last night. I feel groggy and off, and I sit up slowly, running my hands through my hair and rubbing my fingers across my scalp as I try to gather my thoughts.

I had hoped that when I woke up, I'd see everything a bit more clearly. That I'd feel more rational about it all. But I can't shake the leaden feeling in my heart every time I remember that Ivan was at the gala with another woman, even though he was so insistent that they weren't really together. And then, when I remember seeing Nate there with his gorgeous date, there's a sinking feeling added to that.

Scrubbing my hands through my hair again, I slide out of bed, going to the shower. Twenty minutes later, I emerge feeling a little less groggy and slightly more hopeful that Ivan and I will be able to talk this all out when we see each other in a few hours—and then I see my phone next to my bed, lit up with a series of messages.

SARAH: *How are you feeling this morning, babe? Is everything alright?*

. . .

ZOE: *I want pictures of the dress. ASAP. I might use you for some marketing, if that's ok. Also, how was the party??*

NATE: *I'm sorry, Char. If I'd known you would be there last night, I would have warned you. I promise, she's just a coworker...*

Nate: *Char, c'mon. I know you want to talk after seeing me there last night. Just call me.*

JAZ: *Sarah told me Nate was there. Are you okay, babe?*

IVAN: *Charlotte, I'm so sorry. I'm not feeling well. I think I might have eaten something off last night. I can't make our date today. But if you'll text me back, we can reschedule?*

THE LAST MESSAGE sends my heart plummeting to my feet, and I'm struck with the sudden urge to hurl my phone across the room as tears burn at the back of my eyes.

He was lying to me last night. He must have been. I sink down onto the edge of the bed, trying to control my rioting emotions and failing.

The truth is, I realize as I look over the texts, I've let myself get too invested in this budding romance with Ivan, too quickly. And I knew I would. That's why I stuck to my guns so hard about the whole exclusivity thing. But even though I tried to set boundaries for myself and for him, I *was* jealous last night, when I had no right to be. And that, plus my reaction to him rescheduling, is a sign that I need to take a big step back.

I quickly text Sarah, letting her know that I'm fine and thanking her again for taking me, apologizing for leaving so early. I shoot Zoe a message promising her photos, and ask Jaz if she wants to meet for lunch. Nate's messages I ignore. And then I sit there, rereading Ivan's text, chewing on my lip as I type out a response.

CHARLOTTE: *It's fine. Hope you feel better. Maybe next weekend.*

BY THE TIME I've made myself coffee, my phone has buzzed a number of times. Jaz is down for lunch, although she's clearly concerned about my canceled date, and I see a response from Ivan.

IVAN: *I'm so, so sorry, Charlotte. You have no idea. I wouldn't cancel if I could make it, I promise.*

I WANT TO BELIEVE HIM. I really do. But instead of answering, I just fire off a couple of lunch suggestions to Jaz, and curl up on my couch with a muffin and my cup of coffee, taking a couple of painkillers with it to ease my headache.

By one, I'm sitting across from Jaz at our favorite Thai spot, a steaming bowl of tom yum soup in front of me, the fragrant steam making me feel remarkably better before I've even started eating it.

"So he canceled?" Jaz looks at me sympathetically. "I'm sorry, babe. I know you were really excited."

"I was." I drag my spoon through the soup. "He says he's too sick to make it, but I saw him at the gala last night, and he looked fine—"

"What?" Jaz drops her fork, leaning forward with interest. "Sarah told me about Nate, but not about Ivan being there—"

"I didn't say anything about it," I admit. "She was sure I was all shaken up about Nate being there with that woman, and I didn't have the energy to explain the rest of it. I just wanted to go home by that point."

"Understandable. But what was Ivan doing there?"

"I don't know. I—-he's wealthy, obviously. There must have been some connection." I explain all of it to her—my escape up to the balcony, finding Ivan there, the woman that was with him. "He said they weren't there *together*. Just that she was with him because his father wanted him to take her. And to be honest, she really didn't seem to give a shit that I was talking to him—"

"Well, I mean, if you were just *talking*—" Jaz gives me a pointed look, and I can feel my face flush a little.

"He kissed me." I don't think I need to elaborate; I'm pretty sure the look on my face and how red my cheeks are will tell Jaz everything she needs to know about that kiss. And from the smirk on her face, it has.

"Okay, so what's the problem?" she shrugs, twirling noodles around her fork, and I sigh.

"The problem is that he canceled on me today. Claiming to be sick, when like—sixteen hours ago I saw him at a gala, *with another woman*, and he was perfectly fine."

Jaz frowns, stabbing a piece of chicken. "Look, Charlotte, you know I'm never one to give men the benefit of the doubt. But he seemed really into you. That first date went great, and from the look on your face, that kiss was pretty great, too. So maybe he really is sick. Maybe he drank too much and got a bad hangover. Maybe he really did eat something that didn't agree with him." She gives me a lopsided smile. "It's worth giving him a chance, Charlotte. He seems like a pretty good guy."

"Yeah, he does." I let out a sigh, taking a bite of the coconut lemongrass soup and letting it soothe me. "I'll let him stew on it a little and then reschedule the date."

"Attagirl." Jaz grins. "Now, what are we doing with the rest of the day, now that you're all mine for it?"

Jaz and I end up going to a movie instead and grabbing dinner after, and then I drift home, trying not to think about what Ivan and I could be doing right now if he hadn't stood me up. The urge to text him is strong, but I do my best to resist it, focusing on other things instead. Catching up on TV shows, drinking a cup of tea, taking a hot bath. Anything that I can do to relax and unwind instead of thinking about how last night, and Ivan's subsequent cancellation of our date, makes me feel.

Feeling rebellious, I pour myself a glass of wine after my bath, and sit down at my laptop, logging onto the chat site. I haven't gotten onto it in days, because I felt guilty after my date with Ivan. Now, I feel like I need something to remind me not to get so caught up in him. He's already disappointed me once, and I don't want to count on him so much that I miss out on getting to explore. That's what I wanted out of my dating life for a while post-Nate, after all—exploration.

I bite my lip as I log on, seeing Venom's name in bold, telling me he's online. A hot flare of jealousy licks through me, wondering if he's talking to someone else, and I quickly click on his name before doing anything else. All I want right now is for him to talk me through the pleasure that I want to lose myself in.

I want to feel that adrenaline rush, that feeling of doing something bad that I've never allowed myself before.

CuriousDove24: *What are you doing tonight?*

A moment goes by, and my chest tightens, wondering if he really is busy talking to someone else. Or maybe watching someone else's video on the site. Maybe he doesn't think of me as soon as he logs on, the way I think of him every time I think about this site.

And then his name pops up—and a second later, a picture.

Venom69xxx: *I wasn't really doing anything. Just hanging around, thinking about you. But now that I know you're here—*

The picture is dark, but it's unmistakably his hand wrapped around his hard, exposed cock. And he's fucking *huge*. Long and thick, bigger than any dick I've ever seen. I swallow hard, my mouth going dry, staring at the picture for so long that when the wind picks up outside, smacking a tree branch against my window, I jump and let out an embarrassing squeak.

I'm glad he wasn't actually here to hear that.

Venom69xxx: *Did I scare you off, dove? I'm sorry if that was too much, but I thought you'd like to see what you do to me.*

Venom69xxx: *Just thinking about you gets me this hard. I can't imagine how it would feel if you were here in front of me.*

CuriousDove24: *No, I just—you caught me off guard. It's so big.*

Venom69xxx: *Mm, that's what every man wants to hear, dove. I wish I could hear that from your lips. Telling me while you're on your knees how big my cock is. Looking up at me with those pretty eyes, all worried you won't be able to fit it all in your mouth.*

THE NEXT IMAGE that comes through isn't an image at all. It's a brief, few-second clip of his hand, sliding up and down his length. I can hear the wet sound of him stroking, and my thighs squeeze together, as I can't help but imagine that sound is coming from my mouth around him, or from him thrusting into me.

I play the clip again, biting my lip as I rub my fingers over the outside of my panties, teasing myself. His hand is covered in tattoos, but the picture is dark and angled in a way that I can't really tell what they are. I imagine it's on purpose—this is supposed to be anonymous, after all. But I can't imagine he's actually anywhere near me. He probably lives in an entirely different country. The possibility of me running into him is astronomical.

Venom69xxx: *Did you really save your Saturday night for me, dove?*

. . .

I START to tell him that yes, I did. It's not true, but this is all a fantasy, and I feel strange admitting that I actually had plans to spend it with someone else. Venom is hardly someone who would care, but I don't want to tell him he was my second choice.

Before I can stop myself, I start to type out the truth. It's not sexy, and it's not a part of what we're doing here—-but I can't bring myself to make up the story that I should. *What's wrong with me?* I feel like something is. Like I'm obsessing over someone's feelings who couldn't care less what I was really going to do tonight, who doesn't know who I am, who is barely real to me and me to him. Just like I was jealous over Ivan, when he's not mine to be jealous of.

CuriousDove24: *I was supposed to go on an apple orchard date today. But he stood me up. I guess I was lonely.*

Venom69xxx: *He's an idiot, then. I can tell you what I'd do if you asked me out on a date like that, dove.*

I HAVE a feeling that whatever it is, it won't be as innocent as the date that I was supposed to have with Ivan. But I ask, anyway, because now I'm too curious to back out.

CuriousDove24: *What would you do?*

Venom69xxx: *Well, for one, I wouldn't screw it up like that guy. We'd go on the date, dove. Pick apples together like a cute little couple. But then, later that night, we'd sneak back in. When it's dark and quiet, and there's no one else there but us. And then—*

THE SCREEN GOES quiet for a moment, and I swallow hard, the wind outside of my window making my skin prickle. I'm suddenly nervous, jumpy, as if I really am outside in a dark orchard with this man that I don't know. My heart is beating faster, and I feel that ache between my legs intensifying, the need to touch myself building until I don't know if I can take it much longer. But I wait, wanting the tease. The torment. And I know what I'm really waiting for is for him to tell me to do it.

CuriousDove24: *And then, what?*

A picture comes through. It's like the one he sent me last time, of him from the chest up, that mask on his face. Once again, it's dark and blurry enough that I can't really make out any of the tattoos on his chest, but what I'm focused on is his face. That mask, obscuring his features. And when he sends me a second picture, once again of his hand gripping that thick cock of his, I have a feeling I know what he's going to say.

Venom69xxx: *I'd tell you to run, dove. Run through the orchard while I chase you. Until I catch you, and eat you, just like I promised.*
    Venom69xxx: *I imagine you taste sweeter than the apples.*

My hand is under my panties, sliding between my folds, dragging through the wet heat as I find my swollen clit and start to rub. I can imagine all of it, exactly what he's saying, and the fact that it turns me on so much, that I *want* it, makes me feel guilty and ecstatic, all at once.
    Before I can stop myself, I do something I've never done before.
    I reach for my phone, angling it so that I get a shot of my hand inside my panties, making sure there's nothing identifiable in the picture. And then I take another of just my fingers, wet and glistening.
    CuriousDove24: *I wish you could taste me right now. I'm so wet.*
    Venom69xxx: *Oh fuck, dove. You look so good. I want those fingers in*

my mouth. I'm already so close.

Venom69xxx: *Fuck, I just need to come. I can't wait. Imagine me pinning you down in the grass with my cock inside you, and come for me too.*

I GASP as I shove my hand back into my panties, too turned on to go and get one of my toys. I need to come, too, and the idea that I've gotten him so worked up that he can't wait has me on the edge. I feel myself getting closer and closer, and then another clip flashes up into the chat. I reach out with my left hand, clicking on it as my fingers rub frantically over my clit, and let out a shaky moan as it plays.

I watch as his cock stiffens in his hand, his fingers rubbing in quick, sharp strokes over the tip, and I hear him groan as cum arcs from it, his hips thrusting upwards as he comes all over his hand, spattering his fingers as he grips his shaft and strokes himself harder through the orgasm. It sends me over the edge, too, and I play it again as I feel my muscles tense, the pleasure bursting through me as I cry out, a long, whimpering moan spilling from my lips as I come hard to the sight of Venom coming for me.

Breathless, I sit there for a second, coming down from the high. I can still feel the aftershocks quivering through me when I reach out to tell him how good that was—and see, to my disappointment, that he's already logged off.

I bite my lip, trying to shove the feeling away. *It's an Internet chat site for getting off, Charlotte,* I tell myself firmly. *And he got off. What do you think he was going to do, sit and virtually snuggle afterwards?*

I need to get my head on straight. I'm disappointed that a faceless man online logged out abruptly after getting what we were both there for, and while I know it's probably tied to having also been let down by Ivan earlier, I know I'm being ridiculous.

Shoving my chair back, I strip out of my clothes and go to clean up, changing into my pajamas afterward. I make myself a cup of tea, downloading a dating app while I do, and slide into bed, signing in and starting to flip through the profiles of the men signed up there.

Nice, normal men, I tell myself firmly, as I look through them. Men with golden retrievers and pictures of them hiking. Men who have jobs they can tell me about. Men who will suggest apple-picking dates themselves—that *don't* involve stalking me through them at night and fucking me in the grass.

I ignore the jab of disappointment I feel at that thought, and swipe right on a few. Attractive guys, the type that looks like the sort of men I've always dated. Nice, and safe. Men who probably won't rock my world in bed, but who also won't let me down.

The fantasies have been fun. But it's time I start thinking about where my love life is going after the fantasies have been explored.

Before I get in too deep, and can't climb back out.

20

IVAN

I knew Charlotte would be upset that I had to cancel our date. *I was upset that I had to cancel our date.* But there was no way I could go looking the way I did after my father's "lesson" in his office.

Still, even the pain of my injuries couldn't keep me from logging on Saturday night, wondering if she'd get on. If she'd end up there, since she wasn't out with me. Safely back in my own familiar home, in the glow of the computer screens, I'd gone from soft to rock-hard the moment I saw her name pop up.

It felt strange, to commiserate with her about a date that I was supposed to be on with her. It also felt strange, knowing that instead of that date, she was talking to who she believed was another man. And what I said was the truth. I felt like an idiot for missing out on the date with her. I felt like I could have somehow avoided all of this, even though the truth is that there really was nothing I could have done. Trying to get out of taking Sabrina to the gala would have ended badly for me, too. And going along with my father's plans for her was unthinkable.

I'd tell you to run, dove. Run through the orchard while I chase you.

I look up at my ceiling in the morning light through my swollen eye, groaning at the memory. Despite the aching, stabbing, bruised variety of pains ricocheting through my body with every passing moment, just the memory of that conversation is enough to make me hard. And I can't help wondering how many of Charlotte's secret fantasies are things that she would actually want to become a reality.

It's no secret that plenty of people fantasize about things that they'd never want to do in real life, and there's nothing wrong with that, in my opinion. But Charlotte has been so *good* all her life, so proper, and I desperately want to know how much of what she's talked to me about in the secrecy of our online chats is what she *actually* wants.

If she wanted me to chase her through an apple orchard with a mask on, pin her to the grass and fuck her right there, I'd gladly do it. It would be one of the tamer things I've done, actually. And just the thought is enough to make my cock ache, adding that pain to the list of everything else on my body that hurts.

Gritting my teeth, I reach down and push my sweatpants down to my thighs, freeing my already-dripping cock. A quick swipe of my thumb over the thick pre-cum dripping from the swollen, tight head, and I have enough to create a slick, hot slide of my fist over the straining flesh that has my toes curling in seconds.

I imagine Charlotte between my legs as I feed my cock into her pretty mouth, cooing at me that she just wants to make me feel good as I lay back. Obeying my every demand as I wrap my hand in her thick, soft, dark hair, sucking me off until I fill her mouth with my cum.

"*Fuck!*" I growl aloud as my cock explodes, sticky heat coating my fingers as I come in what feels like record time. *At this rate,* I think grimly as I fumble for a tissue on the nightstand, *I'm going to need to jerk off a couple times before our date just so I don't come in my pants the first time I kiss her, like a fucking teenager.*

If I still get a chance for that date. Charlotte is clearly in her *take no bullshit* era when it comes to men, and I can't blame her. Her ex fucked her over in a way that no man should ever treat a woman, and between not telling her about the gala and then missing the date, the rational part of me says that she *should* tell me to fuck off.

But the part of me that's entirely, wholly obsessed with her refuses to allow that to be a possibility.

My phone goes off next to me, just as I'm finishing cleaning up and tucking myself back into my sweatpants, and I reach over for it, groaning as every movement sends pain rocketing through my body. When I look at the screen, I see red.

The tracker that I put into her phone when I gave her my number, the one that allows me to see her phone activity, is coming in handy. Because I can see that she downloaded a dating app—and that she has messages from no fewer than ten guys this morning, all wanting to find a time when they can meet up.

And three of them she's actually messaged back.

I grit my teeth so hard I'm worried they might crack, cursing my father and his bullshit under my breath as I force myself to sit up despite the pain in my ribs. If I'd made it to that date with her yesterday, this wouldn't be happening. She'd still be thinking about *me*, not talking to Joshua, Bryce, and Rick.

All stupid fucking names. All men that I don't intend to let within speaking distance of her. There's no way she's going out with any of them.

I set the phone down, breathing sharply as I try to think. She hasn't set anything up with any of them yet, so there's nothing I can do. Not yet.

I let out another sharp hiss of frustration as I run a hand through my hair, feeling utterly helpless. I don't want to lose her, but the circumstances are working against me, and I can feel her slipping out of my grasp before I've even really had a chance to try to make her mine.

Somewhere in the back of my mind, I can hear the rational part of me murmuring that that should remind me of why she and I aren't meant for each other. Why this can only end with someone getting hurt—her, or me, or both of us.

That if I really cared about her, I'd let her go.

But I *can't*. And I'm far past being rational when it comes to Charlotte.

—

By Wednesday, she still hasn't texted me back about rescheduling. And I can see that she's still talking to Joshua, a reasonably handsome man working in finance who wants to take her out for coffee Saturday morning.

Like hell, is all I can think as I look at the string of messages, pacing back and forth through my house. I haven't left since I came home on Saturday, and while I *like* being home, being here like this feels more like confinement than choice.

It gives me plenty of time to formulate a plan for how to foil Charlotte and Joshua's date, though.

Saturday morning, I dress nicely, putting on jeans and a long-sleeved dark blue henley. I drive my Mustang into the city, parking a few blocks from where I know Charlotte is meeting Joshua for coffee, and walk briskly to the cafe, knowing from the messages that he told her he'd get there a little early to get a table for them. I also know she's running late—some issue with her blow dryer dying.

I see Joshua the minute I walk into the coffee shop. He's sitting a little ways towards the back at a small table, a cup of coffee already in front of him, scrolling through his phone. Without missing a beat, I sit down across from him, and he looks up sharply. There's a smile on his face in the instant that he thinks it's going to be Charlotte sitting down, and then it drops just as quickly when he sees me.

"I'm sorry," he says crisply. "Whatever you're selling, I'm not interested. And I have a date meeting me here, so—"

"Your *date* is why I'm here," I tell him flatly. His eyes are roving over my face, taking in the purple and yellow bruises, the still-healing cuts, and the half-swollen eye. I can see his mind spinning, trying to figure out if there's some connection between Charlotte and how I look, and the panic just behind it. Joshua isn't the kind of man who handles violence well, I can see that from the way he's slightly green just looking at my injuries.

"Nothing to do with all this," I tell him cheerfully. "Just a little mishap, that's all. But Charlotte and I are just having a little disagreement. We haven't made up yet, and I know she's getting back at me by going on this date. So what you're going to do, rather than insert yourself in the middle of it, is get up and leave, right now. Quick as you can, before she shows up and can see you. And to sweeten the deal—" I slip a roll of bills out of my pocket, nudging it across the table to him. "There's five grand there. Cash. Now I know you're worth a good bit more than that, but five grand is five grand, isn't it? Surely you're not so flush that you can't appreciate that amount still."

Joshua's eyebrows have risen nearly to his hairline. "I don't know what this is," he splutters, red spots appearing on his cheekbones. I fight back a chuckle, because I can already see where this is going. I've seen it before, with men I've tortured. Joshua's pride has come out to play, and he's going to try to make a stand—going to try to convince me that he's a bigger man than I am.

Unfortunately, I already know that's not the case.

"This is me telling you to get the fuck out of this coffee shop and take the bribe." I give him a cold smile. "I don't want to resort to threats, Joshua. But Charlotte will be here soon, so if you want the money, I suggest you take it and leave."

"Or what?" His bluster is in full force now, his voice low, but he's glaring at me as if he really thinks this is a fight he can win.

"Joshua, I can go home right now, and in twenty minutes, every one of your accounts will be drained." The cold, pleasant smile is still fixed on my face; if anyone looked over, they'd think we were just talking business. "I don't have to lay a finger on you to hurt you. I could take every cent you have, hack into your car loan, and set it to repossession, plant a fake arrest warrant that would take days and an expensive lawyer for you to sort through, and get it tossed out. I can ruin your life with a few keystrokes, *Josh*. So I suggest you go. She's not worth it."

That last is the first lie I've told him. Charlotte *is* worth it. She's worth all of it and more, and I feel more certain of that than I have of anything in a very long time. But Joshua doesn't know that yet, and if I have my way, he never will.

For one brief second, I think he's going to keep arguing. And then he looks at me—and whatever he sees in my face, he seems to understand that I'm not lying or bluffing.

"Fine." He snatches the money off of the table. "Not worth all that, for a—"

"Careful," I warn him, that cold smile still on my face. "Violence is still on the table, depending on what you say next about Charlotte."

The chilly viciousness in my voice seems to convince him. He shoves the money in his pocket, leaving his coffee as he strides to the front door. I watch as he goes outside, half-jogging down the sidewalk, and reach for the mug, downing it as I watch him go. A cinnamon latte—not half bad.

By the time Charlotte arrives, I've ordered my own coffee—a pumpkin spice latte, because they're good, regardless of what anyone says—and I'm in a corner armchair by the stone fireplace, pretending to read a book I brought along. Instead of actually reading, I'm keeping a covert eye on the door, waiting for her to walk in.

When she does, I can feel my heart skip a beat in my chest. She looks beautiful, as always, dressed in a rust-colored corduroy skirt that stops a couple inches above her knees, a soft-looking cream-colored sweater, and tobacco brown knee-high equestrian boots. Her hair is down, so thick and wavy that I can feel my palms itching with the urge to touch it.

I feel a moment's guilt when I see her look around, and the bright smile that was on her face drops. It's clear she was expecting Joshua to be here, and he's not. I'm also willing to bet he didn't text her—he wasn't a stupid man, and I have a feeling that he was aware I'd know, somehow.

If I was a good man, I would have left her alone. I would have let her have her coffee date with the safe, good, *normal* choice, and I would have quietly exited her life. There is no good ending to this, I know that. *None*.

But as I look at her from over the top of my book, I know that there's no real choice for *me*. Not anymore. Because the hunger I feel when I look at her isn't safe, normal, or good. I *need* her, crave her, and I have a feeling that it's because she's so much different from what I live with day in and day out.

My world is brutal. Ugly. Violent. Charlotte is innocent and good and sweet, and I want to revel in that, to get so close to her that I can't help but feel all of it on my skin—and at the same time, I want to ruin her completely.

She's still standing there just inside the door, looking slightly forlorn, and I close my book, getting up quickly before she can leave.

"Charlotte?"

Her head whips around at the sound of my voice, and her mouth drops open when she sees me—out of shock at seeing me there or at my bruised and battered appearance, I can't be sure which. "Ivan?" Her voice has that same disbelieving quality it had when she found me on the balcony at the gala, and my chest tightens at the thought of that night.

"I was just having some coffee and reading." I hold up the book, and she glances at it for the briefest of seconds before looking back at my face. "You look upset. Is everything okay?"

"No, I—" She blinks rapidly, as if she's trying to get her thoughts straight. "I was supposed to meet someone here for coffee, but I guess he didn't show." She bites her lip, her gaze sweeping over my face again. "Ivan, what happened to you?"

There's genuine concern in her voice. I don't doubt that she's still upset with me over what happened at the gala, and our subsequently canceled date, but she's not so upset that she doesn't care. That gives me a renewed flicker of hope.

"An accident." I rub the back of my neck with one hand, looking sheepish. "Dropped my motorcycle. My ribs are pretty banged up, too. Happened the night of the gala, after I left. That's why—"

Understanding dawns on Charlotte's face. "That's why you

canceled our date." Her eyes widened. "Ivan, why didn't you just tell me? Why did you lie about it?"

I feel another flicker of guilt. *If you only knew, little dove. That's the least of it.* "I was embarrassed," I tell her instead, leaning into the story. It's not as if I can tell her the truth, after all—I can't tell her that my father is a Bratva patriarch, that he punished me for failing to deliver a rival's daughter to men who would sell her into sex slavery. If I said any of that, Charlotte would *run* in the other direction, and she'd be right to do so.

In which case, I might as well have left her to her date with Joshua.

"That's nothing to be embarrassed about." Charlotte laughs. "I'd fall right off if I tried to ride a motorcycle." She bites her lip, and it takes everything in me not to reach down and rub my thumb across the spot where her teeth sank in.

"I wish you would have told me the truth," she says slowly, looking up at me. "I would have understood, if you had. I really would have. We could have just talked everything out. Instead, I thought you were lying about everything. About that woman at the gala. Making up an excuse that you were sick to get out of having to face me." She lets out a sharp breath. "Maybe that wasn't fair for me to just assume all of that. But after what Nate did—"

The guilt is no longer a flicker. It feels like a stab, digging into my chest, reminding me that there is *no* future here. Because I'm lying to her about so much more than what she thinks, and I can't keep it all hidden forever. One day, she'll find out, and it will destroy her.

If I let myself fall too much further, it will destroy me, too. I might already be there.

"I get it. And I'm sorry." I mean it, too. I *am* sorry, for things that she doesn't even know I need to be sorry about.

But not sorry enough to stop.

"Let's have our date," I say abruptly, looking down at her. "Let's get coffee, and go to the orchard, and have the day we planned. Right now."

Charlotte's eyes widen, and I can see her old self, the one who plans everything ahead of time and never does anything impulsive, fighting back against the idea instinctively. But I can also see the moment that she pushes it back, her smile widening as she nods.

"Okay," she says decisively. "Let's do it."

21

IVAN

We both order coffee—another pumpkin spice latte for me and an apple pie latte for her—and start to walk the few blocks to my car. "I'm sorry for just assuming you were being a dick," Charlotte says again as we walk, clutching her coffee as the crisp fall breeze blows her hair around her face. "I should have texted you back. Jaz said I was overreacting."

That guilt stabs into my chest again. "Not overreacting." I look ahead of us, taking a sip of my coffee as I school my features. There's a heavy, hard knot of anger in my chest now—not at her, but at the circumstances. In my *life*, I was born into the world that I was, one of violence and dog-eat-dog survival, and because of it, I can't be with Charlotte the way I want to. I can't have met her as a normal man, one who could woo her and fall for her and be loved in return the way it should be. Instead, I need lies and deceit to be with her, and it can only ever be temporary. "I really do understand. But now we have another shot at it. Let's make the most of it, yeah?"

I glance over at her, and she's smiling as she takes another sip of her coffee. "I'd like that," she says softly. "I still can't believe you agreed to an apple-picking date."

"I can't believe I agreed to help bake a pie." I return her smile. "It's going to be terrible."

"Fortunately, I know how to bake." Charlotte sips at her coffee as we turn the corner to the parking garage. "I'll teach you."

I feel the sharp bite of desire, my cock twitching at the thought of all of the things I want to *teach* her. But today isn't about that.

Today is about something more dangerous than lust.

"Oh wow," Charlotte breathes as we walk up to my car. "That's beautiful."

"It's a '69 Boss 429. Very rare." Very *expensive*, too, but I'm not about to brag. Charlotte doesn't seem to be the type to be impressed by how much I spent on a car, and it's one of the things I like about her. How much money I have isn't what's important to her. "It took me a while to track it down," I add, smoothing a hand over the glossy black hood. "But it's my pride and joy. Favorite car I own."

"I think I like it better than the one you picked me up in for dinner," Charlotte says, her gaze drifting over the car. "It's more—badass, I guess?" She laughs softly. "I don't know. The other one was gorgeous, but this one is—" She drifts off as I open her door for her. "Are you a car guy?"

It takes me a moment to register her question. She's standing between me and the car, her back to the open door, and she's so close that I can smell not only the sweet honey scent of her perfume but also the warmth of her skin. A warmth that I want to reach out and touch, to bury myself in, to wrap around me until it sinks down to the cold depths of my soul. I want her, and standing so close to her, it's difficult to not reach out and try to *take*.

It makes me wonder what she would do, if I tried to kiss her right now. If I urged her into the backseat of the car instead, ate her out right here in the parking garage, in the back of my car. If I pulled her onto my lap, fucked her hard until she screamed for me.

"Ivan?" Charlotte is looking up at me, and there's a quiver of nervousness in her voice. It's as if that prey instinct has slipped out again, warning her away from me instinctively, even as she leans into me, her chin tipped up as if she *wants* me to steal that kiss.

"I want to kiss you right now," I murmur, reaching up to run my finger along the edge of her jaw. I feel her shiver, and I know she's remembering, the same way I am, that kiss in the stairwell. "But I don't want to miss our date a second time."

I take a step back, putting a small amount of distance between us. I see the movement in her throat as she swallows hard, taking a step back as she slides into the car.

I'm hard as hell as I walk around to my side of the car, stiff and uncomfortable in my jeans, and I have to fight the urge to reach down and adjust myself. I slide into the car, turning the key, and as it roars to life, I glance over at Charlotte. "Ready?" I ask, and she nods, the movement a little jerky, as if she's feeling some of the same things I am.

The actual drive is beautiful. I turn the radio to a station playing old bluegrass and country as we drive out of the city, down streets fringed with changing leaves, out to the orchard that Charlotte gave me directions to. It's a Saturday at the peak of fall, so the parking lot is almost full, and Charlotte gives me a guilty look.

"It's going to be really busy," she says apologetically. "Probably a lot of kids. I hope that's okay, and you don't mind—"

"It's fine," I assure her, killing the engine and sliding out to come around and open her door. "All that matters to me is that we're finally getting our day together."

It's the truth. The families and their kids swarming all over the place don't bother me the slightest bit, not when I'm here with Charlotte, doing the thing that she so badly wanted me to come out and do with her. And I realize, as we get our baskets and head out down the path winding through the grass into the trees, that I'm having *fun*.

I'd agreed to this because she wanted it, not because I really wanted to, and I didn't think there was anything wrong with that. Plenty of people did things just because the person they were with wanted them to. But as Charlotte and I start picking apples, trying to figure out what constituted the best ones for picking versus eating, each of us taking turns climbing up to pluck them off and tossing them down to the other, I can feel myself relaxing more and more.

It's the most normal, fun, innocent thing I've ever done. And as out of place as I feel among these other normal couples and families, knowing the darker side to my relationship with Charlotte, knowing all that I'm hiding from her—I find myself more and more able to pretend that it's not there. That *we're* normal.

The smile on her face, the sound of her laughter, the way she gasps when she tosses me an apple, and it almost hits me—all of it makes me feel soft and warm in a way that I've never experienced before. It makes me feel *happy*.

She plucks one last apple, scurrying down and dropping it in the basket. And then, before I can say anything, she leans down, biting into one as she looks up at me, eyes sparkling with laughter, the apple held clenched between her teeth.

I know what she wants me to do. It's absolutely ridiculous, but I find myself leaning forward, taking a bite out of the apple as she does. It drops between us, and I catch it reflexively in my palm, the juice cool and sticky against my hand as I chew the sweet flesh between my teeth.

Knowledge. Sin. *Her*. Everything I want, sweet on my tongue, and I drop the half-eaten apple into the grass between us, one hand cupping her chin as I bring her mouth to mine. She tastes like the apple juice, and I sweep my tongue over her lower lip, pushing it into her mouth the instant her lips part, not caring who else might see us kissing like this.

The feeling of her mouth, soft and wanting against mine, ripples through me with an intensity that's almost painful. I've never wanted anyone the way I want her, never wanted anything so much that I'm willing to do and sacrifice anything to keep it. I know I'm teetering on a dangerous edge, but I can't bring myself to care.

I want to fall with her.

I pull back before the kiss can get too heated, looking down into her widened, desire-glazed eyes as I reach down to take her hand in mine. "Let's go try to bake a pie," I tell her, a smirk on my mouth, and I see her eyes rest there, her gaze so full of need that it takes everything in me not to kiss her again.

"Okay," she says softly, her fingers linking with mine. "Let's go."

An hour and one stop at the grocery store later, I park in the underground lot at Charlotte's building and she leads me to the elevator that will take us up to her floor. I feel a twist of anticipation in my stomach—I haven't been to her apartment yet, and I'm well aware that this is another step forward. A signal of trust on her end that I don't deserve, not with everything I'm doing in order to make this relationship happen.

She unlocks the door, letting us inside, and I'm hit with the scent of sweet fall candles, something that smells like pumpkin and vanilla and honey. "I really like this time of year," she says apologetically, a sheepish smile on her face as she sees me look around for the source of the scent, and that sharp feeling of anger pierces me again.

Not at her. Never at her. But I know that reaction comes from something someone else needled her about. Her asshole ex, probably, making fun of her for liking fall candles.

"Here, you can hang your jacket up." She points at a brass coat rack on the wall next to the door. "I'll take the stuff into the kitchen." She's already shrugged off her jacket, and she takes the bags out of my hand.

When I join her, she's put her hair up and tied on a cute cream-colored apron with a pair of red chickens embroidered on the front of it. She looks impossibly adorable, and I wince as I look at her, my rational mind breaking through the fog of obsession again for just a moment.

What the fuck are you thinking, Ivan? What makes you think you can have someone like her, even for just a little while? What gives you the right to break her heart?

If it was just physical, still, maybe I could walk away. There are plenty of gorgeous women in the world, and I've never had trouble convincing any of them into my bed. But if it was still just physical—I also wouldn't care. I wouldn't feel this stinging guilt as I look at her, knowing I'm leading her down a dead-end path to a cliff's edge, and knowing that I can't stop taking her there.

She turns, holding out a potato peeler, and I quickly school my expression into something neutral, leaning up against the doorframe. "You said you weren't very good at baking. Think you can handle peeling the apples?" she asks teasingly, and I nod, smiling as I reach out to take it.

If only you knew just how good I am with sharp objects, dove, you'd run screaming instead of handing me one.

I take the bag of apples, stationing myself on one side of the counter with a bowl while Charlotte starts working on pie crust on the other. She sets her phone on the corner, opening a music app, and puts on some kind of soft jazz music—it sounds a little like Norah Jones, maybe—and sways back and forth with a smile on her face as she mixes ingredients. Halfway through, I look over from cutting up the apples into small chunks to see she has flour on her nose, and I turn before I can stop myself, reaching out to brush it off.

She goes very still, looking at me. Her lips are parted, and I can tell that just that small touch roused something in her.

Fuck, I want to kiss her. And if I do, I'm not entirely sure we'll stop. But the way she's looking at me—I'm not sure she's going to *want* me to stop, either.

I can feel myself leaning forward, on the verge of doing it. On the verge of reaching for her. And then, the shriek of a timer buzzes through the air, making us both jump, and Charlotte bursts into nervous laughter.

"I think that means it's time to assemble the pie," she says with a laugh, and I take a step back, shoving down my rampant desire as I push the bowl of sugary apples towards her instead.

An hour later, the prettiest and best-smelling apple pie I've ever seen is cooling on the counter, as Charlotte collects her things for us to go out to the movie. "See?" she says teasingly, gesturing at the pie. "I told you we could do it."

"It's all on you," I retort, getting my keys. "On my own, I would have made a complete mess of it."

It all feels so achingly *normal*, the kind of life I've never lived and never really thought I wanted. I've long wanted to get away from my father, from the Bratva life, his boot on my neck, and the things I'm forced to do, but I always pictured myself as a rolling stone after that, going from city to city, never staying in one place or with one person for long. I never pictured myself with someone like Charlotte, doing the kind of things we're doing today. But as we go to the movie theater and get tickets, buy soda and buttery popcorn, and sit next to each other in the slightly creaky seats—I find my chest aching with a longing to keep this normalcy for a little while longer.

It's like she's a breath of fresh air, a sliver of light, and I'm grasping for it even though I know it'll slip away.

She leans into me as we watch the movie, her sweet scent surrounding me, her hair tickling my cheek and neck. Her hand finds its way onto my knee this time, and my fingers link with hers. Her touch sends a jolt of desire through me, but the lust isn't at the forefront, for once. Not right now. At this moment, I'm aching for something different—something far less familiar to me.

When the credits roll and the other people around us start getting up, I turn to look at her. She tilts her head back, looking at me with an expression that I can't entirely read, and a small smile curves the edges of her lips. "Did you have fun today?" she asks softly, so softly that I can barely hear it—but what I can hear is the uncertainty there. The worry that I tolerated all of this, that I've just been counting down the minutes until this very ordinary date is over—and that couldn't be further from the truth.

"I've had more fun today than I've had in a very, very long time." *That's* the truth, and as I say it, as I see her eyes light up in the dimness of the theater, I can't stop myself from kissing her any longer.

I reach out, sliding my hand into her hair, tugging her mouth to mine. She comes easily, willingly, her lips parting against mine as she lets out a soft, gasping breath that turns my cock to steel in an instant, my entire body pulsing with need. My other hand lands on her thigh, gripping just enough to drag another of those breathy gasps from her, and it's all I can do not to pull her into my lap. She tastes salty and sweet, hints of the salty butter still on her lips, and I lick it away, feeling like a teenager desperate to get to second base again as our tongues slide together, and I groan aloud.

She pulls back, and even in the low light, I can see that her face is flushed, her lips prettily swollen and pink from the kiss. "We should get out of here," she says softly, and I feel my entire body react to those few words.

It's not exactly an invitation back to her place, but it's not *not* an invitation. The chance is enough to keep that anticipatory desire throbbing through me as I gather up my coat, holding it in front of myself to hide the awkward bulge in my jeans. My cock feels stiff and uncomfortable, aching to be freed, and I want to bury myself in her so badly it hurts.

We barely make it back to the underground lot at her apartment before I'm kissing her again. I wanted to kiss her at every stop sign, every red light, and the minute I turn the car off, I push my seat back, reaching over to unclip her seatbelt as I slide one arm around her and pull her into my lap.

She gasps, her hair falling in messy waves around her face as she looks down at me. "Ivan—"

"Tell me if you want to stop." My hands are sliding under her sweater, frantic to touch her, my mouth already on hers as I pull her down to me. The weeks of hearing her talk about her fantasies online, of getting myself off to them while I know she's miles away doing the same thing, the sweet torture of being close to her and that kiss in the stairwell—it all boils over, desire burning through me hotly enough to make me feel as if I'm going mad with it, and I know as she squirms in my lap that she can feel how hard I am.

My hands slide higher as her tongue tangles with mine, over the soft cups of her bra, molding them in my hands. I yank the cups down, filling my hands with her bare breasts, feeling the stiff nipples against my palms, and Charlotte moans against my lips, her hips rocking against me, down on the thick ridge of my cock.

She's wearing that corduroy skirt still, and it's pushed up around the tops of her thighs, only the thin fabric of her panties separating her from the rough denim of my jeans. She moans as she rocks down onto me, the hard length of my cock and the stiff material rubbing her through her panties, and the sound makes me throb painfully.

I slide one hand out from under her sweater, tangling my fingers through her hair as I nip lightly at her lower lip. "Do you want to make yourself come on me?" I whisper, arching my hips up against her. *Little dove?* It hangs on my lips, so close to slipping free, and I force the endearment back before I give myself away. "Come on my lap, sweetheart," I murmur, licking along her lower lip as I wrap my hand in her hair. "I know you want to."

I *feel* her tremble against me. I can feel her fighting with herself, the part of her that's a good girl, that doesn't make out with men in parking garages, where anyone could walk by and see. "I don't want to hurt you," she whispers, looking down at my still-healing mouth. "Every time you kiss me, I'm worried—"

"It does hurt," I murmur, pressing my hand against the back of her head. "But I'd rather kiss you and feel that sting than not have your mouth on mine."

My other hand kneads her breast softly, rolling my thumb over her nipple, and her hips grind down against me again. "Make yourself come, Charlotte," I murmur, still teasing her nipple as I shift beneath her, letting her feel the ridge of my cock rubbing against her again. "I want to feel it."

"What—what about you?" she whispers breathlessly, rocking against me as she says it. I can feel her pleasure building, can see it in the red of her cheeks, the hitch in her breathing, the way her hips are starting to move of their own volition, as if she can't stop herself from chasing the release that's hovering just in front of her.

"We'll get to that," I murmur, my lips still very close to hers. "Grind on me just like this, sweetheart, or move those panties aside and get my jeans all wet. I don't care which one. Just come on my lap like a good girl, Charlotte."

She lets out a low, keening moan at that, her hips rocking faster. I tighten my fist in her hair, dragging her mouth to mine, ignoring the bruising pain of her lips against the still-healing wounds on my mouth as she starts to ride me in earnest. Every grind of her hips brings me closer to the edge, too, and I fight back the urge to come, relishing the feeling of her rocking against me as she chases her orgasm.

I'm not sure I've ever seen anything hotter in my life. Her hands fly up, gripping my shoulders as she bucks against me, and her eyes open suddenly, fixed on mine as she pulls back from the kiss, her teeth sinking into her lower lip. "I'm—oh god, Ivan, I'm—"

"*Fuck*. Yes, baby, fucking come for me. Come on my fucking cock—" I pinch her nipple, rolling it as her head falls back, her mouth open as she lets out a shuddering cry, and I swear I fucking *feel* it as she comes. I can swear I feel the heat as her pussy soaks her panties and my jeans, as she rubs her clit frantically against the ridge of my cock, and I grit my teeth, groaning with the desperate need to come, too. I've never been so fucking hard in my life.

She's panting, gripping my shoulders so hard that I can feel her nails digging in. Slowly, her breathing regulates, and when she opens her eyes I don't see the eagerness there any longer.

Instead, I see something very close to panic.

"I—" She licks her lips, tugging her skirt down as far as she can get it to go, looking around the parking garage. My cock feels like it's about to burst through my zipper, and I try to force myself to stop thinking about it, not to think about whether or not she's going to return the favor and instead about what's got her ready to bolt.

"Hey. I'm right here, Charlotte," I murmur, tugging her mouth back to mine with my hand in her hair. But she resists, pulling back, and I let go of her on instinct.

She's still sitting in my lap, her wet pussy right on top of my straining cock, and I think I might be in hell. If so, it's not anything more than I deserve.

"I—I can't believe I did this." She runs her hands through her hair, and her distress starts to push back my desire a little. "We're moving too fast, I think. I said I didn't want to be exclusive, and I was jealous at the gala, and now this—" She leans back, licking her swollen lips nervously. "I've never done anything like this before."

"Hey." I smooth my hand over her hair. "It's okay. If you don't want to do anymore, it's okay." My cock lurches at that, as if to say that it's most definitely *not*, but I do my best to ignore it.

Charlotte scrambles out of my lap, as if that was the go-ahead that she needed to put a stop to this. She grabs her purse, biting her lip, her expression confused and guilty. "I just need some time," she whispers, and I nod, forcing patience past my very *impatient* desire.

"You can have whatever you need," I promise her. "I'll go at your pace, Charlotte. I promise." I glance back at the elevator. "Do you want me to walk you up?"

She shakes her head abruptly. "No, I—probably better if you don't." Her gaze flicks back to my lap, and I know what she's thinking—that if I walk her up, we're going to end up doing this again, but in a place private enough that she won't be able to talk herself into stopping. "Thank you for a—a wonderful day, Ivan," she manages. "I'll talk to you soon, okay?"

Before I can even respond, she's scrambling out of the car, as if she can't get away fast enough. But I know it's not me she's running from.

It's herself, and what she wants.

—

WHEN HER NAME pops up on the chat site a few hours later, I know exactly why. She's running from what she felt with me today—what we both felt—by talking to a stranger. By reminding herself why she wants her freedom.

And goddamn it, I can't stop myself from giving her a taste of that, even as I'm working against my own interests.

I didn't even make it out of my car before I jerked off once I was home, my cock aching from having Charlotte make herself come on it, unable to wait long enough to actually get inside my house. I'd come fast and hard, and now, just seeing her username pop up, I was halfway to stiff again.

CuriousDove24: *I want to know what you'd do after you caught me in the orchard, Venom.*

I READ THE SENTENCE TWICE, my cock fully hard again in an instant, and I'm struck with the strangest sensation I've ever felt in my entire life. I'm painfully jealous—of myself.

Charlotte doesn't know Venom is me. Which means she left me in the car, hard and aching for her, and now she's about to get off to this guy. Something cold and violent slithers through my gut, something that wants to see how far he can push her, even if I can't.

Venom69xxx: *Are you sure you want to know, dove?*

I SWALLOW HARD, easing my cock out of my sweatpants, running my fingers lightly up and down the shaft. I'm going to find out how far her fantasies go tonight. I'm going to see if I can make my little dove fly away—and if it sends her right back into my arms.

CuriousDove24: *Yes. I want to know.*
Venom69xxx: *Pretty birds end up caged. That's what I'd do with you, dove. Take you home and tie you up, keep you locked away for whenever I want a taste. Would you like that? To be kept caged for my pleasure?*
CuriousDove24: *Depends. How much pleasure do I get out of this?*
Venom69xxx: *Oh, dove. As much as I can give you.*
CuriousDove24: *Tell me what you'd do.*
Venom69xxx: *Tell me first, are you touching yourself to this? Thinking*

about me keeping you tied up, hands and feet to a bed, or maybe manacled to a ceiling, waiting on me?

CuriousDove24: *Yes. I have my toy. I'm going to fuck myself with it while you tell me. Pretend it's you filling me up while you tell me how you'd make me come. How I'm going to make you come, too.*

I LET OUT A SHARP, hissing breath, my hand moving over my cock as I close my eyes. She's so much braver behind a screen, so much more willing to tell this faceless man all of the things she wants, while she runs from me after I give her an orgasm. Jealousy licks through me, hot and tangling up inside of me, making me feel like I'm going insane. I can't be jealous of myself, but I am, murderously so, jealous of a persona I created to make her do exactly what she's doing right now.

Venom69xxx: *I think I like the second option, dove. I'd keep you chained to a ceiling, inside a pretty cage. Naked for me. So whenever I wanted, I could put your legs on my shoulders, and eat you out until you came all over my face. Lower you down enough that I could fuck you whichever way I wanted, and then hoist you up again, letting all my cum drip out of you.*

GOD, I'm so fucking close already. I stroke myself harder, close to the edge, and then a picture flashes onto the screen—Charlotte with her panties pulled to one side, her fingers on her clit, and her pussy stretched tightly around a thick silicone dildo.

Not as thick as my cock, is the one thought I manage before I lose control of my orgasm. My cock spurts, hot and wet over my fingers, throbbing as I let out a ragged groan, staring at the sight of her perfect pussy split open by the toy.

I want to fuck her so badly it hurts. I *need* to fuck her. The thought rolls through my mind on repeat, over and over, as I come all over my hand as if I didn't just come hard a couple of hours ago.

. . .

CuriousDove24: *Venom? Are you still there?*

Venom69xxx: *Sorry, dove. That picture made me lose control. You made me come so fucking hard, dove. I couldn't stop it.*

CuriousDove24: *That's really hot, actually. I want to make you lose control like that, for real. Make you come so fast you can't hold it back. You could come all over me and leave me like that. Make me lick it off your cock while it's dripping off of me—*

CuriousDove24: *Oh fuck, I'm going to come too. I'm—*

Before I can stop myself, I smash my hand against the mouse, closing the screen. I know she's going to wonder why I logged off so abruptly, she's going to think it's something she did wrong, but I can't handle another second of it.

I feel like I'm being cheated on with myself, and it's enough to make my head feel like it's splitting in two.

Not least of which because she's not actually doing anything wrong. We're not together. She owes me nothing.

But all I want is her. And apparently, having her halfway as two different men isn't enough for me.

I want all of her, as myself.

And I don't know how much longer I can wait.

22

CHARLOTTE

I want to tell myself that I don't know why I ran from Ivan today. But the truth is, I do know. And it's the reason I ended up on the chat site tonight, talking to Venom, and getting myself off for the second time today.

Ivan terrifies me. Our date today was the best date I've had in a long time, and our dinner together—our first date—is in a close second after that. He's sweet and charming and funny and so incredibly handsome that it's hard to believe he's real. When he kisses me, when he touches me, I feel things that I didn't think existed in reality.

Things that make me do something like grind myself to an orgasm in a man's lap after two dates, in a parking garage where anyone could have walked by and seen us.

I feel like I'm going crazy. I've gone from being the most boring person I know, sheltered and introverted and never, *ever* up for a good time, to someone who does things like *that*. To someone who finds herself online on the dark web at eleven o'clock at night, sending a stranger a filthy picture as she comes to the things he's telling her he wants to do to her.

The kind of things that should scare me, and do, but also make me so wet, so needy, that I came almost as hard as I came for Ivan earlier.

And there's that, too. Twice in one day isn't a thing for me. I've never felt so aroused all the time, my mind filled with fantasies and needs that I've never had before, as if I unlocked a Pandora's box of sexuality that night at Masquerade, and now it's overflowing.

I feel almost obsessed with talking to Venom, with finding out what outrageous fantasy he'll tell me, how far he'll push it, how far I'll let him. As I come down from the high of my orgasm, the fact of that obsession hits me, and I feel a wave of post-orgasm clarity and regret.

I send Ivan away for this. He was a gentleman today, a perfect date, everything I could have asked for and more. I *felt* how desperately he wanted me, rode his erection to a mind-bending orgasm, and then left him hanging. I could have taken him up to my apartment instead, had *real*, undoubtedly incredible sex, for the first time since Nate and I broke up. I could have him in my bed right now.

Instead I've been online, with a faceless man who could actually be anyone, digging deeper into a darker side of myself that I can't seem to stop exploring. It makes me feel freer than I ever have before—but I also feel ashamed. Not of what I'm finding out that I want, but of the fact that I chose it over Ivan. He's *real*, and this man isn't. Not in any way that matters.

On impulse, as I come back from cleaning up, I grab my phone. It's late, and I'm not sure Ivan will be up, but I call him anyway. To my surprise, he picks up almost immediately.

"Charlotte?"

"Hey." I sink back onto my bed, unsure of what I'm doing, or why I'm doing it. "I'm sorry if I woke you up."

He chuckles. "You don't need to worry. I'm a night owl. What are you doing?"

"Thinking about that apple pie we never actually tried. It's on the counter—I felt bad trying it without you."

"Is that your way of asking me out on another date?"

I bite my lip, toying with a loose thread on my duvet. "Maybe."

"What if I said I wanted that date tomorrow?"

"I have brunch with my girlfriends on Sundays," I tell him quickly. "I can't ditch them. They'd never let me live it down, if I canceled on them for a man."

"As well they should." His voice is deep and rich, teasing, with that hint of a Russian accent that makes me feel shivery. "Is brunch all day?"

Something tightens in my stomach—I think I can hear something in his voice, a need that I can't help but think I must be imagining. A man like Ivan wouldn't *need* to see *me* again, but that's what it sounds like. Like he doesn't want to wait.

"No," I say slowly, almost hesitantly. There's something pinging in my head, a sense of alarm, something telling me that there's danger here. But I think I know what that danger is.

I could lose myself to Ivan. My body, my emotions, my heart—they're all in danger, because he's something I've never encountered before. A man who seems to be everything I could possibly want, and it all feels too good to be true. "Maybe, like—until one or two in the afternoon?"

"What about a hike afterward, then? And dinner? Someplace more casual than the last dinner I took you to, since I know now you like that more." There's warmth in his voice as he suggests it, but I can still hear that need, as insane as it seems. "Maybe I can convince you to let me come up for a taste of that apple pie for dessert."

I bite my lip, a jolt of heat going through me. I'm not sure he's really talking about the pie. But that doesn't stop me from whispering *yes*. It might even be part of the reason why I do.

"Yes," I repeat. "That sounds nice. I can text you where we end up going for brunch tomorrow, so you can pick me up afterward. An easy hike, maybe," I caution with a laugh. "I don't know if I want to do anything crazy after mimosas."

"Nothing crazy," he promises. "I'll see you tomorrow, then."

I stare at my phone for a long time after we hang up. I can't help wondering if I should have agreed to the date, if I should have made him wait longer, if I should have made *myself* wait longer. I feel another jab of guilt as I think of Venom, and I wonder if I'm stringing Ivan along by doing this without committing to a relationship. I can still hear him in my head, telling me that once I figure things out, that will be it for us both. It was such a bold declaration, so final, like nothing any man has ever said to me before. No one has ever *wanted* me as much as Ivan seems to.

It's what I thought I wanted—but it's also terrifying, intense and scary, and it makes me want to run towards him and away from him all at once.

I wanted to give myself a chance to indulge this wild side that I'm discovering before I commit to a relationship again. And it's not as if I'm stringing Ivan along with something that could ever be anything real. Venom will only ever be what he is—a name on a screen, a fantasy typed out a handful of words at a time.

Ivan said he'd let me do this at my own pace. That he'd be patient with my uncertainty.

Now, I'm starting to feel like I'm counting on that.

When I pick up my phone in the morning, getting ready for brunch, it's not Ivan's name that I see on the screen first. He's there, his name followed by a quick *good morning, sweetheart, I can't wait to see you later*—but it's preceded by a string of texts from Nate, each one making my stomach drop further than the last.

Nate: *I can't believe you haven't texted or called. Did five years really mean nothing to you?*

Nate: *It was just fucking sex, Char. Just sex with a whore I didn't care about. And you threw our whole fucking relationship away over it.*

Nate: *You're pathetic, honestly. Acting like a child, throwing me out of our apartment because you couldn't handle me treating you with respect. Like a woman I wanted to marry instead of a fucking slut.*

Nate: *How many guys have you gotten on your knees for by now, anyway? Huh?*

Nate: *I'm fucking lucky I didn't marry you, bitch. And I'm going to figure out how to get my apartment back. My name is on it, too, you stupid cunt. You can't stay there much longer. Better hope I don't find you bouncing on some other guy's dick when I get back.*

My face burns, and it takes everything in me not to respond. I *haven't* been with anyone else, not actually—what Ivan and I did in his car is the furthest I've gone other than that night at Masquerade, in reality. That, and my nighttime chatting sessions with Venom is the extent of it. I haven't fucked anyone since Nate left. No one else has actually been in my bed. And reading the messages, thinking that this was a man who once upon a time told me that he loved me, who I was planning on marrying, makes me feel sick.

"You're better off knowing," Jaz says at brunch, when I show her and Zoe and Sarah the messages. "At least now you know who he really is, there's no chance of you going back to him."

"That's true. But it's hard seeing someone's true colors like that," Sarah says, pushing a bite of her waffle around her plate. I know she's thinking of Colin, who she told us called her all kinds of names in their last argument. "It's tough matching that up with the person you used to know."

"It makes me wonder if it's even worth trying again." I drop my phone next to my plate, my half-eaten croque madame sandwich staring up at me. "If someone can be normal for five years and then go insane like this—not to mention the cheating—how can I ever trust anyone? Maybe I shouldn't bother."

"This is about Ivan, isn't it?" Zoe asks, and Jaz nods. She knows about my date today; I told her earlier.

"I'm going out with him after brunch." I poke at the egg on top of my sandwich, watching the yolk run over the bread. "But maybe I shouldn't. Maybe this is all pointless."

"No," Jaz says firmly. "Even if it all goes wrong with Ivan in the end, *trying* is the point. If you just close yourself off, then Nate wins. If he gets in your head that much, then he will have gotten what he really wants. You've got to shake it off and do what *you* want. And if it hurts in the end, it hurts. You get back on the horse."

I cross my eyes at her playfully. "You don't even know how to ride a horse."

"Wrong," Jaz says confidently. "I was quite the equestrian when I was a kid. Quit when I left for college." There's a momentary flicker of nostalgia on her face, and I look at her, surprised. I hadn't thought there was anything about Jaz that I didn't know.

"A girl has to have some secrets," she says, seeing the look on her face. "A little mystery is good for all relationships, not just romantic ones." She winks, filling up her mimosa glass. "Now, let's get you good and drunk before you go hiking. Maybe Ivan will fuck you up against a tree."

"Oh my god!" I gasp, just as Sarah and Zoe erupt in tipsy giggles.

I *am* a little buzzed when Ivan comes to pick me up. The girls can see him from the table we were sitting at, and I can see them leaning, getting a good look at him as he ushers me bemusedly to the car, opening the door for me before walking to the other side. He drove the Mustang again, and I feel a rush of heat, remembering what happened last time.

"Are you sure you're okay to go hiking?" he asks, a slight smirk at the corners of his lips, and I groan.

"I'm fine," I assure him, as he hands me a bottle of water. "A little tipsy, but I'll sober up by the time we get there."

"Okay, then." He doesn't entirely sound like he believes me, but he pulls out onto the road, and I start to gulp down the water, intent on proving him wrong by the time we get to the trail.

I *do* feel sober by the time we get there, and thankfully Ivan stuck to his promise, and picked one of the easy trails. It's not so much a hike as a walking path fringed thickly with colorful trees, and I let out a relieved sigh as he opens my door for me, and I slide out of the car.

"Those leggings are distracting," he murmurs, looking down at my tight dark grey leggings, covered by a long teal tunic sweater and paired with grey sneakers. "I'm going to walk behind you the whole way."

"No you don't," I tease him, grabbing his hand, and I feel him tense briefly, as if he hadn't expected me to. But he relaxes so quickly that I almost think I imagined it, and a moment later we head down the trail hand in hand, the air perfectly chilly, the leaves vibrant all around us.

"I could get used to this," he says softly, his fingers rubbing against my hand, and I look at him with surprise.

"Walking?"

"No." He rolls his eyes teasingly. "Spending time with you. Time like this, where things are quiet and relaxing, and I don't feel like I have to think about anything else." His thumb passes over my knuckles again. "You told me that you think you're boring, Charlotte, but you—" He breaks off abruptly, looking away, and I have the sense that he was about to say something that he thought was too much. Something too emotional for what we are to each other right now.

"What?" I press, before I can stop myself. Something tells me that he was right to pump the brakes on whatever he was about to say, but now I want to know. I feel like I *need* to know. "You can tell me."

He stops, turning towards me, looking down at me with those dark blue eyes that draw me in. "You'll run if I do," he murmurs, and I feel a shiver run down my spine that has nothing to do with the cold.

"Would you chase me?" I whisper, the words coming out more husky than teasing, and I see his eyes darken, his muscled frame looming over me as he reaches out, brushing his fingers over my cheekbone.

"Anywhere," he murmurs, and what was sexual a moment ago suddenly seems terrifyingly romantic, my stomach knotting with apprehension. I want this, and I don't, all at the same time—and I don't know what to do with that.

"What were you going to say?" My voice sticks in my throat, and Ivan looks down at me with an expression I've never seen before.

"You're not boring, Charlotte," he murmurs, his fingers grazing my cheekbone again. "You feel like home."

His hand slides into my hair, tugging me up as his mouth comes crashing down onto mine, heedless of the still-healing cuts on his lips. I think I taste a hint of iron as he kisses me, giving the kiss a dangerous edge, my adrenaline spiking as my tongue slides against his. I feel him backing me up, his hands on my waist, and I burst into sudden laughter as my back hits a tree and I remember what Jaz said.

Ivan pulls back, the moment broken, his face confused. "Why are you laughing?" he asks, and I wince, thinking he's going to be pissed at me for ruining the moment.

"Jaz said you might fuck me up against a tree," I admit between giggles, and Ivan smirks, closing in on me again as he runs one hand down my waist to my hip.

"Would you like that, Charlotte?" he murmurs, brushing his lips over mine again. "Getting fucked out here in the open? I could pull those leggings down and bend you over, or strip you naked and wrap your legs around my waist, fuck you hard right here. You could walk back to the car full of my cum." His hand drops lower, fingers sliding up my thigh. "Is that what you want?"

The fantasy is dangerously close to Venom's promise to chase me through a dark orchard. I shouldn't want it, but that doesn't change the fact that I'm wet, wet enough that I start to worry I might soak through my leggings. I want Ivan to move his hand a little to the left, to press against the spot where I so desperately need it, and I pull away from him instead, my heart racing as I duck under his arm and step back. "Maybe," I whisper, my arms wrapped around myself, and his expression changes from lustful to gentle as he sees the apprehension in mine.

"Maybe a bed, first." He smiles at me, breaking the tension, and laces his fingers through mine again as we keep walking, the normalcy of the afternoon restored.

Except for the part where he told me that I felt like home. It turns over in my head, again and again, and I can't stop thinking about it, long after the moment has passed.

—

By the time we get back from the trail, it's late afternoon, and we're both starving. We find a little pub not far away and stop for an appetizer of fried cheese, with burgers and beer for our meal, and not once does Ivan say anything about how I should watch how much fried food I eat. Instead, we scarf it all down, and when he drives me back to my apartment, I hesitate as he opens my door.

"You should come up for dessert," I tell him. "That apple pie is still in the kitchen. We could watch a movie."

I shower and change as quickly as I can, and come out in my shorts and a long t-shirt to find him in the kitchen, cutting slices of the pie. He turns, and I swear I can see the heat flash in his eyes as they travel all the way down, down to my feet, and back up again.

"This isn't very sexy," I say jokingly, almost apologetically, and Ivan frowns.

"You're sexy in anything you wear." He holds out a plate to me. "Trust me, Charlotte, I'm having just as hard of a time keeping my hands off of you while you're wearing that as I was when you wore that sexy dress on our first date."

I find that hard to believe, even though he *sounds* sincere. But I can feel the weight of his eyes on me as we settle in on the couch with our apple pie and mugs of cider that we'd bought at the orchard, and I put on *Beetlejuice* in the background. There's nothing sexy about any of this, and yet I can feel him looking at me as if he wants to devour me.

As if he wants the taste of me more than anything else.

It reminds me of that night at Masquerade, of the man that I allowed to go down on me, a man I'll almost certainly never meet or see again. But Ivan is giving me that same feeling, and it makes me feel tight and hot all over, like my skin is suddenly too small for my body.

I wonder if I should have let him come up. I have a feeling that things are going to go further tonight, and I won't have the willpower to stop it again. But that raises the question—why do I want to? Sex isn't a promise of forever. It's just pleasure.

And I want to find out what kind of pleasure Ivan has in store for me.

I swallow hard, taking another bite of the pie. "This is good," I mumble around a mouthful of sugary apple and buttery crust, and Ivan nods.

"It is. Thanks to you," he reminds me, and I laugh.

"We'll have to try our hand at some other types. Some kind of berry for Christmas, maybe—" I break off, realizing that I've basically suggested we'll still be seeing each other in the winter, but Ivan doesn't look the slightest bit startled by it.

"I'm all in," he says with a grin, but there's something deeper under those words. I can hear it, the same way that he said *that'll be it for us both,* at dinner that first night.

Too soon to be saying things like that, but I think he meant it, all the same.

"Thank you for—all of this," I say softly. "I know this isn't really your vibe. The hiking and silly movies and eating pie. It's probably not the kind of thing you usually do at all. But it's been a long time since I've had a date who would do this kind of thing with me, so—" I shrug lopsidedly, and Ivan sets his plate aside, his hand resting on my bare knee.

"You're right," he says, and the movie fades into the background as his gaze locks with mine. "It's not my usual thing. Not at all. But with you—I want it to be. I've been happier these past couple of days with you than I have been in a long time, Charlotte. And I don't want it to end anytime soon."

"Why would it?" I bite my lip, wondering why I asked him that, me, who has run away from him, who keeps insisting that there can be no exclusivity between us, not yet. But I want to know what reasons he might have.

He hesitates. "There are things I can't tell you yet, Charlotte."

"About your work? I remember you said it was confidential."

Ivan nods, almost looking relieved. "Yes. But I—I care about you, Charlotte. More than I thought I could, in such a short time. And I don't want this to end. I don't want to stop seeing you, and I want—I want to see where this can go."

The admission sounds vulnerable. He looks younger for a moment as he says it, almost hopeful, and I reach out, brushing my fingers over the back of his hand. "Would you ever lie to me?" The question comes out before I can stop it, the memory of the woman at the gala still in the back of my head. I think I see something strange on Ivan's face for a brief second as I ask it, a sudden tightening of his expression, as if the question has upset him. But it clears so quickly that I think I might have imagined it, and he shakes his head firmly.

"No," he says, leaning forward. He takes my plate out of my hand, setting it on the coffee table as he spills me backwards onto the pile of throw pillows on the couch, a plush ghost that I bought a few days ago suddenly trapped beneath my back. "I never would."

The way he's looking at me, with a sudden, almost desperate need, wrenches at something in my chest that has nothing to do with lust. My legs slide up around his, tangling around his hips, and he rocks forward, pressing against me as his mouth finds mine. My hands slide down his chest, lower, and he suddenly tenses, groaning with a sound that's almost pain.

"Are you alright?" I pull back, and he nods, his jaw tight.

"Just my ribs. From the accident." He tugs up his shirt with one hand, and just above his chiseled abs, I can see the blooming purple and yellow splotches of bruising across his ribcage.

"I'm sorry," I whisper, scooting back a little. Ivan shakes his head, looking down at me with that same need still in his eyes.

"You don't need to apologize. A little pain wouldn't stop me. But—" He hesitates, and I look at him, surprised. I know he wants me. But he looks unsure, and I push myself up to a sitting position, frowning slightly.

"Do you want to stop?"

"God, no." He barks out a laugh, shaking his head. "But I think—I think I probably should. I think you were right, Charlotte. We should take it slow."

I'm so stunned I can't speak. He leans forward, lightly kissing my cheek, and it takes everything in me not to turn my head into the kiss. "I should go," he says quietly. "Before I make a liar out of myself."

He stands up, and I want to protest, but I can't. I did the same thing yesterday, and he let me go without an argument. I can't do less now. But still—I wish he would stay.

"I can't wait to see you again, Charlotte," he murmurs. And then he grabs his jacket, striding towards the door, leaving me there on the couch, stunned.

This wasn't at all how I expected the night to end.

23

IVAN

I've never felt so torn about anything in my life as I do about how I feel when it comes to Charlotte.

What started out as a physical obsession has turned into more. Every moment that I've spent with her has changed it, molded it, until it's grown into something that threatens to take me down, too. I wanted her from the first moment that I saw her, but it's more than that, now.

I genuinely care about her. I'm more than a little afraid that I'm falling in love with her. And none of that can go anywhere.

It doesn't matter. I can't let her go.

I don't log onto the site when I get home. I don't want to know if Charlotte is online, or if she got on hoping to talk to Venom after I left. I can't stand the thought of her getting off to another man—even if that man actually *is* me. She doesn't know it's me, and that's the part that's driving me fucking insane.

I get in the shower, turning the water on as hot as I can stand it, thoughts of her soft mouth and body under mine earlier driving away every other rational thought until I've made myself come thinking about her. I stand there afterward, shuddering with the aftershocks of pleasure, and I tell myself to let her go. To break her heart now so that I don't shatter it later.

My world is too violent for her. She wouldn't want me if she knew half the things I'd done. And she won't want me once she finds out I've lied to her.

In finding a way to have her, I've ensured that I'm always going to eventually lose her.

"Fuck!" I slam a hand against the wall, gritting my teeth as hot water runs over me, head bowed and muscles tense. I've teased her about keeping her in a cage, my pretty little dove, but I've built myself a cell and given her the key. I'm never going to stop wanting her—and the longer this goes on, the worse it will get.

And she's far from the only thing I should be thinking about. I've been putting off meeting with Agent Bradley for as long as I can, but I can't get out of seeing him the next day. I find myself at the diner just after the breakfast rush, sliding into the booth across from him where he's sitting with the same cup of black coffee in front of him.

"You look a bit worse for wear, Kariyev," he says with a raised eyebrow, and I scowl at him.

"My father had feelings about losing Sabrina Petrov. He made sure I was aware of them."

"Well, I'm sure she's grateful for your sacrifice. Although, for a girl like her, witness protection might be almost as bad as the fate your father had planned." He chuckles dryly, as if he's made a funny joke. "No designer heels and hair extensions where we're sending her to hide."

"I'm sure she prefers that to being sold to some billionaire," I tell him coldly, although inwardly, I can't help but feel bad for her. It *is* better, I'm sure of that, but I can't imagine she's going to be happy, wherever it is that she's going. It feels monumentally unfair that our fathers' private quarrel with each other has turned her world upside down, and now she's going to suffer for it, if less so than she would have otherwise.

"These are the names of the men who were there that night, that I know of for sure." I push a piece of paper across the table towards him. "There's also my brother, Lev Kariyev. But good luck trying to take him down. He's my father's heir. You'll need more than this to go after him."

"And what about you?" Something cold and dangerous glitters in Bradley's eyes, as if he thinks he's about to catch me in a plot. "What happens to you if your brother, the heir, goes down?"

I snort at that, leaning back. "If you think I'm doing all of this to orchestrate my brother's fall so I can take over for my father, guess again. He has two other sons before me, and they'd eat each other alive before they'd let me have the spot. I want *out*, Bradley. Not further in."

Bradley raises an eyebrow, but says nothing for a moment. He tucks the paper away, then looks at me coolly across the table. "This is a good start, Kariyev. Next time we talk, I expect more."

"More?" I glare at him. "I told you, I'm not in on the trafficking. Me helping you to get Sabrina out is only going to push me further *out* of it all, not closer. I'm not sure how much more I can get you, besides more of what I've already been doing. Movements, shipment times, that sort of thing."

Bradley stands up, as if he hasn't heard a word I've said. A heavy hand lands on my shoulder. "Figure it out, Kariyev," is all he says. And then he's striding towards the door, the chime of the bell letting me know he's left.

I rest my head against the back of the seat, closing my eyes for a moment, colors swimming in the dark of my vision. Exhaustion sweeps over me, and for a minute, I just want to quit. All of it. I want to leave, and dare any of them to come after me. Even Charlotte, for that brief moment, isn't enough to keep me here.

But they'd find me, eventually. If not my family, then the feds will. I can't run far enough to get away from them, not forever, and I'm not willing to end up in one of their cages.

Which means continuing to play the game I dealt myself into, at least for now.

The worst part of the day is that I have somewhere I'm expected to be tonight. Somewhere where my *family* expects me to be, specifically, and just the thought makes my teeth grate. I want to see Charlotte, to talk to her, to be with her, but there are some family obligations that I can't get out of.

Tonight is one of those.

My father is throwing a party on his yacht. I've been ordered to attend, and I suspect it's so he can see the aftermath of his "lesson." Lev called me with the "invitation" a few days ago, and made it clear that it wasn't one I could decline.

A driver is waiting for me by the time I come downstairs. I got ready at my penthouse, suspecting my father would send a driver. I wonder, as I slide into the back, if he realizes how predictable he actually is. If he knows how easily I can anticipate what he'll do next.

It doesn't matter, I think grimly, smoothing my hands down the crisp fabric of my suit. *I still haven't been able to get away.*

All three of my brothers are at the party. Lev is waiting for me on the dock, just as the yacht is getting ready to sail. My father's excess is already on full display—nearly-naked women carrying drinks and trays with party drugs, billionaires in suits splayed out across couches, women in their laps, snorting lines, doing shots. Music pounds through the air, and I see my father on the far side of the deck, deep in conversation with someone as the yacht pulls away, heading out onto the water for the remainder of the night.

I've been to my father's parties before. I've never minded the drugs and excess before this; I've even partaken in it. A high, a woman, a hit of a drug, or a moment of pleasure—all of that makes being around my family for the duration of something like this much more tolerable. But tonight, it all feels distasteful.

Charlotte has given me a taste of something different. Made me *crave* something different. And now, that something different is all that I want.

I cross the deck to where my father is standing, knowing he'll want to see me. There's no use putting off the inevitable. His stony gaze rakes over me, taking in the nearly healed wounds on my face, and he nods.

"Looking better," he says, and I shrug.

"What can I say? I heal up nicely."

"A good Bratva man knows how to take a punch as well as give one." There's something almost approving in his gaze, as if my ability to take his beating somehow raises me in his approval. The thought turns my stomach, and I have to fight to hide my distaste.

"Take that sour look off your face," he says flatly, and I know I didn't entirely succeed. "I invited you here tonight to let you know that you're forgiven. You've paid your penance, you took your punishment. Now—enjoy." He waves his hand, indicating the party spread out across the yacht. "And talk to Lev before you indulge too much," he adds, his stony gaze holding mine for a moment without blinking. "He has something to tell you."

I can't fucking wait. "Will do," I tell Dima in a clipped voice, turning away to walk across the deck. The night ahead of me feels interminable, especially since I have no interest in the drugs or the women on offer. I grab a shot of vodka off of a passing tray, tossing back the top-shelf alcohol and relishing the burn down my throat. I *might* get drunk. There's no real harm in that, and it might be the only way that I manage to make the night tolerable.

I hear heavy footsteps behind me as I down another shot, and turn to see Lev standing there. "Shit. It's you." I grab another shot before the server can move on. "*Otets* told me to talk to you tonight, before the party went on too long." I have no real desire to know what my brother has to say, but much like the conversation with my father, finding out is inevitable. I might as well get it over with.

The cold smile at the corners of Lev's mouth gives me pause. He leans in, his hand on my arm, gripping it in an almost brotherly embrace as he speaks very close to my ear.

"We know about her, Ivan."

The heat from the alcohol is replaced in an instant, by a cold hand squeezing my chest. "I have no idea what you're talking about," I manage, my voice remarkably smooth despite the fact that it feels as if a fist is wrapped around my heart. "Which *her* are you referring to? There's been quite a few."

Lev's hand tightens on my arm. "Don't play games, Ivan. Little

Charlotte won't last long if you do. I'll take my time with her, if we have to use her against you, but I have a feeling she's very breakable. And you know how I can lose patience sometimes, with my toys. That's why you're the better torturer, brother. I don't have the *finesse*."

My blood is ice, my head pounding. I want to kill him, my hands clenching into fists, and only the knowledge that to do so would certainly result in them taking Charlotte stops me. I take a step back, wresting myself out of his grip, and when I look at him, the expression on his face tells me that he's not bluffing.

"You're up to something, Ivan," Lev says silkily. "*Otets* and I aren't sure what, yet. But there's something in that devious mind of yours, and we intend to make sure you continue using your talents for *us*. So remember, if you step out of line—" He smiles gleefully. "I'll enjoy making you watch while I make an example of her. You can even critique my technique, if you like. I'm sure I could learn a lot."

I want to get the fuck off of the yacht. I want to be as far from Lev, from my father, from my whole fucking family as possible. But I *can't*, and I know that's why they picked now to tell me this, to trap me here on the fucking ship in the middle of this hedonistic display, and remind me who I belong to.

What they will always take from me, if I try to grasp anything else for myself.

When the next server comes past with a tray of shots, I yank it out of his unsuspecting hands, carrying it with me as far from the party as I can get. Leaning against the railing, I down shot after shot, looking down at the dark water and blearily wondering if I could dive over and swim to shore.

By the time the yacht docks again, I'm well and truly drunk. I know my father and Lev have probably noticed, but I'm beyond giving a shit. I drag myself off of the ship and down to the waiting car, falling into the backseat as it takes me back to my penthouse.

For the second time in a row after seeing my father, I end up sitting on the floor of my shower, letting the hot water beat down on me. The cold feeling hasn't left me, icy fingers wrapped around my heart as I think about the fact that my brothers know about Charlotte.

In all my games with her, I foolishly thought they were the one thing I could protect her from. I couldn't protect her from eventually uncovering my lies, or the truth of who I am, or how violent my world is. I couldn't stop either of us from getting hurt, eventually, because of this obsession I've fostered. But I thought I could keep her safe from them.

I should warn her. I should tell her to get away. I should come clean and tell her the danger that she's in, but I'm not sure she'd believe me. The world that I live in, one full of Bratva and mafia, criminals, and kingpins, isn't one that everyone knows about. She might think I'm making it up to justify my lies. She might never speak to me again, but stay put, leaving herself wide open for my family to use her against me.

I could take her away myself. I could make her go with me, until she understands.

I run my hands through my wet hair at the thought, my eyes shut tight. *Until she understands what, exactly?* That I'm falling in love with her? That I want to keep her, even though I have no right to her? That she can trust me to protect her, even though I've only ever told her half the truth at best?

I could keep her captive, but she'd hate me for it. Still, if it's the only way—

I know it's wrong to even consider it. But my imagination is out of control, trying to fathom some way out of this where I don't lose her.

I can't let her go. Not now, and maybe not ever. And I refuse to let my family take her from me.

—

IN THE MORNING, my head is pounding, and I don't feel any more at ease. The anxiety has settled into a ball of ice in my stomach, and I get up despite my headache and nausea, leaving my penthouse to watch Charlotte go to work. The sight of her walking into the building, happy and unbothered, eases the feeling a little, but not enough. She's safe for now, but only until my family decides they need to leverage something against me. And then—

I need her. I need to be close to her, to feel her in my arms, to remember that she's real and safe and *mine*. I'm tempted to fall back on the old staple of meeting her at her spot for lunch, but it doesn't feel like enough. With my heart slamming against my ribs, I pull my phone out, texting her.

IVAN: *I know it's a work night, but meet me for dinner? I want to see you.*
Charlotte: *It's been less than a day and a half since we saw each other.*
Ivan: *Is this too much? I miss you. I shouldn't say that, but I do.*
Charlotte: *No, it's sweet. Dinner it is.*

I PICK her up at six that evening in the Mustang. Instead of going anywhere fancy, I take her to a little place I know of just outside the city, a bistro that has a quiet, rustic vibe, but serves food as good as anything I've had downtown. Logically, I know that if Lev or any of my brothers are following me, just getting outside the city limits won't stop them from watching where I'm going. But it *feels* better, safer, and that's what I need right now.

"Are you alright?" Charlotte asks as we sit down, looking at me with concern in her eyes. "You seem off. Worried about something."

I shrug, glancing down at the menu. Everything here is good, but nothing sounds particularly appetizing. "Work stress." It's not entirely a lie. "I haven't been sleeping well. Just a lot on my mind, I guess."

She tilts her head slightly. "And coming out to have dinner with me makes you feel better?" There's a hint of surprise in her voice, as if that idea seems foreign to her. As if she's never had a boyfriend tell her that his night was made better by having her there.

"Of course it does." I look at her, wanting her to believe this, at least, even if she eventually stops believing anything else I've ever said. "Every time I see you, Charlotte, my day lights up. You are, without a doubt, the best person I've ever known. And when I'm with you, the rest of it—it feels unimportant."

Her eyes widen, and she sets her fork down, looking as if she's struggling with what to say. "That's the sweetest thing anyone has ever said to me," she finally says, softly. "You're a very sweet man, Ivan Vasili."

I want to laugh, then, because no one on earth has ever described me as a *sweet* man. I don't know a single person who ever could, except for, apparently, Charlotte Williams. But that urge dies away on the heels of hearing her say the false name I gave her, the cover that I set up from the very beginning to keep her from knowing who I really am.

"I'm not sure that's true," I tell her instead, reaching across the table to touch her hand. "But I'm glad that you think it is."

For all that she was willing to make small talk over dinner, telling me about her friends and what she's been doing at work, asking me about my hobbies—most of which I can't tell her—she's unusually quiet on the drive back to her apartment. I look over at her when I pull up to the curb, reaching out to rest a hand on her knee.

The tension is thick in the car, but it isn't only the desire that I always feel when I'm near her. It's the weight of all the lies I've woven around us, the weight of my family's threat, and even though Charlotte knows none of that, I have a suspicion that she can feel it, too.

"Charlotte?" I murmur her name, and she turns to look at me, her green eyes luminous in the dim glow filtering in from the streetlights.

"I want you to come up," she says softly. "I know you said you wanted to take it slow, but, Ivan—"

I've already put the car in gear, pulling away from the curb and towards the entrance to the underground lot where I can park. I might have wanted to take things slow the last time I saw her, but that was before my father's threat, before Lev leaned close to my ear and whispered the things he would do to Charlotte if he got ahold of her.

The emotions warring inside of me are too many and too

complex to unravel them all. It's not only possessiveness and jealousy and anger and fear, but others, too—and somewhere in the mix of all of it is the undeniable fact that I care for Charlotte more than I ever meant to. More than I ever should have.

And I *need* her. If she wants me, I can't tell her no.

A good man would walk away, I think as I park the Mustang and kill the engine, my entire body throbbing with anticipation. *A good man would try to get her to go somewhere safe, and then leave.*

But I'm not a good man. For all that I've tried to do good things, deep down, there's sin in my blood. I've been raised in it, steeped in it, and I will never, ever be the kind of man that anyone could call good.

So instead, the moment I open her car door, and she steps out, I wrap my hand in her hair and push her back against the side of the car, my mouth slanting hungrily over hers.

I can feel in every inch of her that she's made the decision to take this all the way. She responds to the kiss without hesitation, her hands sliding over my chest, my shoulders, gripping me beneath my jacket as she arches against me and tangles her tongue with mine. Her breathing is quick and fast, her chest heaving, and I want to pick her up and fuck her right there against the car, without waiting a minute longer.

But I also don't want my first time with her to be like that—quick and rushed and dirty. If I'm lucky enough to get more than that, I'll fuck her in every filthy way she's ever dreamed, but this time—

I pull away from the kiss, as breathless as she is, rock-hard and foggy with lust. She sends my desire into overdrive in a way that no other woman ever has, and right now, all I can think about is getting her upstairs and into bed.

"Come on," Charlotte says softly, grabbing my hand and tugging me towards the elevator, as if she's thinking the same thing. I follow her, and the thought enters my head that this is my last chance to walk away. To do the right thing.

But that ship sailed a long time ago.

We're barely in the elevator before I'm kissing her again, pressing her up against the wall with my hands in her hair as the floors tick upward. She lets out a soft moan against my lips, and I rock my hips against her, letting her feel exactly what she does to me. Exactly what I've been waiting to give her, ever since that first night at Masquerade.

"It's been—" She takes a shaky breath against my mouth, looking up at me with those wide, soft green eyes. "It's been a little while. I haven't been with anyone else since—"

She breaks off, biting her lip, and even though I was almost sure of that, I feel a wave of satisfaction from knowing for sure. That from the night I met her, there has been no one else who has touched her, seduced her, made her come. It's always been me, since that night.

The doors chime, sliding open, and Charlotte leads me down the hall to her door. There's a sudden shyness in her movements as she unlocks it, and as she steps inside, I look down at her, seeing the way she's chewing on her lip, her fingers trembling a little as she drops the keys into the entryway bowl.

"Are you sure about this?" I ask softly, and she nods.

"I'm sure."

My hands land on her waist, turning her, pushing her up against the door as I kiss her again. I've forgotten about any part of me that hurts—all that matters now is feeling her against me, the way her body softens with each drag of my mouth over hers, even as mine tenses and hardens, wanting her with a desperation that makes it hard to go slow.

I pick her up, my hands sliding under the curves of her ass as I lift her up against the door, and her legs go around my waist, kissing her furiously as I grind into her. She lets out another breathless moan, and I remember vividly the way it felt when she came on my lap in the car, working herself to an orgasm as I watched her.

I need to taste her. I need to make her come again, but this time, with my mouth. "Which way is the bedroom?" I murmur against her lips, barely breaking the kiss, and she motions in the direction of it, gesturing as I step away from the door, still carrying her the whole way.

With a quick jerk of my shoulder, I push the door open, walking straight to the bed and spilling her back onto it. She looks up at me, her lips parted, her eyes wide, and I slide my jacket off, letting it fall to the floor as I return her gaze hungrily.

"Last chance," I murmur softly. "Tell me if you want to change your mind, Charlotte. Because once we start—" I let my eyes slide over her, taking in every inch, and I know nothing has ever been as true as what I'm about to say.

"Once we start, there's no going back."

24

CHARLOTTE

A shiver of fear, laced with desire, runs through me at that. This is just sex—but the way he says it makes it sound like so much more than that. Like this *means* so much more than just the pleasure we can get from each other tonight. Like going to bed with him will mark me in some way, make me his—-and maybe even do the same to him.

But that intensity is part of what makes me want him. That *need* in his eyes is part of what's turning me on, making me so wet that I squeeze my thighs together, aching for him to reach down and touch me. I want more than anyone else has ever given me, and it feels like Ivan is offering me that.

It feels like jumping off of a cliff blindfolded. But if I'm hand in hand with him, a part of me thinks I might like the rush of the fall.

I lick my lips nervously, nodding. "I want you," I whisper, and there's a flare of heat in his eyes as he grabs the back of his shirt, yanking it over his head in one smooth motion that makes my eyes fly open even wider than before.

I've never seen him shirtless before. He's fucking gorgeous, chiseled with muscle that makes him look like he's been carved from stone, his skin etched all over with dark tattoos, too many of them for me to focus for long and try to make out what they are. I see a siren, a sea monster, a dark bird, loops and swirls of designs covering his chest and arms, down over his hands, up to his collarbones and stopping there. Marring the swirls of black ink are the still-healing bruises on his ribs, fading to greenish yellow in the aftermath, but my eyes don't linger there for long, either. Instead, I can't help staring at the deep cuts of muscle leading down into his jeans, a stripe of dark blond hair running from his navel down to the button, all trails leading to the place I'm aching to see.

Ivan chuckles, a dark, hungry, almost wolfish sound, as he runs his thumb over the button of his jeans. "Impatient, aren't you?" His voice has deepened, thickened, full of a lust that makes my skin prickle as he steps closer to the foot of the bed. "Your turn, Charlotte. Take off your top."

There's a command in his voice. I can feel the shift in the air, the turn from sweet and gentle to dominating, demanding. This is a different side to Ivan, and I suddenly understand what he meant when he asked if I was sure.

I could still stop this now, if I wanted to. But I can't tell him this isn't what I want—because the commanding tone of his voice, the way I can see him looking at me...this is all what I've fantasized about. What I wanted, when I realized at Masquerade that there were things I'd been missing out on all my life.

I reach down, undoing the first button of my shirt. Ivan's gaze falls to my breasts, watching as I undo each button, that hungry look deepening with each sliver of skin that my shirt reveals. I go slowly, realizing as I do that I like teasing him. I like watching his jaw tighten as I take a little longer with each button, like seeing that muscle leap in his cheek as he lets out a sharp, impatient breath.

Reaching up, I push the sides of my shirt away, revealing the black cotton bra I have on underneath it. "It's not very sexy," I start to say apologetically, and before I can finish, Ivan is on the bed, his hands gripping my knees as he pushes my legs apart and leans over me.

"Never say that." His hands slide up my thighs, pinning me to the bed, and my pulse leaps, a heady cocktail of fear, anticipation, and desire buzzing through my veins. "Anything you wear is sexy, Charlotte. Because it's on *you*."

"And what if I do say it?" I whisper, looking up at him, a dose of daring added to the mix. His eyes gleam, and his hands tighten on me, holding me in place in a way that's clearly meant to show me just how easy it is for him.

"Do you like being punished, Charlotte?" he murmurs, raising an eyebrow. "Because I would like to punish you. If you disobey me, I would enjoy teaching you a lesson. Turning that pretty ass pink with my belt, just so I can look at it arched up in the air while I fuck you from behind." His fingers press against my hipbones, his thumbs sweeping over my denim-clad thighs in an arc, so close to where I want to be touched and still so far away.

My breath catches in my throat. "I don't know," I admit. "I've never—"

"I think there's a lot you haven't done." His hands slide towards the button of my jeans, the look on his face is impatient, eager. "There's a lot I can teach you."

With one sharp motion, he flicks the button open with his thumb, yanking down the zipper. His fingers curl in the waist of my jeans and my panties together, dragging them down my hips and thighs in a smooth motion that bares me so quickly it takes my breath away. In seconds, I'm naked from the hips down, and Ivan loops his arms under my knees, spreading my legs wide so that I'm more exposed to him than I think I've ever been to anyone in my life.

My face flushes hot as I see him stare directly between my legs. "So wet," he whispers, and my blush deepens. "Pretty and pink and swollen, all for me. You're so ready, and I haven't even started."

He leans in, sliding down the bed as he presses my legs down to either side. "Keep them there just like this, *milaya*," he murmurs, and the way he says it sends pinpricks of heat over my skin, the roughness of his accent on the Russian endearment turning me on that much more. "Keep your legs open for me."

My head drops back against the pillows, every inch of my body so sensitized with desire that when he touches me, a shudder of pleasure runs through me. His palms are warm on my inner thighs, sliding up, his thumbs brushing over my sensitive folds the moment before he spreads me open even more, revealing all of my most intimate flesh to his hungry gaze.

"Beautiful," he murmurs, and then his tongue slides over me, and I forget how to breathe.

It feels so good. Wet and hot, long, slow strokes that seem to lick every inch of me with each pass, as he drags the flat of his tongue over my folds, my entrance, up to my clit, rubbing it over that sensitive, swollen point until I'm squirming and gasping underneath him. I reach down, dragging my fingers through his thick hair, and when I feel him groan against me, I realize that he likes it.

"Pull my hair, Charlotte," he murmurs, rolling his eyes up to look at me as he drags his tongue over all my most sensitive spots again. "I like it rough, too. You don't need to worry about hurting me, *milaya*. I'll like whatever you do to me."

It's as if he's turned another key in my inhibitions, with that. His mouth fastens on my clit, sucking at the swollen flesh as his tongue lashes over me, and I knot my hand in his hair, hips rocking against his mouth as I ride his tongue. The pleasure is overwhelming, pushing me to the edge, and as he sucks hard at my clit, my mouth drops open on a cry.

"Ivan! Ivan, I—"

The orgasm hits me before I can finish. My hips buck upwards sharply, grinding on his face as I come hard, my nails digging into his scalp as I scream his name. It's still pulsing through me when I feel him push two fingers inside of me roughly, curling them as he thrusts hard, still rolling his tongue over my clit until he pushes me into—

I don't know if it's a second orgasm, or a continuation of the first. All I know is that I've never felt anything like it. I've never felt anything so good.

When I'm limp and gasping on the bed, my other hand knotted in the duvet, Ivan pulls back. His mouth is glistening with my wetness, his eyes dark with lust, and when he rises up on his knees, I can see the thick ridge of his cock pressing against his jeans. "Get that off," he growls, motioning at my shirt and bra, and I can't obey fast enough. My eyes are glued to the front of his jeans as I fall back naked against the pillows, watching as he yanks the button and zipper of his jeans open, shoving them and his underwear down his hips. His cock springs free, slapping against his abs as he strips the remainder of his clothing off, damp arousal pearling at the tip.

He's huge. I felt him against me, but it looks bigger like this, jutting up between his hips, thick and veined and flushed. Ivan looks down at me, his expression almost feral as he moves forward, straddling my body as his hand wraps around his shaft.

"God, you're fucking gorgeous," he growls, his eyes raking over my bare breasts. He angles his cock down, dragging the smooth, swollen head down the valley of my cleavage, his pre-cum leaving a damp trail as he slides his cock between my breasts. I gasp, arousal flooding me, prickling every inch of my skin as he reaches down, mounding my breasts around the thick length of his cock as he thrusts hard against my chest.

I moan helplessly, unable to stop it. This is what I wanted, for a man I trusted to just *take*, to fuck me the way he wants to, to ravage my body for his pleasure without worrying about whether he *should* or not. I want to be used, to be fucked, to be allowed to do the same to the man I'm in bed with in return, and there's no shame in Ivan's face as he thrusts his cock between my breasts again, groaning at the sensation as his gaze flicks up to my mouth.

"I've wanted to fuck these pretty tits since I saw you in that blue dress the first night we went out," he growls, his thumbs rolling over my nipples as he squeezes my breasts around his cock again. "But I want your mouth more. Are you going to open your mouth like a good girl, Charlotte, and let me put my cock in there?"

A shudder of pleasure runs through me, my hips arching at the filthy words, my pussy flooded with desire. I'm soaked, wetter than I knew it was possible to be, and I look up at him, nodding.

He lets go of my breasts, his cock still lying heavily against my chest as he reaches up, his thumb pressing against my lower lip. "Open up, *milaya*," he murmurs, pushing his thumb into my mouth.

"I want to see those pretty lips wrapped around my cock. I want to feel how good your mouth is."

I don't actually know if it's that good. I haven't done this often, and never like this, on my back, with Ivan hovering over me as he angles his cock against my lips. But from the moment my lips touch the swollen head, my tongue flicking out to lap up the pre-cum pearling there, the sound Ivan makes is one of a man on the verge of coming before he's ready to.

"God, I want to fill your pretty mouth up," he growls, pushing the head between my lips. "I want to see my cum dripping out of your lips. But I want to come in your pussy tonight. So that will just have to wait."

The promise of more, of all the things he has yet to do to me, makes me moan again, around the hot intrusion of his cock between my lips, sliding over my tongue as he pushes it deeper, the sound of his pleasure matching mine. He grips the headboard with one hand, the other letting go of his cock to stroke his knuckles down the side of my face, the expression on his one of taut pleasure and an affection that startles me.

"Good girl," he murmurs. "You take my cock so well. So pretty with your lips wrapped around it. Can I fuck your face, *milaya*? See how far you can take me?"

He's too thick for that. I'm sure of it. I should shake my head, tell him no, but instead, I find myself nodding, eyes wide and teary as Ivan moans with pleasure at my answer, both hands gripping the headboard now as he arches his hips upward, sliding his cock deeper into my throat as my head tips back.

And then he starts to thrust.

Slowly, shallowly, as if he's well aware I've never done this before. But still, I feel myself gagging on each stroke, eyes watering, and I'm so wet, so turned on that I almost feel as if I could come without touching myself. I *want* to touch myself, and I reach down, my fingers sliding in the slick wetness dripping from my pussy as I find my clit and start to rub, matching the rhythm of Ivan fucking my mouth.

"Oh god. *Fuck*," he moans, hips rocking again. "That's right. Make yourself come for me again. Come with my cock in your mouth. And then I'll fuck you the way you need to be fucked."

I moan something unintelligible around his cock, a *god, please, yes* that he can't hear, but that I think he understands. The muscles in my thighs are tightening, that knot of pleasure in my belly unfurling, and I cry out around the thick length of Ivan's cock in my mouth as I feel myself unraveling for a third time, the orgasm exploding through me as I come hard.

He jerks himself free of my mouth, his hand squeezing hard around his shaft as he slides down my body. "Fuck, I almost lost it," he pants, his eyes wide and dark, and another jolt of pleasure arcs through me as I realize what he means.

The thought of him being so aroused that he almost lost control of his orgasm fuels mine, and I shudder again, moaning as he rips open a condom, rolling it down his length in a flash before he pushes my thighs wider, the head of his cock at my dripping, clenching entrance as he pushes into me.

"*God,*" he moans, gripping the headboard as he pushes the swollen tip inside. "Fuck, you're so fucking tight, *fucking hell—*" He goes still for a moment, panting as I clench and flutter around him, the last echoes of my orgasm still rippling through me as the feeling of him filling me up already starts to prime me for another. "God, you have the best pussy I've ever fucking felt, Charlotte."

I have no idea how that could be true, but the way he says it makes me believe him. I moan as he thrusts deeper, inch by inch, his cock filling me to the limit, even as wet as I am, even after three orgasms. With one last jerk of his hips, he seats himself deeply inside of me, looking down at me with lust-glazed eyes as he rocks his body against mine.

"You feel so good," I whisper, and a shudder runs through him.

"So do you." He reaches down, stroking a thumb over my cheek as he rocks against me again, and there's a sudden moment of tenderness in all of the lust, a silence in the midst of the storm. I wrap my legs around his, locking him against me, lifting my hips so that we're rocking together, and Ivan suddenly leans forward, his arm sweeping underneath me as he lifts me up and into his lap.

He runs his hand through my hair as he perches me on him, thrusting up into me with short, shallow strokes, his other arm around my waist holding me down on his cock so that every thrust makes me rub against him, his taut skin grinding against my clit. "You're going to come on me again," he murmurs, his hand cupping the back of my head as he starts to thrust harder. "Ride my cock like you rode me in the car, Charlotte. Come all over it while I'm buried inside of you, and then I'm going to fill you up. I'm waiting on you. Waiting to come, and *god*, I need to come so fucking bad—"

He thrusts as he speaks, the words dripping like honey over my skin, sweet and sticky, his body stimulating mine with every stroke, driving me higher. I love the way he talks to me, the way he fucks me. I love everything about this, and I wrap my arms around his neck, my hands in his hair, kissing him with wild abandon as he drives us both to the edge.

I clench around him, tightening, and Ivan groans. "Right there. Yes. Fuck, baby, I'm going to come with you. Come for me, *yes*—"

His hands clutch at me as the orgasm hits, my back bowing as I grind down on him, my head falling back. I feel his mouth on my neck, my chest, the tops of my breasts as he thrusts into me hard, spilling me back onto the bed as he slams into me once more, and I feel him swell and throb as he holds himself there, coming with me as we both cling to each other.

He stays like that for a moment, panting as we both come down from the high, sweaty skin sticking to each other. He holds himself up on his elbows, enough not to crush me, but I can feel his chest heaving, and after a long moment, he rolls to one side, one hand pressed to his ribs.

"Are you okay?" I manage, looking over at him, and he nods.

"Even if I wasn't, that would have been worth it." He meets my eyes, that familiar cocky smirk on his lips, and I can't help but smile back.

"That was the best sex I ever had," I murmur, and his smirk widens.

"Good. That means you'll want to see me again."

I swat at his arm, letting my head fall back onto the bed. "I would have wanted to see you again, anyway."

I push myself up, slowly, unsure of what to do next. I want to play it cool, to send Ivan home, to treat this as if it means nothing. But I know that's not true. It did mean something. And what I want right now is to roll over and curl into him, and hold him until we both fall asleep.

"You can stay if you want," I murmur, moving closer. Ivan looks over at me, his dark blond hair falling into his face, and I see a regretful expression there.

"I would love nothing more than to do that," he says softly. "But I have to be up early. It's probably better if I don't."

"I—yeah. Sure, of course." I bite my lip, and I start to get up to go and shower, but Ivan grabs my arm, stopping me.

"It's nothing to do with you, Charlotte." He reaches up, pushing my hair back. "I want to stay. I really do. It's just work, I promise. Next time, I'll plan better."

I want to believe him. *God*, with everything in me, I want to believe he's telling the truth. "Okay," I whisper. "I'm holding you to that."

"Good." He leans forward, giving me another kiss, before he reaches down to collect his clothes. "It won't be long, I can promise you that. I already want you again."

I can see that's true, as he gets up and starts to dress. His cock is half-hard, swollen between his legs, and I see it twitch when he looks up at me, that wolfish, hungry expression still on his face.

"Soon, Charlotte." He pulls on his shirt, coming around the bed to kiss me again, his lips lingering against mine for a long, warm moment. "I'll text you."

He grins at me, a promise in that smile and his dark blue eyes, and as I watch him go, I know I can't keep pretending that this isn't a real relationship much longer. Ivan is just waiting on me. I know that much—and all I have to do is let go of my other fantasies. Of the dark, hidden place where I can talk about all the things I think I want but that I'm afraid to ask for, with the man who calls himself Venom, who tells me all the things he wants to do to me in return.

If I want Ivan, I have to give that up. But after what just happened between us, I don't think it will be that hard, after all. I think of the way he touched me, the things he did to me, and I have a sudden, sharp certainty that if I told him all of those fantasies, he wouldn't look at me differently. He wouldn't leave me because of it, or stop wanting me.

He'd have some of his own.

25

IVAN

Leaving Charlotte when she asks me to stay feels nearly impossible. But the danger of Lev following me to her apartment is too great. I don't doubt that there's a chance that he already knows where she is, but I don't want to give him more reason to think that she's useful to get under my skin. If he knows I've advanced to spending the night with her, he'll be even more eager for a reason to use her against me.

So, instead, I drive myself back home, relishing the lingering feeling of her touch all over me, the scent of her clinging to my skin. The reality of being with her had lived up to the fantasy, and more. And I already want her again.

When I get home, I head straight down into the basement. All I want to think about right now is Charlotte, but I have a job to do, too, and I can't neglect it. Now more than ever, I need to make sure that I'm not on the wrong side of the feds, as well as my family.

I consider, for a moment, telling Agent Bradley about Charlotte. I wonder if there's a possibility that he could get her to safety. But she's not a part of this, not a victim of my father's yet, and I think of the way he's looked at me every time we've met, as if he wants nothing more than a reason to bring me down too, along with my family.

He wouldn't help Charlotte. I feel that down in my bones. If he did, there would be a price—likely using her as bait, and just the thought of that makes me feel coldly furious. I'm not going to reveal every secret, every lie to her, ruin any chance of seeing her ever again, all for them to use her as a means to get to my father.

I'd rather fucking die.

The other monitor, the one that I use to track Charlotte's web and phone activity, pings, and my heart drops abruptly. For a moment, I think she's logged on to talk to Venom, and the jealousy I feel is a thick, sick rot in my gut.

But it's not her. It's her fucking ex, texting her. And as I watch the messages appear on the screen, my blood runs cold, then hot with anger, then cold again.

Nate: *I saw you in the car with some fucking guy.*

Nate: *I knew you were being a fucking slut. Fucking him in our bed.*

Nate: *You're going to be fucking homeless, bitch. I'm going to get the condo back.*

Nate: *Fuck you. You think you're too good to text me back? You think me sleeping with some other bitch made you miserable? You have no fucking idea how miserable you can be.*

My hands clench into fists as I read the messages. I scroll back, feeling a stab of guilt that I missed this, that I hadn't seen what he's been saying to her because I've been so caught up in the escalating chaos all around me. I'd seen the messages that he'd sent her at the very beginning—a jealous ex being a dick. I thought he'd leave her alone, when it was clear she wasn't responding. But he's never given up, and I grind my teeth as I read each and every one, my anger spiking with every new slew of messages.

No one is going to talk to her like that and get away with it.

The helpless feeling that I had when my father beat me, when

Lev threatened Charlotte on the yacht, when I talked to Bradley and realized how much more they wanted from me—it all comes rising back up, and I can feel all that anger narrowing in, given direction, given something to focus on.

At first, he was just a pathetic, jealous, bitter ex pissed that he got caught cheating. But now he's watching her, threatening her. And while I'm well aware of my hypocrisy in being pissed that he's stalking Charlotte, I don't fucking care.

She's mine. I can still smell her on my skin, still taste her on my lips. And by the end of tomorrow night, Nate is never going to fucking bother her again.

THE FOLLOWING AFTERNOON, I go to my penthouse, parking in the underground garage, and change in the apartment. I dress in all black —black cargos, a long-sleeved black T-shirt, black gloves, black boots. And next to me, as I dress, sitting on the bed, is a black balaclava and the white skeleton mask that I put on for Charlotte as Venom.

I've been texting her all day. Lighthearted texts, back and forth, neither of us willing to come out and say how much last night meant to either of us. Not over such an impersonal medium. But the next time I see her—

I'm not sure I want to tell her even then. I want to show her, with my hands and mouth and my body, show her how much she means to me. How much I want her. How much just one night with her has made me certain that I have to find some way to keep her.

Keep her safe. Keep her *mine*.

That obsessive thought buzzes in my head as I grab my keys, the balaclava, and the mask, stalking downstairs to my car. I drive across the city, just out to the suburbs, to Nate's brother's house.

The lights are on inside. I park in an alleyway, pocketing my keys and pulling the balaclava over my head, securing the mask. Walking to the line of trees just across the road, I find a vantage point that lets me see into the house, through the large picture windows. I watch patiently as the time ticks past, until the two other adults in the house—a man that I assume is Nate's brother and a woman who must be his wife, based on the quick research I did—get up and walk down a hallway. A light flicks on in a room towards the back of the house, stays on for about thirty minutes, and then turns off. Nate is still in an armchair in the living room, playing what looks like a shooter video game, and I push myself away from the tree that I'm leaning against, prowling slowly toward the house.

It's laughably easy to get in. The garage is detached, which means there's a back door with nothing blocking it. Last night, I checked for any records of a security system on the house, and found none. I pick the lock in a matter of seconds; there are no alarms, nothing to let the residents know I'm here. An astonishing amount of confidence that they're safe.

Which, of course—Nate's brother and his wife are. I have no intention of hurting them. But Nate doesn't need to know that. And by the end of this night, he's most definitely going to be hurt.

I slink into the living room, pressing myself against the wall, silent as the grave. All of Nate's attention is focused on his game, and he doesn't hear me as I sneak up behind the chair, moving in one fluid motion to put a gloved hand over his mouth and my hunting knife to his throat.

"Don't scream," I murmur in his ear. "You're going to come with me. If you do, everyone else in this house will be safe. If you start causing a fuss, then who knows what might happen to them?"

This is the riskiest part. I'm not sure Nate is self-sacrificing enough to keep silent for the sake of his brother and sister-in-law. And I was right to think that—I feel his mouth open under my glove, on the verge of screaming. I rear back, hitting him in the head hard enough to daze him, and he slumps.

Now I'm going to have to wait for him to come back to consciousness. He's a dead weight, and although I'm strong, I'm not as beefy as, say, Lev. But I manage to get Nate up and out of the armchair, hefting him over my shoulder like a sack of potatoes as I leave the game running for noise, slipping back out of the house and across the street to the trees where I was hiding.

I take him further into the tree line, far enough that passing cars won't get a glimpse of us in their headlights. Pushing him up against one of the trees, I zip-tie his hands behind it, stuffing a rag in his mouth to keep him silent as I fumble in my pocket for the vial of ammonia that will bring him back to consciousness.

Nate comes back with a jolt, his eyes wide and muffled, panicked noises coming from behind the gag. The only light out in the chilly night, in this strip of woods, is the moon filtering down between them, illuminating me in a way that I'm sure looks relatively monstrous. All in black, the only thing that can be illuminated is the white mask on my face, and I can see the terror in Nate's eyes as he takes me in.

The bitter smell of piss fills the air, and I realize he's already wet himself. I can't help but laugh at that—it's pathetic. I haven't even touched him yet. But I didn't expect better from him.

"I'm going to take the gag out. If you scream, your dick will be the first thing I cut off. Understand?" I wait for him to give a trembling nod, and then yank the fabric out of his mouth, dropping it to the grass.

"Who—who are you? If you want money—" He sputters the words, his teeth clacking together with fear, and I laugh.

"This isn't about money. It's about Charlotte. You see, I've seen your text messages to her. Not because she showed them to me, but because I figured it out on my own. And I don't like the way you talk to her."

He's wearing a t-shirt and sweatpants, shivering in the cold night, and I cut the clothes away methodically as I speak, not bothering to be careful. I hear him whimper and gasp as my knife nicks his skin, and I chuckle, tossing the clothing down to the grass.

"That's nothing, Nate. Just a little scratch. It will get much worse, I promise." I cut away his boxers, leaving him naked, his dick shriveling in the cold. "Now, we're going to have a conversation." I step forward, pressing my knife tip into the lowest part of his abdomen, right above his dick. "And whether or not you get to keep this depends on how it goes."

Nate is shivering all over now, trembling with terror. I drag the knife lower, holding it against the base of his dick, and reach up with my other hand, grabbing his jaw. "Don't look away from me. Now tell me, what makes you think you can keep texting Charlotte, when she clearly doesn't want to talk to you?"

"She—" His teeth chatter. "She'll come around. She's upset, but she doesn't get it. I didn't ask her to do those things because I *love* her. I respect her too much! And now she's out there letting other men touch her, like a filthy slut." His voice grows stronger, some of his fear receding as he spits out the words that have clearly been festering for some time now. "She didn't appreciate how I treated her. How I made sure to make her feel special. Better than all the other sluts. But now she's fucking some guy—"

I swing, hard, my fist connecting with his face. "I dare you to call her that again." Another swing, hard enough that I hear the cracking sound of his jaw. "You won't be able to speak another word out of this fucking mouth when I'm done with you."

I'd planned to be slow, methodical, but the building stress of the past weeks and months, combined with the way he's talking about Charlotte, tip me over the edge. I *have* to be careful, methodical, when I torture someone, but there's no information I need from Nate, nothing he can give me other than the cathartic feeling of inflicting pain on someone who has hurt Charlotte. I can't hurt my family for threatening her, but I can hurt him, and I hit him again and again, in his face and ribs and stomach, until I finally drag the knife down, scoring a bloody line down the top of his dick. He's so bloodied by that point that the only sound he lets out is a mewling whimper, twitching against the tree, and I press the knife in before jerking it away.

"It'll be a while before you can stick it in anyone else," I hiss. "Think about that, before you ever talk to her again. In fact, just in case the message isn't clear—"

I step closer, pressing the knife into his chest. And as he moans in pain, I etch out the message I don't want him to forget, one letter at a time, into his skin.

Keep your mouth shut.

"There." I step back. "Now, when your brother sees you, you'll have to explain. Good luck with that. And since he'll see my message, too, he'll be able to remind you. A little oversight never hurt anyone, right? God knows I have more than I want to deal with." I pat him on his bleeding cheek, and Nate groans as I shove the gag into his mouth again, cutting through the zip-ties holding his wrists. I sling his bloody body over my shoulder, whistling under my breath as I carry him back to the house, depositing him naked on the back step.

"They'll find you here in the morning," I assure him. "It'll be an uncomfortable night, but you'll get through it. And Nate?" I squat down, tipping his chin up so I can look directly into his face through the mask. "Don't ever breathe her name. Don't go trying to get me back for this. Don't try to figure out who I am. Just remember that you're going to stay out of her life for good." I pat his face again, straightening, and wipe my knife off on his thigh before sliding it back into the sheath on mine.

I wore black for a reason. His blood won't show until I get home and dispose of the clothing, making sure there's no trace of him on me anywhere. I'm good enough that there's no chance this will come back on me. Not unless Nate somehow figures it out, and I don't think he's smart enough for that.

I also don't think he has the balls to do anything about it, if he did.

My spirits considerably lifted, I start walking back to the alleyway where I parked my car. I reach for my keys, looking up—and then freeze in place.

There are three dark figures standing in front of my driver's side door. Three figures, that, as they step a little closer, I see are all three of my brothers.

"What the fuck is this?" I snap, crossing my arms. "Lev, I'm not surprised to see you here being a pain in my ass, but Niki and Ani, I am surprised to see. You don't usually manage to drag them out."

"They're my backup." Lev smiles coldly at me. "I know what you're up to, little brother. We're going to take you back to *otets*, and you're going to confess. You're going to take whatever punishment he decides. If he wants your death, then so be it, slow or fast, whichever pleases him. And if you go along without argument, if you submit, then maybe we'll leave your bitch alone." He smiles, teeth white in the darkness. "Or maybe once you're dead, I'll take her for myself. But you'll never know, will you?"

He moves forward, so quickly that I almost don't have time to dodge him. In the alleyway, there's very little room, and it's three-on-one. Bad odds—but I've never cared about that.

When he swings again, this time, I swing, too. I clock him in the jaw, making his teeth clack together and sending him reeling back, and manage to get my knife free of the sheath as Niki and Ani close in.

I have an advantage here. I can see in their faces that they're afraid of me. That they know I have no love for them, that I'll kill them if I have to in order to get out of here. To get to Charlotte.

"Ivan." There's a reasonable note in Niki's voice, one that suggests he's going to try to talk this out. But I'm in no mood to even give him a chance.

When he steps forward, I slash out with the knife, catching him in the arm. He lets out a startled sound of pain, my willingness to hurt him clearly catching him off guard. Lev is staggering forward, and I look around, gauging the distance between myself and the unlocked car.

A handful of steps. A few feet. That's all I need to manage. I take a breath and barge forward, knife slashing out to one side, my fist connecting with one of my brothers' soft flesh as I strike out to my left, swinging without elegance or grace as I bolt for the car.

I feel blood on my hand. Pain in my ribs. I strike again and again, the motion around me a blur as I grab for the door handle, yanking it out and flinging myself backward into the driver's seat. I kick out with both feet as Lev lunges for me, driving my heels into his gut, grabbing for my keys as I swing upright and snatch the door shut.

There's a howl of pain as I clip someone's fingers as they try to grab it. I slam my hand down on the locks, every movement to start the car vicious, frantic as I gun it down the alley. Ani tries to step forward, and the corner of the hood clips him, knocking him to one side as I floor it, skidding out onto the road as I turn.

They'll go for Charlotte next. But I'm going to get to her first.

26

CHARLOTTE

I feel oddly heavy, the morning after I slept with Ivan. There's a text from him waiting as soon as I get up, a sweet good morning, but the messages from Nate are weighing on me. He saw me last night. He was watching me. Following me.

I remember the way I felt walking home from brunch, the creeping feeling of eyes on me, and how I'd fantasized about my masked man. In this new light, the thought makes my skin crawl, makes me want to get into a shower and scrub myself raw.

It's not how I wanted to feel, the morning after. I wanted to be basking in the afterglow, sunny and happy and floating after the experience I had with Ivan. Instead, Nate's messages make me feel itchy, like I want to scratch my skin off.

I'm tempted to stay home from work, but I know if I do, I'll just fixate on the texts, and how they make me feel. It's better to be busy, to have something to do, so I go to work, feeling like someone is watching me the whole way. That crawling feeling runs up and down my spine, banishing any lingering pleasantness from the night before, and I resent Nate even more for ruining that for me. From taking away what should have been a *good* morning.

I thought that if I ignored him, he'd go away. That he'd get the hint that this was over. But he's only gotten worse, the more time has passed. And even though it's laughable to me that he's so upset over seeing me with someone else after what he did—the texts last night make me worry what he might do about it.

That's another reason to go to work, one that I hate that I'm even thinking about. There, at least, I'm safe from anything he might try to do. I consider asking Jaz if I can stay with her tonight—have a girls' sleepover, but I know the fact that I'm asking on a work night would clue her in that something is wrong. I've told her a little bit about the irritating texts from Nate, but not since they've gotten worse. And I don't want to worry her.

All throughout the day, I try to focus on Ivan—on how good of a night we had last night, on all the things we did that I'd never felt before, on the fact that I now *know* it's possible to feel all of that outside of just fantasies. Whether or not it will last, I have no idea, but for now—for now, it's everything I wanted.

And I want more of it.

I text him throughout the afternoon, both of us dancing around how impactful last night felt, but I can tell he wants to see me again. We talk about possible dates, about a restaurant I want to try, about another hike, *not* after I've been drinking mimosas. I think about how he promised to fuck me up against a tree after we'd done it in a bed, and shiver pleasantly, some of the bad feelings receding.

"Do you want to get tapas after work?" I ask Jaz, when we grab lunch. "I know Zoe is busy, and Sarah is working late, so maybe just us? We could get dinner, even, and try out that new bar. The one with the custom cocktails."

Jaz, ever the spontaneous one, is more than happy to go out on a work night. We go back to my apartment and change, and my phone stays silent, with no new text messages from Nate. None from Ivan in a while, either, but he had mentioned he had a busy work day today. I don't want to seem clingy, so I wait for him to text me, first.

Dinner is great—appetizers and wine at a French fusion spot we both like, and the new custom cocktail bar, designed to create cocktails by spinning a series of wheels to choose the flavors to mix together, is even more fun. Two cocktails in, I've all but forgotten about Nate's threats, pushing them to the back of my mind. He's being an asshole, but he won't actually do anything about it. And in time, I tell myself as I finish my third drink, he'll get over it. He'll realize his threats and blustering isn't working, and he'll leave me alone.

I hug Jaz, getting into an Uber to go home after we cash out, and finally open my phone after leaving it alone for most of the night. It's after midnight, later than we should have stayed out, and I'm startled to see my screen light up with texts.

I'm even more startled to see that they're from Daniel—Nate's brother.

He never really talked to me of his own accord when Nate and I were together, and I don't see why he would start now. I open my messages—and I feel my blood run cold as ice as I begin to read them.

DANIEL: *What the fuck is this, Charlotte? Do you know anything about this?*

Daniel: *Someone broke into our fucking house. Did this to Nate. Is this because he was texting you? Did you set someone on him?*

A PICTURE COMES up on the screen—one that makes me gasp, covering my mouth with my hand. It's Nate—or at least I'm almost sure it is. His face is battered, swollen almost beyond recognition, and in his chest, there's a message carved.

Keep your mouth shut.

Frantically, I text him back.

CHARLOTTE: *No, of course I didn't. He's being a dick, but I would never think to do that. That's horrible. Have you called the police?*

. . .

There's no answer as the Uber pulls up to my building, and I can only imagine that Daniel is probably dealing with them right now. I feel sick at what I saw in the picture—but a tiny part of me, one I'm ashamed to admit, feels the tiniest bit glad that someone got sick of Nate's shit.

That instead of being a bully, he got bullied, for a change.

I bite my lip, pushing the thought away. And as I do, a new, more frightening one takes its place.

Why did Daniel think this was about me? And if it was, who—

I didn't tell anyone but Jaz that Nate was still texting me. And I didn't tell her about the worst ones.

A cold feeling slithers down my spine, a warning, but I don't know what it could be—or who it could be about. Only a feeling that I'm in danger, that something is very wrong. I grip my keys tightly as I head to the elevator, my heart beating hard the entire way up to my floor, and walk quickly to my front door, unlocking it and slipping into the safety of my warm, dark apartment.

But that cold feeling is still there. There's a prickling down the back of my neck, some primal instinct warning me, and I reach out, flicking on the light as I turn away from the door.

There, standing in front of me, is a man in a mask. The same mask that I saw in the pictures Venom sent me, a grinning skull, the rest of him dressed all in black. I open my mouth to scream, fear coursing through me, but he lunges forward, grabbing me before I can with one hand over my mouth and the other around my throat.

I feel something against the pressure point in my neck, a sharp, stinging pain.

And then everything goes black.

Thanks for reading!

I hope you enjoyed book one of the Endless duet! I'm super excited to announce that I now have a subscription plan where you can gain access to the bonus scenes you've come to know and love. Plus, you can also read along as I write new stories, and depending on the plan you choose you'll have access to exclusive short stories and previously published books. Take a look here!

If subscriptions aren't for you, I totally get it. **Text *SPICYREADS* to 737-317-8825** for new release information.

READY FOR THE final chapters of Charlotte and Ivan's love saga, keep reading for a sneak peek, or click here to read as I write or get it now on Amazon!

CHAPTER **One**

Charlotte

When I wake up, for a moment, I have no idea where I am.

My head aches. I don't usually drink enough to get a hangover, but once or twice I've ended up with one, and this feels worse than that ever did. As soon as I open my eyes, a bright sliver of light stinging them and adding to the sharp pain, I close them just as quickly.

But that can't change the fact that I know I'm somewhere other than where I should be. I should be in my apartment, at home, in my own bed. Wherever I am, it's not there—this place smells wrong, clean in an antiseptic way, almost hospital-like, but not quite. Empty, like too-filtered air. Nothing like the soft lavender scent of the room spray I use at home, usually underlaid with the scents of lemon and basil from my cleaning products. The sheets and blanket feel stiff, nothing like the soft, cozy bedding I have at home.

I'm afraid to open my eyes and find out, because then I'm going to have to accept that something has happened. That the man in my apartment, the sudden pressure on my throat, everything swirling dark—that wasn't all some awful dream.

That text from Nate's brother must not have been a dream either, then.

I squeeze my eyes tighter, trying to get that picture out of my head. But I can't. Nate, bloody and stripped naked, a message carved into his chest. I can't imagine who would do such a thing, and why. Nate is an asshole, a pretentious dick with an overinflated sense of self, who thinks he can justify having cheated on me with excuses about *respecting* me too much to ask for what he wanted in bed.

But I can't imagine what would have warranted *that*. A level of violence I've never really imagined existing outside of fiction.

Was it him? Venom? I feel a stab of guilt, thinking that my online fantasies might have led to this. I'm furious with Nate, and I don't want him back in my life, but that doesn't mean that I wanted—*that* to happen to him.

I'm not sure I want that to happen to anyone.

Oh god, is that going to happen to me?

A flare of panic jolts through my chest. I have to open my eyes. I have to be brave, and find out what's happened.

For a moment, just before I open them, I have a brief flicker of hope that maybe I really *did* imagine it. That maybe I'm imagining all the sensory cues that tell me that I'm not in my bedroom, at home.

I blink, letting the light flood in, and all that hope is dashed.

I'm in a hotel room. That much is immediately obvious. A fairly mid-grade one, too, from the looks of it. The bed is covered with a stiff floral-pattern duvet that could have been put in here anytime in the last two decades, and the floor is covered in a beige shag carpet. The walls are cream, the furniture dark pressed wood. There's two small lamps hooked on either side of the bed, their push-button switches underneath the only nod to modernity.

There's no phone. I notice that almost immediately, and I push myself upright, that flare of panic worsening. There are always phones in hotel rooms. *Always.* Someone has removed this one.

I press a hand to my chest as my heart starts to beat faster. The memories of last night come flooding in again, pushing me closer to the edge of what I think *might* be an oncoming panic attack. I don't know. I've never had one before. The closest I think I might have come was the night I found out Nate cheated on me. I've never lived the kind of life that *causes* panic attacks.

I didn't realize just how lucky I was until this moment.

I've been so stupid. I thought there was no way Venom could find me in real life. No way my fantasies could track me down. I thought I was safe, because I knew enough about the internet to cover my tracks. I *work in tech*, for fuck's sake.

But he must have been better. Good enough to find me. Obsessed enough to come after me.

I shouldn't have gone home after getting that text about Nate. I should have gone to Jaz' house. Gone to a hotel. Anything other than walking into my apartment alone, where a man in a mask was waiting to grab me.

Gingerly, I reach up and touch the spot on my neck that's still sore. He must have known where to find a pressure point. *At least he didn't drug me.* The thought makes me let out a choked, near-hysterical laugh—because I can't believe that's legitimately something that just went through my head. That something has happened to make that a reasonable thing for me to think.

My clothes are still on, too. Another good thing. I push the duvet back, frowning as it occurs to me that not only did he not strip me, he —tucked me in?

I was stalked, knocked out, kidnapped, taken to a hotel in god knows where—and then respectfully tucked in with all of my clothes still on until I woke up.

Something feels off about all of this.

Gingerly, I swing my legs out of bed, remembering that I had my phone and purse when I walked into the apartment. I might have dropped them when I was grabbed, but that doesn't stop me from starting to look for them anyway—in the drawer next to the bed, around the desk, the chair, even in the drawers of the dresser. But there's nothing. Just my shoes, which he *did* take off and set next to the bed.

It's then that I realize the shower is running.

I glance at the digital clock next to the bed—it's seven in the morning. Assuming I'm still in the same time zone, no one from work, or Jaz, will have noticed I'm gone yet. The only clue that Jaz might have that something is wrong would be that I didn't text her last night that I made it home.

Carefully, I get up, trying not to make any sound as my feet hit the carpet. My mouth feels dry, and my head still hurts, a dull ache at the base of my neck that makes me reach back and press my fingers against it, wishing for some kind of painkiller.

But I need to try to get out of here. As far as I know, there's no way to lock a hotel room door from the inside to prevent someone getting out—

I try the door handle, and it doesn't budge. I stare at it for a long moment, trying to figure out how that's possible. There's something next to the door, a small black box—

Close to frantic, now, I dig at the side of it with my nails, trying to pry it off. It won't come loose, and I feel my pulse racing faster, my eyes starting to burn with frustrated tears as I yank at the door handle again. Short of pounding on the door with my fists and screaming, I don't know what else to do.

Pivoting, I look towards the window. *How high up are we?* I cross the room as quickly as I can, the carpet muffling my footsteps, and lean up against the window, looking down.

We're on at least the second floor, maybe higher. There's nothing beneath the window but asphalt. If I could get the window open, I wouldn't make it out of that fall unscathed. I'd probably hurt myself badly enough that I wouldn't be able to get help before he got to me again—or even if someone saw me, I might hurt myself badly enough that it wouldn't be worth it.

I want to get out of here. I don't want to end up paralyzed or permanently damaged doing it.

What do people do in situations like this? I don't know. I don't watch true crime or read the kind of books that would tell me the answer to that. I'm trapped, and the sense of panic builds until my thoughts feel foggy, that pounding, dull pain at the back of my head only getting worse—

The sound of the shower switches off.

Fuck. I swallow hard, spinning to face the bathroom door, my hands gripping the windowsill behind me as I look frantically around for something to use as a weapon. I don't want to be defenseless. I don't want—

The door opens, and I brace myself, ready to scream.

My mouth drops open, but no sound comes out as I see Ivan, standing in the doorway wearing nothing but a towel wrapped around his hips.

Click here to read along as I write, or here to download the full ebook from Amazon!

Made in the USA
Monee, IL
24 October 2024